To my lockdown buddies, aka The Virtual Pub Group

1

___

Brightest sunshine, so hot it almost stings the skin. The heart-lifting blue sky soars high above and, always in the background, the lulling boom and swoosh of the turquoise ocean.

Beside Tess on a sun lounger is her husband, Dave. His usually pale and puffy body is starting to change. Walking, swimming and being outside all day means he's turning honey-brown and he's leaner than he's been in years. She looks past Dave to her almost grown-up children, Alex and Natalie, who are relaxed and soaking up the sun. Alex has his headphones on and his eyes shut. He's breathing deeply, hands calmly by his side, no sign of his usual, restless, twitchy energy to be seen. Natalie's hair gets blonder and her tan deeper with every passing day. The biggest change with Natalie is that she's not looking at her phone, or in yet another stroppy rage, instead she's just back from yoga class and she's sipping on a holistic smoothie, bright blue eyes fixed on the bright blue ocean, as she contemplates a swim.

Tess can feel her own heartbeat slowing as her shoulders sink back into the lounger.

Massaged, pampered, organic beachside bliss like this does not come cheap. But she has finally, after too many years of waiting on the sidelines, been raised up to partner level at her accountancy firm and with the enhanced salary and extra bonus, she has, at last, been able to make this perfect holiday of a lifetime happen for her family. They're all together again, but happy, relaxed and really enjoying each other's company. She and Dave are getting on so much better. And the feelings of sadness, loneliness, even hopelessness that have been troubling Tess lately, they're evaporating in the gorgeous heat of these languid, beachy days.

How many weeks would she need to spend here to truly rejuvenate? To reset herself? Rediscover herself and her marriage? Not to mention her waistline and her inner joy?

Was three weeks even enough?

Remember way back, Tess, when you enjoyed wearing a bikini? Had hair halfway down your back? When you had fun, and sex, and big ideas... and a spirit of adventure?

* * *

'Hi Tess, just a heads up that he's here.'

The sight of her colleague, Sophie, at her office door with the warning that the group CEO, John Lloyd, had entered the building snapped Tess instantly from her daydream. She quickly closed the browser window where she'd been comparing luxury Cambodian beach resorts, daydreaming about an unforgettable family holiday, and felt her heart skip a beat.

John Lloyd was here and everyone knew why. He was here to make the new partner a formal offer and discuss terms. Then he'd have some further discussion with the other partners, and then there would be an announcement to the whole Leamington Spa office.

Tess had been mentally preparing for this morning for days

now. She'd been interviewed twice for the partner position, once in Leamington, once in London. Six sharp new items of career clothing now hung in her wardrobe, not to mention the new pair of shoes and the freshly cut and darkened bob, done at eye-watering expense in Leamington's priciest salon.

At last, right at the tail end of her forties, Tess felt ready for the big step up. Yes, she was behind the male colleagues who'd joined when she did, but had become partners several years ago. She suspected this wasn't just because she was a working mother, who kept to her hours meticulously and never worked weekends, but also because she was quiet, hardworking and low key – not any kind of company headline maker. She wasn't 'an innovator' or showy in any way; she increasingly preferred the way she'd always done things and the clients she'd worked with for years. She was at home in a comfortable shoe and loose-fitting trouser suit, rather than anything more attention grabbing. Over the years, she had perhaps become more reserved at work and enjoyed being the diligent details person, ruthlessly good at maths and accounts. She suspected it had been almost two years since she'd last updated her LinkedIn profile.

During all her time at the company, she'd been a full-time working mother, plagued with the guilt that she wasn't doing either the mothering or the full-time working bit as well as she should. She'd hoped that as the children got older it would become easier. But she learnt on the battlefields of the recent years that teenagers were challenging and exhausting, as needy and prone to melo-drama as toddlers and, actually, she'd probably had it best during the primary school years.

Although she kept thinking of him as a student, her twenty-two-year-old son, Alex, was now, after a difficult finals year, a graduate working in London, and her nineteen-year-old daughter, Natalie, was in her first year at uni in Edinburgh. So there was just her husband, Dave, and their old dog, Bella, in the house and Tess could finally see how she could dive much deeper into her career and become the focused, driven, and yes, *important* person in this company that she'd only recently realised she would like to become.

'I've held back,' she'd told the interview panel. 'I didn't think more ambitious career goals would combine with the amount of time I wanted to spend with my family. But my children have left home, the company is more family friendly than ever, and I really want to focus on what I can do for this business now.'

She had thought when she'd said it that it was true, but way at the back of her mind was the suspicion that she was only pursuing this because she couldn't really think how else to spend the next decade and a half of her working life.

Now, waiting anxiously for John Lloyd to turn up in her office and offer her the partnership, she was much more sure that this was what she wanted. She straightened the items on her desk: the notebook, the pens, the small pile of papers. Then she stood up and walked round the small room, adjusting the blind, turning the plant on her desk and wiping the trace of dust from the frames of her accountancy certificates on the wall. Yes, Leamington Spa partner – she was ready. Bring it on.

The phone on her desk beeped and she startled, feeling a rush of nerves.

'Hello, Tess here.'

'Hi, Tess.' It was Katrina at reception. 'Mr Lloyd wants to know if it's okay to come to your office.'

'Yes, yes... of course.' Tess thought she could hear some hint in Katrina's voice. Excitement? Expectation? Everyone was waiting for this announcement. And she knew, from several open discussions, that everyone was expecting it to be her.

Tess stood beside her door, feeling her heart thud. She decided she should open the door in a welcoming gesture. But this was something of a mistake because it was a long corridor and Tess found herself saying hello to John Lloyd before she was sure he was in earshot and then over-smiling at him for the long, long minute it took him to get to the door.

'Hello, Tess, how are you?' the elegant Mr Lloyd, in blue pinstripes and a pink satin tie, asked as he reached her. 'Now, please call me John,' he added.

This felt a little too soon. John Lloyd had only been in the job for four months and at her interview in London, he'd been firmly 'Mr Lloyd' in her mind.

'Hello... John... come on in and take a seat.'

In the corner of her room was a low coffee table for client meetings, with three comfortable chairs surrounding it, so this is where she sat and faced him. She found herself wondering about pink satin as a tie choice... with a gold tie clip. It struck her as a little showy. What would Dave say if she suggested a tie clip? Or a pink satin tie? Or... well... even a tie? The fuss he made on official school ceremony days when teachers had to wear ties.

'So, one point seven million pounds. One... point... seven... million!'

For a moment, Tess had no idea what John Lloyd was talking about. But she was pretty certain it couldn't be her new salary.

'The Hambold review,' he added helpfully.

'Oh, yes... quite a bit of money,' she added.

She guessed £1.7million could buy thirty bars of gold, at current prices, or a super yacht, a New York apartment... maybe even a minor Impressionist painting.

This was how much money she had saved Hambold Mechanical by spotting, not a loophole, just an opportunity – a new tax ruling that the company had not fully understood how to take advantage of until she'd pointed it out and helped them to redraft their annual accounts submission. And the good thing was, she had been conducting an independent accounts review, so the oversight hadn't been made by anyone at her firm. Even better, she'd already heard that the £1.7 million saved wouldn't be spent on super yachts or gold bars, but on expanding the UK operation by creating an extra department and taking on new staff.

'It's the biggest saving we've ever made on an independent review,' John Lloyd was saying, 'We've gained Hambold as a client and we want to make a bit of a fuss about it, Tess.'

'Oh, well... thank you very much... Mr... John,' Tess replied, feeling the slight prickle of embarrassment across her neck and cheeks. 'Good to hear Hambold are pleased with the work.'

'Very pleased. And we're very pleased with you. Now...' he leaned forward and something of a troubled look seemed to settle on his face.

All the hope, expectation and excitement she'd built up around this moment faded on the word 'now...'

He wasn't wearing the right expression. He definitely did not look as if he was about to congratulate her and this was so unexpected, she wondered how on earth she was going to react.

'Although we feel it is very much overdue, you're not going to be made partner,' call-me-John said, quietly, seriously and sincerely, because he was clearly someone used to delivering professionally disappointing news.

Tess was sitting down, but it still felt like a blow to the back of the knees.

'Right...' she heard herself murmur.

'I know this may not be what you expected to hear.'

She managed to repeat. 'Right,' again softly and then focused all her effort on not crying. Not crying. Not at all. No hint of it.

'How would you like to move to something interesting in London, instead?' John Lloyd suggested. 'I'd like you to come back down to head office, have another chat with us and see what might suit you.'

'Well... that's... something I'd not thought about.' She swallowed hard. 'But definitely interesting, John.' Sounding absolutely calm and professional, even when she was in total turmoil on the inside, was something she'd perfected over the years in the job.

'Yes, come down and meet the team there. I'll get Helen to put a date in the diary with you.'

'Great... that sounds great. Thank you,' she said, making eye contact and smiling as brightly as she could.

Tess knew straight away that she would go to London for that meeting, to the swanky, glassy building in the heart of the city. And it would involve as much serious prep as the interviews – with a blow dry, an on-trend outfit, and further deep study of the company website for all the latest up-to-the-nanosecond jargon: *dial back John, we don't have the bandwidth for a pivot, let alone a paradigm shift.* And then, most likely, she would turn the London role down and stay in her Leamington job, because she liked it here. She fitted right in. She liked the town, liked her colleagues, liked her clients – many of whom had been with her for years.

But she wasn't going to be a partner and, further down the line, she wasn't going to be a board member either... unlike her male colleagues. And she couldn't help thinking that it really wasn't fair. She worked hard, and she was excellent at her job. But it seemed to require a degree of thrusting over-confidence to get into the upper ranks, and she didn't have that. Not even a shred of it. She was the quiet person, doomed to be overlooked, despite making the *biggest ever* tax saving on a client review.

And who the hell *was* going to be the new partner, she thought with a burst of outrage? They must be bringing someone in from another branch. She jumped straight to the conclusion that it was bound to be a guy, younger than her, all thrusting over-confidence, ready to do the networking, LinkedIn videos, commutes to London and business leadership that she wasn't thought to be capable of.

Tess knew she should ask John who was getting the partnership and why, about what she'd done or not done to be passed over like this. But instead, she let John talk about her London 'promotion', which she was almost certainly going to turn down.

'So, let's discuss this further when you come down,' John went on, 'And you'll get a decent bonus, of course, that will reflect Hambold joining our client roster. And I'd like to add that you, personally, have done a brilliant job. I want to show you off to the rest of the company; have people inspired by your work.'

Squarely meeting her in the eye, he added: 'I am sorry about the partnership, Tess. Just timing, I suppose...'

Then, putting his hands on his knees and looking as if he was about to stand up and conclude their talk, he added: 'There's someone we believe will be a better fit.'

'Oh... am I allowed to know who?' she asked hesitantly, 'Or do I have to wait for the announcement?'

'No... I think I can let you know. She's with this branch – it's Jamila Khan.'

'Jamila?'

Tess hoped she hadn't allowed too much surprise into her voice. But her first reaction was surprise. Jamila was young, early thirties and relatively new, she'd been in the Leamington office for not quite two years... and, of course, she was very much Tess's junior. But that sour grape was quickly followed by the realisation that Jamila was a really excellent choice.

That was the truth.

Jamila was charismatic and extrovert. She was engaging and unbelievably smart. And yes, she had confidence and definite leadership potential. Tess could understand the choice immediately. Compared to Jamila, Tess realised with a horrible lurch, she was a bit boring and old school. She would have been the comfortable shoe choice, the sensible pump, she thought, toes curling and now she could feel herself blushing again with the shock, the disappointment and the humiliation of it all.

As the fresh wave of upset broke over her, she looked quickly up at the ceiling and wondered how she would avoid crying.

'Jamila will be an excellent partner,' Tess heard herself say, 'really excellent. And I'll look forward to meeting with you and the London team.'

'I totally understand that this is going to be difficult for you,' John Lloyd said with an obvious note of sympathy, 'especially in a small branch like this. You can tell everyone straightaway that you've been offered an opportunity in London.'

Tess nodded.

'Now, I'm going to go and talk to Jamila for half an hour or so, which gives you some time to... umm... let it all sink in,' he added, getting to his feet.

She was nodding vigorously. She thought she might shake the forming tears out of her eyes she was nodding so hard. This was such a sharp and humiliating pain. It made her think of that one time in her life when the guy she had liked so much had turned up to meet her with his brand-new girlfriend.

'And Tess, let's have a call later this week,' John Lloyd said, as he made towards her office door, 'when the announcements are over and we're all adjusted to the news. Because I want to listen to you.'

'Do you?' She wasn't sure what he meant.

'Yes. You'll have me on the line. If there's anything you want to discuss, any ideas you'd like to share, this will be your chance. You've worked here for seventeen years. There's a great deal I can learn from you.'

And that was such a kind thing to say that unfortunately a tear spilled over from the edge of her left eye. But she tilted her head away and, as he left the room, John Lloyd made out that he hadn't noticed.

* * *

For a few moments afterwards, Tess sat at her desk. She glanced at her email – but there was nothing new. She looked through the list of tasks she'd set herself for the morning – all paperwork, nothing immediate. And, quite frankly, she couldn't face any of it. Quite frankly, if her computer burst into flames right at this very moment, it would be a welcome distraction.

'*Seventeen years...*' she repeated to herself. How could it possibly have been so long?

She felt an intense need to leave the office and get some fresh air.

'I've got a quick errand to run, back soon,' she told Katrina, as she whisked through reception, pulling on her raincoat because it was a cold, grey spring day out there.

But once she was outside, she didn't know where to go or what to do with herself. She just wanted to be alone with her torrent of thoughts, so she made for the car park, bleeped open the door of her sensible Volvo, got into the driver's seat and burst into bitter tears.

It wasn't even jealousy. It wasn't a feeling of 'how dare you pick her, when I'd be so much better at this'. No, it was more complicated. Just like seeing that guy – Jason was his name – with his new girlfriend all those years ago. It was such deep disappointment with herself. It was understanding immediately that *of course* that girl with the long, tanned legs in a *cream-coloured* sweater dress was just right for him, and, of course, Jamila would make the perfect, dynamic new Leamington partner. And now Tess was again on the sidelines, so frustrated, disappointed, and so upset with no one but herself.

And she asked herself the impossible question: why couldn't she have been the kind of person they wanted?

There was, of course, a packet of pocket tissues in her handbag, so head down, hoping no one would spot her out here in her car, she cried hard. She'd been crying a lot lately, to be honest. Since Natalie had gone back to her second term at university, the house felt too empty. The evenings were too quiet and there was this saggy lack of momentum to family life that made her feel bored and pointless and... just sad.

And now this.

From sadness to annoyance and back again – lately, she'd begun to wonder if sadness and annoyance were the only emotions she was going to have from now on.

And look at the state of her face! She would have to lock herself into one of the toilet cubicles for some time to get the repair work done before the big, happy company announcement.

Out of habit, she glanced at her phone, where eleven new messages flashed at her.

Dave reminding her to bring home red wine and the sourdough bread he liked. He'd obviously completely forgotten about the partnership announcement being today.

Her mother reporting on Dad's doctor's appointment:

Doc not too worried but yr Dad will need dreaded tube up bottom, LOL Mum xx.

She meant 'loads of love' but still...

Natalie asking too nicely, with too many hug and heart emojis, if it would be okay to use the family Amazon account to buy a new duvet because she was freezing (snow cloud, snowflake, snowman emoji).

The dry cleaners to say she could pick up her suit.

The dentist reminding *her* that Dave had an appointment tomorrow, possibly because they'd given up reminding Dave.

The vet to tell her Bella's worming tablet was available.

Four clients asking for one thing and another.

And finally, in came a message from her colleague, Sophie:

Yes, I'm early but I just wanted to be the first to congratulate you. You're going to be an amazing partner and I'm so happy for you. Sx

'I'm just so tired...' Tess said out loud to her phone, her steering wheel and her pocket hankies.

Remember way back, Tess, when you enjoyed wearing a bikini? Had hair halfway down your back? When you had fun, and sex, and big ideas... and a spirit of adventure?

'Oh... what am I going to do?'

Lavelle's on LaJolita in downtown Los Angeles was *the* current place for evening cocktails, mocktails, smoothies and espressos. Its artisan drinks and plant-packed patio were instant Insta. So River Romero, waiting for the producer who had just agreed to hire her for a lucrative rewrite to show up, decided that for the next string of Thursday evenings, she would spend a couple of hours here to see who she could casually bump into. Like just about every other writer in this town, she could be busier. She was on the lookout for a big project, the lucky commission, or that executive with sway who could make all the difference.

And she was tired of trying to get meetings with these, quite frankly, a-holes. Fed up of getting dressed up, driving across town and waiting in over-styled lounges only to be told by some infant with an earpiece, 'I'm soooo sorry, something urgent has come up for Mr Asshat, and he'll have to rearrange.' Or – even worse – actually getting the meeting, only to hear her carefully crafted pitches crash and burn as a committee of dummies failed to grasp even the very basic concept of what she was pitching.

River, who would admit only to being 'in her thirties', was

becoming aware of an increasingly disheartening situation. Just as she was stepping into her writing prime, just as she had finally figured out what she was doing and how to do it, she was surrounded on all fronts by newbies and dimwits who wouldn't know a great idea or a quality piece of writing if their lives depended on it. And this being LA, almost everyone's lives depended on great ideas and quality writing.

Never mind, she told herself, as she was shown to her table where she ordered a coconut and lavender cooler, hoping it wouldn't be too weird. She did not want to get snarly and bitter, like many a mature writer. Good things happen to good writers all the time, she reminded herself. Her last commission had been a challenge, but she had thrown everything at it, determined to take the opportunity to create quality and worthwhile work. But truth be told, both she and her bank account could do with something meaty, substantial... something *big*. Something that would make all this hustling and scrabbling worthwhile.

'Well, hello there, Phillip Renfield. And how are you doing?' she gushed, delighted to see that a major producer she'd been trying to snag a meeting with for weeks was passing right by her chair. 'I'm River Romero, just to jog your memory in case you've sunk a couple of their pearl martinis.'

'The writer,' she added, as his gaze fell on her without any sign of recognition, 'We worked together on *Spangled*.'

This seemed to work.

'Oh yeah, of course, hello, River. How are you doing?'

'I'm great. But... hey, if you're on your way to the rest room, don't let me stop you. I can catch up with you on the way back.'

He smiled and seemed to like this.

'Nah... on my way out. Are you here on your own?'

'I'm waiting for Steve Kay,' she dropped the well-known producer name, 'and as usual, I'm too early.'

'Steve Kay?' Phillip's interest was pricked, 'Cool. Care for some company while you wait?'

'I'd be honoured.' She waved at the empty chair opposite hers. This guy had been impossible to get a meeting with, she had called his executive assistance at least ten times in the past four weeks, and now here he was, offering to sit down and shoot the breeze. She was definitely going to hang out in this place regularly.

Phillip Renfield was an important producer. He was in his late forties now but expensively preserved – fit, tanned, nice haircut, maybe a touch of Botox to the frown lines, and an expensive linen jacket. He took the seat and rested his folded hands on the table.

'How's it going?' she asked first, 'Your name is all over the trades. You're a very busy guy.' Her smile was warm and she amped up the charm.

'Yeah, I'm having a good run,' he replied, 'there's lots of things happening. I've just wrapped one production and starting a new one next week with great names attached... so, all good, all exciting. How about you?'

'I'm meeting Steve tonight to sign up with him for a nice rewrite, but I have a slate full of projects looking for good homes, so I'm hustling as always.' River followed this with a smile she hoped projected positivity and excitement.

Just to be clear, she certainly didn't want a date, she wanted a chance to pitch to Phillip, but she knew pitching required patience. Most likely, she wouldn't even pitch to him this evening.

'So what's the script rewrite?' Phillip asked, waving over a waitress and ordering a pineapple and passion fruit smoothie for himself. 'And for you?'

'I'm fine with my cooler here, thanks.' When the waitress was gone, River answered his first question, 'Well, I can't say too much, it's still under wraps. I can say it's for the high school/young adult market and we all know how important that audience is.'

'Tell me about it,' Phillip agreed with a smile, 'I've got dragged into making a teen movie that's supposed to be "*High School Musical* meets Shakespeare's *Merchant of Venice*".'

River couldn't suppress her burst of laughter at this, then immediately worried that she'd blown their friendly chat, but Phillip shrugged, smiled and said, 'I know, right.'

They exchanged a look and she remembered how much fun he had been to work with on the movie that was, so far, the biggest hit of her career, but the start of Phillip's very successful career.

'Well... it sounds interesting and pretty different,' she told him.

'So before I got involved, the script that got turned in – no names – was a dog,' he confided. 'And now I need to make sure it gets a serious do-over. I mean, a musical for kids based on a Shakespeare play. Gimme a break. It is going to be hard. But we're going to get some kids fresh out of film school involved and hopefully they'll funk it up and turn it around.'

'Hmmm...' River didn't like to say what she really thought about this idea. Letting some inexperienced juniors loose on a script that was already bad would almost certainly produce something that was even worse. But she didn't want to rain on Phillip's parade this evening, instead she wanted to smoothly pave the way for her to call him up in a day or two, and pitch him a handful of her new ideas.

So they spent a few enjoyable minutes swapping industry gossip and reminiscing about the best days of working together on *Spangled*. Then Phillip glanced at his phone and said he'd love to stay longer, but he had another event lined up tonight. River, in turn, said she better find out what was keeping Steve Kay.

'This has been fun,' Phillip told her as he stood up. 'Call me, run me through your slate and let's see if there's anything I like.'

'That would be amazing. I will. And thank you!' River enthused, 'Have a great evening.'

'You too.'

And so he headed off into the night for a fresh round of producer schmoozing, while River picked up her phone and was dismayed to see a WhatsApp from Steve, especially as the first words were 'Sorry River...'

Sorry River, she said under her breath, *what the fresh freak is this?*

She opened the message and read:

Sorry River. It's a bust. The budget's been pulled for this project. It's not happening. So no point us meeting tonight to discuss. I'll be in touch about something else soon.

What the *actual*...?

Unless technology had caused a delay, the guy had sent this message two minutes ago – exactly twelve minutes after he was supposed to be sitting right here in this bar with her.

She was angry, of course. No, make that she was freaking furious. But she was also so disappointed. This was a harsh business, always fraught with last-minute changes and disappointments. But she'd thought that by now she'd earned the right to something more professional than a lousy blow-out WhatsApp twelve minutes into a meeting that was supposed to celebrate the sign up.

That was supposed to have been a good job with a decent paycheck attached. And now she was left staring at a message that it was a bust. She was so angry and insulted she didn't dare to reply. She was frightened of how much bridge-burning abuse she could hurl in under thirty words.

The truth was, her bank account was running low, lower than it had been for years. The warning lights were starting to flash. She'd long ago sold her swanky apartment, bought on the *Spangled* success money. Now she was facing the real worry that she might never be able to move out of the much cheaper place she'd bought with a generous helping hand from her brother. She needed something to work out soon.

And now the waitress was hovering at River's elbow with the check. And *jeezus*... that's how much they charged for mocktails in here? What in the world did a drink with actual alcohol in it cost? And yes, Phillip had, of course, left her to pick up the bill. That was the price of being the pitcher in this town.

River opened her purse and made the painful payment by card. She needed new work. She needed to land something exciting, packed with potential and *big*. She needed the last few years of scraping about doing script polishes and rewrites, even comedy sketches, to all finally come good.

3

'I thought you handled it so professionally, Tess, very well done. Your off-the-cuff speech about Jamila was gracious and generous.'

'Thank you,' Tess replied, 'and thank you for coming to me and talking it through beforehand, John, that made everything easier.'

The dust had settled on the partnership announcement, made two days ago now. Tess was beginning to feel that although she wasn't over it, she could sort of handle it. A sparkling-wine-soaked evening out with Sophie had helped and so too, had the three-course commiseration dinner with all her favourite food that Dave had made for her when she'd told him all about it: 'I know you can't be sad if you're eating spaghetti alle vongole.' And he was sort of right. But then he'd ruined it by saying: 'You don't want to be a partner anyway. All the ones I've met through your work are complete tossers.' When the truth was that she did want to progress up the ranks but in a different kind of way.

And now she was making the call to John Lloyd that he had suggested. All the upset and soul-searching prompted by not getting the promotion had finally given Tess an idea and now that she was about to discuss it with John, she hoped her nerve wouldn't let her down.

'So,' he continued, 'I said I would listen to you and now's your chance. Is there anything you'd like to discuss? Any opportunities you'd like to take? Anything you want to raise? You've been here for a long time. You have so much insight.'

There was only one thing on her mind, but it was not the kind of ambitious, eyes-on-the-prize suggestion that 'call-me-John' would be expecting.

Her glance fell on the collection of magazines that was stacking up on the shelf beside her neat desk. She wanted to go to the other side of the world for the first time ever. She wanted to be somewhere completely different; feel sugary white sand between her toes as she gazed out over turquoise water. She wanted to see rainbow-coloured fish dart past her legs as she walked into the sea. She wanted to stand in front of mysterious and ancient temples, and join the hustle of those frantic cities she'd only ever seen on TV. She wanted to go on a family adventure with Dave, Alex and Natalie.

She wanted to feel properly free and unburdened of the day to day. Above all, she needed some serious time off work to do this. Not just the annual two, at best three, week trip that would leave her jet-lagged and exhausted. No, this was going to be a proper summer holiday, like the seven week long hiatus that Dave, a school art teacher, was able to take every year.

This was her big chance to ask because John would want to do her a favour after the disappointment of the partnership. But she had to frame it right, not try to explain to her CEO that she wanted to reconnect with her children once again, because there had been a time, not so long ago really, when she had known every tiny little detail about their lives, but now she was lucky to speak to them for thirty minutes once a week. The CEO also wouldn't want to hear that she needed to spend time with Dave when they weren't just talking about doing the groceries, or what was for supper. Or were the kids okay? And when were the gutters last cleaned out? And did the car tax need to be renewed? And why leave the empty cracker box on the shelf when there were no crackers left? And all those other necessary, but utterly mundane, details of long-time-married life.

Above all, *she* needed a change. Family life, which had sustained and surrounded her for twenty-two years, had come to an abrupt end. It was only a short time ago that she and Dave had first dropped Natalie off at university, when Tess had managed to smile bravely through the goodbyes, but then cried almost all of the 322 miles home. The day-to-day rush and busy-ness of running a family; the natural trajectory propelling you all forward through the school years – making the team, getting the grades, choosing your subjects, passing your exams, new friends, birthday parties, planning the school holidays, buying uniforms and party dresses, agonising over uni choices... it was all over.

More than anything, Tess longed for time away, to be some-where brand new so she could come to terms with it; make some kind of sense, some kind of plan for this new chapter, this whole new era of life that seemed to have arrived far too soon.

And an idea had come to her in the aftermath of the Jamila partnership shock. So now she summoned her confidence and her scattered knowledge of current business speak and began. 'You know, John, I do have an idea, but it's a little left-of-field.'

'I'm all ears, Tess. I love left-of-field. Fire away.'

'I'm a midlifer, John. I know that fifty-three per cent of employees at the company are my age and older – that's a lot of people – and we're at risk of getting set in our ways. We can be change averse, technophobic and reluctant to embrace the new. We can lose our enthusiasm for making progress and improvements at work. Lose our drive. So... I'd like to suggest taking a sabbatical over the summer – unpaid is fine – because I want to take a proper block of time away from the office to travel. I want to explore ideas around how to stay enthusiastic about work, no matter what your age; how to remain open to new ideas; how to embrace tech when you're over forty-five. And obviously, I'll share my learning with the whole company when I get back. I hope I can help to inspire the company's more... well... senior members.'

There was a pause.

Tess held her breath and felt the prickling intensify across her face as she wondered if she'd just made the most ridiculous suggestion of all time. Her CEO had offered her a promotion, a chance to step up to a bigger job in London, and she'd just pitched him a sabbatical idea and more than hinted that she was losing her enthusiasm for work.

The pause went on and Tess curled her toes.

'Well, well...' John Lloyd said finally. 'Now that is left-of-field and not at all what I'd expected, but good for you.'

Tess felt as if she could breathe again.

'I say yes. I say take your break, take three months off, have a proper sabbatical... and paid,' he added, to her relief, 'visit horizons new and come back to us with a raft of fresh ideas.' She heard the encouragement in his voice, 'I'm a midlifer myself, so I'll want to learn from your project. And congratulations, Tess, thank you for making us all look so good at our jobs.'

As she put the phone down, a grin split Tess's face. A happy, relieved, yes, even triumphant grin – and it was a long time since she'd grinned like this. Three. Whole. Months. Off. *Paid*.

This was incredible. And absolutely long enough for the lavish, adventurous, thrilling travelling holiday she had in mind – temples of Vietnam, beaches of Cambodia – followed by six weeks of in-depth research for the 'midlife project' she'd come up with. Both truly inspired ideas that had somehow bubbled up from the depths of her upset and despair.

The only cloud on the horizon was that she hadn't actually mentioned this idea to Dave yet. And Dave, who hated to fly, who loved holidays either in his own back garden, or involving vast quantities of cheese in France, was going to think she had completely lost the plot.

4

In her long experience of trying to get through to producers, River had found that it was usually the third call that was the charm. When you called an office for the third time in a morning, the perky executive assistant was generally done with putting you off with bullshit excuses and would actually ask her boss, in this case Phillip Renfield, whether or not he wanted to speak to you.

'Hi River, thanks for calling.' When she heard Phillip's voice coming out of her mobile speaker, she could actually have given a little jump for joy. 'I've got a meeting in ten, but why don't you hit me with some outlines, I'll tell you what I like and then you can send me the full storylines. Does that sound okay?'

He sounded very busy, of course, professional, but definitely open to hearing from her.

'Phillip, I'm not going to pitch you anything...'

Now she was sure she had his attention.

'Instead, I want you to give the "*High School Musical* meets *Merchant of Venice*" gig to me. I literally cannot stop thinking about it. In the right hands, I think it could be amazing. The play is about racism and exclusion and injustice... in a school setting, with musical sing-alongs, it could be incredibly powerful. Plus, I *know* Shakespeare. Someone cultured should be working on this, someone who can translate everything that was genius about that play and make it totally relevant for today's audience.'

With barely a pause for breath, she went on: 'And high school kids... they can't make it to the end of a TikTok video, so this has got to grab them, entertain them and make them think, without preaching any kind of lesson at them. I'm thinking I take the script you have to England. I actually go to Shakespeare country. I immerse myself in it all. Go to the theatre, visit Shakespeare's birth-place, get the feel.

'Maybe I could script up a little documentary aimed at kids that releases at the same time as the movie? Plus, you know me, Phillip, you know I'll be way less of a pain to work with than a bunch of kids out of film school. I mean, let's have an ideation session with the film school kids, I bet they could come up with things we'd never have thought of, but then you need a grown-up to create an excellent script.'

She paused. Screwed up her eyes... and waited for his reply.

You could never tell with a pitch. She'd been rehearsing it all morning. She thought she'd delivered well, with the right level of expertise and enthusiasm. She thought her ideas were great. But you could never tell with a pitch.

The pause went on. Long enough for River to wonder if she'd made a complete fool of herself. Or worse, that she'd sounded desperate for work...

Then finally, Phillip said, 'I love it.'

And River felt almost faint with relief.

'I love your ideas, I love your energy, and best of all, I love the way you're solving one major headache for me.'

Wow! River couldn't help thinking, her emotions switching direction in a split second, *and that's the way I reel 'em in.*

'But this is a big project. I don't expect a final draft of the script until August/September. Can we make the figures work, River? I don't have a generous budget for this. I might not be able to afford you.'

He then hit her with a suggested fee that made her jaw drop. This was his definition of a not-generous budget? She needed to work with him a lot more often. She could definitely go to England, write a script, write a documentary and have months of spare money literally sloshing around in her bank account for that.

But careful, careful, wasn't the rule to always negotiate? River didn't have an agent. She'd fallen out in too spectacular a fashion with too many agents in the past, so now she did her agenting herself.

'Well...' she said.

And now it was her turn to pause.

Sometimes, people offered you more money without you even needing to say a word, she'd discovered. Sometimes you just... had to... pause...

She let that pause go on almost uncomfortably. She waited for him to say something.

'Okay, I can probably go up a little,' he said finally, 'Let me see what I can do. I'll come back to you today.'

'Thank you, Phillip. This is going to be amazing. I'm really very excited.'

'Yeah, me too, right!'

'I want to get to the source. I mean, the Shakespeare guy's material has lasted over four hundred years. We're still quoting it, still performing it, so he must be doing something right. I think the inspiration for making this script awesome is going to be in England.'

'Actually, I'll be in London for a few weeks in the summer,' Phillip volunteered.

'I bet all kinds of really great people will be there too,' River said, feeling an idea coming together. 'If I'm going to be renting a place – I should have a garden party. Mix it up. Invite some cool LA people, some theatre people and anyone else interesting I can find along the way.'

'You know how to hold a good party, I remember,' Phillip said.

'Yes I do, thank you! Hey, I should let you go, Phillip, you have a meeting. We'll talk very soon and I'm so thrilled to be working with you again!'

When the call was over, River looked up from her desk, well, actually it was a café table but in one of the quietest, calmest cafés she knew, all shades of greenish blues. And when she was working here, she ordered two espressos an hour, plus tips, to keep everyone happy, so it was practically a desk.

Okay, this project was not signed yet, so she couldn't celebrate. But it looked really good. It looked like a done deal and she was so happy, she could shout. Or maybe sing... since she was now going to be writing a musical... a '*High School Musical* meets *Merchant of Venice*'... what the actual hell? How was this going to work? She had no idea. But she was a smart, very creative person, so surely she could figure it out.

And a party... an English garden party. She needed to think about that too. How to find other guests, she wondered... she'd look up the actors, writers and theatre producers involved in the Shakespeare plays she would go and see. She'd put feelers out with her friends. The main thing was not to have too many writers at her party. Writers, *goddammit*: wonderful people... terrible people... they'd swig down all the booze, they'd tell hilarious stories and then move on to the deepest, darkest opinions that would depress the hell out of everyone, and then they'd corner all the producers and steal the commissions from under her nose. *Writers!*

And where the heck was Shakespeare country anyway? Where

did he live? Where did they put on all those plays every summer? Wasn't it in London somewhere?

She tapped the questions into her phone and was soon looking at a map of Stratford-upon-Avon in Warwickshire. Warwickshire? Where was that? It didn't look anywhere near London at all. It looked miles and miles and miles from anywhere except Birmingham. She didn't know much about England, but she did know that *no one* was going to travel to a garden party near Birmingham.

5

'An elephant care centre? Do you think that's something you'd like to visit?' Tess turned to ask her husband, 'I mean... I'm not really so keen, but Natalie might really like that. It might even be something she could put on her CV.'

Natalie was studying Biology at uni, because it was her best subject at school, but she had only the vaguest idea of what she wanted to do when she graduated.

'*Elephant care*?' Dave perched his reading glasses on his head and looked up from the book he was reading beside her in bed, 'I don't think any of us is qualified to give elephants any kind of care.'

'No, I know that, but this tour I'm looking at of northern Thailand takes in Bangkok, Chiang Rai, Chiang Mai – and includes visits to hilltop temples, a local hill-tribe village, plus an elephant care centre.'

Dave continued to look at her and now she suspected that the debate they'd been having for the last three weeks was about to break out again.

'Look, Tess, is this *really* a good idea?' He was using his most kind and sympathetic tone, as if she was one of his pupils who had made a mistake, but that was okay, because he was here to help her now, 'I mean... Thailand, Vietnam, Cambodia... these places are so far away...'

'That's the idea, Dave.'

'We'll be on seventeen-hour flights with stopovers. We'll have jetlag and maybe deep vein thrombosis... and then when we get there, people always get food poisoning, amoebic dysentery, tape worms, mugged and all kinds of disasters when they travel to countries like this. I mean, it just doesn't sound relaxing at all. Don't you want to unwind? To really relax?'

'I want to travel,' she countered, 'I've never had the chance to go travelling and I'm planning to book all kinds of relaxing things in between the travel and the sightseeing. Look at the website for this eco spa...'

Tess turned her laptop screen to face him, so he could see the luscious blue and bright green images from this particular corner of paradise as she read aloud from the spa's website: 'Swim in the freshwater pools, heated to different therapeutic temperatures; unwind in our scented flower gardens as you enjoy our range of creative and relaxing treatments.'

'Oh God,' Dave eye-rolled, 'but that's probably the kind of spa where they only serve you a slice of watermelon every other day, so that you can lose the two stone required to make you think it was worth the money.'

'Dave? Would I take you somewhere that only served watermelon?' she asked. 'We all know you'd be absolutely miserable!'

But really, she thought as she turned back to her screen and gave a furtive eye roll of her own, a week of watermelon-based meals would probably be a great idea for Dave. His middle-age spread was spreading so rapidly that even his pyjama trousers were starting to look stretched.

'And what about the cost?' he protested, 'I mean, I know you're getting paid for the break and I know you're expecting a good bonus, but we have Natalie at university; we want to give Alex some money to get a place of his own, and we'd also like to retire in the not-too-distant future, so maybe we shouldn't be blowing thousands and thousands of pounds on a six-week holiday. Six weeks! My whole summer... I just don't know if that's how I want to spend it. You know I always want to do some...'

'Painting,' she snapped, 'Yes, I know, Dave.' He had now opened a long and festering wound and she was going to have to point out a few home truths: 'In the run up to every single summer holidays, you buy paint, you buy canvasses, you buy new brushes and then somehow, every year, the entire holiday goes past and you don't even paint one single sodding thing.'

It was a low blow. She knew it would upset him, but he was upsetting her.

Yes, of course it was expensive. But wasn't she allowed to spend her money on what she wanted? And she wanted a six-week adventure, a wonderful family holiday... the holiday of a lifetime. She wanted to see Hoh Chi Min City, in all its frantic glory, then cruise the Mekong Delta, and marvel at its floating markets. She wanted to go to Phnom Penh in Cambodia. Siem Reap and Angkor Wat – the largest temple in the world – were on her list of glorious destinations. She wanted to stand in front of Angkor Wat, and drink in the sight of ancient tree roots draped over even more ancient buildings.

And she wanted to do all of this with her family standing by her side. She was paying, so why shouldn't she make this happen? Why couldn't they all get excited about it? She hadn't felt so excited about anything for a long time.

Was it really too much to ask her husband of twenty-three years to show some enthusiasm? To be all for it, instead of doing his best to convince her not to do it?

'You have no idea how much the children always got in the way in the summer...' was Dave's excuse on the painting front.

'The children? In your way? Natalie is nineteen. She spent most of last summer in the US,' Tess couldn't help pointing out.

'Yes, but you don't know about the creative process...' he protested, 'you've got to have headspace... you've got to...'

'If you'd really wanted to paint in the summer holidays, you would have found the time,' she contradicted him. And she knew he would find this hurtful, but really, what she was saying was true. He couldn't keep pretending he was some sort of stifled genius who would flourish just as soon as he had the right amount of time... whatever that was. He was an art teacher at a great school who liked to spend the summer holidays lolling around in the garden then cooking a nice dinner. He was definitely not the creative cool kid she'd married all those years ago, when he had plans to... oh, what did all that matter? They were here now in their lovely house in the English countryside, a teacher and an accountant with two really great kids. What did it matter about youthful plans and dreams? That was all another lifetime ago.

'I think Natalie and Alex will love the idea of this holiday,' she said, to get the conversation back on track.

'What I want to suggest is three weeks without them, three weeks when it's just us on this holiday,' she glanced at her husband, 'and then they come out and join us for three weeks. I thought three weeks of just the two of us... might be quite good for us,' she added.

But Dave wasn't going to be drawn into a boggy discussion about 'the state of us' just before bedtime. He gave her a curt smile and then turned back to his book... historical crime fiction would be her guess, one of his favourite genres: 'Foxy Miss Scarlett in the stately home library with the antique silver-plated candlestick'.

'What about the house?' he asked, 'Six weeks is a long time to leave the house empty.'

And that was true... maybe their cleaner could come in once a week to check on it... maybe a neighbour, too. Tess hadn't solved this problem yet.

'Let's talk about this tomorrow,' Dave said.

'Fine.'

On a break at work earlier in the day, she'd followed a link and wasted three minutes and forty-five seconds of her life watching an earnest anthropology professor rubbing a wooden stick into a notch on a wooden board in order to finally, after long and painful effort, create a tiny spark that smouldered in the dried grass and bark chips he'd prepared. It had made her think of the state of her marriage. A great deal of effort for very little spark or flame.

She and Dave were very fond of one another; they got along; they generally agreed on things; they ran their home and their family and their lives well together. But she was beginning to seriously wonder if that was enough. They'd been together for twenty-three years, and the last five, maybe even six years had been very testing. The teenage years – the rows with the teenagers, the rows about the teenagers – and the sudden death of Dave's mother just two years after his father's death. It had all been very turbulent.

They'd had too many arguments, far too little couple time, and now they were in this holding pattern of generally getting along well – okay, when they weren't annoying the heck out of each other – in their groove, quite comfortable, with the odd prickly argument, but Tess found herself wondering: where did the passion go? The fun? What were she and Dave really looking forward to now?

These thoughts bothered her a lot. But infuriatingly, they didn't seem to bother Dave at all. Now that the children had left home, it was as if he couldn't wait to be retired and snoozing on the sofa in his slippers. *Retirement*, for God's sake? She wasn't even fifty yet!

Several times a day, Tess quoted to herself the opening line of the Elizabeth Barrett Browning poem read out at their wedding, but she replaced 'How do I love thee? Let me count the ways', with 'How do you annoy me? Let me count the ways.'

Like a room last decorated over twenty years ago, or an untended garden, their relationship desperately needed concerted attention. But neither of them wanted to make the time or the effort to do it.

'Goodnight, Tess,' he said after he'd read a few more pages of his book, then he turned out the table lamp at his side.

'Goodnight,' she replied.

* * *

Later, when she was sure Dave was asleep, she stole out of bed to get Bella, the beloved family Labrador, nearly fourteen years old now. Bella was a bit smelly, drooling and arthritic, but she was absolutely adored. Although her hearing wasn't sharp, she still heard Tess calling to her from the top of the stairs: 'Come on, girlie, come on up.' So the old dog ambled up the staircase and followed Tess into the bedroom. There, Tess helped Bella up onto the sofa then wrapped a cosy fleece blanket around her. When Tess got back into bed, she felt comforted listening to the two different rhythms of breathing in the room.

Her thoughts turned again to how busy and obvious life had felt when the children were young, as they all progressed in a bustle from one year and one step to the next. Now, the house was too quiet, too organised, too perfect, and too... just sad. Natalie was a blur of energy, noise and action too sorely missed. Her long, thoughtful conversations with quiet Alex, now in his first post-uni job, were also an aching gap in her life.

She missed the daily mothering: the feeding, the explaining, reassuring, encouraging, everyday chatting, and the little acts of love, from stocking up on Natalie's favourite snack in the supermarket, to folding a freshly washed t-shirt for Alex.

She had so much enjoyed being the mother captain of the family ship, the centre point in her children's lives. And she wasn't sure how to replace that pivotal role.

'Oh, God...' she thought, 'this must be my midlife crisis. And I'm trying to solve it with an eye-wateringly expensive family holiday.'

Quickly followed by: 'Maybe an eye-wateringly expensive family holiday will solve it... I'm willing to give it a try.'

And then the brainwave: 'Why don't we cover some of the cost of the holiday by renting the house out while we're away?'

6

'Your host has cancelled your booking. We've made some other suggestions for your visit to Stratford-upon-Avon, England.'

This had been the distressing message River had found waiting in her inbox.

After firing the host an appropriately acidic email and blasting her in the review section:

> This flake has cancelled my holiday, no warning, no explanation, so I'm just making sure everyone reading the review section gets to know. Quid pro quo, cupcake, quid pro quo.

River set about finding somewhere else to stay during her July visit to Shakespeare's hallowed town. Turned out July was the month when all the plays were on, so her plan was to begin the rewrite now, and make good progress, then use her time in England to add colour and plenty of original work, plus collect material for the documentary, of course.

She and Phillip had signed the deal. The first instalment of money was due, and she had now read the whole script. It was *so* much more terrible than she could ever have imagined.

She'd also endured the ideation session with the straight-outta-film-school babies. They'd been truly sweet, but their suggestions for new comedy and action scenes were lame. Although two ideas, for Shylock to rap his most famous speech and to make white pupils the minority in this high school, weren't too bad, more research was required.

She scrolled through the Airbnb suggestions for Stratford-upon-Avon. Almost everything looked ugly, tasteless or too small.

The place that had fallen through had been so stylish, with power showers, two TVs, a big garden with decking and garden furniture, and it was well away from the road. Now she couldn't find anything with any of these comforts. She needed peace and quiet, comfort and calm. How else was she going to get the script finished and the documentary written?

Godammit, she whispered under her breath, so as not to disturb the white-haired ladies at the table next to hers, sipping soya chai lattes after their power walk round the neighbourhood. What was the matter with English people? Look at these horrible houses, everything so beige or so grey. Wasn't the weather bad enough in England without decorating your entire house in beige and grey? And peach-coloured towels! She was staying nowhere with peach towels left over from the 1980s.

There was only one thing to do – she increased the price bracket on her search. And lo and behold, there, at the very tippy top of her price range appeared the perfect English house... oh, *more*, so much more than she was looking for. Like the centrefold spread from *House Beautiful*, a wooden front door, some kind of purple flowering plant trailing down the side of the house and inside, one room more beautiful than the next: dark polished wooden floors, sumptuous navy sofas, good art, a delightful bedroom, a serious cook's white country kitchen and a garden packed with flowers, all set up with a barbeque and outdoor sofas and armchairs.

This was where she had to go. What would it be like to live in a house like that, just for a while? She wanted a slice of that perfect English lifestyle. But, oh, the price was steep, steep, steep. Even for a screenwriter with a big project on the go.

Maybe she could strike a week off her stay? She scrolled on through the house description and saw that the place came with use of a car included. So she would save on car rental... maybe that would make it just about possible?

She looked through the photos of the garden again and considered the swanky party she was planning, with Phillip and actors from the theatre and all the other available cool people that she could round up from a hundred-mile radius.

Surely that would be good for her career? Surely not just staying in this house, but also hosting the party could be written off as an expense? Corporate hospitality... maybe? She tried to imagine the incredulous look she would get from Irma, her accountant, who once a year tried to make sense of River's chaotic files, packed with receipts and invoices.

Yes, surely it would all be classed as an expense. River held her breath and sent an enquiry to the owner. No, she definitely couldn't afford it, certainly not before the first instalment came in from Phillip. But sometimes very good things happened when you took a risk, when you went out on a limb, and stretched yourself.

And she had struggled of late. She had lost good commissions, done work that was crappy and below the going rate because she was desperate. She'd even stopped seeing a lot of old friends because... well, reasons, but one of those reasons was that their success made her feel low. She was due some better luck. River had the definite feeling that very soon, it was going to be her turn.

7

FOUR MONTHS LATER

'Three months... you're going to be away for *three entire months*? I'm sorry but I still can't take that in.' Sophie shook her head and lifted another forkful to her mouth.

Tess and Sophie were having their usual last Friday of the month working lunch in the Italian restaurant round the corner from the office. This was when they enjoyed a lengthy and civilised meal with wine and discussed the month at work, talking through the gripes, problems or grievances, and occasionally patting themselves on the back for things well done. The work discussion was followed with talk about their families and more personal things. Tess's sabbatical and her 'holiday of a lifetime' had been the hot topic of conversation for some time now, especially as she now had only three weeks left in the office. For Sophie, whose children were between the ages of ten and sixteen, the idea of such a long holiday, so far away, was unbelievably exotic.

'I do know that it is completely outrageous,' Tess agreed, still not quite daring to believe that it was all going to happen, the longed-for sabbatical, with the six weeks of carefully plotted travel round all the most beautiful places in Cambodia, Vietnam and Thailand, plus a further six weeks back at home to recover and put together her 'midlifer project'. This holiday, so long in the planning, was now really almost here. She could hardly believe it.

Sophie had helped with the heavy lifting at work – the rearranging of project dates and deadlines, and the organising of cover. Someone was even coming up from the London office for a month to help out. Then Tess had indulged fully in the planning of the trip itself – where to go, where to stay (from eco beach huts to luxurious spas), what to do, what not to miss.

For most of the spring, it had become almost a hobby, something she did in the evenings and at the weekends, something on the scale of a major work project that had required a whiteboard, post-it notes and its very own files and folders on her laptop. There was even a Pinterest board of beaches, each one more vibrantly turquoise-blue than the last.

Yes, it had taken quite some time to talk Dave fully round to the idea of the trip. She'd had to promise more beaches, relaxing breaks between the travelling stints, 'safe' food, and some kind of legal tranquilliser for the flights. And when he felt these things were being taken care of, he had finally begun to get enthusiastic. Alex and Natalie had started to get interested, too. They'd opened up email links and WhatsApp pictures, they'd told her which hotels, tourist attractions and areas they preferred over others, but no one had been quite as involved, as zealous even, about the whole thing as Tess. This was her thing, and it was her gift to her family. Not only had she organised everything, but she had paid for it too from her Hambold bonus.

She wanted this holiday to be something exciting, adventurous and unforgettable – something that took them completely away from themselves, from the ordinary everyday, an adventure they would all remember forever. So she'd relished the plotting and the planning and had even withdrawn some lifetime savings to make this very special dream trip come fully to life.

She knew that she was trying to recapture lost time with her children. She wished now that she'd spent so much more time with them during the seemingly endless days of the summer holidays. Instead, she'd usually managed three weeks at most. Two weeks on a family holiday and then a third week when they prepped for school, shopping for uniforms, shoes, new pencil cases and lunchboxes, visiting the dentist. At the time, she'd been grateful and only a little jealous to leave Dave at home running art projects, friend visits, bake-offs and day trips, but now that her children had left school, had, to be honest, left home, she regretted the unfettered summertime that she hadn't spent with them.

Surely, somehow, she and her colleagues could have made a plan to have given them all much more of the summer off? Didn't businesses in Scandinavia shut up shop for the whole of August so everyone could swim and fish at their lake hut? And those economies didn't exactly come to a standstill.

What had seemed *so* important about work back then that she'd been able to suit up, pack her laptop bag and leave the house every morning to go and sift through some company's accounts? And why had a senior accountant and a head of art between them not been able to salary sacrifice a few weeks of pay for some extra summer holiday time?

Because, looking back, there hadn't been an unlimited number of summers. And, of course, she loved grown-up Alex and Natalie, loved them both fiercely, but when she allowed herself to think about it, she missed their childhoods very much and wished she'd wrung more out of the available time with them.

So this was an attempt to make up for it, before the children were fully grown up and gone. And she would spend the first three weeks of the holiday alone with her husband for the first time in years. She hoped this would give them time to take a fresh look at their worn and saggy relationship, their comfortable old pyjama-bottom of a marriage, and have a think about where they were and where they might be headed.

'So what's this American like, who's renting Ambleside while you're away?' Sophie asked, bringing Tess back from her thoughts. 'And why is one lone American renting your beautiful big house?'

'She's a screenwriter from Los Angeles...' Tess said, pride and excitement in her voice. 'Do you remember that film *Spangled?*'

'Oh yes, I do. That was funny, and smart and really good,' Sophie added.

'So renting Ambleside for the summer is probably small change for her.'

Although their children were at different ages and at different schools, Tess and Sophie had shared long conversations about all kinds of critical childhood and parenting moments: secondary school choices, the pros and cons of braces, maths exam results, acne treatment, whether or not fifteen-year-olds should be allowed to visit their boyfriends' homes, screen time, and other assorted parental minefields.

They never discussed their marriages though, it occurred to Tess. Work, of course, children, yes, homes, yes, wider families, yes, current TV viewing, naturally, but husbands and marriages were topics only mentioned in a superficial way.

Did Sophie suspect that Tess wasn't happy with the state of her marriage? That was as much as Tess would admit to herself... that she wasn't happy with the current 'state'. She definitely thought of the situation as temporary. She hoped it was temporary and that one day soon, it would pass. But if she thought back to when she had last felt really proud and happy to be Dave's wife, it seemed a very long time ago... years ago, in fact.

And sometimes she wondered if they could be heading towards a pivotal moment, a make-or-break decision.

'Is it nearly four?' Sophie exclaimed. 'I've got to get back to my desk for an hour, then I'm on football taxi duty at five thirty.'

Sometimes these reminders of busy family life gave Tess a pang, but occasionally – like today – the thought of going home to a calm house completely free of all child taxi duties was really quite nice.

'And who's going to look after your old doggie while you're away?' Sophie asked as she tried to attract the waiter's attention.

Even as Tess replied, talking in glowing terms about the pet sitter, who was going to take Bella into her home and look after her really carefully, she could feel her stomach clench slightly.

This was the glitch in the plan; the one poorly tied loose end. Bella. The old girl had lost so many teeth, her food was a senior dog paste that Tess sometimes spoon fed to her, if her appetite was poor. Bella needed a dose of painkiller for her arthritis twice a day, but she still whimpered when she squatted or got up from her bed because her hips were stiff and sore.

Tess knew that Bella wasn't going to last forever, and the thought that Bella might die when they were away on the holiday was terrible.

* * *

Too much wine, she thought, in the back of the taxi home, speeding through a green blur of hedgerow and country lanes. Too much wine... she was sluggish and sleepy. She would take her duvet down to the sofa; get floppy old Bella snuggled up beside her, put the TV on and fall asleep for half an hour.

'It's this turn here,' she told the taxi driver, because these twisty back roads were easily confused, 'and then the first on the left.'

Several minutes later, the taxi rolled up the smooth reclaimed red brick slope of the driveway and came to a halt.

This was Ambleside.

This was home.

And she *loved* her house. Ambleside was one of the loves of her life and had been ever since she'd first set eyes on it. Such a handsome 1930s building, with a freshly painted white exterior, gloss black proper wood-framed windows and a shiny oak front door framed with trailing lilac wisteria flowers. This was her family's home. And had been for eighteen years now.

They'd moved in when Alex was four and Natalie just a year and a half. They'd taken out a vast mortgage that had caused her panicked middle-of-the-night wake ups as she saw nothing but decades of poring over spreadsheets ahead to pay it off. And all that hard physical *labour*... stripping out mildewing woodchip, rotted bathroom panelling, ancient, stinking carpet. Uncovering rotted joists, patches of hidden damp, collapsed drains and even, on a particularly terrible Sunday evening, a nest of grey, furless baby rats in the low attic. They'd had to hit the leftover Christmas brandy after that discovery. Wine just hadn't been enough.

For almost a year, buying the house had felt like a dreadful, ruinous mistake. But all that pain was long forgotten now, she thought, putting her sturdy metal key into the familiar lock. Room by room, the house had been re-made around them into their true family home.

There had been updates now and then since the first major renovation: the nursery wallpaper had been replaced with stark white for a teenaged Alex and pastel blue with flowers for Natalie. And in the last year or two, Tess's attention had shifted from sourcing perfect curtains and kitchen tiles out into the garden.

Today, as soon as she stepped into the hallway, she could tell that something wasn't right. It was the smell – the sharp back-of-the-throat tang of vomit. Dave was away on a school trip until tomorrow, so only Bella, the family dog, was home.

'Bella,' she called, 'where are you, my lovely?'

She hurried into the sitting room where Bella's big, comfortable bed and blankets were pulled up close to the radiator.

Tess's eye travelled from the first pile of sick along to the second and third and finally to Bella in a heap in her basket.

She rushed over to the trembling dog and knelt down beside her.

'What's up, my darling?' Tess said, running her fingers over the warm, velvety head, 'are you not feeling well?'

Bella's head lifted slightly, she managed a brief whimper, and her old, clouded eyes met Tess's.

And Tess was instantly filled with dread.

'No...' she whispered, 'oh no, Bella.'

* * *

'Well, you'll have to bring her in,' the receptionist at the vet's told her in a voice that sounded clipped and unsympathetic.

'I can't bring her in,' Tess said, 'she's too ill. It will cause her too much pain.' Plus, at the back of her mind was the realisation that she'd drunk the best part of a bottle of Chablis, so was in no fit state to drive the car.

'Isn't there anyone who can come out and see her... even later today? Any time really, I'll be here with her.'

'No, we're closing at five thirty and we don't do house visits,' came the reply.

'Right... okay... and is there anyone I can phone if things get worse?'

'Yeah... we'll put the answering machine on and it'll give you the emergency number. But you'll have to go to them. They don't do house visits either.'

Tess ran her hand over the dog's soft head and suddenly tears were spilling down her cheeks.

'Right, fine,' she said, 'thank you.' Then she hung up.

Bella was still trembling and whining softly in her basket. The cooling sick was congealing on the grey carpet. But vets didn't do house visits any more. Despite the overwhelming sense of sadness, Tess knew she had to do something.

Okay, first things first. She went to the kitchen cupboard where she kept Bella's arthritis pain relief. She took a teaspoon from the drawer and filled Bella's bowl with fresh water. Then, for a few minutes, she ministered to the sick dog. She tenderly squeezed a double dose of medicine into her mouth. Then she dribbled teaspoons of the cool water over Bella's parched-looking tongue.

She stroked the dog's ears and after a while, Bella's trembling and whimpering quietened and she seemed to fall asleep.

Tess went to the kitchen and put together a sponge, a towel and a bucket of soapy water. Back in the sitting room, she tucked one of Bella's blankets over her, then scraped and scrubbed at the carpet.

When that was finished, she brought her duvet down, lay on the sofa and, just like Bella, fell asleep – only to wake with a start an hour or so later to a terrible deep, dark wail. She couldn't understand for a moment what it was or where it was. A frightening, gutteral sound... like the cries women made in childbirth. She looked round the room and saw Bella lying on her side, close to her bed, her legs stiff and stretched out, wailing in pain.

Tess felt panicked. She turned first of all to her phone lying on the floor beside the sofa. She wondered if she should phone Dave, hundreds of miles away looking after school children on a trip to St Ives. Maybe she should phone her own children... but what would they do? What could they do? How could they help her or Bella?

This was going to be down to her. She would somehow have to step up and handle this. She would cope with this because mothers always find the strength to do these things – to give birth, to tend to the babies and the sick and to stay with the dying.

'Hello, Bella, hello, darling,' she said, kneeling beside the dog and running her hand gently, tenderly, comfortingly over the dog's head and side.

For almost an hour, Tess tried to comfort the beloved dog, she fed her medicine, she ran water over her dry, panting tongue, and she listened to the harsh rasp in Bella's throat.

Then she knew she had to get help. Surely she would be okay to drive to the vet now? And get the pain relief the dog needed.

She phoned the number, jotted down the emergency contact details, made the second call and that was how she came to be driving slowly down a series of narrow roads with poor, aching, groaning Bella in the flattened front seat, wrapped in Tess's fluffy dressing gown. Tess had one hand on the steering wheel, one hand on the dog's head. She was talking reassuringly and as kindly as she could. She wished and wished this wasn't happening, and she felt the enormity of this trip.

This might be her last car ride with their dog.

How many thousands of car rides had she made before with this lovely, gentle soul? Trips to the park, trips to the forest, the children giggling in the back seat, and Bella barking happily from the boot. In all the joy of taking small children and a delightful doggie to the beach, how could you possibly imagine that there would be a journey like this in the future?

And just like that, very fond and funny memories rushed into her mind. The time Bella got lost on a country park walk and she and Natalie shouted so hard and for so long that they actually lost their voices for the rest of the day. And Alex had been so worried that he couldn't go for a walk for months afterwards unless Bella

was on the lead. The time Bella jumped up to the kitchen countertop and managed to wolf down an entire chicken just out of the
oven. Tess had spent several minutes searching for that chicken,
convinced she must have put it somewhere, before she'd finally
realised what had happened. They'd had to go for fish and chips
instead. For months, Natalie would mention it every time they had
chicken: 'Remember when Bella ate the *whole* chicken, Mummy.
The *whole* chicken, in one big gulp.'

By the time Tess pulled up in the animal hospital's car park,
Bella was wailing again, stretching out in pain and retching. Tess
wasn't going to leave her here like this, so she tooted her horn a few
times, hoping this would bring someone out.

Sure enough, a receptionist came to the doorway and asked:
'Yes? Can I help you?'

'I phoned... it's my dog... she's really ill. And I don't think I can
move her.'

She was told that the vet would be out as soon as he could. So
Tess went back into the car and spent several long minutes holding
the dog's old head in her hands, talking to her and trying to soothe
her. But the panting and whining made it clear that Bella was in
deep pain.

The vet, when he arrived at the car door in pale blue scrubs,
looked young and a little tired.

'Hello there, I'm Stan,' he said, 'So... it's not going so well here.'

Stan knelt down at the door and gave Bella an initial examination. He put his stethoscope against her heart and against her stomach. He listened long and carefully. Then he took time to ask Tess
detailed questions and consider her answers. He asked how old
Bella was.

'So, what's the matter with her?' Tess asked when the questions
seemed to have come to an end. She realised she was trembling,
too, frightened of the answer.

'I'm really sorry, but I'm pretty certain that she's dying,' came the reply. 'I think her kidneys have failed. She's in a lot of pain and I'm going to give her a sedative now to help.'

He picked up the scruff of Bella's neck and injected deftly.

Surprisingly quickly, Bella's body relaxed, her breathing deepened, and the whimpering quietened. This meant that Tess could shift her focus from Bella's precious old head to what Stan was saying.

'She needs to go to sleep now, doesn't she?' Tess asked, 'I mean... it's time... to let her go?'

She heard her voice break on the final words and, for several moments, she had to struggle hard to keep her face from crumpling.

'Yes, I think that would be the kindest thing you could do for her now,' Stan replied.

'Do we need to bring her in to the surgery?' Tess asked, her voice hoarse.

'No, we'll not move her now,' Stan replied, 'she looks comfortable. You get into the seat beside her and I'll go and get what I need. I'll be about ten minutes... would you like some more time, or does that sound okay?'

Oh, the kindness of that question.

Tess heard herself say, 'Ten minutes is fine.' But nothing about this was fine at all.

She put her hands around the old dog's face and used every one of the last remaining minutes to hold Bella and tell her what a wonderful dog she was. How much she was loved and how much fun she'd brought to them all. She named every family member in turn and thought she could see Bella's ears twitch at the mention of Alex, then Natalie and Dave. She smoothed Bella's ears, ran her hand down the warm fur and tried not to think about anything other than keeping Bella comfortable.

* * *

And that was how Bella died, with her head in Tess's lap, with Tess's hands around her head and Tess holding back tears as she murmured gentle and comforting words of love.

For some time afterwards, Tess sat in the car beside Bella's body, without the calming rise and fall of Bella's breath, and she tried to imagine her home without Bella's presence. It would all be so unbearably neat and organised and tidy... not even any dog hair. Tears streamed down her face as she considered the loss of Alex, Natalie and now even Bella from her daily life. No dog hair, no jumble of trainers to trip over in the hallway, no damp towels on the stairs, make-up stains on the sink, no dog lead hanging by the door. It was the end of an era, well before she was ready for it to end.

There was paperwork to sign and Bella was taken out of the car, still – at Tess's request – wrapped in her dressing gown. Bella and the dressing gown would be cremated and Tess would have to come back on Wednesday to collect the ashes. In the reception area, in the dazed aftermath of this trauma, Tess drank down a bitter, gritty coffee from the vending machine.

The receptionist asked if she was okay to drive, or did she need a taxi?

Tess felt barely able to answer the question. But she nevertheless convinced herself that she would be fine to drive. And drive through those familiar country lanes she did, in the dark, through a blizzard of tears. Crying so hard she could feel water pooling in the hollow at the base of her neck, and snot streaming from her nose. She hardly noticed the journey, but she did feel the shock of arriving home, knowing there was no Bella there to greet her and never would be again.

This thought was so sad that she shut the front door and crumpled to the ground, where she keened her grief for many long minutes.

When she finally stood up, she saw that it was after 11 p.m. She had no idea how it had got so late. There was a text on her phone from Dave to say goodnight because he was going to bed early... or, more likely, sneaking to the hotel bar with the rest of his frazzled colleagues.

She couldn't bear to call him or her children. Let them think that all was well and Bella was sleeping peacefully in her bed, for one more night, at least. Tess drank some water, then went through a half-baked version of her usual bedtime routine.

When she lay back on her pillow, she heard the quiet and felt intensely alone. No Dave breathing peacefully beside her, no footsteps in the corridor of a teenager going to bed late. No Bella on semi-watchful sentry duty downstairs. Her unhappiness lay like a weight on her chest.

'I can't go on like this...' Tess told herself. 'Something has to change.'

8

It was after 7 p.m. when Tess heard Dave's car pulling up in the driveway. She was on the sofa, her eyes swollen with crying, her nose swollen with crying, her head pounding with both crying and the half bottle of wine she'd drunk alongside her cheese toastie supper.

'Helloooo!' he called cheerily from the front door. 'Daddy's home! Where are my lovely girls?'

He meant her and Bella, which just made Tess burst into a fresh round of tears.

'In here,' she croaked.

Dave came into the room. He was stocky and broad-shouldered, his hair a bit overgrown, wearing his trademark denims with a colourful shirt and the black woollen coat she'd bought him for Christmas. He'd trimmed back his short salt-and-pepper beard while he'd been away.

Dave took one look at her, dropped the bags he was carrying and rushed over.

'Oh, Tess, what's the matter? What's happened? Is it...?'

'It's Bella,' she said, before he got into a panic about the children or anyone else, 'I'm so sorry... but she's... she's...'

Her shoulders heaved and it took some effort to say the dreaded words: 'She's died.'

Dave dropped down onto his haunches in front of her. His expression was astonished, full of concern and always so kind. Whatever else Dave could do to wind her up into the kind of fury that long-term married parents may feel for one another now and then, he could always be relied on to be kind. And she felt very glad to see him.

'Oh, Tess... that's awful. Why didn't you call? Why didn't you tell me? What happened?'

She made room for him on the sofa, felt the weight of his arm around her shoulder, leaned into him and, a little consoled now, told him all about Bella's last day on earth.

When she was finished, he held her tightly and told her that she should have phoned, should have let him help her through it all. 'You shouldn't have had to do this all on your own,' he said, almost annoyed.

She put her hand into his and squeezed. 'I know,' she said, 'but you were busy, responsible for other people's children. I didn't want you to worry, or be distracted, or tired.'

He squeezed back and sighed.

'The poor old doggie,' he said quietly, 'dear me, so many happy years with Bella. So... that just leaves us, then... dear, oh dear.'

She saw the tearing in his eyes and with a broken, 'I know,' Tess burst into yet another round of tears.

'Oh, God,' she said, 'when am I going to stop crying?'

'Probably not for a few days,' he said, blinking away his own tears, 'remember when my mum...'

She nodded, not wanting him to go on. When Dave's lovely mum had died suddenly three years ago, she had not been able to stop crying for two weeks solid. It became almost comical... cooking while crying, cleaning the bath while crying, taking a work conference call while crying, bringing water bottles on every car trip because the risk of dehydration was real.

She knew already that she was going to miss the everyday, constant presence of Bella for a long time.

'Maybe we'll get another dog,' Dave said, 'when we're ready...'

But she shook her head. Just now, the idea of being so fond and so distraught all over again was terrible. The abrupt ring of the home landline was an intrusion into their mournful quiet.

'I'll get it,' Dave said, already up on his feet.

'Hello, Alex, how are you doing?'

Tess sat up and instantly felt a little better. This was Alex, their twenty-two-year-old, who rarely called, so it was always a treat to talk to him.

'Good... good... good to hear it... that's great...' Dave was saying.

Tess let Dave talk, of course, but she was impatient to get hold of the receiver herself and listen to Alex's voice, to hear how things were really going for him. He prided himself on being independent and strong, but she worried about him. She remembered from her own experience that the first years out of uni could be really hard. The world of work was not usually all that you thought it would be.

'Hello, my darling,' she said, when it was finally her turn to talk, 'how are you doing?'

'I'm good... it's all good,' he said, but she listened hard to hear what he really sounded like. And she thought his voice was definitely bright, but maybe tired too.

'Long days?' she asked. 'I hope you're not working too hard.'

'No, it's really fine. It's going well.'

She asked about London. Where had he been? What had he done? And enjoyed his replies, full of detail and description.

'I'm really looking forward to seeing you,' she told him, 'and really catching up with you and Natalie on the holiday.'

'Mum...' just the word was enough. She read the tone and in her mind she could already see *roadblock ahead*.

'What is it?'

'Mum... I don't want this to be hard... I really don't want to let you down.'

'But... Alex... you can't...' she warned him.

'Mum... it's just not going to work for me... I can't get that amount of time off. All the senior staff take time off in the summer. The juniors have to cover.'

'But I told you to ask for it weeks ago, months ago... I told you to tell them it was exceptional circumstances... Alex! You can't let me down on this. The holiday is only three weeks away now...'

'Please don't cry, Mum,' he said. 'Please don't do that.'

She hadn't even realised she was, because since this morning she'd cried more than she hadn't.

'Look... I can probably take a week, maybe even ten days. Why don't I come for the last part of it?'

'But you'll miss out on so much... I mean, travelling across Vietnam and into Cambodia. You'll miss all of that. Do you really want to miss that? It's all booked, all paid for... I know it sounds like such a cliché, but it really will be the holiday of a lifetime!'

Her voice sounded high and shrill. And she sounded angry, which wasn't right, because she wasn't angry, she was distraught and a little desperate. She so wanted him to be there with them. Why didn't he get that? Yes, maybe three weeks was too much to ask from a fiercely independent twenty-two-year-old. But he'd agreed, he'd said yes and he'd sounded really enthusiastic when she'd first started planning all of this.

'Can I think about it?' he asked and she could feel herself

balling her hand in frustration. It was his pet phrase, his get-out clause, his decision-ducking tactic.

'Yes... please think about it. I'll call you tomorrow. And I love you, Alex.'

Only when she replaced the receiver did she realise she hadn't even told him about Bella.

She turned to Dave and began with, 'Alex...'

'I think I gathered. Look, give him a bit of time and I'll try to talk to him as well. Why don't you give Natalie a call?' he suggested, knowing this might be a soothing move. When Natalie's exams had finished in May, she'd gone out to the south of Spain to teach English and seemed to be having an amazing time.

'I think I'll round up Bella's things and put them into the attic,' Dave added.

Was it worth putting them in the attic, Tess wondered? Shouldn't they give them to a dog shelter or something like that? Right now, the thought of having another dog was impossible. And it wouldn't be any less tragic to come across Bella's things years later in the attic. But as she couldn't bear to part with them today, she found herself agreeing with Dave.

Then she couldn't help reminding him. 'Use the proper metal ladder, not that rickety old wooden one, and when you're ready I'll come and hold it steady for you. There's that floorboard gap, and I don't want you to...'

'Okay, okay,' Dave said, almost out of the room. 'I'll call for you.'

* * *

It was a long conversation between mother and daughter. It was emotional and then quite fraught. Natalie wanted to know all about Bella's death and cried down the line, which made Tess cry too.

'Oh, I just can't stop myself at the moment...' Tess declared. 'I'm a permanent bloody water feature... and another really upsetting thing is that Alex doesn't seem to want to come on the full holiday. He's talking about only coming for the last ten days at most.'

Tess had certainly expected Natalie to be upset about Bella. But she had not expected the long, guilty pause she heard now. Followed by: 'Mum... I've been meaning to talk to you about the holiday. I think three weeks is going to be too long for me.'

For a few moments, Tess was too taken aback to speak, then came a rush of angry thoughts. *Meaning to talk to me? Just when was she planning to mention it? Too long? Three weeks was too long? Was she planning to just pop over to Thailand for the weekend of a lifetime maybe? And all this time and money I've spent already!*

'You know that this trip starts in three weeks' time and I've been planning it for months? You do know that, don't you?' Tess asked, trying not to lose her cool. 'You know that it's all booked and every last detail is sorted and paid for and you could have just mentioned *ages and ages* ago that you weren't happy with the three-week plan.'

Natalie was having such a good time and so determined to stay for the whole summer that Tess was beginning to suspect there was a romantic reason for wanting to ditch the family holiday.

'I mean I can't just go cancelling and rearranging and spoiling everything because you've got a passing whim to go and do something else,' Tess added, realising that staying cool and calm was going to be just about impossible.

'Well... I just think a week or two-week commitment for a family holiday would be a bit more normal...' Natalie went on. 'Mum, three weeks, plus all the days of jetlag... that's a lot of time to give up for...'

'*Give up?*' Tess was really trying to rein in her anger now.

'You and Dad should go,' Natalie added. 'You both deserve a break. Treat it like a second honeymoon...'

'I thought we'd all agreed to go on this holiday,' Tess said, not sure if she was more upset than angry, 'I thought we were all really excited about it... I thought we'd all have an amazing time...' she heard the dry sob in her voice and felt that she had run out of tears.

Now she could hear Dave calling for her and she really had to finish this call and go to give him a hand. Good grief, this day was turning almost as bad as yesterday.

'Natalie, I have to go now. Please think hard about this and I'll speak to you tomorrow, okay?' With a final, 'Loads of love,' Tess ended the call.

She got up from the sofa, thinking general 'ungrateful bloody wretches' thoughts about her children and stomped into the hallway. She turned to head up the narrow staircase to the upper floor, and just as she rounded the corner to the attic landing, she saw that Dave had, despite her instructions, taken the wonky old wooden ladder, and not the weighty metal one. He was already at the top of it with Bella's large dog bed in both of his hands and, to Tess, that bloody ladder looked a little unbalanced.

'Dave, for God's sake,' she complained.

Unbelievably irritated with him, she hurried forward to take a steadying hold of the rungs, just as the cardboard patch smoothing out the floorboard underneath the rug finally squashed under the weight of the ladder, and sank just a sudden half a centimetre.

Tess saw the movement and quickly grabbed hold of the ladder, but this only added to Dave's sense of unbalance. The dog's basket flew out of his hands and then his arms flailed as he tried to rebalance and she attempted to grab him, but with an alarmed, 'Whoooaaaaaaahh!' which she thought was pretty restrained, considering, he span backwards off the ladder, crashed straight into the wobbly bannister, which promptly collapsed and sent him over the edge of the landing and onto the stairs below.

'Dave!' she screamed.

9

'He's fractured three ribs and broken his ankle. He also has concussion. He can't remember who Donald Trump is. He can't remember Donald Trump... can you imagine? That was one of the scariest things...' Tess realised she was talking at high speed in a jumbled rush to Alex and maybe he needed her to slow down, so he could take this all in. 'He's going to be okay,' she said, pausing to make sure that bit was sinking in, 'that's the main thing. He's definitely going to be okay... on crutches for few weeks... but... okay.'

It was Monday, almost lunchtime, and everything felt almost all right and quite manageable again after the turmoil of yesterday evening. But she couldn't help replaying the events over and over again in her mind. Crouching beside Dave on the stairs, calling his name, feeling certain he was dead... or about to die.

For a few moments, he'd made no sound at all. And all she could think was, *don't die, don't die, please just do not die*. And in those moments, literally nothing else had mattered. She had just wanted her loving husband, Alex and Natalie's wonderful dad, to please, *please* be alive.

Then very quiet groans had followed.

She'd tried to remember anything at all useful about first aid, but could only come up with: 'Don't move the patient if broken bones are suspected.' She was very glad that his head was higher up the stairs than his body. If he'd been the other way round, she would have had no idea whether she was supposed to move him or not.

She'd got 999 on the phone and they'd been just as calming, useful and reassuring as she could possibly have wanted. But it had still felt like a very long wait for the ambulance. And getting Dave, in a neck brace, on the edge of consciousness, and in so much pain, down the narrow staircase had been excruciating.

'What's your name, then?' they'd asked cheerily to keep him talking. 'And what were you up to in the attic, then?'

'I'm Dave... Who are you? Where are we going?'

Even when they gave him answers, he would ask the same questions again after a few moments, revealing his confusion and disorientation, as Tess had panicked about brain swellings and severe head injuries.

For the next seven hours, every one of her thoughts had been about Dave and was he going to be OK, until finally, just before 4 a.m., a surprisingly chirpy A&E doctor had come to talk to her in the little inner sanctum waiting room about X-ray results, blood tests and the head scan.

'He's most likely going to be just fine...' the doctor had told her and she'd felt almost faint with relief.

'But sore and not very mobile for a few weeks. He's going to have a plaster cast, crutches, the works. He won't be absolutely back on his feet for about two months. So you're going to have to think about how to cope with that. Do you have a downstairs bathroom?'

'Mum, that sounds terrible,' Alex said, interrupting her stream of thoughts, 'for you and for Dad.'

'Yes... it was... it is.' Tess was still reeling. This was her second call. She'd already relayed the full accident story to a sleepy and astonished Natalie, who almost certainly had someone in bed beside her – a detail that Tess couldn't really think about right now. She was trying to park the thought, telling herself she would come back to it later.

'I still can't believe it's happened,' she told her son.

'Dad's definitely doing okay?'

'Yes... he is... he's on a load of painkillers, very drowsy, so I've not been able to get much out of him. But I'll be back at the hospital later and I'll report back. Or give him a call yourself.'

'Yeah... of course. Bloody hell,' he repeated. 'So I suppose the holiday's completely off then?'

The holiday.

The holiday...

'The *holiday*...' she whispered.

She hadn't even got that far in her thoughts. She took this as a sign of how shocked she'd been by what had happened.

'The holiday?' she repeated.

The holiday? *Was there any way? Any chance?*

'Oh my God...' she whispered.

At first, her mind scrambled for solutions, as she tried to come up with ways to make this still possible. Surely people could fly with plaster casts? And hotels must have facilities for people on crutches... or would a wheelchair be better? But then... what about the planned white-water rafting? Or the week of trekking into the hills and travelling through the jungle? Even enjoying the wonderful sandy beaches of Thailand...

It was going to be impossible for Dave.

All that time spent planning, all those late-night internet trawls, booking a string of special places and experiences and all kinds of lovely things to treat her family with.

All those careful, lovingly made plans were just crumpled up and gone now.

The sugary sand, the turquoise sea, the ancient temples...

'Alex...' she wailed, 'it's all *ruined*...'

'Mum... it's going to be okay. Don't worry about it.'

And then, possibly trying to cheer her up, he added: 'Knowing you, you had totally fantastic insurance.'

'Oh... that's so... so... not the point!' There was a lump in her throat and the heat of tears welling in her eyes.

'Well, it's quite a good point, Mum. Now you get a full refund and you've got three months off work to look after Dad.'

She absolutely loved her son, would walk barefoot to the ends of the earth for him. But in that exact moment, she could quite cheerfully have throttled him.

'Alex, I wanted us all to have an amazing holiday. An unforgettable holiday. The...'

'Holiday of a lifetime, I know, Mum. I'm sure we will, sometime.'

Sometime! Now she wanted to laugh. *Sometime*...

He made it sound as if one summer was as good as the next, as if there would always be another time. When she was certain that this was it, this was the last chance for it to be just the four of them and that was it, already gone.

Their last summer as a foursome would now be last year, when they went to Croatia and Natalie was grumpy for the entire ten days because her boyfriend had broken his phone and couldn't talk to her and she'd burned to a crisp on day two, plus Alex had sulked in his room because he'd got a 2.2 in his degree and couldn't understand why, and thought it was the worst fate to befall anyone ever.

'I'm really very upset about this,' she told her son. 'I mean I'm upset about Dad, of course I'm upset about Dad and for Dad... but he *had* to use that bloody wooden ladder, didn't he? Had to use the *wooden* one... I'm going to drive the bloody thing to the dump later today. No, I'm going to personally smash it up into pieces and burn it in the garden chimenea.'

She heard the wobble in her voice and felt very sorry for herself. Several weeks at home looking after Dave... well, of course she would have to do it... or... four weeks at the very least, then maybe forget about the sabbatical and return to work early. It certainly wasn't what she had planned. Not for the first time, her family had made sure she wasn't doing what she had planned to be doing.

'Are you okay, Mum?' Alex asked.

'Oh... I'll be fine. Just have to get on with it, I suppose. How about you, Alex, are you okay?'

'Me? Totally fine.'

'It's not easy, your first proper job. You're allowed not to be okay all of the time.'

'I'm fine... really.'

'Okay, I love you and I'll see you soon. Maybe you'd like to come up and visit your dad.'

'Yeah... of course... I'll call him. You take care...'

* * *

Alex ended the call and stared for a moment or two at the phone in his hand. How could he say what was really on his mind?

How could Alex tell his mother how bad things were? How could he soften the blow and stop her heart from breaking? Especially now that she had this Dad disaster to deal with.

He sat back in his chair and stared at the ceiling, which was decorated with a brown stain of damp. He was twenty-two years old, and his life was falling apart.

Alex lived by himself in a tiny bedsit on the outskirts of Croydon. Well, he was sub-letting this bedsit from someone he'd met on

Gumtree. The guy was travelling for five months and wanted to make sure the bedsit wouldn't gain an unwelcome squatter while he was away. His room contained a single bed, a small desk probably bought from Ikea at least twenty years ago, and a flimsy wardrobe with his clothes. There was a small window that overlooked a construction site. Beyond the door of his room was a small kitchenette and a barely functioning shared bathroom.

His parents did not know he had moved to this place. His parents did not know that he had left his job only nine weeks after he'd started it, because it was unbearable. Everything about his life right now was unbearable. He was supposed to be on the first rung of a respectable career, but actually he was living on meagre benefits in a shambles.

At night, the orange glare of streetlights bored into the room, filling it with dark shadows, and a huge, hulking metal crane blocked the view of the horizon. Every time Alex saw this crane, he was reminded of a toy he'd had as a child, a wooden crane that could pick up objects with a magnet. *That was a nice little toy, red and made of wood, with a little lever to pull things up. I really liked it. Not like this one – so huge and rusted and faceless, and horrible to look at.*

He was now sure that this was how life was: things started out so simple, then snarled up and became so complicated and twisted. *Look at the way this thing blocks out the sky! God, how did things get like this?*

Alex was a tall, thin and thoughtful young man, with wavy strawberry blonde hair, and a permanently anxious expression. He had the look of someone who had once been good looking, but hadn't been able to take care of himself. His skin was pale from lack of time outside, his hair was dry and stuck up at odd angles. His clothes weren't old, but they were overworn and underwashed.

Every morning he woke up late, stayed in bed for a few hours watching movies on his phone, then finally got up, and having missed breakfast, went straight to the shopping centre to find some lunch. He only ever ordered something horrible, a Subway or a McDonalds, and he would chew through this disgusting lunch on his own on a park bench, looking the perfect picture of misery, and sincerely wishing he hadn't wasted his fiver, and had instead gone hungry.

After this, he rolled by Tesco to pick up some drink. He often bought wine, because his parents used to let him drink it, and it reminded him of home. Then he would spend the evening watching obscure movies, or reading even more obscure books, and desperately trying to drink enough to forget who he was and what he was doing. Or what he wasn't doing. He definitely wasn't working in that oh-so promising graduate trainee job with that oh-so impressive city firm. And he wasn't doing anything else instead... because he had no idea what else to do and he couldn't face all the busy-ness and business of working life. For five miserable weeks, he'd sat in that swanky London office, enduring the insultingly menial tasks he was given. He wanted to shout at his po-faced manager: 'I've written a 20,000-word dissertation on the macro-economic consequences of Bitcoin!' as he was handed another photocopying task.

And finally, one lunch break, he went out for a sandwich and realised he didn't have to go back. So he didn't. He never phoned in to explain and he never answered any calls from the place either. Let them figure it out.

Usually, he went to bed without dinner, but there was hardly any point in going to bed, because at night, he couldn't sleep.

This was not at all how he had imagined his big move to London would be.

His grown-up life, as he'd pictured it, was filled with so much more promise and opportunity. He always used to hope for adventure, excitement and a future full of good things, or at the very least, days spent doing something worthwhile.

As soon as he finally put away his phone, turned off the light, laid his head on the pillow and tried to drift off, after his lethargic and monotonous day of doing so little, he could find no peace. The most awful thoughts drifted out of the darkness. He saw his parents arguing and shouting at him years ago, when it looked as if he was going to do badly in his A Levels. They'd found him tutors; they'd helped him into uni, and in his final, stressful uni year, they'd stepped in again to make sure he got through it. He imagined how furious they would be with him, if after all their efforts to get him into this career opening, they found out that he'd failed at it.

And of course, he thought of death. Death, death, death, he could not escape it.

'What will it feel like?' he wondered. 'What comes next?'

'Is this really all there is? Will I really just have another sixty years of sitting around eating Chinese food and pissing about, before it's all over? What kind of madness is this?'

Alex couldn't stand these questions and usually threw off his grimy duvet and paced around the room, waiting for dawn, when all of this might go away. And usually when the first light began to creep in through the window, he felt calmer, and was able to drift off at about five in the morning.

He was so alone. His head ached with the pain and the embarrassment of his condition. No help. No help from anywhere. What was he going to do?

So now that the call to his mother was over, he sat perfectly still on his bed. The giant crane loomed over the room, its great iron bars casting unnatural, triangular shadows on the walls.

Alex felt trapped in a cage.

10

River was having breakfast in one of her regular places, a chic and sunny café only a block from her apartment. But the grapefruit was too tart and her coffee was lukewarm and weak, *weak*... was there a worse crime than making coffee too weak? And even with sunglasses on, the glare of the early morning light was hurting her head.

She was pecking at her laptop and looking with dread at her financial spreadsheet. She was waiting for two outstanding payments to come in, including the one from Phillip Renfield, which still had not made land. But a very substantial tax bill was due. How could she have earned so little in the past year and yet owe so much tax? She'd already called Irma and had an angry, baffling conversation about past earnings and rollovers and accumulated taxes, which had been just unimaginably awful. And handsome Dylan, who had said he would look after her dogs when she was in England, had just messaged to say:

Hey great news, I got a job 😊, but 😟 I can't sit for your dogs.

She had stared at his stupid smiley and unsmiley faces for a full minute before this message had truly sunk in.

Then she'd dialled his number.

'Dylan, what the actual freaking fuck is this?' were her opening words.

Dylan struggled for a response.

'Are you seriously letting me down on the dog-sitting, that we've only had arranged for like, forever?' she demanded.

'I'm sorry,' he managed.

'You are actually serious?'

'It's a great opportunity, I've got this part with...'

'I truly don't care,' she snapped. 'Look, Dylan, when you have promised to look after someone's dogs for six weeks, you don't send some emoji-laden piece of sad sackery when you've decided to wimp out. You pick up the goddam phone and explain it, properly, like a goddam human being. You maybe even suggest another "resting" actor friend who could do the job instead. That's how you keep your important friends sweet, instead of making them incredibly *pissed* at you.'

She hung up, waved the waitress over and sent back both her grapefruit and her coffee. Just like her, they were too bitter.

Her phone rang and the name that flashed up was 'Tess, English house'.

Finally, something nice to deal with.

'Hi, Tess, how are you doing?' River began, 'I am so excited... and it's now only two and a half weeks until take off. Do you know that? I've been obsessing over the BBC's weather forecasts and it's looking great. Sunny, but so much cooler than over here. In the seventies... perfect English garden party weather.'

'Yeees...' Tess didn't sound so sure and River guessed this was because English people never knew what the temperature meant in

Fahrenheit, because they were always using Centigrade and literally *no one* ever knew how to convert one into the other.

'River... I'm afraid my husband, Dave, has been in an accident.'

'You're kidding me...'

River listened with growing horror as Tess listed the body parts Dave had broken or damaged, and outlined the prognosis and the medical advice.

'He's in a lot of pain and he can't travel. So... we can't go on our holiday. I'm afraid this means we'll have to stay in the house, so Dave can be at home and recover. This is obviously really disappointing news for all of us...' Tess went on, 'So... well... we can't rent you our home any more. Obviously, I'm so, so sorry about all of this. I'm really sorry...'

River just sat, perfectly still. She saw the waitress behind the counter pouring her a fresh cup of coffee. She saw a guy in those bright, tight cycling shorts that were currently a thing walk past the window. Was this conversation for real? Was this English woman honestly telling her that the English holiday couldn't happen? But what about the script? And all the Shakespeare plays she'd booked to see? And the garden party? And just the pure unadulterated peace of weeks and weeks of being in a beautiful place, undisturbed and writing, writing, writing, until it all came out right?

'Hello... River, are you still there?' Tess asked anxiously.

River was so angry that she couldn't actually form the words. And for her, that was very rare, almost unique.

Instead she heard herself uttering a terrible, wounded, furious 'Aaaaiiiiiiieeeeeeeee,' sound down the phone.

Tess was clearly too startled to make a response. *Good*, River thought. And then the words gushed back in a furious torrent.

'I can't have the house?' River began, 'I can't have the *house*? How do you think you can do this to me? What is the matter with you?' Her anger ramped up with every question. 'And just where do you expect me to find another place? It's summer, high season? Everywhere's booked. The whole of England will be stuffed full. I booked this place *four months ago* and believe me when I tell you it wasn't my first choice, or even my fifteenth! But everything else was gone! You *cannot* do this to me...' Her voice was clear, loud and strident and yes, everyone in the place was looking at her but WTF, this was not going to happen. 'You will not do this to me. Take my money and go stay somewhere else. Jesus... sort this out, lady. Sort it out or I will sue you.'

There was a strangled gasp or sob, perhaps, from the other end of the line. So River managed: 'Sorry to hear about your husband.'

And then she hung up.

Jeeezus freaking God. What was the matter with everyone? Why couldn't people stick to the plan? Keep their commitments? Pay their *freaking* invoices on time?

She punched in the number of the first TV company that still hadn't paid for the rewrite done nearly five months ago now.

'Accounts, please,' she snapped. Once the right person had been located, she informed her: 'Hi, my name is River Romero and yes, I am calling again. I'd like you to know that the head of the Guild of Writers is a close personal friend of mine. Do you want me to explain to him how the multi-million-dollar-making Awesome Tech TV empire treats its writers?

'I am a writer, who has done a great job and deserves to be paid, okay? I am not a piece of used toilet paper stuck to the heel of your shoe. Okay? Are we clear? Right. So, let's get this bill paid today and there will be no need for you to take out a restraining order on me. Right, okay. Thank you. You have a nice day.'

The invoice department at Phillip Renfield's production company got a similar call.

And in the middle of that second call, River had that wonderful out-of-body, flash of inspiration moment that almost made all the many wearisome aspects of being a creative person just about bearable.

Once her second call was over, she dialled 'Tess, English house' back and prepared to apologise profusely.

'Hi Tess, it's River. Look, I absolutely apologise,' River said, as soon as Tess had picked up. As an impulsive, and often incredibly furious person, River was very used to apologising.

'I'm so very sorry your husband has had this accident. That's really terrible. And your wonderful holiday is ruined, that's also terrible, *awful*... I am truly sorry for you all. And I was very rude, but I guess I was just really surprised.'

'Yes, so was I,' Tess said quietly.

'Your wonderful holiday...' River said, truly sympathetic for this woman now. A six-week Asian adventure, completely ruined. 'Please tell me you had insurance,' she added.

'Yes, but...'

'That doesn't make up for it, oh my gosh, I know. But at least...'

'Yes,' Tess agreed.

'So, I've been thinking and thinking about how we could possibly turn this around, because I *have* to come to England. I have a huge project and I can only do it right in Stratford-upon-Avon and as you know, the entire county is fully booked for the summer. So... here's the plan...' River took a breath and almost thought that she should cross her fingers before she began.

'I'm going to fly to England and live in your home, as agreed, and as already paid for. You and your husband are going to fly to LA and live in my apartment. You don't need to pay me anything for this. So you'll have all your insurance money, six weeks booked off work, and a free holiday in one of the greatest cities in the world. How could you refuse? And by the way, my apartment is gorgeous, with a pool. I'll send you pictures. You will love it, I promise.'

'Dave can't fly,' Tess said immediately. 'That's the point, River.

He's broken his ribs and his ankle. For the next month at least, he can only hobble about on crutches. Otherwise, yes, we would try and salvage some of what's left of our holiday.'

In a quiet voice, knowing she had to pitch this right, River asked: 'So, Tess, why don't you come to LA? It's a fantastic city – you'll totally love it. And you'll have an amazing holiday,'

'River, I have to look after Dave.'

River could hear the aching disappointment in Tess's voice and knew that she might just have an opening.

'But do you really?' River asked. 'You're not a nurse. Isn't there a friend or family member he could stay with? Or what about getting an actual nurse, who could help? In a few weeks, he won't be in such bad shape... and you had planned a real adventure for the summer. You've booked all that time off work. Jeez... that must have been absolute hell to organise. So why don't you come over here and have that adventure... for yourself?'

11

'So, how did she take it?'

Dave's face was drained and strangely yellowish against the stark white of his hospital pillow. There were purple circles under his eyes and the beard around his chubby jowls was already looking overgrown. Dave had never been an athletic, or even mildly sporty guy. He'd been slim when he was young because he'd smoked all kinds of things, had never eaten much and liked to party hard. But in the last four or five years, his hobbies of drinking quality wine, watching quality TV dramas and cooking quality dinners were making him increasingly heavy.

Tess used to do everything she could to encourage him to follow her lead in at least walking regularly and holding the worst of the middle-age weight gain at bay, but now she was resigned to her chubby husband, although it could still be something of a shock to see the full extent of his girth, as she did now because the thin hospital gown was exposing his thick side.

'River took it very badly,' Tess admitted. 'She actually shouted at me. It was really unpleasant. And now she's insisting that she still comes over.'

'What, and stays with us?' Dave laughed at the idea.

'No... she thinks you should move somewhere else to someone who can look after you. And I should go to her apartment in LA.'

Dave, lying in a hospital bed, uncomfortable, and plaster-casted, still managed a joyful laugh at this, although it hurt his ribs quite a lot.

'Move somewhere else, like this? You go to LA? Good grief. She sounds completely insane. What did you say?'

'Well... I...' Tess met Dave's eyes.

Three months. How could she possibly spend the three months she had worked so hard to plan, putting arrangements in place at work, and even setting up a weekly rota of visiting friends to make sure her mum and dad didn't miss her too much... how could she now spend all that precious, hard-won time looking after Dave and pottering about her house?

But she had to look after Dave. Everyone expected it of her and she expected it of herself.

'I said I'd have to get back to her,' Tess said, feeling uncertain and oddly defeated.

'She can't have the house,' Dave said. 'You'll have to make that clear. Refund her money. Tell her this definitely won't work.'

But still Tess protested. 'She has to come to Stratford for work. She's got a big writing project on. It's going to be very hard for her to find anywhere. Is there anyone we can think of who might have a place where she can stay?'

'Not for six weeks, Tess, that's impossible.'

And suddenly Tess felt tears slipping down her cheeks. She tried to brush them away quickly, but Dave saw and put his hands over hers.

'What's the matter?' he asked.

'What's the matter?' she repeated the question angrily. 'Every-thing is *ruined*, completely ruined! I was so looking forward to this summer. It was all I could think about. All I've been thinking about for months! I wanted to have a wonderful time, a proper adventure with you and the children – and now it's a total disaster!

'And the worst thing is, none of you seem to even care! It turns out Alex and Natalie didn't want to come anyway, and you *had* to use the bloody wooden ladder that should have been thrown out years ago, even when I told you, you shouldn't,' she couldn't help the outburst, 'and my lovely dog is dead...' this prompted a fresh spill of tears, 'and now I have some dreadful American woman shouting at me over the phone because she wants to live in my house for the summer. And I can't go anywhere! When I'm desperate to go somewhere. That's what's the bloody matter!'

'I'm really sorry,' Dave said.

But it just didn't feel like enough.

* * *

Can you fly with a broken ankle? Can you fly with broken ribs?

The internet advice was not exactly encouraging.

Is LA wheelchair friendly?

What to do in LA in a wheelchair.

These questions lead her down entirely different internet rabbit holes. There were vast art galleries and museums in LA, stunning white buildings, all glass and steel, surrounded by perfectly green lawns and improbably blue sky. There were beaches and public pools – she had expected that. But public parks, galleries and hundreds of miles of hiking trails and forest, she'd not been aware of all this.

The pictures that River had sent of her apartment were also lovely. It was open plan, in soothing shades of cream and white, with a big, comfortable sofa, several bookcases and a lovely antique wooden desk. There was a large, tiled balcony filled with plants that overlooked the pool courtyard. Tess pictured herself mixing up a smoothie in the apartment, throwing a kimono over her swimsuit and then heading downstairs for a cooling swim before she settled down onto the sun lounger to enjoy her drink and plan her adventures for the day ahead.

She was scrolling and scrolling through LA images of pools, beaches, hillsides, sunsets and bright lights, when Natalie called. She wanted to know how her dad was doing because his phone signal in the hospital was terrible and it was almost impossible to get through to him.

'Why don't you come back and see him?' Tess asked. 'He would love that.'

'Yee-ees.' Natalie didn't exactly sound sure of this. 'Maybe a long weekend?'

'Are you so busy out there? You can't even be spared for a week?'

'Well, no... I can't really. The school is so busy. And they've asked me to stay on for the whole of the summer, now that we're not going away.'

'But you're definitely okay?' Tess wasn't quite sure why she was asking. The Natalie she was looking at on Skype was smiling, sun-kissed, relaxed and full of joy and energy. Happy. Just as you wanted all your children to be. What was the saying? 'You're only as happy as your unhappiest child.' Natalie was obviously happy and that made Tess feel very happy for her too.

'Have you met someone special out there?' Tess asked.

The way Natalie laughed and broke off eye contact answered the question.

'Maybe...' she said with an excited grin.

'Spanish?' Tess asked, flashing forward to a future where she had to get on a plane every time she wanted to see her daughter in person. Then immediately telling herself to calm down. Wasn't everyone allowed a dreamy summer romance at Natalie's age?

'No... he's one of the student teachers,' Natalie replied, 'he's from Scotland and he's actually called Hamish!'

And they both laughed because it seemed too much.

'I know,' Natalie said, '*Hamish*... he sounds like a little old man in a tweed hat, but he's really tall and blonde and... lovely.'

'That sounds very nice.'

'Yeah...'

To Tess's knowledge, there hadn't been a boyfriend since an unhappy breakup at the end of Natalie's final school year.

'Is he helping to mend your heart?' she asked gently.

'He is. He's just... awesome. I really, really like him.'

'Is he at uni too?'

'Well, not anywhere near me, he's got a football scholarship to a US college in Florida... so that's quite far away.'

'Oh... yes, it is...'

'We're trying not to think about that too much,' Natalie added quickly. 'We're just, you know, enjoying the moment.'

'Are you okay? Do we need to talk about... anything?'

'Anything' meant all the tricky stuff that you might want to talk to your mum about, or more likely your best friend. Over many frank and awkward conversations, they'd built the understanding that Natalie was allowed privacy, of course, but Tess was always there for her if she wanted to talk anything through.

'I'm not rushing into *anything*... okay, Mum?'

'Are you sure you're okay? You know I always want you to be happy and in control...'

'Yes, I know,' Natalie said, 'and not to get too carried away to ever forget about safe sex.'

'No...'

Although Tess would have loved to be the kind of parent who could have breezy sex-chats with her daughter, it was always awkward and just a bit weird. But still she persevered because she was sure it was the right thing to do.

'I will talk to you if I need to. And...' Natalie's smile curved upwards, 'thanks for asking.'

Tess smiled back. She hoped it was enough, and knew that, at least, it was far better than the one and only 'sex talk' she'd had with her mother: 'Tess, have you learned about human reproduction in biology class?'

'Yes,' Tess, aged about twelve, had replied, although it wasn't true, but she was now in a panicked confusion of her own, her only thought being, 'Please don't talk about this!'

'Oh, well... that's all right, then,' her mother had said with obvious relief and moved the conversation quickly on to other things.

And that was it! AIDS, contraception, rape, date rape... Tess's mother had never felt the need to air any of these issues with her daughter, ever.

'So... what are you going to do with your time off, now that Dad's managed to hospitalise himself?' Natalie asked, interrupting her thoughts.

Tess snorted at the question. 'Well, I'll be looking after him, of course. He's not going to be able to do much for quite some time.'

'Muuum... he won't need you to hang around for the whole time. He'll be hopping about on his crutches pretty soon and he'll manage. You should go off and do something exciting on your own, for a change.'

'What do you mean he won't need me? Have you ever tried to make yourself a cup of tea on crutches? It's not exactly easy, you know. Cooking on crutches, showering, going to the loo... he's going to need help with everything.'

'Mum! Maybe if he'd broken both his arms as well. But he hasn't. Look, you don't need to be there all the time. He has friends;

he has auntie Jackie. He can get Deliveroo if he's desperate. Maybe you can even get cups of tea on Deliveroo now, bet you can. You should go and do something, for yourself. I mean, maybe you should still go on the holiday? You were so excited about it, so looking forward to it. Maybe you should just pack your bags and go. Dad will manage, and think about what an adventure you could have. You'll have a year's worth of stories to tell us.'

'I can't go on the holiday...'

'Why not?'

'Because of your dad...'

'We'll put all kinds of good things and good people on Dad.'

'It would look really selfish of me...' Tess protested.

'Really? You've been looking after all of us for over twenty years, would it really be so bad to take two months off?'

'But...'

'Are you scared to go on your own?'

'Of course I'm not scared.'

'When did you last travel somewhere by yourself?'

'Well... I...'

Absolutely nothing came to mind. She'd not travelled by herself since... since... she was a student.

'I think you might be too scared,' Natalie said, but she meant it kindly. 'Think about it, Mum, it could be amazing.'

* * *

Are you scared?

The question hovered over her head all evening as she made supper for herself, as she went out for a dogless walk by herself, as she googled Los Angeles far into the night, even though she knew she'd be exhausted at work tomorrow morning.

All by myself...

She didn't want to be 'All By Myself'. Last year, she was still the frantically busy working mum of a school-aged child. There were still school holiday dates, parents' evenings and exam revision traumas taking up her time. Now, her big family reunion had collapsed and her daughter was urging her to go off all by herself.

But Tess didn't want that, couldn't they see? She wanted to be with them. She wanted Natalie and Alex making sarcastic jokes over dinner, Nat rolling her eyes, Alex quoting *Peep Show* and all of them laughing at old, worn and beloved family jokes. It now felt as if her family had exploded, all the elements flung far out into orbit: Alex in London – although they saw so little of him, it may as well have been the moon. Natalie in Spain. Bella, the dear departed.

And poor old Dave...

You were supposed to go through some sort of romantic rekindling with your husband when your children left home, weren't you? But that had definitely not happened yet. They still seemed stuck in their parent roles. Their stressed, devoted, busy parent roles. When they talked, it was about family things, children things, house things. There were no fresh topics of conversation. There were a handful of friends that they liked to see together, but they also had their own groups of 'the boys' and 'the girls' that they went out with separately.

As a couple, they were last on holiday together without the children seven years ago on a minibreak to Devon, where the rain did not stop for the whole three days, and they played Scrabble, admittedly several pretty intense games, instead of having sex.

In all honesty, Tess knew her marriage could be a lot better, but she also knew it could be a lot worse. So mainly, she didn't worry about it too much. It was on the back burner, in a holding pattern. And surely at this stage of family life, people sort of settled? Didn't they? They accepted that romance wasn't a big part of life and sex even less so.

It was so very hard to think sexy thoughts about a man when you laundered his extra-large pants and could hear him break wind in the en suite. That bloody en suite... as if married life wasn't enough of a challenge without a hole in your bedroom wall so you could hear your spouse's every move in the bathroom.

But, but, but... she hadn't expected everything to get quite so old couple-ish by now. Wasn't the internet full of sixty-something women going on about their amazing sex lives? But she was always too tired, too stressed or too busy to think about sex.

Make tea, not love. Talk to the children... run a spreadsheet... do the ironing... nurture the houseplants. That was where her interests lay now. In all honesty, sex felt past its sell-by date.

So... she rated herself as a really good mother, a pretty good accountant, but probably, if there was some wifely A Level, she suspected she would only scrape a B.

Her phone rang and she saw Dave's number.

'Hello, sweetheart, how are you doing?' she asked.

'Well... could be worse, I suppose. That's one thing about being here, there's always someone who's worse off than you are. I'm trying to make the best of it... and I was thinking about the summer.'

'The summer that's not going to happen any more... ah, well.' She didn't want to go on about it, she was sure she'd made him feel quite guilty enough.

'Well, not the way we'd planned,' he said. 'And we means mainly you, Tess, you did all the planning. You did all the work and I feel for you.'

She let out a sigh and tried not to feel too sorry about it all.

'Are you wallowing?' he asked.

'Yes, I am wallowing and I'm allowed to wallow,' she said, 'I really miss the dog...' but Bella was just part of it. She already missed looking forward to the holiday... she had no idea how she would deal with the coming and going of the departure date... and, oh, *everything* was just a bit much right now.

'I think you should go to Los Angeles,' Dave said.

This suggestion made her almost angry. 'Oh, you do, do you? Think I should just toddle off to the other side of the world and get out of everyone's hair, maybe? Stop annoying you all?' she asked.

'Tess... we all love you, but I did not want to go on your big holiday.'

'Dave!'

'Well, I didn't. You just twisted everyone's arm.'

'I can't believe you... any of you! Who wouldn't want something like that?' she protested angrily. 'What's the matter with you all?'

'You're the one who wants the big change, the big adventure. You should go. I mean, it's not Cambodia, but it's LA. It's pretty bloody exciting.'

'Oh, I should just go? You're still on morphine, aren't you?'

'Yes, I'm still on morphine, and it is awesome, but this is not the morphine talking.'

'What about our couple time? Our together time? Do you want to get out of that too?'

'Well... maybe that wouldn't be such a bad thing, would it?' he said. 'Maybe what we need is some time apart rather than a three-week trip together.'

'Oh... I see...' she felt a little bit blindsided. It was one thing for her to think that they could do with some time apart, but now here was Dave telling her he'd like space. First the children and now him – did no one have any further need for her?

'But... you're in a plaster cast and you'll be on crutches... how will you manage without me?' she protested.

'I know this may come as a big surprise, but maybe I'll manage just fine,' Dave replied.

'I see,' she repeated, suddenly wondering if they were talking about for six weeks, or forever.

'I've been thinking about it,' Dave went on. 'In a week's time, if the ribs heal up nicely, I'll be up and about on crutches, so once I've got used to them I think I could move into the summerhouse at the bottom of the garden. There's running water already and I'll get a little hob and a fridge and round the back, I'll have a chemical toilet installed, temporarily of course.'

'The summerhouse? A little hob... and a chemical toilet?'

This really was the morphine talking. 'Dave, *seriously*, you've got a plaster cast on your foot for the next six weeks at least.'

'I've got full use of both arms,' he insisted. 'Thank goodness for that. And I've made a decision for me... I'm not going to tour Southeast Asia, lovely as it would have been, I am finally going to spend the whole summer painting... because there is literally nothing else I can do.'

'Oh... *painting...*'

The last time he'd mentioned it, she'd bitten his head off. But this time, she bit her tongue. Dave had been meaning to paint all summer for about... well... ever since Alex was born, probably. All those long summer holidays an art teacher gets, but how quickly they all seemed to be used up with childcare, life admin, chores, flat-out exhaustion, and all the other things that come with being a grown-up and a parent.

This time she didn't dismiss his painting idea. This time she thought about it from his point of view. Painting was quite obviously still unfinished business for Dave. After all these years, there was maybe still a part of him that believed he was not only an art teacher, but also an artist.

Dave had gone to a world-famous London art school and his class had been one of those golden years that had spawned not just one, but a handful of incredibly successful artists. Artists who were well known today – their important works displayed in galleries, and selling for huge prices. Maybe there was a nagging feeling at the back of Dave's mind that he could have been one of them. He'd been in the group all those years ago. He'd had the ideas and the talent.

When Dave had left art school, he'd spent a whole year painting in a shared studio, and that was when he and Tess had met at a party. He'd made ends meet by working part-time at a supermarket before his father had intervened, leaning hard on Dave to train as a teacher so that he could earn himself a respectable salary. Then marriage to Tess and baby Alex had followed before Dave was out of his twenties. And painting, really getting right into the heart of painting again, that was something Tess knew Dave had put on hold, year after year, promising himself as every fresh summer holiday approached that this year he would find the time.

Maybe at last, this year, he really would manage it.

'Plus...' Dave went on, while these thoughts rose up in Tess's mind, 'I think you could do with an adventure. You maybe really need an adventure. You're the one who wanted that big, exciting holiday the most. And... you know, I do think that some space and doing different things could do us a lot of good.'

And there was a phrase all loaded with discussions they'd had and needed to have.

The space could do us good.

Dave was a very loving husband. She never doubted him. She was never, ever going to come home to find Dave in bed with another woman, or with his bags packed up, telling her he was leaving. It would never happen. No matter how much they might drive each other to distraction. He took his family very seriously.

But they both knew things between them were completely lacklustre. They loved one other and they annoyed the living daylights out of one other. Some days, they could barely be in the same room together. And they couldn't seem to get out of this pattern, this low-gear marriage that bumped along uneasily. Maybe he was right... maybe space would do them good.

Maybe they didn't need quality time together on an Asian adventure; maybe they needed time apart. Maybe he needed a summer of painting in the glorified shed at the bottom of the garden and she needed an adventure all of her own.

Maybe she needed to try and remember who she was and what she liked and what she wanted to do.

'But Dave,' still she protested, 'I can't just leave you in the summerhouse, while you're... *broken*. You'll need someone to bring you food, make you food, maybe even dress you... I mean, are chemical toilets even big enough for people with crutches?'

'A disabled chemical toilet, then. No, I've been lying here, thinking it all through carefully... big t-shirts, sweatpant shorts, slip on shoes. I'll get my sister to come round and check on me. I'll get a couple of the neighbours to drop by if I'm really stuck. And I will make lots of healthy one-pot meals and soups. Maybe even salads. You'll come back from LA and maybe I'll be half the man I was. LA, Tess! Think about it. Not everyone gets the chance of a trip like that. In fact, don't limit yourself to LA, use it as a base, go and explore the West Coast.

'And Natalie has said she'll come and see me for a weekend or two,' he added. 'She can stay at Sophie's and come and visit me. Maybe even take me out on some trips. But really, I want to be left on my own,' Dave said, 'so I finally have absolutely no excuse but to dig out the paint and the brushes again and really spend some time on it.'

'And what about Alex?' Tess asked. 'I really think he needs some care and attention from us. I can't tell if he's really as okay as he says he is... I worry about him.'

'You always worry about everyone.' Dave added, 'Look, we'll

both phone Alex all the time. He can come up here and stay with friends whenever he likes. Maybe he can even go over to LA and visit you.'

'Oh! That's a good idea...'

Tess wondered if she could convince Alex to come. Sun and beaches, somewhere new and exciting – these things would be so good for her moody overthinker of a son.

'Just do this, Tess,' Dave urged her. 'Press go, book the tickets, and we'll all muddle along without you, somehow. Just go for it. Do it for yourself.'

Once she'd said goodbye to him, she took a long time to think it over. She could go for a bit, she told herself... she could go for a fort-night... it wasn't so far away... if she didn't like it at all, or Dave needed her, she could come back. She walked all around her house, straightening cushions, watering house plants, making a mental note of the jobs that still had to be done... and realised she was prepping for River to be here.

And River could only be here if Tess went to LA.

Finally, before she could backtrack on herself, she picked up her phone and dialled River's number.

'Hello, Tess, I hope you've got some good news for me,' was River's opener. It made Tess smile.

'Yes... as a matter of fact I do. You can come over and spend the summer in our house.'

River gave an excited shout.

'One thing will be different. My husband, Dave, will be living in the summerhouse at the bottom of the garden. I hope that's not a problem, he'll have a little kitchen and bathroom there. He'll be right out of your way.'

'Okaaaaay... I guess that could work.'

'And I'm going to fly to LA,' Tess suddenly felt a little breathless at the thought, 'and stay in your apartment.'

'That is amazing... oh my God, that's totally amazing. I am so excited for you!'

'Yes, me too...' *I think,* Tess couldn't help adding mentally.

'You are going to love it here. Truly, you are going to have the most wonderful time.'

12

And then came the day when there was no more prep left to do. Ambleside was gleamingly ready to receive its houseguest. The bannister had been repaired, every loose screw had been tightened, every painting straightened, every pillow was plumped, every towel was fluffed, every guest soap unwrapped and there were vases with flowers in all the right places. The surfaces shone. All the kinks, wrinkles and wonky bits had been sorted and... it was time.

Dave's summerhouse adventure had already begun. He'd spent his first night there, to make sure everything worked and he could get in and out of his bed, his chair and his toilet. His tiny kitchenette was stocked with enough for two days when the cleaning lady, Angela, would drop in with fresh supplies. Paints, pastels, canvases and an easel were all packed into one corner, ready for the summer of creation.

Tess's bags were packed, her passport and boarding card were in her handbag, her taxi to the train station was ordered and Dave was hopping around her, going through the travel checklist, almost impatient for her to go.

But oh, the panic she felt when the moment of leaving came. She checked through her bag just one more time, and once more again. She asked her husband another round of final questions: was he going to be okay? Could he really manage? Should she be leaving?

'Yes, yes and yes,' he insisted, smiling fondly at her.

'Come here,' he urged, propping himself against the kitchen counter so he could give her a bear hug.

Holding Dave felt like the best and safest place in the world at that moment and now she had no idea why she'd thought it would be a good idea to fly to the other side of the world from him, especially when he was still recovering.

'This is a terrible idea,' she whispered against his neck.

'It's a great idea. You don't want to hang around with old peg-leg. I'm going to enjoy the peace and the quiet. You are going to experience a whole new city, a whole new world. Go off. Enjoy it. Do not feel guilty about me for one minute. I'm going to have a ball.'

'I don't want to go, Dave,' she heard herself suddenly protesting. 'It's an eleven-hour flight, and I've never done a long flight on my own. The last long-haul we did, I was sick twice.'

'Tess... don't be mad. You're the most capable grown up I know. If anyone can do this, it's you. Go and have an adventure. I will really, really look forward to having you back, my love,' he hugged her hard with these words, 'but now you need to go.'

No, she didn't! She really didn't *have* to go. She could change her mind; she could stay. Why was Dave so keen on making her go? Were they going to split up? Was this a trial run to see how they enjoyed their time apart? And what did he mean, he was going to have 'a ball'? What was he planning when she was away?

'Are you sure you'll be all right?' she asked him.

'Yes!'

'Are you sure I'll be all right?' was her next question.

'You? Of course you'll be all right. Go off and have a great time.'

She screwed up her eyes for courage, but didn't quite want to let go. This would be it – this would be their last hug for weeks and weeks.

When she finally let go, she left the house as slowly as possible, clinging to the metaphorical doorposts.

But then she was in the taxi, speeding through lanes with hedgerows so lush, so green, so overspilling with cow parsley and blossom and hawthorn that your heart could break. She was still so sad not to be going away with her family, the way she'd planned for so long. But maybe she could feel the first prickling of excitement. Maybe this could really be an adventure... and an adventure all of her own.

* * *

Tess sat on the arranged terrace, at the arranged time, having hauled one suitcase and one piece of hand luggage onto the underground and up the escalators and along a busy pavement. It was, on reflection, a mad idea to be meeting on his lunch break on her way to Gatwick. She was exhausted by the hassle of dragging her luggage across town. But she felt she had to see him in person before she left. She was, in fact, a little desperate to see him.

And now, just a few minutes late, she picked him out, loping with his big stride along the pavement towards her.

As he drew closer, she took in the details. His hair looked dry and overgrown and as soon as he spotted her, she suspected from his tense smile that she was going to get nervy, irritated Alex, not joyful and funny Alex. He was mercurial, always had been. When he was feeling happy and positive, he could be an energetic and enthusiastic delight to be with. But when he was gloomy or low, he could be tense, snappy, irritable and frustrated.

Never mind, Tess told herself, over the years she'd learned many ways to bring him round. She stood up to hug and kiss her son hello, holding him close for as long as he allowed her to.

'It's lovely to see you,' she told him, grinning, looking at him up close and taking in all the details. His face was freshly shaved and he was dressed in the regulation young workers' uniform of dark skinny trousers, a white shirt and a jacket too loose and boxy for his slim frame. His blonde hair was short at the sides, but unruly on top. Although the sun was shining brightly and the weather had been good for week after week, Alex was winter pale with dark circles under his eyes.

'How are you doing, darling?' she asked him, once he'd settled in his chair.

'Good, I'm good... how about you? Going off on this big adventure!'

'Yes!' and as she talked him through her plans for the next few weeks, he relaxed into his chair a little and his smile warmed up, but then when she asked how his work was going, the tension immediately came back to his face and his posture.

'It's fine... interesting,' he told her, as they glanced through menus and made the lunch order. 'They do keep us really busy, which is good.'

'Yes, you look as if you've hardly spent five minutes outside in this weather.'

'Yeah... well, my hay fever's been terrible,' he said, running a hand through his hair. 'Worst summer ever, in fact.'

'Oh dear... and you're taking the...' she began gently, knowing he didn't like her interference.

'Yes, Mum,' he interrupted with a roll of his eyes.

Their food arrived and she expected Alex to fall on it, as he would always have done as a teenager and then as a permanently hungry student. Instead, he sliced it up carefully and forked up the odd mouthful, but as they talked, the pauses between mouthfuls became longer and longer. And there was still plenty of food on his plate when he let the waiter carry it away.

'You're not hungry?' she couldn't help asking.

'No... had a muffin with my coffee not that long ago. Sorry.'

He was fiddling with his cuffs, checking his watch and just couldn't seem to settle in his chair.

'Is it okay for you to come out and meet me for lunch?' she asked, wondering if he was nervous to be out of the office for too long. 'Do you need to be back soon?'

'No, it's fine, it's absolutely fine,' he replied, sounding annoyed.

She asked more about work, the people there, was he making new friends? And he answered everything but still with the same stressed, annoyed tone. His answers didn't give the detail she'd been hoping for. They sort of kept her at arm's length and it just didn't sound as if he was having a great time.

She'd hoped there would be news of new friends, a girlfriend even, and nights out with work colleagues, and busy weekends of London fun. Tess's first job had been a five-year stint in London and it had been an action-packed, exhilarating time. Three years into it, she'd fallen in love with Dave. Instead, Alex talked a lot about going for walks, enjoying the scenery, finding quiet boltholes in the urban jungle. And that would all be fine, if he seemed happy about it.

But the simple, sad fact was that he didn't look happy. He was still fidgeting and looking off into the distance instead of meeting her gaze. But all her attempts to ask if he was okay, in different ways, were met with an irritated 'I'm fine'. She thought back and wondered if he'd been happier at university... maybe he'd seemed a little happier then... well, not in that dreadful final year when he'd turned himself into a stressed-out wreck and he'd had to move home to study for his finals. She didn't think he'd been really, fully happy for some time. Not in the relaxed, bouncy, care-free way that Natalie could be happy. But there was always going to be a difference. Alex was naturally more wary, cautious and tense.

'Alex, it is a good job you've landed...' she began.

'I know, I know,' he countered. 'I'm grateful to have it.'

'No, sweetheart, what I want to say is, if it's not the right one for you, you can change it. And if London isn't the right place for you, you can move.' She put her hand gently on his forearm and told him, 'Come back home and recharge if you need to. You will always be welcome, darling. You always have a home with us, whenever you need it.'

Alex nodded.

'I know,' he said finally, 'but I think I'm okay. I'm just... I'm trying to work things out. And I think it's going okay.'

'I'm always here for you...' she said and then couldn't help laughing at herself. 'Listen to me, I already sound Californian, but I really do mean it.'

'Imagine how you'll sound after six weeks in LA?' he said and she so enjoyed the return of his grin.

'Why don't you come out and see me? I have a second bedroom. And a pool! We can go to the beach. And we can go to the movies, of course. And we can do all the high-brow arty things that you like to do.'

'In LA?' he scoffed.

'Honestly, they have the most incredible art museums. I've been looking everything up. Come and see me?' she asked again, but she suspected she wasn't going to get a commitment.

'Hmmm...' he gave her a smile. 'I'll think about it,' he said finally, 'it does sound nice.'

'I'll send you daily pool photos until you will be begging to come over. Have you made any other plans for the summer?' she asked.

'No,' was his simple reply. He didn't elaborate.

'You are going to get some time off, though?' she asked.

'Yes, a week, maybe even two... should be okay.'

'Come to LA... please? I'm sure after a week or so I'll be desperate to have someone to keep me company.'

'Okay, Mum, I'll think about it...' He sounded ready to tip over into irritation with her again.

This was followed by: 'Mum... are you and Dad okay?'

'What do you mean?' she asked defensively.

'Well... you know... as a couple.'

She was about to brush it off with an 'of course,' or 'don't be silly' reply, but his light brown eyes focused on hers and asked her to be honest.

'We've had some difficult times,' she admitted, 'it's really hard work being parents...' Alex gave an eye roll, but she carried on, 'and we've had a lot to adjust to with you both moving away from home. I'm not sure we're adjusting very well. And I hope... we both hope that some time apart might help. But... to be honest, we're not great at the moment. But we both want things to get better.'

Was that true, she asked herself as she said it? Did she honestly want things to get better? Or were her thoughts turning more often to life without Dave... life after Dave? Was she mentally rehearsing for divorce?

'Does that help?' she asked gently.

'Yeah,' Alex said and the lines of concern between his eyebrows relaxed a little.

And Tess tried to imagine what it would be like to tell Alex and Natalie if she and Dave were going to split up. It would be horrendous, the worst conversation of her life. Maybe it would make them look back over their childhood and question so many times when they'd assumed they'd been part of a happy family. But could she carry on being unhappy, for the sake of keeping everyone else happy?

'Good luck, especially with your holiday. It's not very you.'

'What do you mean?'

'Well, just going off somewhere, without much planning... and on your own. It isn't very you.'

She had to admit that was probably true, especially the bit about not planning.

'Well... I'm trying something different... trying to shake myself up a little. Now tell me what you've been reading. Anything interesting?' She knew how much he got into new books and loved to talk about them.

'Yes.' His face brightened up immediately as he began: 'I've discovered this South Korean writer...'

The hour was soon over and it was time for Tess to catch her train to the airport. Alex insisted on helping her with her bags all the way to the underground, although she worried he would be late back to work.

'They know I'm meeting you. They know it's a one-off, so don't fret,' he assured her.

And then it was time for her to hug him goodbye, which made her tearful.

'Please look after yourself, darling,' she told him, 'you can be in touch any time. And I'll phone you. It's not easy being your age and trying to work out what you want to do. I know it's not easy.'

'Take care, Mum.'

'You too. We love you,' she told him, hugging him hard.

Tess watched as he walked across the station, up the stairs and out into the stark sunshine of a July afternoon. He was wearing trainers, she noticed, as he reached the top steps.

She thought she'd seen some mention of his work dress code

banning trainers... and this thought was a troubling undertow to all the other things swirling round her mind on her way to the airport. Until she finally put it to rest by telling herself that maybe the code was relaxed in the summer. And anyway she would ask him the next time they spoke.

Yes, of course, she would ask him.

13

River was exhausted. Taxi, plane, train, train, taxi... it was all blurring into a jumble that she was beginning to think would never end. She needed sleep, or maybe more caffeine, nicotine even; she needed to pee and/or maybe to be sick. And when was this twisting, turning, churning car ride ever going to end?

There was an abrupt jerk on the brakes and, finally, the car began to slow.

'Here we are, ma'am... this is Ambleside,' the taxi driver announced as they pulled to a halt. 'Looks like a lovely place to stay.'

River pushed her sunglasses on top of her head and opened her blurry, gritty, exhausted eyes.

Oh. My. Gosh.

Her eyes widened to take in the beauty of Tess and Dave's family home. It wasn't just like in the photos; oh no, it was so much better. It looked bigger. It looked thicker, and much more solid, as if it had been here for hundreds of years and would be here for hundreds more. The plant trained to grow up and around the charming wooden front door was flowering in big clumps of pale lilac. The front garden, the hedges, the setting around the house... everything was so ludicrously luscious and green.

The taxi driver pulled into the paved driveway and got out of the car to help her with the luggage in the back. There were two medium-sized suitcases, but she'd kept her handbag and precious laptop bag in the front seat right beside her. Her two-year old MacBook, her hands and her wrists were her 'tools' that she guarded carefully. The MacBook, although she tried to back up regularly, was jam-packed with all of her projects – past, present and future. The hands and wrists were the physical means to channel her thoughts directly from her mind to her fingertips, to the computer screen. How anyone had got anything written in an era of typewriters was a mystery to River. Imagine no delete? No copy, cut and paste. And then before typewriters, imagine having to deal with only pen and paper? Holy mother... Tolstoy's wife having to copy out *War and Peace* by hand, not just once but over and over again, so that he had *spare* manuscripts. Shakespeare writing by candlelight on parchment made from the skins of baby cows!

Really, a modern writer had no excuse not to be writing tens of thousands of words a week, with the current tools at hand. Mind you, they also had to battle with the internet: an infinite warren of rabbit holes of distraction, available at the merest tap of the touchpad.

River reined her mind back in from this cascade of thoughts right back here to the present. She got out of the car and watched as a man on crutches opened the front door. He was stocky with a greyish beard and darker, shaggy, collar-length hair and the kind of outdoor tan that ends at the open neck of a shirt and its rolled up sleeves. He looked a little bit like a rock band roadie on holiday. He looked like quite a lot of fun, actually. She was guessing this was Dave.

'Hello, you must be River. You made it! How lovely to see you,' he began, and his smile was warm and enthusiastic.

'I sure did. It's absolutely awesome to be here.'

'I'm Dave,' he said leaning forward, elbow on the top of his crutch so that he could shake her hand.

Big, warm handshake, big, warm guy... River was thinking as she held eye contact and smiled broadly.

Dave took a long, appreciative look at River. She was tall and skinny, Latino-looking with cascades of hair in shades of mahogany, caramel, rust and blonde. Golden bangles tinkled on her wrist, golden hoops hung from her ears. Skinny jeans, ankle boots, a conker brown leather jacket and a creamy shirt made up her simple, but slightly rock'n'roll outfit. Her smile broke across the honey-coloured skin of her face and highlighted high cheekbones and pearly teeth.

'How was your journey?' he asked.

'Absolute freaking hell,' she replied. 'I'm never going on a plane or a train again. Sorry, but I'm gonna have to move in here for good.'

They both laughed at this.

She paid the taxi driver and as Dave apologised that he could do nothing to help, she wheeled the bags towards the front door.

'Right,' she said, 'you first, let's do the tour. I am so excited!'

With a burst of surprise, Dave realised he was too.

* * *

'So... number 1635 must be on this stretch,' the taxi driver announced, indicating and pulling off the three-lane highway into a side road that ran along the front of a row of faceless six-storey high apartment blocks. They had that grimy look that concrete, railings and awnings get when exposed to a dirty, dusty road for year after year with little rain to wash the grime away.

Tess squinted her eyes against the glaring sun and looked at the numbers: 1625, 1630... 1635. *Really? Are you absolutely sure?* She wanted to ask the driver. But somehow, she was sure. She hadn't expected River's home to be on such a busy road, that was true. But maybe in LA the loveliest of apartments were tucked behind workaday façades like this one. This place had a pool, for goodness' sake, so it could hardly be shabby.

The taxi parked up and the driver wanted to be paid before he opened the boot and got out her bags. Maybe he'd had too many bad experiences. Although she wasn't sure how exactly he was expecting her to do a runner with a large suitcase.

She paid the fare, adding a tip, and steered her bag to the front door. It was just after 2 p.m. LA time and the heat glared off the concrete at her. There was a sliver of a key to locate from a tiny lock-box, then she had to open River Romero's mailbox and retrieve the envelope with the proper apartment keys. Once she'd done this, she spent a moment or two trying different keys on the front door until she had success. Then, trailing her bag behind her, she stepped into a lobby as unloved and grimy as the front of the building. Ahead of her was a table overspilling with junk mail, and two windows leading out towards the back of the building that were so dirty, she couldn't tell what lay beyond.

She knew River's apartment was on the top floor, so she called the disappointingly dreary lift and took it up. On the top floor, a corridor of dark wooden doors greeted her and she sought out number 44.

As she took the key and made a first pass at the locks, a rumbling, barking sound started up from the other side. Tess double-checked, this was definitely door number 44... and the key was turning in the lock. There was more barking, right up against the door now and scratching sounds as two excited dogs anticipated the return of their owner.

Dogs... but River hadn't said anything about dogs?

Maybe with the exhaustion of jetlag, Tess was imagining dogs. She listened carefully and definitely heard scratching and barking. Despite really liking dogs, Tess was now very unsure. Dogs were very territorial. What if these ones were not happy to see her?

'Hello, doggies,' she said cheerfully, as the final key turned and she knew the door would now open, 'hello there... hello, hello... good boys or maybe good girls...'

The door was just a few inches ajar and already two furry white snouts were poking out, sniffing and whining with excitement.

She pushed her suitcase in first, then followed, careful not to open the door far enough to let the dogs scramble out.

As soon as the door was shut, she was face to face with two very excited, very furry dogs. They were so big. One reared right up, planting its paws on her chest. She just about screamed in fright, thinking it was going to attack. But no, this appeared to be friendly. Now the other one joined in, and Tess was caught up in a blur of white fur, fluff, dog tongue, dog teeth and terrible, terrible dog breath.

They were so big, so heavy, she worried they were going to knock her over.

'Down now, down,' she said in the firm-but-fair voice she'd not had to use since Bella was a very young dog.

'Down!'

Finally, the dogs seemed to get the message.

Why were there dogs here? Was she sure she was in the right place? But the keys had opened the door. Dogs...

It felt like about 100 hours since she'd had any sleep, or anything nice to eat and she could not cope with great big, surprise, bouncy dogs, not just right at this moment.

She wheeled the suitcase through the wide entrance space that was home to a dining table, chairs and a whole lot of coat and shoe clobber and into a spacious open-plan living space with a kitchen along the left-hand side. It should have been a wonderful space, with its huge window leading out onto a balcony, but to Tess's dismay, it was an absolutely astonishing mess. She actually gasped out loud at the state of the place.

The two sofas were piled high with books and papers, shoes and clothes. The kitchen counters were just as cluttered with dirty pots, plates and glasses, gadgets and more stacked bundles of papers, newspapers, magazines, mail and books.

There was a desk near the window that was completely covered, almost a foot high in paper, and there was a further jumble of books and clobber stacked underneath it. Everywhere, there were ashtrays piled high with butts. And worse, foil food trays with the congealed remains of meals had been used as ashtrays too. Tess was afraid to go into the bedroom or the bathroom because of what she suspected she would find there. Okay, at least there were dogs, she reassured herself, that meant there wouldn't be... *vermin*.

As the dogs continued to follow her, she put her head gingerly round the bedroom door, she saw a wardrobe, doors ajar, with clothes falling from their hangers. More clothes were heaped on the floor and the bed. More ashtrays abandoned at the bedside. An overflowing wicker laundry basket had a lid balanced on top of the heap of clothes inside. The bathroom was an equal mess, and it looked damp and slimy, so she pulled the door shut quickly.

She moved a pile of books to the floor and sat down on the corner of the sofa. From here, she looked out through grimy glass onto the balcony. She saw that the glass door was open by about twelve inches, to let the dogs go in and out, and out there on the balcony, amid pots with the withered remains of dead plants, were many large, meaty dog turds drying in the sun. Some were fresh, some were fully desiccated, many were in various in-between stages. This was a skin-crawling level of mess.

She thought of the fresh flowers she'd put out in her lovely house to welcome River home. She thought of the little guest soaps newly unwrapped in the soap dishes, the fluffy white towels, the tiles all scrubbed to sparkling by Angela, their long-serving cleaner, the kitchen, white, bright and shiny.

She went to stand at the filthy window, to take a look at what was down in the courtyard, because the one good thing she'd worked out was that this apartment didn't face onto the busy multi-laned road. There, beyond the dog-dirtied balcony, she saw the saddest, grubbiest swimming pool she could have imagined. It had been drained of its water and there were leaves, twigs and plastic bags collecting in heaps across the bottom. Three faded, broken loungers surrounded it, along with several dead palm trees in dirty pots.

She collapsed back onto the sofa again, feeling tears of anger and disappointment leap up into her eyes. She was *so* tired, she just wanted to get into a calm, cool bed and sleep for the next twenty-four hours straight. She didn't want to have to deal with panting, stinking dogs and this rancid, stinking flat.

'River, you absolutely useless bloody cow!' she said out loud.

14

River carried her bags one by one into the house.

She saw the gleaming wooden parquet beneath her feet as she followed Dave through the pristine whiteness into a gorgeous sitting room with luxurious sofas and curtains, all muted greys and heathery tweeds. There were flowers and branches in vases and, beyond the room, a view of a luscious green lawn and more flowers.

'Oh my goodness, it's absolutely beautiful,' she exclaimed. 'What a delightful home you've created.'

Dave smiled. 'It's all down to Tess. She thinks she doesn't have a creative bone in her body, but she has a great eye for interior design. The kitchen is in here...'

River followed him into the lovely white wooden country kitchen that she recognised from the photographs. And she half listened as he explained how to use the hob, the oven, the microwave.

'Do you have a blender?' she asked, because as a rule, she didn't really cook. She just kind of blended – juices, smoothies and soups – and ate out.

And smoked.

She wondered when would be a good time to ask where she could smoke because, quite frankly, she'd not yet found anywhere in England where she could smoke and it had been a goddam twenty-seven hours or something since she'd had a cigarette.

'I'd show you round upstairs, but... the crutches,' Dave explained.

'Yes, of course. I'll be fine. So... where do you stay?'

'I'm all moved into the summerhouse, down at the bottom of the garden, quite tucked away from the house. So I won't bother you at all. I've got running water, a refreshing cold shower, my kitchen and my chemical loo. I'm enjoying it. It feels like a holiday, especially if this weather keeps up.'

'And how are your injuries? Are you healing up okay?'

'Well... there's a bit of a way to go... but I'm coming on fine.'

'If I need anything, or can't figure anything out... is it okay to come and ask you?' River wondered.

'Yes, of course, I don't want to get in your way. But I'm here if you need me,' Dave said with a kind smile. 'The odd friend might come up and visit, or take me out for a trip, so there may be a little bit of coming and going from the garden. But, please, make yourself totally at home. And you're insured to use the car, of course. The keys are hanging on the hook beside the front door.'

'Stick shift?' River asked warily.

'No, it's actually an automatic. So hopefully Tess will get on all right with your one.'

'Oh... yes... of course.'

She looked around at this beautiful home, with its plush sofas and cushions and immaculately arranged bookcases. There was unusually good artwork on the walls and the plants were all so green and pampered. Upstairs, she was sure the beds would be made up with crisp white linen and plump duvets. And the bathrooms would be spotlessly glossy.

She had long suspected that she wasn't much of a homemaker, or even a housekeeper, but Tess's home was bringing her rudely face to face with this reality. Before coming here, she had thought her apartment wasn't too bad... a bit messy, sure, but she was a creative person. She had to have a creative place. But now... here... looking around this tranquil oasis, she was suddenly certain that she could do her best work here. Not in the chaos, frenzy and upheaval of apartment number forty-four at 1635. Well, to be honest, she never worked there any more. She couldn't face it. She only worked in cafés, quiet bars and bookstores.

'Dave? Are you going to speak to Tess soon?' she asked.

'Yes... I was going to try her right now, in fact. Let her know you've arrived safely and see if she's got to your place all right.'

'Could you please tell her that... well, I left in a hurry... I've been very busy with work... and I'm sorry, but my place is... it's... it's kind of a total hot mess compared with your home. And I want to apologise to her for that. I mean it, I want to say sorry, truly.'

Dave smiled, met her eyes again for longer than he meant to, and then gave as much of a shrug as he could with the crutches.

'Oh, don't worry about that. I mean, you're letting her stay there for free. I know Tess, she'll have it all organised and put to rights in under an hour.'

'Please apologise to her for me,' Tess said. 'And tell her, her home, *your* home, is just stunning, beautiful, and I'm going to love staying here.'

It looked as if Dave was going to leave her now, so she had to ask.

'Dave... I'm really sorry, I know you don't want anyone smoking in the house and I totally, totally get that... but is there anywhere where it would be okay to smoke in the garden?'

'Oh!' Dave turned to her with what she thought was something of a mischievous look. 'Do you still *smoke*? I don't know anyone who still smokes...'

'I know, I'm sorry... I'm an LA cliché, I have wheatgrass, spirulina and three Marlboros for breakfast.'

'No, no, not at all...' he said, highly amused. 'I'm going to dig out my old glass ashtray for you and we'll set you up with a little smoking den on the patio. I gave up smoking twenty-two years ago, when my son was born... *still* miss it. *Still* inhale deeply when I walk past a smoker.'

'Well, let's get out there and give you a cigarette... you know that one won't hurt, right? And I won't tell Tess if you don't.'

* * *

Tess was desperate, *desperate* for sleep. Her eyes were burning in her head and she felt dizzy. But surely the dogs needed to get out. How long had they been in here? Did they need to be fed? Or watered? Were there any instructions about them at all? Did she even dare to take them both out on a lead? They looked very strong and excitable. She searched all around the mess for any kind of information that River might have left. Finally, under a fruit bowl on the kitchen countertop that was home to one withered apple and a black banana, she found a scribbled list headed 'TESS'. She scanned it quickly for dogs. And there was the blessed info:

Tess,

I am so, so sorry about the dogs. They were supposed to go stay with a friend of my regular dog sitter, but she bailed at the last minute. I have been able to get another walker, Tom, to help. He will come and walk the dogs twice a day, but they will have to stay in the apartment. They are really sweet and friendly, and won't give you any trouble. You can call Tom anytime, if you're having any trouble. His number is over the page along with all the feeding instructions. So sorry again... leaving has been a freaking nightmare!

She punched Tom's number into her phone and when the reply came, she tried not to sound too crazed.

'Hi, hi, is that Tom? Hi. I'm Tess, I'm from England. I've arrived at River's flat... apartment from England. Tom, could you possibly take her dogs for a few hours? They seem desperate for exercise and I'm so tired... I've just got off the plane from England and I have to sleep or I think I'm going to...' It was too late, she was already sobbing. 'I'm so sorry,' she went on, 'I'm not usually like this. I'll be fine to look after the dogs, but just not today. Not this afternoon. Are you free at all? Can you come round?'

'Hey, Tess... welcome to Los Angeles,' came the most laid back drawl, 'yeah... sure... I can be there in like thirty minutes. Is that cool?'

'Oh, thank you, thank you so much, thank you. Thanks again.'

'It's cool.'

In the thirty minutes that she waited for Tom to arrive, Tess concentrated on the bedroom. One by one, she took the items from the bed. Used, grubby things – underpants, for crying out loud – she picked up with her fingertips and tossed in the direction of the washing basket, everything else, she hung onto hangers, or pushed into drawers. She felt quite overwhelmed with emotion when she found a box of clean linen under the bed, so she could change the crumpled pillowcases and sheets. Then she tackled the clothes on the floor, again tossing to the laundry basket, or hanging in the wardrobe. She ventured into the bathroom and used the grotty towel, hanging lopsided on a hook, to wipe clean the sink and the mirror. She scrubbed at the toilet with the brush. Then she sat down to pee and realised there was no toilet paper.

'I bloody well hate you, River,' she shouted furiously out loud.

When the doorbell rang, mercifully it wasn't too hard to work out how to use the intercom and let Tom in.

* * *

She noted only a few details about him during their brief chat. He was ludicrously buff and tanned with such a young and handsome face. He sported tight shorts and a tight, lime green t-shirt, and seemed incredibly polite. He kept calling her 'ma'am': 'yes ma'am', 'that's right ma'am', 'for sure, ma'am'. And most importantly of all, he was taking the dogs away for a full four hours – plus he knew their names, Burton and Wilder, and showed her which was which. He would take them for longer, he told her sadly, but he had an audition.

An *audition*... of course! Because she was in LA now and people just casually had to go off to auditions. And some part of her, beneath the layers of exhaustion, wanted to give just a teeny little scream of excitement at this. Because she really was in LA now and the dogwalker had an audition, or maybe that should be, there was an actor walking the dogs.

Once Tom and the dogs had left, she locked the door, drank down a long glass of lukewarm water from the tap, then texted Dave:

All good here, darling. Please don't call I have to sleeeeep xxx

She pulled down the blind, then closed the curtain in front of it and fell onto the clean, newly made bed.

Her last thought was: sleep, oh God, sleep. Please, please just let me sleep.

* * *

River had toured the upstairs fully, with its sloped ceiling, skylights and perfect décor. She had seen the two bathrooms with rolled white towels and fresh pats of soap. She had peeked into a girl's room with tasteful flowered wallpaper and immaculately organised shelves of photos, books, trophies and treasured toys. There was a boy's room too, neat as a pin, with a tartan blanket on the bed, and a wall of books and posters. Then the calm, dark master bedroom, all laid out for River with any photos and personal treasures that might have once been here carefully tucked away, so now there was just restful, ironed white linen, a jug of the lilac flowers from the front of the house and two big white reading lamps on either side of the generous bed.

Oh God, it was heaven. When she got back home, her room was going to be *exactly* like this one.

She closed the thick, lined, grey plaid curtains. The room was peaceful, silent and dark enough for her not to need her eye mask. She took off all her clothes and got in between the cool, smooth sheets.

This was the most soothing bed she had climbed into for a long time. She lay back on the pillow but did not feel the sense of calm or release that she was hoping for. Instead, she felt a wave of acute sadness and envy. This was a perfect home. The home of people who'd obviously made a success of their careers, their marriage and their families. And even though she told herself every day that she was free, she was doing the work she loved, and she had never wanted to be tied down with children, or a husband, or commitments, she still felt hot tears fall from the corners of her eyes because right now, her life was so much more of a mess than she could ever have imagined.

'For chrissake, cupcake,' she told herself sternly, 'you're just exhausted and emotional. Take a melatonin pill and get some goddam sleep.'

* * *

Tess woke with a start and was immediately aware of a face... a big, pale face covered with fur. She nearly screamed in fright, then her eyes opened fully and she took in the small, hot room, made sense of the dog's head next to hers, and remembered that she was in LA. She vaguely remembered Tom turning up with the dogs and how she'd gone straight back to sleep afterwards. She looked at her phone and tried to work out if the 6.45 showing was UK time, LA time, morning or evening. She had no idea. She went to the window, pulled back the curtain and saw pale blue sky and the abandoned pool. Morning? Or evening? She was none the wiser.

But did it matter? She was on holiday... on her own... no schedule... no rules... no one to please but herself. She could adjust to LA time as quickly or as slowly as she wanted. After all, she was going to be here for quite some time.

Something of a plan of action was forming for today... or tonight, or whatever it was. She would go out and buy some groceries in the shop she'd noticed from the taxi window. Then she would drink several cups of strong tea – a stash of her favourite teabags was in her suitcase – and maybe eat toast... yes, she'd buy bread, butter and jam. All kinds of staples would have to be brought in, because she'd already looked in the small and elderly fridge and there was nothing but three bags of coffee and some ancient veg in there.

Then, fortified by the tea and toast, she would clean this place from top to bottom, even if it took the first two entire days of her holiday, because that way she could actually start to enjoy living here for the next six weeks.

It was as if the thought of *six weeks* was finally settling on her. It was such a long time... of course she had all kinds of ideas and plans about where to go and what to do and how to keep busy. But she was also beginning to realise how much quiet time there would be and how, for week after week, she would be able to do exactly what she wanted, when she wanted to.

If she wanted to stay in and read all day, she could. If she wanted to eat chocolate for dinner, she could. And if she wanted to scrub at someone else's windows for enough hours to make them jolly well gleam, no one was here to stop her. Tess had run her family and her home and her responsible full-time job incredibly well, using almost all the minutes of every day, for over twenty years. So a six-week stretch of doing exactly what she wanted was almost dizzying, too much to take in all at once.

What would she do?

What would she do with herself?

For herself?

By herself?

She had lists and plans, of course. There were so many sights to see on her checklist. And she had the first inklings of other ideas too... she'd always wanted to be fitter but had never found the time. Surely, right here in LA with the glorious weather and all these body beautifuls, this would be the ideal place to start?

And she would go to art galleries and take the fully guided tours so that she could learn much more about modern art and try to understand what Dave and the artists he had gone to college with were all about.

She would read more.

Look at all the books bulging from every corner in this place. Clearly River never stopped reading. Surely she'd find all kinds of interesting things on the bookshelves here? And she could go to the bookshop and get an American copy of... *Anna Karenina*, maybe, and *The Great Gatsby*... and several other classics that she'd always thought she should read.

And she would think... about herself... her marriage... and what she really wanted for this next phase of life. Because she did know that she wanted to be happier than she was right now.

Way at the back of her mind was just the slightest ripple of unease about how she was going to get settled in and get around here... LA felt quite different. The drive from the airport had taken her through an alien landscape of low-rise blocks and dense motorway networks. It was much more urban and inner city than she'd expected and *much* more urban and inner city than Leamington Spa and the country roads to Ambleside. She tried to imagine driving a car across those six, seven-lane freeways and she felt daunted. This was a car city, there was no other way to get around to her knowledge, so somehow, she was going to have to work out how to do this. Otherwise... she'd be in River's flat and walking round River's neighbourhood for the whole of her holiday.

But first things first, she had to make this place nice, comfortable, *liveable* for her time here.

She looked around the flat again and started to make a plan. If she got big laundry bags, she could store River's papers neatly out of sight. There was an obvious space close to the desk where another tall bookcase could stand and accommodate all the books River obviously read. Tess would get that organised for her.

Her fingers were already itching to make a list. She found a pen and paper easily, then she poked gingerly around the cupboards to see what basics were needed: toilet paper, for sure, washing-up liquid, milk... some new cleaning cloths for that balcony window. It would be so much lighter inside the apartment when that window was thoroughly clean.

And the balcony... dear God, she would have to deal with the balcony. Where did the dogs pee? Where did River walk them? Tess went to her phone and looked at Google Maps. There seemed to be some little square of greenery not too many blocks away.

She wondered about River's state of mind. Did River like living like this, in so much chaos? Was she so busy that she couldn't find time to do her home chores? Maybe she was so focused on her work that she didn't even notice her surroundings... maybe you just stopped making the bed one day, and then didn't have time to wash up the next day, until gradually, you had a problem that was going to take a lot of effort to fix.

She immediately felt sorry for her rage at the woman. But she was glad that trusty Angela would be cleaning Ambleside every week. There wasn't any chance that her lovely home would look anything like this when she returned. But even as she made her list and her plan of attack, Tess couldn't quite push down her horror at the balcony, the slimy vegetables in the fridge and the greyish layer of dirt over everything in the bathroom. Who could live like this?

15

It was approaching 11.30 on a sunny Saturday morning and Alex had just woken up from a dreadful night of rolling, pitching and only fitfully sleeping. He caught sight of his reflection in the room's small mirror and stared at it. He looked so much thinner and less healthy than when he'd first left home a few years ago. He hadn't washed for days. His eyes were lined with dark shadows. He looked like a boy, with his face that still refused to grow a beard, and his sad, confused eyes. A boy who'd somehow wandered away from home and ended up where he was never meant to be.

Suddenly his phone started ringing. Alex jumped up. Disaster!

He ran wildly around the room. His father was calling him on Skype, and if Alex answered the call with his room in the state it was in, he might give the old man a heart attack. He flung dirty clothes, discarded packaging, and empty bottles into one corner of the room. He then threw himself onto the bed and, after quickly trying to flatten down his hair, he answered the call.

His father appeared on the screen, surrounded by blindingly bright sunshine and luscious greenery. Was that really what the weather was like in Warwickshire today?

'Hi, Dad,' Alex began and his voice sounded rusty. This was the first time he'd used it in over twenty-four hours.

'Hi, Alex, how are you doing? I thought you'd finally be up by now,' said his father. The picture blurred, obscuring his dad's face.

'How are you? How's the leg and everything?' said Alex, already wondering what else he was going to talk about for the next ten or fifteen minutes and how he could make this conversation go away.

'Well... some way to go on that front,' his dad replied. 'I'm hobbling about on crutches, enjoying life in the summerhouse and the Californian writer, the houseguest, seems to be settling in quite well. I've hardly seen her at all. I think she's been sleeping off her jetlag. I know your mum's arrived at the place in LA, but that's all I've heard so far. She probably has jetlag too.'

Alex was aware that he also had a jetlag of sorts. The world around him was operating on a different time zone to his.

'How's work going?' his dad asked.

'Er, great,' said Alex. *Think of something to talk about, quickly... anything.* He cast his mind about for some sort of corporate term, anything that he could mention.

'We've been creating mission statements this week...' he offered, 'all about the big ideas, the operational goals.'

'Oh, that sounds good,' said his dad.

Yes... like everything in corp world, it sounded pretty impressive, but in fact it was absolute horse shit that would involve mind-numbing hours in meeting rooms, writing words on flipcharts that had no actual basis in reality.

'And how's the social life?' his dad asked next. 'Were you out last night?'

'Yeah... a few drinks with people from work. Nothing too exciting.'

'And still all quiet on the romantic front?' his dad asked with a smile.

'All quiet,' Alex repeated.

His dad shook his head to signal his disbelief. Alex had heard the 'you're such a handsome guy with so much going on up top, I don't get it' chat many times and hoped it wasn't coming again.

'Dating in the age of anxiety,' his dad said finally, 'it can't be easy.'

After further stilted conversation, when they plucked at conversational straws like the price of beer in London, what Camden was like in his dad's day, and live music not being what it once was, Alex made an excuse about needing to get out to buy food and they both said goodbye.

Once the call was over, Alex slumped down on the bed, until he was enveloped in the soft, musty pillows that badly needed to be cleaned. Everything was strange between him and his father. He wondered when it had become like that. When did it turn from 'Daddy, my hero' into Dad, the stranger I can't reveal one single truth to? It must have developed over years from one tiny misunderstanding and disappointment into another, repeated over and over again, until they didn't know how to begin to understand what was going on with one another.

Alex had literally no idea how to begin a conversation with his father about what was happening in his life, or more realistically, in his head. Because that was where he lived his life now, in his head, inside this tiny room. No, there was no help to be had from his dad. His dad enjoyed life. His dad was straightforward and un-tortured, and his dad just really didn't understand why everything was so difficult and stressful and sad for Alex. His dad remembered being young in London as one non-stop party and only wished that Alex was having as good a time as he did.

'You're only young once,' his dad would tell him with a wink, 'make the most of it!'

Alex couldn't remember when he'd last had a really good

conversation with his dad... but to be honest, he didn't think now that there was any help to be had from anyone. He felt so alone, so lost and confused. His head ached with the pain and also with the embarrassment of his condition.

No help. No possibility of help from anywhere. What was he going to do?

He went out briefly for food and drink, then all afternoon he lay on his bed, the light coming in through the ugly brown blind became bright and hot, and then gradually faded, before turning red, and then a dark orange as the streetlights came on again.

As night fell, the noise of people talking, shouting and arguing in the street below came up to him. The giant crane loomed over the room, casting unnatural, triangular shadows on the walls, making Alex feel once again like he was trapped in a cage.

The hours of darkness were the worst, when he fretted himself into a state where it was impossible to sleep. His phone, with its stupid but cheerful little distractions from his misery, was the life raft that he clung to through those hours, until finally the sky began to light up with dawn and then, when everyone else was waking up, that was when he found he could sleep.

Hours later, he finally got up. According to the clock on the wall, it was four minutes after three in the afternoon and, according to his phone, an email had landed that had finally offered him a plan. First of all, he took his sturdy backpack out from under his bed, then he went round the room and packed into it an assortment of the things he considered important.

Then he sat down at the desk, took up the beautiful fountain pen he'd been given for his twenty-first birthday and wrote a few, short lines to his sister.

Dear Natalie,
I'm so sorry but I'm going to go away for a while. I don't want

*you to worry about me. I'll be totally fine and when I come back, I
know I'll be in a much better state.*

*Please tell Mum and Dad that I really do love them and I know
how hard they've tried for me. But I just have to sort myself out.*

I'll give you my contact details as soon as I can.

I love you all very much.

Alexander

Then he realised a note was ridiculous. He couldn't leave it
here, because his family didn't know where he lived. He couldn't
send it because he'd have to find an envelope and stamps... plus
Natalie was in Spain and he didn't even know her address. Instead,
he'd have to email her with this note, which just wasn't the same.
So instead, he folded it up and tucked it into his pocket.

Then Alex shouldered his backpack, checked the room over
and left, locking the door behind him. He'd been accepted to do
voluntary work that came with accommodation on a farm in
Devon. He wasn't sure if he wanted to sign up for the work, but he'd
decided to make the train journey to the remote, rural location to
see if he liked it there.

One thing was certain – he had no intention of ever coming
back here.

16

When River finally woke up from the deep, deep jetlag and mela-tonin-induced sleep she'd been lost to for the past ten hours, she opened her eyes and couldn't understand why everything was so dark. And the pillow... the sheet... why was everything so smooth?

Where was she? What had happened?

Then she gradually remembered that, of course, she'd been on the plane... and she now was in England in the wonderful house! She saw the outline of bright sunshine around the thick bedroom curtains and groped for her phone, which told her that the morning had almost gone. Her first day in England and she'd already missed the morning. That thought was enough to have her throwing off the duvet and hurrying to wash.

Showered, her dark hair blow-dried, she dressed in a carefully chosen outfit she hoped projected 'international, creative woman of mystery and intrigue': a light knit V-neck top with black and white stripes and wide-legged black linen cropped leg trousers. Then she headed to the kitchen where she went into battle with an unfa-miliar coffeemaker, eventually finding instructions on YouTube, ate two oranges and some truly dry and appalling cereal bar called a Weetabix.

She had absolutely no doubt about what she wanted to do on her first day here. She was a Californian in a hurry. She was going to go straight to Stratford-upon-Avon to visit Shakespeare's birthplace and Anne Hathaway's cottage. She was also going to go and visit the famous theatre, although the plays she was going to see, including *The Merchant of Venice*, were later on in her holiday.

She also planned to walk along the river, and up and down those quaint little streets so that she could breathe it all in. She might even eat one of those luscious English cream teas instead of lunch – with real, full-fat, dairy cream. The kind of thing she hadn't allowed herself to eat since 2006.

When she had imagined herself driving from Ambleside to Stratford, she had pictured narrow country lanes, dodging tractors pulling trailers loaded with hay bales, with horses and cows grazing in fields. And, in fact, there were country lanes for the first fifteen minutes or so, which was good as she got used to the borrowed SUV, much chunkier than her little girl-about-town-mobile. But then she hit what was actually quite a complex freeway situation, with her phone only advising on lane changes very, very late. Maybe her phone was directing her on a time-lag from LA.

It was further driving trauma when she arrived in Stratford and found the car parks only had spaces designed for doll-sized cars. So she narrowly avoided scraping the borrowed car. All this adrenaline needed to be dampened down with a full cream tea at the first teashop she walked into. River had never in her life seen a cake shop like it. There were walls of cakes, layers and layers, shelves of cakes... and the cream! Clearly an entire herd of cows was producing cream for this shop.

'Please tell me you keep a defibrillator on the wall,' she joked with the waitress who took her order. 'I mean this has got to be cholesterol central.'

'Yeah, we do actually,' the waitress confirmed, a little charmlessly, but River guessed this was because the tearoom was too busy for random conversations.

She ate one scone, loaded with dense whipped cream and raspberry jam and washed it down with a full pot of tea, black no milk, because there's only so much lactose a person can deal with at once. As she ate, instead of looking at her phone, she looked round the café, packed with tourists filming themselves, their cakes, each other, the view from the window, basically relentlessly filming everything.

When she was completely full of cream, scone, jam and tea, she set off on her first walk around the streets of Stratford. There were touches of full-on touristy cheesiness, but she also felt strangely moved by how old the houses looked and how most weren't perfectly preserved. There were doors that needed a fresh coat of paint and the occasional untidy front garden. It was so strange to think that people really lived here in these tiny dolls' houses with bundles of sticks on the roofs. Little houses built from wonky planks of wood and lumps of clay, hundreds and hundreds of years ago, and so many of them were still here.

The queues at the front of Shakespeare's home and Anne Hathaway's cottage helped her to decide to come back another day. She would come early, when it was quiet and she could enjoy standing in such historic places in peace and quiet. Now, she wandered down to the riverfront and stood outside one of the major theatres enjoying the view, so peaceful with swans gliding along the surface of the water. Her eyes took in the plays and the top-billed actors. And right there, to her absolute astonishment, was a name she'd never expected to see on the front of a theatre, let alone in Stratford-upon-Avon, in England.

But there it was:

Franklyn Gregory – limited run – SOLD OUT.

Franklyn Gregory... Franklyn Gregory?

Franklyn was currently enjoying standout Hollywood success. He was forty-eight and riding a phenomenal wave of smash hit movies, and now a TV series, that had all begun eight years ago with his breakout role in a low-budget crime thriller. Franklyn had the obligatory beautiful-and-talented wife, plus a darling eight-year-old daughter.

But there was a time before the daughter, the wife, and before the major success, when there had been another very important person in Franklyn Gregory's life... and that person was her... River Romero.

Looking at his name looming down on her from one of the major theatres, River couldn't help pulling up the lapels of her jacket and tugging her hair over her face a little.

'Oh boy,' she said to herself. 'Franklyn freaking Gregory... *this* I did not expect.'

17

Tess's first full day in LA was not going to go the way she had planned. Before she arrived, she'd thought day one might involve a swim in the pool before breakfast on the balcony, followed by a trip out to an inspiring cultural institution. Day one was also supposed to involve exploring local juice bars and the nearest hiking route or beach... and maybe enjoying a cocktail out in the evening while she planned her research for her work project.

But now that day one was here, the reality of it was: get up, walk big, over-excited dogs round the block separately while accosting other dog walkers for poo bags, who all seem to have teeny chihuahuas or dachshunds. Manage to get two poo bags barely big enough for the job, plus learn essential information about location of poo bins and nearby dog-friendly parks.

Go to store on corner and buy every kind of essential: from things to eat and drink, to cleaning stuff, cleaning cloths... and bathroom supplies. Drag it all back in two enormous laundry bags, then begin the Herculean task of making River's place the kind of home she had thought she would be spending six weeks in.

Tess's lovely family home, Ambleside, was cleaned most weeks of the year by Angela, the trusted cleaning lady, but Tess was not at all shy of the heavy lifting of cleaning work. So, in River's apartment she began with the kitchen, then moved on to the bathroom, spraying and scrubbing until there was a light haze of cleaning fluid fumes.

She spent almost an hour on the bathroom alone, where with an onslaught of bleach, grout cleaner and stain-removing stuff she worked away until it squeaked with cleanliness. Tess even threw out the mouldy shower curtain and bathmat and installed tasteful white-and-blue replacements she'd found at the store. And yes, there was satisfaction to be had in turning such a grubby space into a clean and welcoming place, but Tess also felt disappointment as she scrubbed between the tiles with the cheap toothbrush she'd bought for this purpose. Why hadn't River felt the same need that Tess had to have her home ready to welcome her guest? It made Tess wonder if she was going to be cleaning up after people and sorting out their messes for the rest of her life. Maybe that was the aura she gave off: capable, boring old Tess, can cope with whatever you throw at her, soaker-up of dramas, sorter out of messes – leave it to Tess, she can deal with it.

She even dropped a tear or two of self-pity before she told herself off. So what if she had to spend a day or two cleaning, and some time every day looking after *unexpected* dogs? She was here, wasn't she? She was going to have much more time to herself than she'd ever had before. She was going to spend time on herself and sorting out her own things, for once.

In the living space and bedroom, much tidying, storing and cleaning of surfaces was done. River's endless piles of books and papers were neatly rounded up and stacked into the bookcases and the two laundry bags.

Fortified by several tea breaks, Tess went on to wash the grimy windows and she de-clogged the elderly vacuum cleaner, coaxing it back into effective life, so she could suck up some of the clouds of dust and dog hair drifting around the floors, the sofas, under the beds and in all the nooks and crannies of the rooms. Then she vacuumed blinds and bookshelves and the tops of cupboards. She disturbed layers and layers of dust, causing the particles to hang in the bright beams of sunshine and make her sneeze violently.

As she worked her way through every necessary job, the flat began to look lovely. She set fruit out in a little bowl in the kitchen. New soap and rolls of toilet paper went into the clean bathroom. She rearranged the antique desk and its orthopaedic-looking chair to make better use of the space and the light. She picked interesting books from the bookcase that she wanted to browse and set them out on the coffee table. She found two small vases in the process of the kitchen tidy and made a note to bring flowers back from her next trip to the store. She put freshly vacuumed rugs out for the dogs to sit on when they came back from the long walk they were on with Tom.

And then there was only one ghastly chore left...

The poo-filled balcony would have to be cleared and fully washed down so that she could wash the outside of the big window and sit at the little café table and chair set out there, not to mention teach the dogs that this was definitely *not* their toilet any more.

It was a nice size of balcony – maybe three, even four, metres long and a metre and a half wide. The wooden table and chair out there looked grubby, bleached by the sun and unloved. She would solve that with a quick wash down and a little pot plant... but before that, it was the fifteen or so dollops of dog mess, in varying stages of dryness that had to be tackled first.

Well, Tess... fixer of messes, dealer of dramas, scooper of other people's dogs' poo... you deal with this and then surely you get a break from cleaning up after others, she reasoned with herself? Just one last, monumental effort.

It was a horrible job but it was worth it to reclaim that balcony, surely? The balcony would be a lovely space, where she could sit and read, think and daydream in the sunshine. A lot of the thick, extra-large poo bags she'd bought were going to be needed, but she could definitely do this. She would find something that could act as a shovel, a kitchen utensil if that was all that was available, and she would swathe it in poo bag. She'd also wear gloves swathed in poo bags. Then she'd round up all these horrible dog dollops, seal them up in a bin bag and then get that bag out of the flat and into the outdoor bins as quickly as possible. The balcony would then be fully bleached and scrubbed.

This was not going to be at all nice, but it would be worth it.

Gloved, bagged, armed with a double bin bag and a well-wrapped frying pan spatula, she headed out onto the balcony. She dealt with the drier dollops first, building her bravery. Spatula under, transfer into bag, don't think about it too much. She was used to dealing with dog poo, she'd had her own dog for years – that thought accompanied by the now familiar pang of pain as she thought of Bella. But scooping up your own dog's freshly delivered... well, it was like changing other children's nappies, there was an added layer of horribleness when it wasn't your own dog or child.

When the driest clumps were rounded up, it was time to hold her breath and brace herself for the grosser, stickier stuff. After offloading the first mound into the bin bag, she decided that the kitchen spatula she was using would be going into the bin too, after this and she would buy River a new one.

Mound by grisly mound, she shovelled, holding her breath, trying not to look too closely where possible. She tried to develop a deft flick to move the heaps quickly into the bag. The flexible, rubbery spatula was actually pretty good for this and her flicks were getting practised. When the flat rubber surface was right under mound, just a quick snap of the wrist would splat the mound straight into bag. This method was working well until, like every beginner happy with their progress, she grew just a little too confident. She put the spatula in place, snapped her wrist hard and the soggy mound flew not into the bin bag opening, but straight above it, flying with force into the balcony's left side railing. There, it broke apart, some poo splattering against the metal rails, some carrying on with its trajectory.

Tess stood up and looked over the rail. The balconies on this building had been cleverly staggered, to allow more variation of sunshine and shade, and to give a more attractive look to the front of building. But as she peered over, she realised this meant things could fall from one balcony to another. And the dog poo had dropped from this balcony onto the one below.

On the neat and tidy balcony below, with lush pot plants and a bigger table covered with a jaunty red tablecloth, someone had set out a soft and comfortable pair of black lace-up shoes. Dance shoes... jazz shoes... maybe? A large dollop of poo had splatted beside the shoes and another large dollop had made a direct hit, on both the outside and the inside of one shoe. Tess was too surprised to do anything. She just stared, open-mouthed.

But then a dark head of hair appeared and she pulled back from the railing.

She heard the loud, angry: '*What the actual...?*'

And dropped her horrible utensil and bags and stepped inside.

Bloody hell... *bloody hell*... what was she supposed to do now? In Britain, you could go and apologise about things like this and hope that people would usually be understanding, forgive a neighbour's mistakes, or eccentricities even. But here, she'd seen enough US TV to know that Americans often didn't hold back; typically, they let you feel the full force of their anger... and they often had guns.

Tess suddenly felt very new here... on unfamiliar territory and alone. *Oh, come on...* she told herself. *I'll just go downstairs and apologise, wholeheartedly, totally sincerely... and offer to clean up.* Yes, that was the right thing to do. Go down a floor, knock on the door and sort this out straightaway.

She took her gloves off, then realised she'd need her poo-clean kit. The gloves and the bin bag and the wrapped spatula – she'd wrap it up in another bag. She was just getting ready to go out when she heard the doorbell ring long and loud. This was followed by fierce, impatient knocking at the door.

'That's it! That is the final freaking straw with those dogs!' a furious voice insisted from the other side of the door.

'Open up! Open this door! Or I will knock a freaking hole in it! Do you have any idea? These shoes... these shoes were given to me by Savion Glover.'

The voice got even angrier, even higher: 'By Savion himself! They can never be replaced! So open this goddam door!'

River had eaten cereal for breakfast; she'd been out for a brief walk in the dewy, early morning sunshine; there was a large cup of dark, steaming coffee at her side; her laptop was open and blinking expectantly at her; and now that River was all set, all prepared, all *required* to write... she didn't know where to start.

It wasn't that her mind was a blank. No, her mind was a constant whirlpool of thoughts and ideas, a tangle of words and phrases. She opened the document with her notes for improving the rewrite she'd created so far. At the top of the page, she'd typed in capitals: 'THIS *ALL* SUCKS', but now she wasn't sure if she'd meant the script, or her ideas for improving it.

'Okay, calm down, calm the freak down,' she told herself, 'we've done this before. We can do it again. It's just a question of beginning, of finding the way in... the key.'

She stared hard at her notes for several long minutes:

The character of Portia isn't right, we just don't like her.

What to do about all this girls dressing up as boys? How to make that relevant? Transgender?

The ending... I hate the ending.

Followed by:

Actually, I hate this entire play.

And that was the big, fat problem right there. She'd re-read *The Merchant of Venice*, and then she'd watched an excellent film version. And now she was booked in to see the show up close in Stratford. But she didn't like the play. It was ancient and stuffy, and try as she might she couldn't see anything fresh or new in it at all. The Jewish guy got punished at the end – for being Jewish. There was no redemption for him. It was all just a huge, stinking mess of prejudice. Half of his fortune was stolen from him and half was given to his daughter because she was giving up being Jewish and marrying a Christian – which was seen as a major relief. What on earth could River do with an ending like that? And in a film for teenagers?

In the current version of the script, the final scene showed a big group hug and a song and dance routine and none of these major problems were addressed.

She took a big gulp of coffee, sighed, looked out of the window and then couldn't resist checking her Twitter feed... followed by her Instagram... then even her Facebook. There was Phillip Renfield posting a picture of the view from his 5 a.m. hike: 'Starting early, feeling positive'. Oh, and one of her ex-agents was having a humblebrag about 'inking a deal' between one of his writers and the producer-of-the-moment: #oursuccess. And on she scrolled through all these glimpses into lives that looked so much more considered, successful and downright more beautiful than her own. She should be tweeting/posting too, of course. Maybe a nice shot of her laptop and her cup of coffee:

#workinghard on amazing script for @PhillipRen #excited #Shakespeareforteens, or whatever. But she wouldn't, because that kind of thing always made her feel like a big, phoney show-off.

She stared at her notes for another ten minutes, but feeling nothing but irritation, her mind drifted to a calming trip to eBay where she stalked vintage Ralph Lauren items and used G-star jeans. Oh, just look at that navy cashmere blazer, US size 6 – perfect and to die for. Still, a buy it now price of $220, that was a lot for elderly and possibly moth-holed cashmere.

To River's disgust, the entire morning evaporated, somewhere between Instagram, Facebook, eBay and her notes, and she had made no further progress on the script rewrite.

Finally, she put the laptop into sleep mode, picked up her empty mug and stalked angrily down to the kitchen. From the sliding glass doors there, she could see the garden was bathed in sunlight and it was all so impossibly green. Green grass, green bushes, green plants; there were some flowers, yes, but above all, the impression was deliciously green – so different to the sandy, parched views in LA, punctuated only by the dusty, spiky beige and blue of desert plants that could cope with the heat.

She opened the sliding door and stepped out into this soft, lush green world. For several moments, she stood and drank it in, feeling her shoulders lower and the sun fall onto her face. She stretched out her arms and smiled, sure she was alone. Then she remembered the summerhouse at the bottom of the garden, and Dave, and felt an urge to find out what he was up to.

So, she crossed the lawn and approached the door of the robust wooden house. Then she rapped on the glass window and called out, 'Hi!'

It took a few moments for Dave to open the door. He looked a little rumpled, hospital-issue crutch under one arm, hair on end, his t-shirt creased and saggy. 'Is everything okay?' he asked with concern.

'Yeah, sure, everything is fine... with the house, anyway. The house is awesome,' she assured him. 'I was just about to brew up another round of coffee and I thought you might like some.'

'Oh... that's very kind,' he told her, 'but I don't want to put you to any trouble, don't want to bother you in any way at all. The idea is that I am not here; I am the invisible man unless required.'

River peered past Dave and tried to get some impression of what the summerhouse was like inside. All she could see was a large table behind him with a stack of white canvases, a glass vase filled with paintbrushes and a pile of paint tubes.

'How's the painting going?' she asked.

'Oh... I'm just getting started, setting everything out really... canvases on one side, all my new paints and old brushes on the other. Just getting prepped... and... all set up.'

He sounded a little guilty.

River understood that feeling exactly. All prepped... all set up... and no idea where to start.

'How's the writing?' he asked in turn.

She shrugged and gave an exasperated sigh. 'Sucking the big time today, I can tell you that for free. Want to sit and have a coffee with me? Those chairs over there look desperate to be used.'

'That sounds very civilised.' Dave followed her gaze to the woven armchairs with comfortable cushions set on either side of a cast iron café table on the sunny corner of decking, all organised by Tess several years ago.

'Is that British for yes?' River asked, teasing gently.

When the coffee was ready, River and Dave settled down into the armchairs and relaxed in the gentle English sunshine.

After a little preamble chat about the loveliness of the garden and all the hard work Tess had put into it, River had a question for

Dave she was burning to ask: 'So how long is it since you last painted something?'

'Well... in my classes, I'm demonstrating things all the time to my pupils,' Dave began. 'I'm sploshing about and showing how to do lines and frameworks and techniques, so it's not as if I've stopped painting...'

River nodded, then added: 'Hmmmm, but that is different. That's like me giving other people edits and suggestions and helping them to fix their work. But starting from the cold, blank page with your own idea, that is a world of difference. Having an idea in your head and then working to bring that idea out, in the best possible way you can, without disappointing yourself too much in the process, that is a whole different ball game. So...' River leaned forward, curious now. 'How long has it been since you did that? Painted your very own thing, from the beginning, from your very own idea?'

Dave looked down into his coffee, as if he was hoping to find an answer in there.

'Well... if we're talking about starting from scratch and painting a brand-new thing... it's certainly been a while...'

River didn't interrupt, hoping he would take the time to work it out.

'It's been about... how old is Alex now? He's twenty-two... *good grief*... well, in that case it's been about twenty years.'

'Woah!' River exclaimed. 'That is a really long time.' But then she smiled at him encouragingly. 'Well, good for you, Dave! Good for you to want to start painting again. That's huge.'

'And possibly quite difficult,' Dave said, sounding gloomy. 'Possibly much more difficult than I could have imagined.'

Dave wanted to add something about how his critical faculties had now totally outstripped his painting abilities, but he worried that he would sound completely arsy.

'Well, I guess you'll just have to start somewhere,' River said, shaking the first cigarette of the day out of her pack. 'Want one?' she offered.

'No... no, thanks...' Dave was still holding out on her offers. But he was preparing to enjoy sniffing at the second-hand smoke, though.

'Maybe don't expect too much of yourself. If you were getting back into a car for the first time in twenty years, you wouldn't rush out to drive down a freeway, would you? You would drive up and down a B-road for a while and get used to it all again.'

Dave smiled at her. 'I like that,' he said, 'that's good advice.'

'So what was going on when you were last painting regularly?' she asked, 'And what happened to make you stop?' As she waited for the answer to this question, she lit up with her battered old brass lighter and carefully positioned the ashtray Dave had given her on her side of the café table.

'This is okay, right?' she asked. 'The smoking, I mean... well, and maybe I should ask if it's okay to ask you about this stuff too?'

Dave waved his hand. 'Yeah, it's all fine.'

'And how's your leg? I should have asked about that,' she said, sending smoke out of the corner of her mouth away from him.

'The ankle seems to be okay,' he replied, 'and it's hurting a lot less when I cough and laugh – the ribs,' he reminded her, 'it's so itchy under the plaster, though. I'm trying to devise ways to stick something down there and give myself a scratch. But, anyway, you want to know when was I last painting a lot? That's easy: I went to art school in London in the early 1990s. And can I just state for the record – my parents were furious. Absolutely furious!'

This made River laugh.

'Oh, same,' she said, 'nothing freaks parents out more than telling them you're planning a creative career.'

'And I got good marks at school,' he said, a little touched that she'd asked about his past and was clearly interested to hear more, 'so they wanted me to become an accountant, or a lawyer, something respectable, something that paid a lot better than my dad's job driving a bus, or my mum's job in social services. And who can blame them?'

River gave a shrug of agreement.

'So when I said I was going to art school – and in those days, the fees were all paid, you didn't need your parents' permission – they just about threw me out of the house. Dad didn't speak to me for nearly a year.'

'Oh, that's harsh,' River sympathised. 'I come from a very talkative family. They will shout and rant at you, but *not speaking*... that would kill them.'

'All credit to him, he did come round,' Dave went on. 'Along with my mum, he came to our end-of-year show, and he spoke to the tutors and got a better understanding that this was a real thing. There were art professors and lecturers. There were gallery owners and artists who made a living.'

'He must be proud of you now,' River said, 'respectable school art teacher married to a successful professional and living in this gorgeous place.'

'And not forgetting the two wonderful children – yes, I think he would be.' Dave smiled, enjoying her compliment, then thoughtfully added, 'He's been dead for quite a while now. Had a heart attack in the supermarket. All those people around and no one knew how to do cardiac first aid. If anyone had been able to do anything helpful, we might have had him around for another five years.'

'Oh my gosh, I'm so sorry,' River said then added, 'we lost my dad in similar circumstances. He had a heart attack in the cinema. And we can't blame the movie – it hadn't even started. But again, no one did anything for him except dial 911.'

It was Dave's turn to be sorry.

'I was so angry,' River went on, 'you'll get to know that about me – it's my go-to emotion – I went on a first responder course the month after he died. Please tell me you still have your mom?'

'No... she died two years ago. They weren't the healthiest pair – smoked a lot – sorry,' he added quickly, but River just shrugged. 'Still, you expect people to make it to seventy these days. But neither of them did.'

'You've already lost your dad and then your mom... that is so sad. That must have been so hard to deal with. I'm very sorry,' River said.

Her sympathy touched him. Yes, his parents' deaths had been hard to cope with. And they'd come at such busy times for his own family... Tess frantic at work, his own children and his pupils busy with school exams, so that somehow the process of grieving, coping and coming to terms with it all had felt rushed. Looking back, he often thought they should have put the brakes on everything for a few weeks and he should definitely have taken more time off, especially when his mum went too.

'Anyway...' Dave took a little moment to gather his thoughts before he spoke again. 'So painting was a really big part of my life at art school and for two or three years afterwards.'

'So what kind of painting did you do?' River asked and, enjoying her interest, Dave told her about being part of a group of young artists who were creating public works of art: murals, huge sculptures and inter-active events.

'It was important to get people involved,' he said, 'take art out of the galleries and into real spaces where people could interact and take part in it, and we were really trying to make a difference. Some things worked very well... some things not so much,' he admitted.

'Well, that's the way with creative stuff,' River assured him, 'some flies, some bombs... and usually, no one even knows why.'

'But it was a precarious way to make a living,' Dave said, 'and, in the end, that just got to me.' He drained the last of his coffee. 'I got married to Tess, who was doing really well, moving up the rungs and having this young, corporate accountant life, while I was totally erratic. I'd have one month at home doing nothing, then two months on the Isle of Skye creating a public monument with a light show for its launch.'

'Wow, that sounds pretty cool,' River said.

'Yeah... for a time it really was,' Dave shot her a smile, 'but then, when Tess was on maternity leave with Alex, and I was either out of London or out of work, it just wasn't cool any more. She had to go back to work early because they needed her, then she got offered a great opportunity up here... and, within a year, we were living in Leamington Spa and she was a full-time working mum and I was teaching art at a very nice grammar school.'

'Well done, Dave,' River said, 'you've created a lovely, comfortable life.'

'Yes...' Dave was agreeing but he didn't sound completely sure.

'But you must feel there is still art inside of you that you want to get out,' River understood, 'because that's what drives all of us creative people... there's something inside that we want to drag out into the daylight. Well, that and paying the bills, obviously.'

'Yes,' he caught her eye and held the look, 'I suppose that is exactly it. There's still some unfinished business. Still pictures in my head that I would like to make.'

'Still something you'd like to say,' River said, but at the same time wondered what she was trying to say with her *Merchant of Venice* for teens... sometimes not everything you create is a piece of art. Sometimes it just has to be quality entertainment.

'Ah... well, I don't know about that.' He gave a shrug and a dry laugh. 'My radical "art is for the masses" statements are probably behind me.'

'There's no shame in having a regular job that you're proud of,' River told him, 'believe me, I've considered it often enough. And loads of my writer friends work a second job. I bet all your art school buddies are the same, huh? People had to get jobs and make a living and leave being Andy Warhol to Andy Warhol, I guess?'

Dave let out a long sigh. In many ways, if that were true, it might be easier, but knowing he was with one of the few people who would probably sympathise, he admitted, 'That would be better, but actually, the people I was rushing around Skye with, working twenty-two hours a day to set up light shows and over-water sculptures and huge city artscapes... they're still doing it. They're doing really well, fantastically well, and my guess is you will have heard of them.'

'Really? Who?' River was intrigued.

Dave reeled off three names. Two certainly rang a bell with River, but the third, *everyone* knew the third.

'You went to college with Van Saint?' she asked, eyes wide.

'Yup.'

'You did installations and sculptures and stuff with *him*?'

'Yup.'

River now cast her mind to the paintings inside the house. She'd picked up straight away that they were carefully chosen, quality works, but now she realised that she'd been looking at some seriously expensive, original stuff.

'That's pretty cool, Dave.'

'Yup.'

'So... let me guess, you must be just a little sorry that you stopped working with him and decided to go and be a teacher?' she asked, even though it wasn't the kindest question.

'Ah, well... as you say, I have a very nice life and a lovely family...' he paused, 'but that can be quite a hard question to answer.'

'And did Tess make you quit the artistic lifestyle? Is that a bit of a sore point between you?'

This question startled Dave. How do decisions get made in a marriage? One person has an idea; you discuss it, you think about it... Tess had wanted them all to be happy: her, Dave and baby Alex. Leaving making art for teaching art had seemed like a good solution. Tess had encouraged him but hadn't forced him in any way.

'It was a joint decision and to be honest, Tess doesn't ever mention it,' Dave admitted. And he realised that over one cup of coffee, River had sought out two of the most tender areas of his life – the death of his parents and the fact that he'd stopped creating art, even though he was good at it, and had never found a way back in all these years.

'Well, hey, if it's any consolation,' River began, 'I was Franklyn Gregory's girlfriend for three years. We broke up because he wanted to get married and have children, but I think I prefer dogs.'

Dave turned wide eyes in her direction. After an astonished pause, he couldn't help blurting out: 'You were Franklyn Gregory's girlfriend? For three years? Hold on, hold on... I need to hear some more about this!'

19

Tess was frozen to the spot. Maybe if she didn't move, didn't make a sound, he would go away. But the voice on the other side of the door was still shouting:

'I know you're in there! Open up!'

The fear of being a strange person, in a strange country, who didn't know the rules and didn't know what could happen next, gripped her.

'Okay, that's it,' the voice said, 'I'm going to call the super!'

Super? Was that some sort of building supervisor? This seemed to give her the shake she needed and she suddenly felt a boost of confidence – surely no axe-wielding maniac would call the 'super'? That sounded almost quite a reasonable thing to do. Maybe she could summon her best business voice and talk this over with him as calmly as possible. Maybe this man's bark was worse than his bite.

Sounding as English as she possible could, she said, 'Just one moment please, I'm going to unlock the door.'

She turned the key, loosened the large bolt and slowly, heart hammering in her throat, pulled the apartment's front door towards her. There in the hallway stood a tall, lean and upright black man with tight salt-and-pepper cropped hair, broad shoulders and a surprised expression on his handsome face.

'You are not River Romero,' he said.

'No, hello, I'm Tess. I'm River's houseguest. I'm going to be staying here for a few weeks. River's gone to England,' Tess said, drawing herself up.

'Hmmm. So, did you throw dog shit onto my balcony?'

This man had a deep and melodious voice, far too classy for that question. It sounded a little like Morgan Freeman was asking her.

'I am so extremely sorry about that,' Tess began, 'I was cleaning the balcony, which was a horrible mess, and a... well... poo... fell over the edge. I am so sorry. I was just getting my cleaning things together to come down and offer to clean it up for you.'

'*A poo? Fell over the edge*?' the man repeated.

'Yes. It was a complete accident and I'm so sorry,' Tess repeated, 'I want to put that right straight away. I've got bags and a scoop out on the balcony that I can bring down.'

'A poo...' the man repeated. 'Over here we say poop, or crap, or shit by the way... FYI...'

'Right...'

'This dog crap fell on a very special, very, *very* special pair of dance shoes. I don't know if your tools, whatever they are, are going to be able to clean this up.'

'Why don't I get my things together and come over?' she offered.

For a moment or two, the man looked beyond her and into River's apartment.

'I have to say, you have really cleaned up in here. The last time I came to talk to River about her dogs, this place was one great, hot mess.'

'Yes... I've had to completely sort it out. I think she must have left in a hurry.' This was the most tactful way Tess could think of putting it.

'Yeah... that sounds like her. She is always in a hurry. Look...' He put his hands on his hips and gave something of a sigh. 'I can see you're trying to sort that woman's crap out... literally.'

'No... not really,' Tess began. In fact she was just trying to take a relaxing holiday. But absolutely not one single relaxing thing had happened so far.

'Well, I can see you didn't mean any harm,' he clarified. 'So why don't I clean up my own balcony and my own shoes and if I have any problem, I will come back to you. What do you think of that?'

Tess got the impression that far from being an angry, hot-headed man, this was a pretty reasonable, and probably quite nice man, who had perhaps been pushed just a bit too far by River in the past.

'Well, if you're absolutely sure you're okay with that? I really am happy to help out,' she told him.

'Yes... I think I'm going to be fine with that. I'm not sure I want any kind of dog crap removal tools coming through my apartment.' These words did come with something of a smile.

'No... probably not,' she said. 'Look, I really am sorry. What number is your apartment?' she asked, thinking ahead to the bunch of flowers, box of chocolates, or other little gift she would leave on his doorstep later today.

'I'm Larry Jones and I live at number 33.'

'Hi Larry, nice to meet you. I'm Tess Simpson and I'll be here for another six weeks. I'm going to try to train the dogs not to use the balcony, so hopefully this won't happen again. By the way, you're the first person I've met in the building, so I hope you don't mind me asking, but what has happened to the pool?'

At this, Larry rolled his eyes. 'Oh, the pool, now that is a long story.'

* * *

When Larry had gone, Tess finished some other chores in the apartment. But this was only minor dusting the slats of the blinds type stuff. All the critical areas, the heavy lifting of cleaning this absolute rat-hole of a place, was almost completely finished now and she was aware that she needed to get outside. She'd been in LA for over forty-eight hours now and she'd only stepped outside once to go to the shop. In all honesty, she was surprised by how overwhelmed she felt by the outside world. It was so hot, so dirty, dusty and busy out there. And she didn't know where to go or how she could get there without using River's car, which she'd not even gone to look for yet.

She realised that she was completely out of her comfort zone. Busy, busy, organised Tess, who could cope with client meetings, client deadlines, stroppy teenagers, a ludicrously overloaded timetable and all sorts of demands and expectations, was suddenly wondering if she could leave an apartment.

This just wasn't like her and she couldn't understand what was happening. What was it about out there that was keeping her held back and stuck inside? It felt so alien and different and she felt so far away from all of her usual people, places and supports. She was truly out of her comfort zone and there was nothing familiar to fall back on. All at once, she realised how rarely she left that zone and did things that were new or difficult. Maybe part of the reason her life had become so routine was that she had become so routine.

'This is ridiculous,' she told herself, 'you came here for an adventure, so you've got to start somewhere...' Okay, she did at least know one person in LA, so that one person would have to give her the hand that she maybe needed. She called up Tom's number on her phone.

'Hi Tom, this is Tess... in River's apartment. Yes... the malamutes. Well... I was just wondering...'

Then rather hesitantly, she explained to him that when he came to give them their walk round the neighbourhood, would he be able to walk her round the neighbourhood too?

'I just don't know where anything is,' she said. 'Where do I take the dogs? Where do I buy something good to eat? Where's the best coffee place? I'm sure you could give me some pointers, just get me started.'

Tom was charmingly enthusiastic and promised he would be there soon, so that put Tess into a different kind of fuss, and she headed to the bedroom to change, wondering what she should wear for the weather and this first trip around the neighbourhood.

She decided on a flowing, floral linen shift type of dress. Then she brushed and fluffed up her hair, and added comfortable, new, white sneakers and a jaunty basket to her outfit.

Yes, she thought, surveying herself in the slim sliver of mirror – that looks fine: summery, breezy, colourful. Then she began the slow process of anointing her delicate skin with factor fifty sunscreen. Ye gods, didn't every single bottle ever produced promise to be non-greasy, with no white marks and wasn't it always a great big lie? She looked at herself in the mirror with much less enthusiasm now. Her legs, her arms, her face and neck all looked pale and waxy. Everything became worse when Tom rang the doorbell, the dogs got all excited and rushed around her legs, shedding white hairs into the layer of sun cream. Good grief.

'So... I don't often walk around these blocks,' Tom was telling her as they set off at a jaunty pace with a dog each. 'I usually put the dogs into the car and drive them out to the nearest hiking trail and let them run. But there are some pretty good dog parks nearby so let's go check them out and I'll show you the good places to stop and shop on the way.' In his perfect fit blue cycle shorts and black t-shirt, he was just as neat and dapper as she remembered.

Ten minutes into this walk, Tess couldn't understand why she hadn't brought sunglasses. The glare from the bright white sky, from the pavement, from even the windscreens of passing cars was hurting her eyes. Plus, her sweat was mixing with the sunscreen to form oily dribbles already running between her shoulder blades and down her sides. Too late now, she realised that the thick linen shift was all wrong for summer in LA. It was designed for gentle British Julys, for temperatures in the high teens and low twenties, when your dress needed a bit of heft against the cool breeze. Here, the occasional passerby they met on the 'sidewalk' was wearing vest tops, shorts, or breezy skirts made of light clouds of material with deep slits to benefit from any passing waft of air.

And her feet were melting in the heavy plastic sneakers, while Los Angelenos wore flipflops, strappy sandals or sneakers made of mesh. Tess's hair stuck to the back of her neck, as she regretted not securing her thick locks in a ponytail or bun so that the breeze could bring coolness to her sweating and overheated parts.

Meanwhile, Tom was walking faster and faster. Burton's lead was tied to his waist and he was keeping up a stream of useful and entertaining chat: 'So that's the coffee shop I totally recommend,' he said, pointing across the road, 'They serve truly awesome chilled chai lattes, or just your regular hot cups of black Java. Whatever you want, they have it there and it is served with the minimum of sass.'

'Do they let dogs in?' she wondered.

'I always do take out, so I don't know. I guess they might let you sit out on the terrace with these two doggos,' Tom replied. 'But let's face it, there is a lot of fluffy, doggie real estate attached to these guys. It may be too much for one small café to handle.'

'Now over there,' he pointed again, 'That's the best Mexican round here. So go and enjoy dinner there one night, or order take-out. Next door is the awesome vegan place and over on the other side of the road, great Chinese. So, everything you need, basically, within an easy walk of your apartment. Okay, and we turn right here, because this is the cutest dog park and there is also just the nicest Korean grocery store on the corner.'

They walked into a square, not with green grass, as Tess might have expected, but paved with flowerbeds and some space for benches, a kiosk and colourful plants in pots. There were other dogs bounding about inside a fenced enclosure. And this is where Tom took River's dogs and deftly unclipped them. The dogs knew immediately where they were and what to do and Wilder began to bounce around playfully, while Burton took a dump.

'Oh, Mr Burton, not again!' Tom exclaimed, nimbly whipping out his dog mess bag from a zipped pocket at the back of his shorts and dealing with the situation. Ah, well, Tess couldn't help thinking, at least that was one less for the balcony.

'Hey Tom! It is so great to see you! Hiiiii!'

Some teeny-tiny Los Angelena skipped up to Tom in her teeny skirt and teeny waist with her teeny-tiny dog in tow.

'I heard you've got a second read-through for the Ackerman project.'

'Oh yeah, pretty cool huh?'

'*In-cred-i-ble*,' she gushed, 'it would be amazing to get a part on that. Uh-mazing.'

And so they stood there, these two impossibly beautiful people, grinning at each other. Then teeny-tiny girl realised that Tess must be with Tom.

'Oh hi,' she said, turning her radiant, soft skinned, pink-lipped, flawlessly white-toothed smile on Tess: 'You must be Tom's mom... how awesome to meet you.'

* * *

As she sat on the apartment sofa, blowing the fan directly at her sticky face, Tess tried to decide why she'd been so offended by this comment. It wasn't as if the age gap between her and Tom was too small. She guessed that he was probably in his late twenties, and she was forty-nine, so really she *could* have been his mom. It wasn't at all unreasonable. But it just made her feel so old, and uncool and unglamorous.

And God, this dress, she looked down at the linen flowers with disdain. What had she been thinking? She realised with a jolt that for some time now, she'd allowed herself to drift into the arena of camouflaging clothes instead of flattering ones.

Okay, that was enough wallowing. She needed to make a nice evening plan for herself. She had bought food at the Korean grocery and she was going to cook. Then when she'd eaten, she wouldn't be able to speak to anyone in her family, because they would all be asleep, but she would send them a long group email, full of her adventures in LaLa land so far.

She had just chopped up her exotic mix of vegetables and was setting the wok on the hob when she was surprised to hear a tap on the apartment's front door.

'Hi, who's there?' she called out.

'Hi, Tess? It's me, Larry. We met earlier today. I hope it's okay to ask a question.'

She undid the locks and the bolt and as she prepared to pull the door open, she had to ask: 'This isn't a trick, I hope... you're not going to revenge splatter me, are you?'

'Nope,' came the simple reply.

Larry stood in the doorway, a little taller and broader than she remembered, but also much friendlier too. She liked his smile. It was warm and kind; it went right up to his eyes and crinkled the corners.

'Hello, again,' he said, 'had a good day?'

'Yes... so hot though, I don't know if I'm going to get used to this heat.'

'This *heat*?' he asked. 'Tess, you ain't seen nothing yet. Been anywhere interesting?'

'Just round the neighbourhood,' she told him, 'But I like the sound of the hiking trails. I think I'll take myself out there with the dogs very soon.'

'Cool... well, there was something that I just wanted to check with you. Did you say River was away for the next few weeks?'

Tess nodded.

'Well... just how long exactly?'

'We've arranged to swap houses for six weeks. We might even both agree to extend if we need to.'

'*Six* weeks?' he repeated. 'I don't get it. After our last argument about the dogs, she arranged to do one-on-one dance lessons with me to make up. She has a twelve-lesson, six-week course booked with me about to start and payment is due.'

He looked pretty annoyed again.

'Was that woman just fobbing me off?' he asked. ''Cos she sounded really genuine, really sorry. And I believed that she was going to make it up with me.'

Dance lessons... this explained a lot to Tess: Larry's upright posture, broad shoulders, and the strong but sinuous muscles.

'You're a dance teacher?' she asked.

'Yeah... I'm guessing that could be a little obvious, what with me offering dance lessons, an' all.'

'What kind of dance?' she asked.

Larry looked almost a little offended.

'All kinds! Ballet, classical and modern, tap, tango, jazz... if you want to dance it, I can teach it to you. But what am I going to do about River?'

There were two reasons why one obvious solution suddenly

came to Tess. She still felt guilty about the dollop of dog poop on Larry's balcony and those very special shoes... and, following her afternoon out, she felt lumpy, un-dainty and gallumphy. And there was Larry, gracefully upright with his perfect posture, sinuous, taking up his space in the world so beautifully.

Plus, she was here in LA to do different things, to spoil herself and to try out all kinds of things she didn't even know yet that she wanted to do. And learning how to dance in LA, well, that sounded adventurous... even a little bit glamorous.

'What about if I take the dance lessons, Larry? Since River is going to be away. I could pay you and I could do those lessons... if that would be okay with you?'

Larry looked a little taken aback.

'Do you have the time?' he asked, followed with: 'Is this something you want to do?'

Now it was Tess's turn to ask the question: 'Do you think you can teach me anything?'

'Yes, of course,' he answered, without hesitation.

'Well, I'm keen to learn... I really would like to learn some new moves.'

'What kind of new moves?' he asked, looking almost a little uneasy.

'Oh... I don't know, but is there any chance you could teach even someone like me something just a little bit... *wow*?'

20

River powered down the laptop once again and shut it with a snap. She had spent the morning writing and fretting about writing, and nothing was turning out right.

She stomped down to the kitchen and tried to decide if more coffee was needed, although she was already jittery, or if it was already time to make lunch. The clock told her it was 12.30. Just about lunch... although still shaken up with jetlag, she didn't really know what she wanted. In the fridge, which had been so thoughtfully filled by Tess before she left, there were tomatoes, peppers, lettuce, cheeses... so she could throw those things together, make a lunch and this afternoon, she would take herself back to Stratford. She would go and visit Shakespeare's house this time, never mind the queues. Maybe that would somehow help.

When her salad and cheese plate was loaded up, she opened the kitchen doors and headed for the chairs on the decking once again, although this day was cloudier and cooler.

Dave was already seated at one of the chairs out there.

'Oh, hello! Don't mind me, I was just leaving,' he said, reaching for his crutch and preparing to stand up.

'No, please, stay... that's if you'd like to... my morning has been horrible and it would be nice to have someone to talk to.'

'About writing?' he asked.

'Not necessarily!' she said, pushing her fork into her salad. 'In fact, probably anything but writing.'

'I could ask you the question everyone asks you...' Dave was smiling at her as he said this.

'No! Not that one! Not the one about "where do you get your ideas?" No!'

'Yes! Where do you get your ideas?'

'Why do people ask that stuff?' River wondered, in between chews. 'These tomatoes are amazing, by the way. How is Tess settling into my far less lovely apartment? Have you spoken to her? Should I call her and tell her what to go and see outside and stuff?'

'I've only had some messages,' Dave admitted, 'she's been really jet-lagged, sleeping all over the place. Hopefully, I'll speak to her soon. So come on, writer friend, ideas – where do you get them?'

'Right now, I don't even know because I'm staring at this script, I'm staring at my notes... I'm staring at the freaking screen and there are no ideas to be had. Nothing. Nada. I've tried a long walk, a long shower, overdosing on coffee... so now I'm going to try and jumpstart the thought process by going back to Stratford this afternoon. Maybe another gigantic cream scone will help me.'

'Nice.'

'But if you want my usual answer to this question: every shred of my existence, every single thing I've ever thought or felt goes into my work. I'm always mining every square inch of my life for material. Writing never feels easy, there's always a lot of thinking, worrying, fretting and struggle versus a tiny little bit when some of it "just flows". There is absolutely no writing by numbers, ever. Even the dumbest crap, and, believe me, I've written some of that too, if you don't believe it and feel it, no one else will.'

She stopped talking and put another forkful of food into her mouth.

'So...' Dave had another question for her, 'are you going to have to put your whole self into *High School Musical* meets *Merchant of Venice*?' There was something of a teasing smile on his face as he asked this.

'Ah ha... good question,' she smiled back at him, 'well, yeah, my teenage self, I guess. I need to channel my teenage self... that's probably exactly how to think about it.'

'So... what do I need to put into my paintings?' Dave asked next, and somehow, behind the friendly smile, River could read the burning question.

'Hmmm... you're not finding it so easy, then?'

'No,' Dave admitted.

'Well... you'll need to work that out,' River told him. 'No one's forcing you to do this. You're on holiday, you've got a broken ankle; you could literally be sitting on your ass doing nothing and no one would judge you. So if there's something you want to say, or just something you want to make... spend the time working on it, working it out. That's what I'm doing... working on it.'

Dave had to admit, at least to himself, that he'd expected the painting to be less work and more fun... maybe when he worked out what he wanted to do, it would improve.

'You know, at home in LA, I keep a framed quote on the bookcase that I can see when I look up from my desk,' River went on. 'It reads: "It is the work that matters, not the applause that follows", and for creative people, that's the key. You have to really love doing the work. Everything else is what my mom calls "pure gravy". The quote, by the way, was Captain Robert Falcon Scott of the Antarctic – led a doomed mission, died in a snowstorm, so not your standard manufacturer of Californian motivational quotes. But I'm fine with that.'

This made Dave laugh enough for the ribs to twinge. River was much more fun than he'd expected. He'd not thought there would be any interaction between him and the Californian houseguest at all, to be honest. But this was working out very well and he was feeling genuinely inspired by her advice.

'I'm heading off to Stratford soon... do you need anything, shall I bring you some groceries?'

'No, no, absolutely not. You are the guest. You are to be at ease, enjoying the run of the place. I'm going out with my sister this afternoon. So have a great time and we'll catch up soon.'

'Thanks,' she nodded, 'And Dave...' an idea had just come into River's head. 'I'd enjoy making you dinner one evening. Would you like that? I just can't say I love eating on my own all the time.'

'Gosh... dinner?' Dave was taken by surprise and flattered that this witty and attractive woman would want to cook for him and spend more time with him. There was only one reply he wanted to make. 'I'd like that very much, thank you. I'll check the weather and we can pick a day to go al fresco.'

'Great idea.'

As River scooped up her plate and glass and headed back to the house, Dave tucked his crutch under his arm and hobbled back towards the summerhouse. Once inside, he sat down heavily on the chair and looked at the pile of, as yet untouched, canvases. He had the paint. He had the canvas. He had all the undisturbed time he could possibly ask for. There was absolutely nothing stopping him. But he felt as if everything and anything he would put on these canvases would be a mess and a mistake.

What had River said? 'It's the work that matters'.

Okay... so right now, right away, he was going to take out a plate and load it with paint, then, very slowly, with a tiny brush maybe, he was going to paint one small canvas entirely blue. Or maybe

green... or what about mixing that bright cobalt with a touch of the
dark emerald...?

* * *

Meanwhile, River put on a fresh outfit, brushed her hair and did
her make-up carefully. She added a lavish cloud of scent for morale
and with only the slightest hint of the question at the back of her
mind... *what if* I bumped into Franklyn? She shooed it right away
again – as if Franklyn would be just strolling round town. He probably didn't make a single move without a butler and a full security
detail. Then she got into the car for another visit to Shakespeare's
hometown.

The house where Shakespeare was born turned out to be small,
very old, and completely unassuming. There was wood panelling, a
big fireplace and a cradle. The double bed looked very small for
two people; a tankard stood on the mantelpiece... and there was not
really much else. But then, people hardly had any belongings when
Shakespeare was alive, maybe a Bible, some clothes and shoes,
tools for the garden and the kitchen, some pots and that was probably about all.

As she looked around the humble rooms, she got a powerful
sense of how long ago this was. Shakespeare was writing as the 1500s
turned into the 1600s... over 400 years ago. The words written then...
with a quill pen and a pot of ink, the characters and scenes he
dreamed of in a humble little house like this were still performed,
quoted and admired today. As she walked through the ancient little
house, it made his achievement all the more real for her, all the more
dazzling and extraordinary. She felt moved to the verge of tears.

She thought of her script rewrite. It was currently a lousy script
that mashed a school production of *The Merchant of Venice* with

some really lame storyline about a group of immigrant school kids being picked on.

'If they prick us do we not bleed?' was quoted a few times and the inevitable, clichéd 'we're all the same, let's get along together' happy ending was visible from the opening lines of the damned thing.

'The idea, I guess,' Phillip had instructed her, 'is we skim *The Merchant*, picking the best bits, the edited highlights. But we're making modern entertainment for modern kids, so we keep the Shakespeare stuff short and sweet.'

River had already read the first version several times. She'd drawn out plans and notes for how to improve it and had those notes read by the script editor. And she'd done a first draft rewrite. But in her mind, something else was still missing: real flavour, a new way to tell this old story... maybe even real inspiration. And somehow she'd thought she could find it here.

The truth was, she didn't really know what exactly to do, or how exactly she was going to rescue this story. And she knew from experience that if you don't have a crystal-clear idea of what you're going to write, you will be scrabbling down there in the weeds for weeks, trying to find something good and coming up with absolutely nothing. There was no choice but to keep thinking about it and keep trying to solve the problem. She was determined not to make some kind of bad hack job of it. The good, no, maybe even great, idea would come. She just had to keep trying, and above all, keep thinking.

In the shop area of Shakespeare's house, there was a rather lacklustre collection of souvenirs – key rings, bookmarks and paperweights with Shakespeare's head embossed on them all. There was also a bookcase of cheap paperback copies of the individual plays and the collected works.

She picked up *The Merchant of Venice* and opened up the grainy pages. Her eyes fell on the lines:

> If it were as easy as to know what were good to do, chapels had been churches and poor men's cottages princes' palaces.

Oh boy.

That was breathtaking.

If it were as easy as to *know* what were good to do…

Yes. That was the problem exactly. She didn't yet know what would be good to do. And even when she did know, she would still have to do it. Still have to write the goddam thing and make every single *line* really good, every single *word* really good.

How could she make it really exciting and moving and good? *Really* good? She needed to write something really good this time. No more hack jobs for the pay packet. Whatever had come together and worked so well for *Spangled*, she had to make all of that happen again.

Being here, where Shakespeare had lived and worked all those hundreds of years ago, would surely help. Wouldn't it?

She walked, once again, slowly and deliberately through the little wooden rooms. She imagined the much smaller people living here, in the smokiness of the fire, with their many dogs and cats, and the very plain food they had to carefully grow, catch, harvest and cook – vegetable soups and the odd chunk of meat, an occasional spoonful of honey as a treat.

Somehow, the baby born here hundreds of years ago began to think, began to imagine and began to write, words tumbling into his mind and flowing out from his pen. And people right across the world were still reading his words today. It was just incredible when you really thought about it.

River walked out into the back garden and took in the flowers rocking in the breeze, the rows of vegetables, and this view of the humble house from the garden. How had William Shakespeare conjured up such a vast world from such a humble beginning? He had written about kings, queens and emperors and captured all the secrets of the human heart. His words still stood because they were still true. They told the most important stories, and revealed the smallest secrets.

She didn't want to make some cheesy LA version of what he had created. Even if this was a crappy project for a highly commercial production company, and even if she just needed the money, she wanted to make something good out of it, something special and something true. But that was probably going to be even harder than she thought it would be.

She hardly wanted to admit to herself how desperate she was for this to turn out really well. Her career wasn't where it could be, where it should be. She'd been overlooked, forgotten about really – you could hardly find *Spangled* on any of the movie channels any more – and she was determined to make the best possible use of this chance. But Shakespeare... re-writing Shakespeare was a big ask. She didn't know yet if she was going to be able to step up.

'*River*? River Romero? Is that you? Yes... it is you! What in the world are you doing in Stratford?'

She turned away from the view of the house that had caught her attention and pushed her sunglasses to the top of her head to get a better look in the direction of this oh-so familiar voice.

He was a little older, of course, but fit, tanned, and suiting the careful transition to steely grey hair. The ageing process was generally so much kinder to male film stars than female ones. He'd no doubt had some light peeling here and some Botox there to lessen the cragginess and here he was, looking handsome, expensive and groomed in his caramel suede jacket.

Unfortunately, it was far too late to duck, or to run and hide.

In her head, she shrieked: 'What the actual *freaking fuck*? What are *you* doing *here*?' while thanking the tiny inner voice that had made her sort her hair, pick the fresh outfit, add the smoky eyes and spritz on the good stuff.

Out loud, she managed to say, 'Oh, hey, Franklyn... that jacket will not help you in the English rain, buddy.'

And she was pleased with the line, even thought it was a little snarky and not the kind of thing you're supposed to say when you randomly cross paths with the enviably successful previous love of your life, who you maybe should have settled down with, but instead you chose to walk away aged twenty-nine... and of course, you've occasionally revisited your decision and wondered what might have been, if you'd chosen differently.

What did you wear to a dance lesson? Leggings, a sports bra and a baggy t-shirt was what Tess had decided on. Then she'd added her ankle socks and running shoes, and yes, she had considered a last-minute online purchase of dance shoes, but then thought maybe her new dance teacher could advise.

She put her hair up in a messy ponytail, settled the dogs down with a treat, then left the apartment and went down the stairs to number 33. She knocked briskly and it only took Larry a few moments to answer.

'Hi, Tess, you're right on time,' he greeted her. She was relieved to see he was in a loose t-shirt too, along with some cropped sweat-pants. The only obvious signs of 'dance teacher' came from the soft, well-worn, leather jazz shoes laced onto his feet, his effortlessly upright posture and the sculpted muscles on his arms.

'Hi Larry... well... this is... quite exciting!' she said, although actually she felt oddly nervous and exposed.

'I hope so, come in.'

She stepped into an apartment that was almost identical in layout to River's. A generous L-shaped space with an open kitchen in the corner, then a calm and ordered living room opposite the generous windows that led out onto the balcony.

But in Larry's apartment, the wide entry space, where River had a dining room table and chairs, was empty and a ballet barre and tall mirrors had been put in place along the wall.

'Welcome to my very own in-house studio.'

'Your apartment is lovely,' Tess told him and it was true. It was decorated in warm, welcoming shades of taupe and beige with bright bursts of colour like the orange kitchen doors and the emerald green sofa. It felt warm, bright and inspiring, but Tess couldn't shake her growing nervousness.

'Okay, so the idea is we don't hang about here, we start straight in and we talk as we move. Does that sound okay to you?'

'Erm... yes... you say move... you do realise that I'm a total beginner? I haven't a clue how to do anything.'

'Everyone says that and it's not true!' Larry countered, as he moved gracefully into the centre of the space. 'We all know how to dance, we've just forgotten, because we've got all adult and rigid and set in our ways. My job is to show you how to undo that. So let's just stand here.' He motioned to a spot close to the mirror, beside the barre, so Tess put down her handbag and went and stood there.

All adult and rigid and set in our ways... Tess was beginning to think that this was exactly her problem and not just when it came to dancing. How was she going to loosen up... in so many areas? Did she even want to? Could she? What was future Tess going to be like? The questions swirled as Larry stood in front of her and put his hands on her shoulders.

'Okay, first of all, shoulders dowwwwwn,' he said, pressing gently to help them on their downward journey, 'and neck and head lifting up from the shoulders. Very good... and now arms out to the side and moving gently up and down like this...'

As Tess tried to copy Larry's elegant movements, he asked her: 'So tell me what you do for exercise every week?'

'Well... not as much as I should,' she admitted. 'I used to walk the dog twice a day, but she died a month ago...'

'Oh no, I'm so sorry,' he broke in.

'Thank you... it was really sad. And she had slowed down a lot, so I suppose it wasn't the exercise it used to be.'

'And what else?' Larry asked, making a little correction to the way she was raising her arm.

'Well...' Tess searched her mind. 'There were some yoga classes over the winter, but I found it all quite boring. Tinkly bell music... and I'm not at all supple.'

'So some slow dog walks... oh boy,' Larry said, looking disappointed in her, 'so we're starting from a pretty low base here then. You let me know if anything gets too tough for you, okay?'

This felt like another LA insult. She had come here to rejuvenate, relax and develop fresh ideas. But for a moment Tess wondered if going to Thailand might have been more gentle.

She tried to copy his deep leg bends, then the leg lifts and the bends from the waist. The backs of her legs burned, and her arms were already exhausted from what she assumed must be just the warm up. She guessed that Larry was several years older than her, but he was moving gracefully and entirely effortlessly. Not for the first time, Tess wondered why she'd never found the time in her life to take her fitness seriously. It would only have taken an hour a day... forty minutes, even.

The children... the job... the house... the garden... it all took an unbelievable amount of time and energy. And, in all honesty, she never ever felt that a run or a dance or an online class would revive her after a long day. She usually felt that the sofa, a large glass of wine and a bowl of crisps were what was required to revive her. Or, at the very least, reward her.

'Let's put some music on and step it up,' Larry suggested, once they seemed to have gone through every kind of painful bend-lift-stretch-and-hold combination that the human mind could create. 'What kind of music do you like?'

And now Tess's mind was blank. What kind of music did she like? Not the dirge-like stuff that Alex played, or the bouncy pop that followed Natalie all around the house; she wasn't much of a fan of Dave's music either, he still liked to bring out the 1990 Art School soulful classics.

'Um... I don't really know...' she admitted.

'You don't know! Of course you know! You must know,' Larry insisted.

But she shook her head and felt at a loss. There just hadn't been time for her music, for years. She couldn't remember when she last actively listened to music and she didn't want to mention songs she had liked ten or twenty years ago... it would be embarrassing and just make her feel completely out of touch.

'Okay... I'm going to put on my white-girl playlist and you can tell me if you like it. Follow my lead, we're going to do some core and butt moves now because every dancer needs those muscles.'

And to the strains of 'Uptown Funk' – *'too hot, hot damn'* – Tess followed Larry, move by tortuous move, and worked hard.

'Just thirty-second bursts,' Larry told her, 'Throw everything at it for thirty seconds and then rest up.'

Soon, she was rosy faced and sweating, but Larry was encouraging. 'Not bad...' he told her, as the warming up and stretching out session was done, the muscles were nice and warm, so now it was time to start some real dance moves. So, he began. 'Arms up, leg out to the side, bend the knee and gentle, controlled jump...' Larry made it look elegant and easy.

He turned Tess towards the mirror and demonstrated once again. Then she made her first attempt and to her horror, not only

was it far more difficult than it looked, but there, galumphing in front of the mirror, was Nelly the graceless elephant.

'Oh my God!' she exclaimed. 'That was awful! I was completely terrible. Horrible! Hopeless!'

'No, no, no,' Larry assured her, 'just give it another try, think: lift up the spine, chin up, shoulders down and light on the feet and graceful...'

Tess tried once again but whatever she thought she could do in her head, her body had a completely different idea. She looked so clumsy, she could cry. Lumping and bumping about in leggings and Dave's grey t-shirt.

'*Too hot... hot damn!*'

She was definitely not *too hot*... well, not in that sense. Hot and bothered maybe.

What on earth was she doing? What was she doing *here*? In this room? In this city? In this country? What on earth did she think she was doing? Her brain spiralled into a despairing little crisis. And what had happened to her figure? She'd not faced up to the boobs and the bulges quite so directly before. She'd once been fit and relatively sleek and the kind of person who managed a run at the weekend and an exercise class on a Wednesday, a regular swim, a four-mile round walk with a young and excited Bella pulling her along.

When did she get so... aaargh... mumsy? Teenage children, young adult children; it all started to suck the life out of you – those endless emotional conversations and arguments and dramas and difficulties. Lifts here, there and everywhere, the constant trips to the supermarket to make sure the fridge and the cupboards were full. And don't mention office life with all its sitting and meetings and endless cups of tea and biscuit runs.

This is where it had all left her – lumpy, shapeless and clumsy.

What's happened to *me*, she couldn't help asking herself? Tess,

the responsible one, who was always picking up or running after everyone else... never leaving one moment in the day for herself. Usually so capable... so in control... but not here in a dance class. Not doing this.

Her face was turning scarlet with heat and embarrassment. She'd never seen herself quite so clearly as a frump and a clumsy frump at that. But here she was, standing in front of the mirror, attempting the simplest step and making an absolute twaddle of it. Hot tears leapt up to the back of her eyes and her throat burned. Where have I gone, she wondered? What about *me*?

'I have to go,' she told Larry. 'I'm very sorry, but this is not for me. I can't do this. I don't want to do this. It just isn't going to work,' she blurted out, flustered.

Larry looked genuinely surprised.

'Hey, Tess, it's okay... it's totally okay,' he exclaimed. 'Honestly, you're doing fine. If you don't like the step or the song, we'll change it... we can start simple.'

But she was already fumbling with the door, desperate to get out into the corridor, so he wouldn't see her tears.

22

River sat behind the steering wheel of the parked car and watched people come and go. She was in a supermarket car park. The weather was grey and everyone who passed looked kind of grey or beige too. Her heart had just about stopped racing from the encounter with Franklyn and now she was left with the tumble of thoughts that he had provoked.

It wasn't that she was still in love with him, of course not. It wasn't that she was sorry she had fallen out of love with him and they had broken up. No, that wasn't it either. It was pure and simple success envy.

When they'd been together, he'd been an actor who was starting to get the breaks and the success and she was a writer who was doing the same. Their career trajectory had looked so assured. They had made it look easy... work hard for a few years, accept a few rejections and then get your foot on the bottom rungs of the ladder of success and start climbing.

Now Franklyn was a massive star. He played the lead in block-buster movies and major TV series. His face beamed out at you from magazines at the checkout; he had catchphrases that people turned into online memes. And meanwhile, she was still hustling from job to job with breaks between work that made her just about insane with anxiety. Could Franklyn have helped her out when she had started to struggle? Well, in fact, he had tried. He had called up out of the blue one day, over a year after they'd split, and asked if she wanted to join the writing team on some project he was putting together. But, of course, River had played the proud and angry card; she'd been insulted that he'd handed her a bone like this. So she'd told him she was busy, and couldn't take it on.

'C'mon, River,' he'd told her, 'this is not a favour; this is a good, solid project and you'd do it really well. We need your voice on this one.'

But no, she'd stuck it out and turned him down. And he'd never come back to her with any kind of work offer again.

'Maybe I should have taken the freaking job!' she said to herself, out loud, 'Maybe if I'd taken that job, I would not be sitting in a supermarket car park in the rain.'

She tried to imagine what Franklyn's Stratford accommodation was like... he must be staying in an enormous house; his wife and two daughters were probably there too. There was most likely a driver... to take Franklyn to Stratford and his family on day trips and shopping trips to London. There was probably a housekeeper and a chef... maybe a personal trainer and a personal assistant... and no doubt his phone buzzed and beeped and rang all day long with exciting calls and opportunities and Very Important People who wanted to speak to him ASAP.

There was a tap on the car window right beside her head. A man's face was close to the glass and he was obviously keen to speak to her. She considered him for a moment. He didn't look overly crazy, in fact, he was wearing a bright yellow vest and possibly had some kind of official duty to perform. So she pressed the window button, but nothing happened as the engine was off. Should she turn the engine on and then lower the window? Instead, she opted for opening the door.

'Hi, yes? Can I help you?' she went with a strict and officious tone, to ward of any kind of craziness.

'Good afternoon, madam, are you planning to do any shopping with us today?'

'What?'

'Well, you've been parked here for two hours and fifty-six minutes and in four minutes time, you'll be liable for a £80 fine. As you can see from the signage placed in strategic positions all around the car park, this car park is for customers only and there is a three-hour maximum time limit.'

'What?' she demanded.

The man merely pointed to a huge bright yellow sign attached to a lamppost just two feet away from the car, that she hadn't noticed at all. In LA, you drove somewhere and you parked. That was it, no hassle, no complications. The whole of the UK was determined to make driving and parking two of the most difficult activities a human could pursue. Climate change, though. So surely that was a good thing?

'I can't see any evidence that you have shopped. Are you intending to shop here?' he asked.

'What? No! Well... yes, maybe.' She considered that getting something nice to eat tonight might be good compensation for this afternoon.

'Can I suggest that you drive out of the car park, park on the road outside and then come in and get the shopping?'

'What? No! Can't I just get my shopping now?'

'I don't think you would be able to shop in three minutes and forty-five seconds, though, would you?'

'No, but you're not going to give me a ticket now are you? I'll only be ten, maybe fifteen minutes over.'

'There are cameras...'

'Oh, for freak's sake! Never mind the cameras. I'm a human being; I take it that you're a human being. Are we going to let the machines control us? Look...' Her temper was rising now. 'I'm going to go into that store and buy a good amount of groceries. Not like a candy bar. Then I'm going to come out and drive my car away without getting a ticket. Does that sound okay to you?'

The man repeated: 'There are cameras. And you have been in the car park for almost three hours.'

'Gimme a break,' River said and went into the store.

It was a happy twenty minutes or so later that she got to the checkout with a basket full of ingredients for the gourmet dinner that she had decided to cook, not just for herself, but to invite Dave along to as well. Surely he couldn't be eating well in that shed. What did he cook on? A camping stove? And yes, she had noticed the regular Deliveroo drivers pulling up at the front of the house, but then, as no doubt instructed, going round to the back. So she had bought steaks and veggies and big potatoes to slice into fries. Two bottles of hearty Bordeaux, butter, eggs and slabs of dark chocolate, so she could make chocolate mousse. And she would pick up a fresh pack of twenty Marlboros from the prohibition-style kiosk where they handed out cigarettes from behind metal shutters. Now this was going to be dinner!

She would send Dave a message from the car: 'Cancel your Deliveroo, I bought two steaks and I'm cooking one of them up for you.'

As she approached the car, bags in hand, she could see the big yellow and black sticker on the windscreen. And all that cheerful bonhomie that had built up during her food shop immediately disappeared in a puff of fury. That guy! That guy had booked her. She immediately began to scan the car park, but there was no sign of him.

This was too much. She clicked open the trunk and set her bags down inside. She was a familiar and seething mess of fury, disappointment and frustration. She certainly didn't think Franklyn was dealing with anything as annoying as this today. Freaking Franklyn and his perfect life and his perfect family and his astonishing success.

And then that feeling was stealing up on her, the one she did almost anything to avoid, the low, chilling creep that nothing was going to go right for her, and everything was always going to be a mess. But she just couldn't allow herself to spiral down because she could get lost in the feeling, drown in it and not know how to find her way back to shore.

'Oh *God*, Drew.' She allowed herself a brief moment. 'I really miss you. And life is such a pain in the ass sometimes.'

And there was only one way to nip that feeling in the bud. She searched inside the grocery bag until she found what she was looking for, then taking aim, she pelted a fresh egg at the parking notice. As it splatted straight into the middle of the sign and then slowly began to slide down the metal, the satisfying burn of anger expressed kindled a heat in her heart and soul again.

'Fuck you,' she told the sign. Then she ripped the ticket from the windscreen, tossed it to the ground and drove out of the place.

23

'What do you think about this idea... I go to a cool, LA hair salon for a makeover? Do you think that would be a good idea? Or is it a mad idea? It's definitely going to be a very expensive idea.'

'Yes, Mum, do it!' Natalie enthused. 'Definitely!'

Tess was on a sunny bench, with the panting dogs at her feet, watching people go in and out of a salon. She liked the look of this salon because there were bold black and white headshots in the window, displayed beside two big pieces of graffiti art. One thing she hadn't expected about LA was all the colour-explosion graffiti: entire building walls taken up with huge cartoon murals. Compared to the muted greys and greens of England, LA hit you in the face with neon shades of blue, pink and yellow. Everything felt noisier, brasher and brighter. At first, it had felt overwhelming, but Tess was beginning to find it energising. Even inspiring.

'I'm loving the sunshine,' she told Natalie. 'I bet you are too.'

'Totally.'

'Doesn't it make everything feel so much more cheerful and optimistic? I take my time in the sun... enjoy the walks, sit on the benches, soak up the rays. In England, we're always rushing about to get out of the cold and the rain.' Although, as she said those words, Tess thought of the corner in the Ambleside garden that she'd lovingly created with decking, comfortable chairs, the café table and the chimenea, so that they could take their time and enjoy the sun on the days when it shone.

'And what about you, Natalie?' she asked her daughter. 'What's happening? How's the romance going?'

Natalie had to giggle down the line: 'It's lovely,' she admitted, 'he's so lovely and I really, *really* like him.'

'And is everything okay?' Tess asked. 'Is there anything you need to talk to me about, darling... because I'm a long way away but I'm always here for you, you know that, don't you?'

'Yes... I'm fine,' Natalie insisted, 'I'm taking care of myself.'

There was suddenly so much that Tess felt she wanted to say. First serious boyfriends... first lovers... there was so much that mothers needed to tell daughters, that the experienced needed to pass on to the inexperienced. From small things to really major things, you couldn't just not mention them because it was a bit awkward and embarrassing. This was Natalie, one of the great loves of Tess's life.

'I'm really not good at sex talks...' Tess began.

'Noooooo, Mum,' Natalie protested.

'But I always wanted to be and I'm just going to have to keep giving this a go, honey... so hear me out for a few minutes, okay?'

'Muuuum, there is the internet, you know.'

'Yes, of course, there is the internet! But the internet doesn't love you to pieces; the internet didn't nurture you from a tiny baby to the lovely young person you are now!'

'True.'

'Okay, here goes... I'm quite glad we're on the phone now. And maybe you know all of this already... but I'm going to go for it anyway because I love you. Okay, there's contraception, of course, you have to do that, you can't take chances, and please make sure you're doing what's right for you. If you want you can talk over the pros and cons of...'

'No, that's fine, Mum, honestly.'

'But also,' Tess went on, summoning her courage, 'I want you to know that sex should always feel great and it should always be about what you want to do. Yes, when you start it's pretty awkward and fumbly and... lubrication, the stuff that comes in a tube, is your friend...'

Natalie squeaked and Tess could feel herself blush, she couldn't believe she was saying this out loud to her daughter, but she realised she had to; she wanted to – this was an act of real love, so she carried on: 'It should always be what you want to do and it has to feel right to you. Everyone you're with has to know that and respect that. And you get to say all the time, all the way through, what you like and want. Sex is nothing like they show on screen, where women just lie there and men are amazing and know exactly what to do and it's perfect every time. No... it's much more like... dancing... learning to dance together and finding out what kind of dances you like.'

Tess was pleased with herself for coming up with that. Yes, that was right. It did take time to really work out what you and your partner wanted and what you were both good at. And sometimes you had to try some new dances too.

'And sometimes you have to try new... dances,' she added, 'and sometimes no one wants to dance at all.'

Her and Dave, she thought... on opposite ends of the dance floor pretending that it didn't matter, but it did. It mattered a lot. Could it ever be solved? Or were they only going to have sex again if they found new people to be with?

'Are you finished?' Natalie wondered.

'No, one other thing... drink lots of water and take showers with gentle soap. Sex can give you bladder infections and they are zero fun.'

'Are you finished now?' Natalie asked.

Tess felt both a sense of relief and quite proud of herself. Yes, she had covered the major points... and it hadn't been too bad. Importantly, she'd paved the way for future conversations. 'I'm sure I'll think of other things and then I'll send you embarrassing emails or phone at awkward times to tell you,' she told her daughter.

'Okay!' was Natalie's first response, followed by a shy: 'Thanks, Mum.'

'You can talk to me any time, about anything, even if it is awkward,' Tess told her. 'We'll get through it. And I love you.'

'What about Alex?' Natalie asked next. 'I haven't spoken to him for weeks. How is he getting on?'

'I saw him in London... but I've not got him on the phone since then.'

'He's so weird,' Natalie said, and Tess immediately protested, 'but he is,' Natalie insisted, 'everything's always such a big secret. He never tells us about anything.'

'Hmmm...' Tess wasn't really agreeing. She knew Alex well enough to know that it hadn't always been like this. As a little boy, he'd loved to tell you about everything, he'd chatted away constantly and enjoyed making everyone laugh. He always wanted to share all the details of the book he'd read, the model he'd built, the joke he'd learned in the playground – even if it wasn't exactly suitable for mummy ears.

He'd been open and engaging and engaged. And somehow, that side of him had shut down around about sixteen or seventeen. 'It's just a phase,' she'd told herself back then, 'he's going through teenage stuff. He's angsting. I just have to stand by and be supportive and he'll come out the other side.'

And then, out of the blue, Alex's final year at school had been a near disaster. Just when it looked like he was going to do really badly in all his A Levels, they'd had to swoop in, with tutors and supervised study... and all those angry rows and recriminations. It had been horrible. Then he'd gone to uni in Birmingham and seemed to be happy-ish, but never as happy as before. And in his final uni year, the same drama – stress and panic mixed with this weird apathy that he didn't care about exams, didn't care about studying, didn't really care about anything, and they'd had to step in again. They'd brought him home and helped with his studying again and just looked after him so that he could get the work done and not have to think about much else. Then half a year after uni, he'd gone to this job, which was a good job and she would be very pleased for him and proud, if she could just believe that it was what he wanted and that he was happy there.

Here they were, almost seven years since he was a carefree fifteen-year-old, and still there was a whole part of Alex that she didn't feel she could come anywhere near.

How did he feel? She didn't really know.

How was life going for him? 'Fine,' he would reply in that flat voice that wasn't his real voice. Was this just a sort of apathetic teenage/cynical voice that he'd put on as a teen and now couldn't seem to shake off again. He'd been so enthusiastic about things, so able to light her and Dave up with his passions, interests and discoveries. She'd thought he would do something interesting in science. She'd thought he would love uni, find himself and come to life again, earnestly discussing things deep into the night with fellow souls.

But actually, Alex had found uni disappointing and discouraging: an endless to-do list with stressy deadlines around assignments, projects, essays and exams. With his job, the same apathy, dullness, and lack of energy prevailed. What did he really want?

She didn't know. What was he really thinking? No matter how she tried, she couldn't get him to tell her.

'I'll phone him,' she assured her daughter. 'I'll track him down and find out what is going on.'

'And what about your hair, Mum?' Natalie asked. 'Just go to the funky salon, but promise me you won't go blonde. Absolutely no middle-aged blonde lady moment for you, okay?'

Tess laughed at this. 'But I'm so brunette, I am a dyed-in-the-wool, literally, brunette. Okay, love you. Don't get sunburned, or heart-broken.'

'No and no and love you too, Mum.'

* * *

Tess considered the salon for a few more moments. She decided that just walking in, hair bundled up in a scrunchy, wearing the floral English summer dress and with the big hairy dogs, probably wasn't an option. Someone terrifying in toothpick jeans would probably eviscerate her with a sweep of their disdainful eyes and a flick of their hair.

So instead, she decided to call and book an appointment. This turned out to be so much trickier than doing the same thing in the UK. There were so many more questions.

'Do we *know* you? Have you been before? What is your hair *like*? What *treatments* do you want? What *products* do you use? *What* is your hair currently dyed with?' And finally: 'Well... we might have an opening in, like, four weeks' time. Do you want to book that? And we can put you on the wait list. That means if anyone cancels, we call you, if you can come at short notice.'

Tess made a booking that was for the day before she was due to fly home and put her name down on the wait list.

Then she tried her son's number and got voicemail once again:

'Hello darling, it's Mum. Can you just give me a little call back, please? I'm on the other side of the world. If you don't phone, I'm just going to worry... and keep on phoning. So please, darling, just give me a call.'

For several long moments, she looked at her phone and willed him to call back. But it remained silent. She thought of all the times in the past when she'd freaked herself out about Alex's lack of contact. And he had always been fine. There had always been a rational, although maybe thoughtless, explanation.

So, no, she wasn't going to drive herself mad about his silence now.

24

'That was a delicious, dee-licious steak!' Dave told River, very appreciatively, 'Where did you get it?'

'Oh... some grocery store in town. They tried to give me a parking ticket,' River admitted.

'They're very strict about parking in supermarket car parks, because of all the tourists. So what did you do?' Dave asked.

'Swore, ripped it up and threw an egg at the parking sign.'

Dave, who was full of good food and had drunk the best part of a bottle of red, roared with laughter at this news.

'Well, ten out of ten for doing what everybody wants to do,' he said, 'but you might find that what with the car having a number plate and the car park having cameras, that the parking ticket comes to us in the post anyway, so I'll look out for that.'

'Oh, I didn't think of that,' River said in all honesty and cast her mind to a pile of paperwork on her desk in LA. 'Important admin', aka 'things she never really bothered about too much unless it was a red hot, steaming emergency', in which case, people usually called loudly, or sent letters clearly marked DO NOT IGNORE.

'Okay, I'm going to make coffee,' she said, 'and then you're going to tell me all about your painting. Have you started yet? How's it going? What are you painting? I want all the deets...'

As River came back into the garden carrying a tray with cups and the cafetière full of steaming full-strength, she saw that he had drained the wine bottle and refilled his glass.

'Such a lush,' she ticked him off.

'Yes, I know.'

'And you didn't even ask if I wanted more?'

'Oh my God... I'm so sorry. I'm so used to being the one that drinks all the wine...'

'Okay... I will think about forgiving you. So... the painting?'

'Well, I've started,' he announced. 'I just picked up a canvas and a brush and started... like you said. You've just got to begin some-where. So I created a plain blue square. And then I added different shades of blue, so many different shades. And then I moved on to other little pieces of canvas until I felt the courage to tackle a big one. And now I'm surrounded by all these pictures of blue, all different sizes, and shades and textures. I'm getting quite excited about textures of paint again, layering, and laying it on thickly, pulling the brush through it. I love paint!' he enthused.

'In fact, I love all of this. I genuinely have not had so much fun to myself for years. If you'd told me how much I was going to enjoy this, I would never have believed you. I genuinely feel young again,' Dave said with a grin. 'I'm sloughing off the daddy years... and the teacher stress. I'm remembering what it's like to feel creative and excited again... and oh, my goodness, listen to me. I better have some more coffee, because this is clearly the wine talking... or gush-ing, more like.'

River was laughing. 'That's great!' she said. 'When it flows, when everything's going well with the creative process, it's amazing... but I'm sure you know the dark and difficult side of it too.'

'You know, I was still in my twenties when I was last doing this and I don't know if I did have much of the dark side. Maybe I'm just too much of an optimist, too much of a happy person in general.'

'Lucky you,' was River's verdict on this, 'So...' she poured out two cups of coffee, 'I had quite the day in Stratford today... guess who I bumped into in Shakespeare's house?'

'The bard himself?' Dave joked.

'No, someone possibly even more well known...'

'No!' Dave was wide-eyed now. 'Not Franklyn Gregory?'

'Oh yes, Franklyn Gregory himself, in all his glory.'

And River went on to tell Dave about the encounter in detail.

'How did it feel to see him again...' Dave wanted to know. 'I mean, I take it, it's been a while?'

'Yes... it has been quite a few years. And I thought I was kind of fine about it... but afterwards, well... that's when I was throwing angry eggs around the car park.'

'But why?' Dave had to ask.

'Why? Why am I angry? Because...' River teased a cigarette out of her brand-new packet and after lighting it, said: 'He just wasn't that special. He was a good actor and he worked hard at it, but why did the world choose him?'

'Well... you could ask that about the superstars in every field,' Dave countered. 'It's probably a combination of talent, effort, and sheer luck. No need to beat yourself up about it.'

'But I was right there,' River protested, 'in the same places, at the same time... so it's kind of hard not to... anyway, I don't want to go on about it.' She inhaled, then let out a long and reflective plume of smoke. 'I want to plan a garden party and, guess what? Maybe Franklyn will come along... with his wife!'

'Here? To this garden?' Dave's astonishment was obvious. 'Franklyn might come *here*? Good grief! Will we need to hire body-guards and crowd control?' Dave was only partially joking.

'Ah ha ha!' River laughed. 'No! He'll probably swoop down with a driver and a casual strongman and stay for a Hollywood twenty minutes, which is long enough to shake the hand of everyone that's of any importance and then sweep off again. In fact, what am I talking about? He almost definitely won't come. But my producer will probably come, so I could invite some actors that he knows, who are in Stratford right now and then I was thinking... what about artists?'

River was getting properly into this garden party idea now: 'What about your artist friends? This will be a couple of weeks from now. Why don't you invite them? You can talk to them about painting and getting started again and see what advice they give you. Wouldn't it be great to reconnect after all this time apart?'

And maybe because Dave was well fed and full of wine, this idea that he would usually have laughed off straight away warmed him, went straight to his heart, and sounded like a really great plan.

'I love that!' he gushed. 'Yes! It's been years and *years* since I've seen some of them, but it would be fantastic to reconnect and have a properly arty party, full of creative types. My God, a party at Ambleside without one single accountant! Absolutely no one like that is allowed to come! And that's final. I have spoken to enough men in grey suits, and women for that matter, to last a lifetime.'

And as he tried to imagine an arty party at Ambleside, Dave wondered why he'd let himself get so out of touch with his old friends. Tess was the party instigator and organiser, of course, and her parties were lovely, but they were full of people from her work... and her circle. He didn't even think it was deliberate... she just assumed he met his friends in the pub. Also, her parties were never rip-roaring fun. And Dave, drinking wine late into the night with his new, glamorous scriptwriter friend, was beginning to think that a little bit of rip-roaring fun would do him good.

'Right...' River straightened up and began to look efficient, 'let's party plan! Break open your phone, your iPad, whatever; we need to make an epic party plan: a guest list, a gazebo, cakes, food, booooooze. And what about music... shall we have a DJ?' She swayed in her seat to demonstrate. 'And a dance floor?' she broke out a few hand dance moves.

'God, I love this, I love it!' Dave exclaimed.

As River lit up her fifth, or maybe fifteenth cigarette of the evening, Dave looked at it longingly.

'Have one,' River said, as if it was nothing.

'I'm on high blood pressure medication...' he admitted.

'One won't kill you.' River shook her packet gently so that one cigarette slid half out in Dave's direction.

'But Tess would,' Dave said.

Mentally, he held out for another three or four seconds... then he picked the cigarette out of the pack with his thumb and forefinger. It had been so long and yet this movement still felt familiar.

He took the cigarette and raised it to his lips as River approached with her clunky old Zippo lighter.

'Yeah, but right now...' River began.

Reckless, Dave thought as he inhaled smoke for the first time in almost twenty years... absolutely *reckless*.

'Tess is on the other side of the world.'

25

The hairdresser called – out of the blue, the very next day – to ask if Tess could be there at 11 a.m. because of a cancellation. She'd had plans for the day and weighed up for a moment or two if the plans could hold and if she could do the LA haircut thing. She decided that yes, she could. She could! It was just hair – if it was hideous, or ridiculous, it would regrow. And, it was just money, if it was outrageously, burn-a-hole in the wallet expensive, well... it would be a regret, but she would earn it back. She wanted a change... in everything. And visiting the funky LA hairdresser was part of that change.

'Yes!' she told the receptionist. 'That's great! I can be there at 11 a.m.'

So she rushed around putting on a different outfit and more thorough make-up, getting the dogs out for a little jaunt although they would be with Tom at lunchtime, then she left River's apartment and hurried in the direction of the swanky salon.

She was there on the stroke of 11 a.m. and walked into the reception area. From there, she was directed to a comfortable sofa and given a glass of iced water and a selection of pristine new magazines, which was just as well as she now began an extended wait. Who knew what Miguel, her 'senior style artist' was up to this morning? Maybe he was posting on SnapChat, or playing Fortnite? Maybe he was dealing with an extremely demanding LA Diva who was making him re-blowdry her entire head, but wait Tess must. After twenty minutes, she went to check with the receptionist that Miguel was, in fact, alive and well, and planning to see her sometime before the end of time.

'Oh, of course,' she was assured, 'he's just dealing with something unexpected and he'll be right with you.' But another twenty minutes crept by before, finally, she was greeted by a very friendly girl with swishy waist-length green and blue hair, who wrapped her into a gown then tucked her into a chair in front of a mirror. Again, she was assured that Miguel would be there in an instant. But still Miguel was delayed. And now there was no iced water, and no magazines to flip through. Tess looked at herself in the mirror, as she knew she was supposed to. Hairdressers were the most powerful psychologists of all. They knew women, all their foibles, desires, inner secrets and insecurities. And she knew that she had been placed in this chair, in front of this mirror, with an overhead spotlight shining on her roots to make her feel as insecure as possible. Miguel, like the handsome star of the am-dram production, was no doubt hidden away off stage waiting to make his grand entrance, to swoop down, dazzle her and make it all better.

She faced herself square on in the mirror. Her hair wasn't a particularly bad point. It was dark brown, thick and straightish. It fell to her collarbone in a layered bob – a version of the cut Courtney Cox had sported on *Friends* all those years ago. In fact, Tess wasn't sure she'd had much in the way of a radical change since requesting 'the Courtney' back in the 1990s. Despite a regular eight-weekly hairdressing schedule, and a box of those stupid little eye-shadow powders you touched your roots up with, she had a half centimetre of hair at her parting that was whiter than she expected, although maybe that was the effect of the glaring spotlight.

And beneath the hair, she wasn't too downbeat about the changes that age was bringing. Her skin was holding up because she was pale and a fan of sunscreen. Well, her jawline and neck were starting to look a little more like her mother's and those lines, the ones that went from nose to mouth and mouth to chin, were beginning to deepen. She took issue with her boobs... and properly didn't like them. Weight seemed to gather only on her stomach and her boobs and this weight had expanded a generous bosom into a shelf that was far too *matronly* for her liking. The shelf required jacket alterations and strategic buttons and hooks on work shirts. It called for underwear that was more like scaffolding than lingerie.

Lingerie... her thoughts snagged on that word. When had she last worn nice lingerie? Or planned any kind of romantic encounter with the man she was supposed to be in love with? What was she supposed to do about the fact that she just didn't want to? What did you do when you loved someone but were no longer in love? Could anything be salvaged at this stage? Or would it be much better for them both to move on? These were the questions that plagued her. Went round and round in her head. Would these weeks on her own bring her answers? It was too early to tell.

'So, hi there! It is Tess, right? Hello, I'm Miguel, I am your creative style artist.'

So, here he was at last. And, finally, this haircut could begin.

Miguel was a lean guy in jeans and a vibrant shirt. He looked Latino and a little older than she expected, wore those clear-framed glasses and had a touch of grey in his 1950s style crew cut with a quiff.

'Hi Miguel, nice to meet you... what kept you?' she had to ask.

'Oh! You're British! That's a bit different. It's been some time since I last cut a British lady's hair. Right, I am going to look at your hair carefully and you are going to talk to me. Okay, let's go.'

And with that, he skated right over his lateness, settled onto the wheeled stool and with his neat comb began to lift sections of her hair and feel, look and evaluate it.

'So... I'm in LA for a long holiday... by myself,' Tess began. 'It's the first time I've been here. It's the first time I've gone on holiday by myself... in fact. I got a sabbatical from work for a few months and I was going to go on this big trip with my husband and my kids, who aren't really kids any more, they're young adults... I was thinking Thailand, Cambodia...'

What was she doing? Why was she telling him all this? Couldn't she just have left it at here in LA on holiday?

'Wow, that sounds amazing,' Miguel broke in.

'Yes... I know, but no one wanted to come.'

Shut up, Tess!

'Really?'

She met his eyes in the mirror and felt a tug at the back of her throat. Oh help, she wasn't going to cry about this here in a hair-dresser's chair, thousands of miles from home? No!

'I don't think it was me,' she added with a half shrug, 'everyone just had other things they wanted to do... busy lives... and a great long family trip didn't... didn't do it for them.'

'Even your husband?' Miguel asked.

'Dave wanted to stay at home... he always wants to stay at home... and then he broke his ankle, so he had to stay at home.'

Perhaps sensing this was a sensitive area, Miguel encouraged her with the words: 'So, you came to LA by yourself, that's an amazing idea. So what are you doing now you're here?'

Walking dogs and tidying my hostess's dump of a flat, Tess decided to leave that bit out.

'Taking time for myself...' she said, 'which is a new thing for me.

This is my first week and I'm just exploring the neighbourhood, but planning to see art, go to the beach, go hiking...' and when this sounded a bit dull, she added: 'I've started a dance class...'

'That's so brave! And exciting,' he exclaimed.

'Yes... I was hoping it would be. But it's actually scarier than I expected. Dancing is hard when you've been sitting at a desk for years. And, of course, I'm here for a brand-new haircut,' she said. 'So, what do you think?'

Miguel was still running his fingers through the hair, squeezing it between his hands and really sizing it up.

'Okay, some questions from me now,' he said and they both looked at Tess's reflection in the mirror.

'I'm thinking you have quite a corporate job,' he began.

'Yes,' she agreed. 'I'm a senior accountant for the local branch of a big firm.' But not a partner, she thought, but didn't say it aloud.

'And I'm guessing you've not changed your hairstyle for a while?'

'No... not really.'

'Or the colour?'

'I suppose not,' she said looking at the dark brown football Miguel had in his hands.

'And you're not very good with styling tools?'

'No.'

How had he guessed?

'And you don't use a hair mask much?'

'No again... sorry.'

'And you swim in chlorinated water?'

When were the LA insults going to stop? Really... was it so unusual not to use hair tools? Or a hair mask? Or do whatever it was you were supposed to do to your hair when you went in the pool? These people were so unbelievably high maintenance and rude.

When she confirmed this, he shook his head.

'Tess, Tess, Tess... this is not good. Okay, so the first thing you're going to promise me is that from now on, Tuesday night is mask night. No one does anything on Tuesday nights, so now you can just put it into the weekly schedule. On Tuesdays, you go to bed with the mask I will give you on your hair every week. Okay?'

Tess nodded meekly. Well, she could try, couldn't she? For a week or two anyway... see if it made any difference.

'Promise number two: don't swim in chlorinated water.'

'Really?' She wasn't sure if she was ready to take orders like this about her life from a hairdresser.

'You can swim in rivers, swim in the sea! If you *have* to swim in the pool, then put the hair mask on, then a tight ponytail, and two tight swimming caps on top – not one, two. I'm serious!'

Tess would have liked to give him some instructions of her own, like, 'How about buying yourself a watch and turning up for your clients on time for a change...' and 'Whoever sold you that shirt was having a laugh,' but as this man was wielding the scissors over her hair, she simply nodded in meek agreement once again.

'So, once we do the cut and the colour, I'm going to show you some simple styling tricks, and you will practise until you're good at them. This is not rocket science, clever accounting lady, this is just hair styling. You can do it!'

She found herself smiling at him, warming to him and, all importantly, trusting him.

'So...' he was ruffling through her hair, 'this is nice, thick hair, strong hair, but it's *dry*. It has a nice wave; it's a good length for you. We'll go a little shorter, but only a touch. So... we need a haircut that is fresh, that is LA; this is the new you. You need a style that puts a spring in your step, makes you happy to look in the mirror, happy you came to see me. And I think I want to add just something extra, something just a little wild for your LA sabbatical that will fade right away by the time it's back to work. How does that sound?'

Tess couldn't help smiling.

'That sounds wonderful,' she said, while thinking: can he do all that with one haircut? This was definitely a change from Loulou in Leamington, who kept a note of her colour on file and told her last time that she'd been using the same one for the past eight years.

'Okay, leave it with me,' Miguel said. 'I'm going to go and make up some colours.'

And then he was gone.

And Tess was left somewhat open-mouthed in the chair. *Leave it with me? Was that it?* Didn't she get any further say in the matter? What if he was planning a blue and green display, like the girl who'd taken her to the chair?

When Miguel came back with a trolley full of colour dishes and an assistant, Tess took it up with him.

'Aren't we going to discuss the colours?' she asked. 'Look at some options, maybe? I'd quite like to know what you have in mind.'

'Nope,' he said, but with a charming smile. 'I can tell you're a busy, busy boss lady. You're running your life, running everyone's life, busy, busy, making all the decisions, all the time. So just for today, I want you to sit back and leave it to me.'

What?!

Leave it to him? The man in the silky turquoise leopard-print shirt?

And quite frankly, no she was not making all the decisions. Otherwise she would have landed that partnership, somehow, on her terms... and she'd be in Thailand or Cambodia with her family. No, unfortunately, people made their own decisions. And you had to hope they weren't too far away from what you wanted... or that you could learn to live with them.

'You will love this, I promise,' Miguel added. 'If not, you can walk out of here without paying one cent. How does that sound?'

Tess cast her eye over the trolley, it was full of black plastic dishes with white, blueish and caramel-coloured creams. Was this madness? She could just take her gown off and walk away now. Instead, she decided to try to relax down into her chair and, for once, let a hairdresser get on with what they wanted to do.

'Okay,' she told Miguel, 'it's a deal... I'm not sure why I'm agreeing to this... but okay... over to you.'

And for the next forty minutes or so, her hair was painted with the creams and bundled into foils while Miguel told her all about his favourite beaches and gave her some ideas on where to hike with the dogs. Then she sat and waited as the dyes took effect. She could smell bleach... yes, there was definitely bleach involved. She had never bleached her hair before and didn't really know what to think about this. Would it be coppery? Gingery? What was the final effect he was going to create? How much would she hate it? Before she could return to work, was she going to have to ask Loulou to look up the files and dye her hair back to the exact colour it was before?

After some time, the colour was checked and then she was off to the neck-straining sink for foils to be pulled out and a lengthy lathering and rinsing process. The smell of bleach was strong... making her eyes water. Natalie's warning was running through her mind: 'Promise me you won't go blonde. Absolutely no middle-aged blonde lady moment for you, okay?'

Rinsing, lathering, rinsing, lathering... half of LA's available water for the day must have been poured on her head by now. And then squeezing and towelling and more potions and brushes were brought to the sink. Now something that smelled of delicious strawberry flavouring was being painted on. And plastic was wrapped round and then, finally, she could sit up, and more magazines and iced water were brought, and she was told to sit for fifteen minutes to let everything take effect.

After this, a final round of rinse-lather-rinse was done. And now, as she sat bundled in her towel, Miguel asked if he could cut, then blow dry and style her hair *away from the mirror* for maximum surprise. In fact, he suggested that she just keep her eyes down, or ideally closed, until he was done.

By now, Tess was a strange combination of excited and exhausted. She would have paid double if she could leave right now and be finished... be done! Maybe she was overcome with bleach fumes, but she agreed to the mirrorless request; anything to bring this session, now entering its third hour, to a close. And, she looked downwards, through slightly closed eyes, at the magazine on her lap. She read words about so and so's plans for an unforgettable summer on Nantucket island, but none of it meant anything to her. Her heart rate felt a little elevated and she wondered what on earth she had allowed to happen here. She'd let some hip LA hairdresser loose, completely unsupervised, on her hair! Her head was pushed down so he could trim the back of her hair, but she opened her eyes wide and tried to take in a side view. Bright baby blonde strands! It was so shocking, she thought maybe she should just close her eyes again.

Okay, okay, she told herself... hadn't she already reasoned that she could dye whatever Miguel had done straight back to her usual colour again. And surely whatever this weekly mask was, it could undo the damage of a severe bleach job. She kept her eyes shut tight through the cutting, through the blasting of the dryer and the finickity fiddling of what she guessed was a hot curling tong.

At last, the frenzy of activity around her head slowed and then, after a final tweak or two, it stopped.

'Oh my gosh,' Miguel said. 'Tess, I'm almost nervous about showing you now, but I have got to tell you, I absolutely love it.'

'*You're* nervous?' Tess said. 'I'm frightened to open my eyes.'

'Wait, wait,' Miguel said and they whizzed her, in her chair, to a different place.

'Okay, you have a mirror now,' Miguel told her, 'it's time to take a look.'

So there, she finally opened her eyes and stared and stared some more at her reflection.

It was terrible...

But it was also wonderful...

It was laugh-out-loud outrageous... and totally *wrong*.

But maybe... it was also totally *right*...

She couldn't decide. She was so shocked!

She was a blonde, definitely a blonde.

A bright, straw blonde, but with a deep, punky two inches of dark roots. She had a fringe... a *fringe*?! Something she'd not looked out from under since she was twelve. And then there was all this twisting, turning movement of gentle corkscrew curls... and... oh good lord... was that pink? *Pink*? Oh yes, indeed... the bottom half of her hair had been dip-dyed a beautiful shade of coppery pink. In the course of one morning, she had gone from Courtney Cox to Courtney Love.

'Oh my God...' she whispered.

'But it's oh my God good, right?' Miguel asked.

He was squatting so that his face was level with hers as they looked in the mirror.

'You look ten years younger, Tess. It's a cliché, but in this case, it's true. You look late thirties, less serious, less weighed down. You look like someone who is enjoying life again.'

'Pink?' she said.

'This shade washes out in around twenty washes. So it can be totally gone by the time you get back to the office. But if you love it, come back in a fortnight and we'll put something more permanent in.'

'Blonde?' she said. 'I wasn't expecting to go blonde...'

'You're remembering our talk about weekly masks and avoiding chlorine? Plus, I've left roots, so you'll only need a little top up every three months or so. I can write down the details of what I've done for your stylist back home.'

'And curls?' she said.

'Yes,' Miguel held up the curling wand, 'now, we're going to do just a tiny mini tutorial. This is a curling wand, not a Geiger counter. You are a smart lady, and you can work out how to use this.'

'Pink and blonde with curls?' Tess was still transfixed by her reflection. She would have to re-think her make-up... she would have to re-think her clothes... maybe she would have to re-think her choice of career. And her children? Dave? Her office? What would any of them make of this?

In something of a daze, she over-thanked Miguel and his assistant. She endured the mini curling tutorial and then, finally, it was time to leave the chair. Miguel kissed her goodbye and she paid the gigantic bill, plus tip... *about twenty per cent*, the receptionist informed her when she asked what was right.

And as she stepped out into the blasting sunshine of a summer's day in Studio City, LA, she put her hand every now and then to her bouncy blonde curls just to check that they were definitely real. She felt shocked, but she also felt amazing! Somewhere underneath her enormous sense of surprise, she knew that this was the push she had needed. This was the first of many pushes. Blonde and pink-haired Tess was ready to be bolder and braver. She'd been almost ready for this haircut and Miguel had made it real. She was ready for other things too... it was time to not just step but to jump out of

her comfort zone. Time for new things, new beginnings... a whole
new chapter.

Natalie!!!!! Wait till you see my hair!!!!

she messaged, and couldn't help noticing that there was still no
word from Alex.

26

It was nearly 5 p.m. and River was heading out to Stratford shortly to see the first of the Shakespeare plays she had tickets for: *The Tempest*. She was feeling quite positive about the day she'd had so far. In the morning, she'd gone for a long walk across country paths suggested by Dave. Then she'd stretched out, showered and made a very nutritious and wholesome brunch before drinking three coffees and smoking four cigarettes in the garden to get herself into the proper writing frame. Five whole hours of wrestling with the script and the script notes had followed. She was positive about the structuring work she'd done, the dialogue she'd written and the opening scene she'd worked on. But still the feeling that she'd not yet hit the nail on the head, not yet unlocked the key to this whole rewrite nagged at her.

Deckchairs on the Titanic was the phrase that kept coming to mind and bothering her a lot. Was she merely rearranging the deckchairs on this script, while ignoring the fact that the whole thing was doomed to sink beneath the waves? If she didn't steer it well past the imminent icebergs, it was going to be just another sucky script made into another sucky teen movie. And her career might well go down with the ship.

Her phone flashed with a message and her heart sank when she saw it was from Phillip.

How's it going, superstar? Hope you have something we can look at? Wanting to show agent and talent attached how script is shaping up so they can get excited and sign up. Have anything yet? Even a few scenes? Just a full outline? Lemme know.

Just a full outline? Weren't they always asking for 'just' the outline? Didn't they realise that the outline was the hardest bit. The outline was the plot, the beats, the twists, the characters? The outline was the bit you sweated blood over. Once the outline was good, well then, it wasn't exactly plain sailing, but at least you had a sound map for your journey.

She messaged back:

I can get you an opening scene tomorrow, does that sound okay? Still working on outline... feel I'm about to make a breakthrough with that. Keep the faith. Gonna be a good one.

Then she messaged:

My English garden party? Do the dates I sent work for you? My old friend, Franklyn Gregory, is hoping to come along.

As she'd suspected, the reply was instantaneous. Well, dawn had broken in LA and Phillip was always working.

Franklyn's coming?

Well, he said he would try. And let's face it, not much else happening in Stratford.

He's in Stratford this summer?!

Yeah… this is where all the cool kids are. It's adorable. You should try it.

What date can F do?

He's OK'ed both of these. I'd say Sun though. A safer bet than Fri for theatre people. That's theataaaaaaaa. We're in luvvie England now.

Marking my diary now. Flying to London tomorrow. Look forward to hanging with you R.

Yup, gonna be cool. Wait till you see my house and garden. The roses!!! I wanna live in England just to be surrounded by these roses.

It wasn't logical to think that she would bump into Franklyn on every trip to Stratford, but as River got ready to go out for the evening, she paid extra care and attention. When she was finished, she was pleased with the effect. It was arty rock and roll, her favourite look: leather leggings, silky blouse, big earrings, straight hair and a particularly luscious deep rose lipstick. Ankle boots with the highest heel she could manage for driving were the finishing touch.

As she was heading to the car, she ran into Dave. He had a crutch under one arm and a watering can in the other hand.

'Should you be doing that?' she asked.

'What?'

'One-crutch watering?'

'Totally fine,' he assured her. 'If I let things in the garden die, Tess will probably break my other ankle, so that would be riskier. Have a great evening!' he said with a wave of the watering can: 'Is it a hot date?'

'No...' she laughed, but enjoyed the implied compliment, 'the-ataaaaa darling, theataaaa.'

'But of course... enjoy!'

* * *

So many tourists! Tourists in the streets where she jostled for a parking space, tourists on the pavements, tourists outside the theatre, inside the theatre and in every single row of the theatre. Almost everyone with their phone out taking selfies and videos and waving at the folks online.

River settled into her seat and read though the programme carefully, trying to ignore the savages on either side of her, who were obviously here to see tonight's celebrity actors in the flesh, and not for the Shakespeare experience.

She'd never read or seen *The Tempest* before, but as the curtain went up and the play unfolded before her, she was surprised to find herself deeply moved by the acting, the plot and oh, the words, the words, the gorgeous words and phrases raining down on the audience.

In the darkness, eyes fixed on the stage, River drank in the words and the rhythms of the language. Yes, it was old-fashioned and the meaning of some of the phrases passed her by, but the wonderful torrent washed over her: *We are such stuff as dreams are made on, and our little life is rounded with a sleep.*

She found herself thinking back to high school and the growing realisation that she was going to be a writer, because she was determined to try to bring the ideas, and the characters and stories she'd created, to life. She was going to try to explain just what it was like to be in someone else's head, seeing the world through their eyes.

To her parents' horror, she'd gone to a dramatic arts college in New York, and, at first, she had tried her hand at acting, directing, even film editing, but it was always writing that called her back. She loved it best and it loved her right back. Of all the tools she could use, words were the ones that proved not the easiest, that was for sure, but the ones she wanted to come back to again and again. And the delightful solitude of writing. The quiet time away from every other demand the world makes, weaving stories out of imagination and thin air... and coffee, plenty of coffee.

Her parents never wanted this life for her. Like her brothers and sisters, River was supposed to find a solid profession. Her Latino-American family was full of cops and nurses, a teacher and a social services worker... these were responsible, public service kind of folks. They all lived in and around New York. They hung out with each other on Sundays, visited her Mom on Mother's Day, took the grandkids round. Whereas she was off in LA on her own. Yes, they were all so proud of her when *Spangled* was a big hit. It was something visible they could see; they could smell the proverbial success. 'Here's our Hollywood superstar!' ... 'Our daughter *wrote* that...' She could tell that for a few years, at least, they stopped worrying about her and her career, let alone her lifestyle choices.

But then when she sold the gorgeous apartment, when she reported only small TV writing assignments... well, then they began to worry all over again. And recently there had even been talk of, 'You can come back to New York... move in for a while... find your feet...' It was horrendous. It was just so dreadful to be approaching forty – the big four-oh – and feel that the life you'd spent almost twenty years trying to create for yourself could be slipping away.

As the play moved on through the final act, River was in love with the sheer romance of theatre: the lights... the costumes... and the poetry. She could feel tears dropping onto her cheeks. Theatre... it didn't even make any sense in this completely digital world, where everyone had a Netflix subscription and could watch whatever they wanted, whenever they wanted. But nevertheless, theatre was a dream, the daydream... the romance. Oh... but how could you ever explain this to people? That you were in love with the dream of writing really good stories, and you continued to chase this dream despite the costs, when other people had pensions, mortgages, dependable healthcare and savings accounts, not to mention ten-year to retirement 'runways'.

Oh jeeezus, her career was a mess, her life was a mess and definitely her finances were a mess. She should sell her current apartment and re-think. But she couldn't even do that because of the terrible situation with the pool and the apartment management... and why was she even thinking about all this crap when, *'Full fathom five thy father lies / Of his bones are coral made / Those are pearls that were his eyes...'*

What the hell was she going to do about the script? How was she going to get it to turn out right? And what was she going to send to Phillip?

This was serious. It felt like a final chance. If this didn't work out well... maybe she would have to quit.

27

Alex opened his eyes. It took him several moments to re-orientate himself. He was looking at his ceiling... it was greyish white. Did that mean it was early evening? Or early morning? What time had he fallen asleep? How long had he been asleep for? What had he been doing before he fell asleep? His brain felt slow and sticky as he tried to think through the answers to all these questions.

Down on the dusty floor beside his bed was his phone, so he picked that up and looked at the time. It was 1.56 p.m. He vaguely noted the stack of messages, WhatsApps and even actual voicemails that would have to be attended to and he noticed the date too. It was high summer. Out there on the other side of the pulled-down blind, there was sunshine and ice creams, paddling pools and holiday trips, sunglasses and swimming shorts, suntan lotion and waves. He couldn't stand it. Maybe it would be a little easier to feel so miserable when it was cold and wintery and everyone else was more wrapped up and miserable too. But to be so unhappy when out there was this bright, shiny, strobe-lit summer world was horrible, awful.

He glanced around the room for prompts about what had

happened before he'd fallen asleep at around dawn. There were four empty cider cans standing in a row on his bedside table. In fact, he was so thirsty now that he gave the nearest one a shake and on finding some fluid down at the bottom, he tipped the can to his lips and drank down the flat, sour apple-ish goo.

He could still see the note he'd left his sister in a scrunched-up ball on the floor. There was no bin in this cramped room, so rubbish just had to fall where it landed and sit there. He'd had a plan to go away in the hope that it would make things better. He'd thought he would get on a train and get out of London, go somewhere new... to the countryside... get fresh air... greenery... see new scenes, and meet new people. He'd answered an ad for work on a farm in Devon. He'd written his note to Natalie, packed his bag, locked his room behind him... then he'd set off down the road, taken the bus and then the underground train to Liverpool Street station, but it was 6 p.m., and he hadn't expected all this rush and flurry of people. People in suits, people in shiny shoes, carrying briefcases, talking into their phones, rushing to platforms, jostling down the stairs. It had completely overwhelmed him. Who could be bothered to do all this? To get up and rush for trains to get to work, where they would rush from one thing to the next, and then rush onto the train and home again. Jesus Christ! He wanted to scream at everyone: fuck off and die. Fuck off. Go home. Leave me in peace. Calm the fuck down!! And a rush-hour train ticket to Devon, even one way, turned out to cost far more money than he had. So, he'd turned on his heel, found some quiet little pub where he'd drunk much of the train ticket money and waited until everything was much calmer and then he had gone back 'home'. Not home really. This horrible little room where nothing happened, and nothing changed. But at least he was left alone. No one bothered him here. No one interfered. But now he had no idea what he was going to do.

He looked at the messages his parents had left him. He didn't want them to worry about him, that was the first thing. And he didn't want his parents to know that he'd left his job, that was the second thing. And he certainly didn't want his parents to know how bad he was feeling, how hopeless and pointless and... he struggled to think of a word that summed it up. He just didn't care, about anything or anyone or even about himself.

Everything felt like too much effort.

Every single thing.

He didn't even want to wake up in the morning. He didn't want to get out of bed and begin the tedium of this day; the effort of dragging himself through from hour to hour... working out what to eat, what to drink, how to fill the everlasting minutes of every hour. And then all through the night, he could not bear the struggle to fall back to sleep all over again.

He didn't believe there was anyone he could turn to for help, because he didn't think this could be fixed. His long, pointless life just stretched out before him and he had no idea what he wanted to do with it. He knew he was supposed to earn money and have a good job and he'd been on track to do that. But everything about that job had been so boring and meaningless that he'd found himself staring out of the office window during meetings, and all he could think was: *is this it?* Is this what I studied so hard for? Is this why I have a degree? Is this why I read a whole bookshelf of economic theory? Surely this can't be it? He'd shadowed several more senior people during his early weeks in the office and what they did all day hadn't looked any more interesting. They were in charge of more... more money, more people, more projects, but their meetings and routines looked just as boring as Alex's.

And then came the fateful day when he was given a whole pile of photocopying to do, so he'd just slipped out at lunchtime and never gone back. All phone calls from his previous office had been ignored. Even the plaintive emails asking him if he was terminating his employment contract and could he get in touch to arrange a formal end... he'd deleted them.

Fuck off. Leave me alone. That was all he wanted to say to the world. Fuck off!!

He picked up his stupid phone. He despised it, even though he already knew he would spend most of today searching desperately online via this idiotic little machine for anything to distract him, entertain him, amuse him, inform him. Anything... *anything* to take away the bored loneliness of being in this room. He was too exhausted to go out, and too cynical to want to do anything else. He was too snarled up and fragile to even want to tell his own mum and dad, who he knew loved him very much, about how it really was for him.

He looked at all the messages his mother had sent. She'd most likely be asleep now.

I'm fine, Mum, don't worry about me. Speak soon xx

I'm fine, Dad, don't worry about me. Speak soon xx

I'm fine, Natalie, don't worry about me. Speak soon xx

There, that was done. That would get everyone off his case for at least a day or two.

Now, somehow, he had to manage to live through the rest of this day. Somehow, he had to fill the one hour that came after the other. Why was it all so hard? When had it last felt good to wake up and have a whole day ahead of him? He couldn't remember.

It had begun to occur to him that maybe it would just be so much easier if he didn't have to wake up, didn't have to face each and every day ever again.

28

Maybe the pink and blonde curls had made her braver, but soon after the haircut, Tess got in touch with Larry and said she wanted a second dance lesson.

'No, no, we'll redo the first one,' Larry insisted. 'I think we just did a bit too much too soon. I'll go easy with you and you will be fine.'

So now she was back at his apartment and once her new hair had been properly admired, the lesson began.

'Okay, lady,' he said, walking her over to the barre area, 'let's keep at the front of our minds that there is no one in the world who doesn't want to know how to dance better.'

First of all, they stretched and warmed up, with Tess following Larry's moves. It was sunny and warmer than she remembered in the room because he wanted her muscles to loosen and become more pliable.

'I want you to bend and sweat, honey,' he told her, 'bend and sweat. Right, we're just going to do arms and shoulders today,' he assured her, 'nothing scary... just going to learn how to be loose, how to move and flow.'

The music was different this time too, slower and more soulful but still pop music: still music that reminded her of good times, good moods, good vibes. So she found herself smiling as she raised her arms up and then let them flow downwards again.

'Oh, those desk shoulders!' Larry complained. He took hold of her hands and shook her arms gently. He took hold of her shoulders and then her neck and tried to help lengthen, loosen and stretch. One shoulder in each hand, he moved them from side to side, one forward, one back.

'That's it, go with it, loosen, relax, shake it out... I'm finding it hard to believe that you are only forty-nine.'

Larry no doubt thought he was being playful and jokey, but once again, he'd pushed Tess too far. She saw herself in the mirror, and the hair was good, no doubt about that. But below the hair, there was still a stiff and somewhat lumpy middle-aged lady trying to dance. Her arms moved awkwardly, her legs just did not do what she wanted them to do and once again, it was too much. She felt utterly humiliated all over again and once again felt like she might cry.

'Oh, woah, not again,' Larry said, very gently. 'I am such a clown, Tess. I'm so sorry; I did not mean to hurt your feelings. Woah, let me get you a Kleenex and then we are going to pull up a chair, right over here, at my kitchen counter and I'm going to make you a tea. We need a break anyway. We definitely need a break.'

And so Tess blew her nose, dried her eyes and sat down at the chair offered to her. Meanwhile, Larry put the kettle on and busied himself warming a dark and quirky looking teapot with a woven handle.

'I like to make jasmine tea,' he said, 'is that okay with you?'

'That sounds lovely,' she said, 'and I'm sorry. I feel like I'm being such a drama queen.'

This made him laugh: 'Oh no, definitely not. A little fragile maybe, but nothing like a drama queen. Believe me, I know a drama queen when I see one.'

The dark, metal teapot was warmed before Larry carefully spooned in green jasmine tea and then poured in boiling water from a height.

'It's about adding oxygen,' he explained as she looked on curiously. He then set two handmade, pottery cups without handles on the counter for them.

And then, maybe because the tea was beautifully made and soothing, maybe because the sun was shining into the apartment, touching the plants, the bookcase, the paintings on the wall... maybe because Larry sat at the end of the counter, not opposite her, and maybe because she felt in need of a new friend and Larry seemed like such a wise and sympathetic soul, she found herself unburdening a little.

'I'm so out of my comfort zone in a dance lesson,' she said.

Larry nodded, but told her not to worry. 'Every minute that you're dancing, you're improving. I give you my word.'

She liked his deep voice. You could trust a voice like that; really believe in it.

'I'm out of my comfort zone everywhere I turn over here,' she added. 'I'm on my own, without my family and they've been around me all day, every day for... over twenty years. I've been away from the world of work, a world that I understand pretty well, for weeks... and I'm supposed to come back with some sort of new action plan... and I've no idea what that is going to be yet.

'And I'm going to turn fifty later this year,' Tess went on. 'And I just *hate* the thought of that. I mean *fifty*... does anyone enjoy that? Does anyone ever image themselves reaching that age?'

'I'm fifty-four,' Larry told her, 'it's not so bad. Better than not reaching fifty-four. That's what I tell myself.'

'And my kids have left home,' she said, and looked up at him.

She hoped she didn't have to explain this any further. She hoped he could just understand how much her world had shifted and how everything was different now and she didn't really know what the new way ahead was going to be like... or what she even wanted it to be like.

'That must feel like the end of an era...' he said. And she was glad that he didn't follow it up with talk of new beginnings, or chapters or even eras. Because really, she was only just starting to get used to the end bit.

'And I'm here in LA on my own, because I just don't know if I want to be married to my husband any more,' she blurted out, surprising herself, because she certainly hadn't planned to say this. She'd never even shared anything like this with any good friends.

'I just don't know if we love each other enough to keep it going for the years and years ahead,' she added.

Larry gave a gentle nod, which encouraged Tess to add, 'But, I just don't know. I mean, I love him and the four of us are a family... but... we've let so many things build up and... there's not much spark left between us. I thought that if I spent time with myself, time doing new things, getting back in touch with myself... that maybe I'd be able to work out what I want. When I'm at home, rushing about and doing all the everyday things, it's very hard to put my head up over the parapet and try to work out what I want.'

She didn't really expect Larry to say anything to this. In fact, she was about to apologise for this great big, uncharacteristic overshare, but then Larry gave a deep and sonorous 'Hmmmmmmmm,' which was very reassuring.

'Dance lessons are going to help,' he said finally.

This wasn't the comment she'd expected, but she managed: 'Do you think so?' in response.

'Yes, because... and I've seen it before... when you dance, you're out of your comfort zone, physically,' Larry said, 'and that mirrors being out of your comfort zone, mentally. So you start to get comfortable with your dance moves, then you grow confident in your new abilities, and then maybe you'll start to grow your mental confidence too. You'll grow more confident about making those big decisions. Instead of not knowing what you want, or worrying that you're not sure if you know, you'll trust yourself.' With a shrug, he added: 'You'll say, "Well, I'm going to try *this*" and you'll feel fine about trying it. Instead of chewing everything over one hundred times and not knowing which way to turn.'

Tess took a sip of her tea, considered his words, and then asked: 'Do you think you should make small changes, step by step? Or do you think you should jump right into a big change?'

'Hmmmmm...' Larry was giving this some thought before answering. Tess moved her forearm into the patch of sunlight on the countertop and felt its warmth. She wondered if she would like to live in a place where it was hot and sunny almost all of the time. Or would she miss all the changes that the seasons brought? Autumn leaves, soft greys and rain, and the anticipation of spring after a dark and everlasting winter.

'It depends,' Larry said finally. 'I suppose if you're making a change like getting in shape, you're going to make small changes every day until you get there. But if you were leaving a relationship, I guess you'd be best packing up and getting on with the move.'

But then he seemed to be thinking it through some more, just as she was.

'But if you really want to get in shape,' he began, 'you could start working out for hours every day. That would get you there real quick. Because telling yourself you'll do thirty minutes every second day, well, you might forget, you might be too tired... so the change might never happen.

'And just say you wanted to fall back in love with your husband again...' he went on, 'that's not going to happen overnight. You're going to have to start doing nice things together, saying good words to one another, talking through the previous hurts and working them out, and finding a way to put that spark, that joy back in. So maybe it's not that straightforward,' he said, topping up their cups of tea. 'But maybe you have to do both – you have to make a big change, a big decision about the direction you're going to go in and then you have to make all the little changes to sustain it.

'But I do know, when people have got into a bad situation, it can take a long time to get out. Longer than anyone expects... but you're making me think now... maybe there's always a way to give it a jumpstart.'

And Tess was thinking along these lines too. Small habit changes were boring... whereas one trip to LA, one adventurous haircut and one completely out-of-the-comfort-zone dance lesson... these things were moving her on dramatically. It did feel as if her thinking could shift. New ideas were popping into her head about all kinds of things. She knew she couldn't go back from this holiday to life as it was before. Big changes had to happen. Some sort of radical open-heart surgery had to be done to her marriage, or it had to come to a dignified close. And her work... Alex... and the other things she was worried about. She had to make fresh approaches. She didn't know what these were yet, but she was going to start working on it all.

'Thanks for listening to me,' she told Larry.

'No problem,' he said with a smile.

'What about you?' she asked. 'Everyone has comfort zones. Where are you out of yours?'

Larry put both hands protectively around his teacup and gave a gentle laugh. 'Well, I am deeply single. So that should tell you something. I have a fifteen-year-old son, who I think I should see more of, but whenever we get together, we seem to get into those nagging kind of fights I remember having with my dad. And it's so painful for both of us that... I'm not in a rush to do it again.'

Tess could only sympathise: 'Ah, fifteen-year-olds... they can be difficult... just wait until they're sixteen... seventeen... and beyond.'

'Yes, I truly cannot wait for that...' Larry said grimly.

'When we were going through the teenage years... I did loads of things wrong,' Tess admitted. 'I should have just tried to enjoy my time with my children, and encourage them in whatever they were into, but instead, I was literally obsessed about what university they were going to go to and what they were going to study. It honestly seemed like the most important thing in the world. As if somehow, if I could get a child into Cambridge or Durham University that would be mission accomplished – I would have done a great job and their lives would be completely sorted.'

Tess had a lump in her throat just thinking about it: 'I must have completely stressed them out and put so much pressure on them to study and do well in their exams. I think I made them feel that not achieving this supposed pinnacle was going to be a total failure. And what happened? Alex had a terrible last year at school and only scraped the results he needed. And even though I had so much sympathy for him and only wanted to help him sort things out... and make it all better... I was also kind of embarrassed. I didn't want to talk to anyone about it.'

And now Tess was thinking about that painful year... nagging and arguing with Alex to study, being blindsided by his terrible prelim results and then scrambling to get him three different tutors to help repair the damage in time.

If she had to point to the times in their marriage when she and Dave had disagreed and not been able to reconcile their differences, then Alex's final year at school and his final year at uni were both big examples. Getting tutors and hovering over Alex to help him through was a waste of time, money and effort as far as Dave was concerned. If Alex wasn't ready to take these things on himself, then he wasn't ready and they couldn't force him. Plus, she remembered bitterly, Dave had thrown in some choice examples of students of his who'd been helped at every step only to fail when they were finally left to do things by themselves.

Dave had thought Alex should somehow be left to pick himself up and make up his own mind about whether he wanted to study or not. Tess had thought a confused eighteen-year-old was in no position to make serious decisions about his future. And if a stressed-out twenty-one-year old needed help to get through his finals, then she was going to give it to him.

'He needs good grades,' Tess had shouted at her husband, 'if he has the grades, he'll be able to do whatever he wants. And he deserves good grades,' she'd also argued, 'he's really bright.'

Unresolved arguments are the drip, drip, drip of corrosive acid on a relationship. And they'd had many unresolved arguments over the years, certainly not just about Alex. Dave had always hoped they would move back to London, whereas Tess was happy in Leamington. Maybe Dave also thought he would become an artist again, whereas Tess was sure he would not. And Dave didn't take her career nearly as seriously as she did. He couldn't understand why she would want to move up from where she was. Plus, he didn't like her parents much – that was another thing – whereas she had loved his, especially his mum, dearly. Natalie... Tess thought now... they hardly ever disagreed about Natalie. They often disagreed *with* Natalie, but their sunny daughter, who managed to be equally close to both parents, was a strong element of family bonding.

'I can't give any advice about parenting or marriages,' Larry said, interrupting her thoughts, 'I'm not good at either of them. But I guess it's like cars...'

'Cars?!' she exclaimed.

'Yeah, you've got to be doing that repair and maintenance stuff all the time: changing the oil, topping up the screen wash, getting new tyres, replacing the brakes, *all the time*... or else you're going to hear a little squeak or a rattle and then the next thing, there's bumping and scraping you just can't ignore and you are either headed for a serious repair or you are going to break down and be sitting on the roadside.'

'Or thinking about trading in for a newer model,' Tess said.

'Exactly!' Larry laughed. 'But just like with cars, we never take the little things seriously enough, we leave it till it's too late and then the whole goddam engine explodes on you. Which is how I would describe my case, by the way. She was throwing my stuff out of the window into the street by the end. It wasn't pretty. No wonder I live by myself. No one would want to go through something like that more than once.'

Tess tried to imagine it. She tried to think of Larry's wife throwing his classic dance shoes out as he hopped about on the pavement, dodging cars, to pick them up. But instead, she saw herself throwing Dave's collection of very shabby old t-shirts out of the bedroom window and onto the lawn, while he stood in the garden in his pyjamas and told her: 'For goodness' sake, Tess, this is a bit of an over-reaction, isn't it?'

'Relationships are hard,' she said, 'except when they're new and then they're really easy and absolute bliss. If only you could bottle that bit and keep it to sprinkle over yourselves when you're old and sour and grumpy with each other.'

'Divorce is hard too,' Larry said. 'I guess you choose your hard.'

That comment stopped Tess in her tracks: '*I guess you choose your hard.*'

This was a fork in the road. She could choose to divorce, or she could choose to make her marriage better. Neither would be easy, but which would make her happier? That was the question she couldn't yet answer.

It was obvious that she couldn't stay still, standing where she was in this horrible, uncertain unhappiness. And it wasn't just her choice. What about Dave? Was he sitting in the summerhouse thinking about this choice too? Would they pick the same path? Which one would make him happier?

She looked up at Larry and realised she didn't want to talk about this any more, so instead, she asked him, 'What else is outside your comfort zone?'

He gave a deep sigh and admitted: 'Finances, I guess... I'm pretty terrible with taxes and savings and 401(k) accounts and all that stuff. And the result is that I'll be teaching my students how to make a tidy move until the day I drop.'

Tess could feel her ever-ready-to-help antennae prick up at this. A tax return was to her what a plié was to Larry – effortless. Surely helping Larry would be about sorting tax returns, timing pension payments for maximum benefit and setting up some low-to-medium risk investments. She could definitely help him with this.

'Larry, have I told you that I'm a trained accountant?' she ventured gently, 'I'm pretty good at all that kind of thing.'

'Well... we can maybe talk about that another day,' Larry conceded, 'but right now, you are playing hooky from my class and it is time for us to get back to the barre.'

And so they did.

And something about their heart-to-heart helped with Tess's dancing. She was finally looser, able to go with the music and throw herself into it more. To music that was faster and louder, they continued to work on arms and shoulders and deep knee bends until Tess's t-shirt was staining with sweat.

'This is so hard,' she complained, but already she could roll, rock and move her arms and shoulders in entirely new and different ways.

'Okay, one last game to end with. You're going to like this, just

...aced on a pretty white and green napkin on a white china plate ...ith gold around the edge. So elegant.

Now, where to sit... where to sit? The front of the café was ...ompletely full, but it looked like there was seating tucked away at ...he back too, so she headed there. The walkway between tables and ...chairs was tight and with her laptop bag over one shoulder and ...handbag over the other, plus coffee mug and plate in her hands, this was trickier than she'd anticipated. Why did they not have waiter service? Why was everyone in England obsessed with standing in front of the cake display and then carrying their food and drink to their table themselves? Was this all about dodging tipping?

'Hey! Careful!'

Her laptop bag clipped some guy on the shoulder.

'I'm so sorry,' she apologised, knowing it was a weighty bag. She over-corrected to the right, which had the entirely unexpected result of sliding her handbag off her right shoulder.

This was a heavy handbag, containing her phone, wallet, ciga-rettes, lighter, lipsticks, the novel she'd stuffed in there at the last moment, not to mention other random items. She had a split second to brace the cheesecake-carrying hand but there was very little she could do. The strap of the bag landed on her forearm and catapulted the cake from the plate. Maybe if it hadn't been sitting on a soft and slidey napkin, she'd have stood a chance. But the cake took off, turned over and landed whipped cream side down on the caramel suede-jacketed arm of a man with his back to her, who had a blue baseball cap jammed down over his head.

The funny thing was, he didn't even need to turn round fo River to see who it was. She just knew. She recognised the hand, th posture, the back of his neck... maybe even the expensive sued sleeve too.

'Oh my gosh, I am so sorry...' she began, placing her coffee cu

trust me – absolutely no freaking out and crying, promise!' Larry encouraged her.

'So, down on your hands and knees, just like a kid. That's all we're trying to do here; remember the looseness and the freedom of movement and sense of play that we had as kids. Okay, so down like this...'

Tess crouched down and then got onto her hands and knees, uneasy about what he was about to ask of her.

'And then you're going to prowl round the space, just like a cat. Not a kitty cat, a big cat... a leopard or a panther, on the prowl. Sometimes your head will be up, you'll be surveying the plain. Sometimes your head will be down as you sniff the ground. You might arch your back now and then and you're definitely going to extend those front legs...' Larry demonstrated each move. 'And light, light... keep it oh-so light on those paws.'

No, Tess wasn't convinced immediately, and her first thought was *I don't want to make a tit of myself.* But the dancing had gone so well that she decided to at least try properly. So she began to stalk around the space on all fours, feeling just a touch more panther-like with every move. Her shoulders were loose, her back arched and stretched and she felt the extension of her arms was graceful. For the first time in a very long time, she was aware of the way she was moving. She was aware of the space she was taking up and she liked the way she felt.

She was aware of her body, all of it, from her fingertips to her toes. And it felt good to move like this.

'Very good, panther lady!' Larry encouraged her, 'and stretch out the back, and arch and stalk. I love it! And we are going to stop right there, on a happy note, and before any sort of spinal disc injury occurs.'

Tess shook her arms and legs loose once again, as instructed.

She was grinning with the pleasure of this achievement, as they arranged the next lesson.

'And what about you make an appointment with me, Larry?' she asked.

'What kind of...?' he began, but then remembered exactly what he had confided in her.

'I can come over and you can make us a cup of beautiful tea and first of all we just talk about where you are financially and where you want to be. That's all. Then after that, we start putting together the paperwork and the online files and then we set up whatever accounts might be needed and make sure you're up to date with...'

To Tess's astonishment, Larry pressed his fingers to his eyes and just shook his head. 'No, no, no...' he insisted. 'No! It's too difficult. It's so messed up... and if I do anything now, I'll trigger back payments I can't possibly afford. No Tess, definitely not.'

And with that he held open his front door and then she was on the other side of it as it shut abruptly.

Comfort zones, she thought as she walked back to River's apartment. This was exactly the same for him as when she had rushed out of her first dance lesson. She hoped he would come to see it that way and realise that she could help him as much as he was helping her.

29

'Can I have a black coffee and the baked strawberry cheesecake please?'

'Do you want extra whipped cream with that?'

River considered... the cake was probably already an entire day's worth of calories, so did it make any sense to stint on the cream? No, probably not. Probably she should just get a little jug of double cream to pour into her coffee as well and be done with it. So far, the day had gone well. She'd walked around Stratford, then she'd found a quiet theatre café where she had worked hard for several very productive hours. Now she was in need of sugar and cream, so she'd come back to the outrageously over-the-top cake café to satisfy the cravings. It was approaching 3.30 p.m., potentially peak cake time, and the café was full.

She declined the tray on offer and took the coffee mug in one hand, plate with cheesecake in the other. Strawberry cheesecake... now that was a slice of New York childhood memories on a plate, right there. And it looked so luscious – the firm creaminess of the cake, shiny, jelly-coated strawberries on top and then that unrestrained dollop of glossy whipped cream. And the whole thing on his table so she could crouch down to scoop up cake, aware of the fuss breaking out around her.

Franklyn, who had clearly been enjoying a slice of forbidden dairy and calorie-laden treat alone in the baseball hat of anonymity, turned round and looked at her with a mix of irritation and surprise.

'Good grief, River,' he exclaimed, but in a stage whisper, obviously anxious for the famous Franklyn voice not to reach too many ears.

'I'm sorry... I had no idea...'

'Damage limitation,' he hissed and passed her several clean napkins, as she remembered how it would drive her wild that whenever they ate out, he would take eight, ten, twelve napkins to the table with every course to clean his hands, his mouth, the table, even the plate sometimes. Not that she wanted to dive deep into Franklyn's weird childhood right now... she'd leave that to Oprah.

River scooped the cake back onto her plate and wiped the floor clean, while Franklyn napkin-ed his jacket sleeve.

'Sit down,' he hissed at her, gesturing to the seat opposite his.

She obeyed but if he was hoping things were just going to quiet right down, so they could have a cosy chat about the delightfulness of English cream cakes, he was mistaken. The Franklyn cat was out of the bag and now there were at least four camera phones pointed in their direction.

River glanced at Franklyn, whose jaw muscles were flexing with tension.

'I'm so sorry,' she whispered, 'I had no idea...' she told him again, feeling somehow guilty, although this was both a coincidence and an accident.

'I think some people had noticed and had started to film before you... landed,' he whispered.

Just that one little scowl of disapproval sent in her direction and she instantly remembered what a diva he was. Yes... it had always been all about Franklyn, which is why she wasn't his wife or the mother of his daughter. She hoped Franklyn loved and appreciated his wife very much.

'Mr Gregory? Is that really you?'

The camera phone holders were coming closer... soon the whole place was going to know he was here and in this narrow space at the back of the café, there was a real danger of crushing in a stampede situation.

'Don't you have security?' she asked in a loud whisper.

'In the car, parked across the street. He's lactose intolerant.'

As Franklyn hunched down into his jacket under his hat, River decided it was time to take action. 'Woah, woah, guys... let's give Mr Gregory a moment now. Thanks so much for your attention,' she said, standing up and not putting her hands in front of the cameras exactly, but sort of steering people back from him.

'Thank you so much. Mr Gregory is so grateful for your attention, but I think he'd quite like to get home and clean up his jacket now. Thanks so much.' This seemed to be working. People were lowering their phones and heading back towards their tables, the space around River and Franklyn was beginning to clear.

'Do you have any cash?' Franklyn asked her.

'You're going to hit me with the bill for this?' River couldn't believe it.

'I only have a card and I don't want to stick around. We need to get out of here.'

This was true. People were still looking their way, fingers itchy to take more footage and get it up out there on social media just as quickly as they could. In fact, that guy over there, he looked as if he was already hitting upload. There was nothing she could do. She was going to be the woman who threw cheesecake at Franklyn Gregory for the rest of all time.

She might have worried about this one a whole lot more if at that moment she hadn't heard a rough gulping, barking sound along with something much more high-pitched as a woman called out in a loud, southern US accent.

'Oh Herb! Herb... what's the matter? Oh, heeelp!'

Both River, Franklyn and every other set of eyes in the café turned to the table in the corner where a portly man and woman were midway through one of the understandably legendary cream gateaux. At first glance it looked as if Herb might be choking, he was deep red in the face and the gulping, barking sounds were coming from his open mouth, but the clutching at his left shoulder rather than his throat was telling a different story.

As River had oh-so-light-heartedly predicted on first setting foot in this place, Herb was the guest who was having an actual real-life coronary.

River had taken full first responder training in the month after her father's heart attack. She knew what she needed to do. And like every other person who has been on the training course, she hoped, prayed, plea-bargained with whoever may possibly be listening up there to please, please, *please* let there be someone else right here in this café who could do this instead of her.

'We need a doctor,' she heard the café owner say behind her, 'is anyone a doctor?' he asked loudly, sounding very anxious.

There was deafening silence. For a moment or two, River heard her blood pulse in her ears with fright, then she breathed in, out, and she couldn't exactly say a sense of calm descended on her, but a sense of clarity, yes.

'Call an ambulance,' River said, turning to the café owner to address him directly, 'can you call it, right now, please?'

'Get your security guy,' she told Franklyn, 'we need this place cleared.'

Then in four purposeful strides she was at Herb's side as he collapsed and fell to the floor.

'Okay, Herb, don't worry, we got this, okay,' she said and marvelled at how calm she sounded. But back at the academy of the arts she had once played a cop, so maybe that was helping.

'Are you a doctor?' his wife asked, her voice shrill and terrified.

'Yes, ma'am,' River said, not because she wanted to lie or big herself up, but because she thought it might help Herb and Mrs Herb right now.

Pushing tables and chairs out of the way, she got Herb flat on the floor. She tipped his head back so his airway could get maximum breath, but he had stopped breathing.

'Herb! Herb!' his wife shrieked. 'Oh my God! He's dead!'

River had a sense of movement behind her.

Another American voice, this one deep and authoritative, was asking people to 'let's give them some space now; yes sir, yes ma'am, if we could ask you to step outside and let us get him the help he needs.' She guessed Franklyn's security guy had arrived.

The clamour and noise rose as people upped and clattered out of the café and then it fell back again. River didn't waste time looking around to see who was left watching, she knew she had to focus on Herb.

He was not breathing. She took hold of his fleshy chin and opened his mouth. There was a smear of cream on his tongue, but it didn't look as if anything was stuck in his throat. He was not choking. He'd had a cardiac arrest.

'Is the ambulance on its way?' she asked, her voice still sounding so much calmer than she felt.

'Yes,' someone replied.

'Okay, we've got to do CPR until it gets here and we may even have to get your defib off the wall. Okay.'

River didn't take her eyes off Herb. He was definitely not breathing. She had not seen his chest rise or fall once in the time she'd been kneeling here. She remembered that cardiac victims might snore or grunt or make the odd breath, but that didn't matter, the important thing was to massage his heart and get the blood moving round his system again because if she could help to pump it round, there was still enough oxygen in his blood to keep his brain and other organs alive.

'Okay, Herb, hello there, I'm River, I'm from LA, California, how about you?'

'We're from Knoxville,' Mrs Herb said, the note of panic still obvious in her voice. 'Knoxville, Tennessee.'

River locked one hand on top of the other, the way she'd been taught in class and located the centre of his chest. The massive heart of Herb. She looked at his face. He was a big guy, a fleshy mountain of a guy. Maybe he was a lovely man who really cared for his kids, maybe he ran a business back in Knoxville... maybe thirty local people relied on Herb to pay their wages every month.

'Right, Herb, let's do this, okay.'

And with all her strength and energy, River began to push down and release right on top of Herb's heart. Just as she'd been taught, she kept the Bee Gees' 'Stayin' Alive' song right at the front of her mind because, apparently, the beat of that song was a really good beat to pump to.

'Ooooh, ooooh, ooooh, ooooh, stayin' alive, stayin' alive,' she whispered under her breath, 'Oooooh, oooh, oooh, oooh, stayin' aliiiiiiiive...'

She wasn't sure what she expected... ideally, for Herb to open his eyes, splutter and jump to life again. But nothing happened at all. Herb lay there, flat out, not moving, not breathing. His wife sobbed and shook right by River's side. And she pumped, ooooh, ooooh, ooooh, ooooh, up and down, up and down. Second after vital second. She tried to picture the blood flowing up Herb's neck and into his brain, bathing all those vital brain cells in oxygen.

The instruction in class had been to keep this up until the ambulance arrived. But after about a minute or so, River realised how much effort this was going to be. Sweat was breaking out on her brow and she was breathing hard. She might have expected her arms to hurt, but in fact, she was feeling the burn in her butt cheeks, with the effort of kneeling by Herb's side and moving herself up and down.

'The person on the other end of the line would like to speak to you.'

The café owner was approaching her with his mobile phone outstretched.

'Put it against my ear,' River instructed, 'I have to keep going with this.'

For a few moments there was a comedy of errors while the café guy tried to hold the phone in the rhythm that River was moving to, but he kept missing.

Finally, River jammed the phone between her ear and her shoulder while she kept pumping.

'Hello, I understand you're carrying out CPR on the patient,' the voice down the line began.

'Any sign of that ambulance yet?' River asked, trying to keep the edge of panic and desperation out of her voice.

'We think it will be with you in around ten minutes.'

In her head, she replied: *Ten minutes! Are you freaking shitting me?*

But Mrs Herb's mascara was running down her face and staining her cream-coloured top. So, that kind of comment was going to help no one.

'Well, the sooner the better,' she said instead.

'The gentleman I was just talking to said there is a defibrillator in the café; the patient's best chance for survival is for you to attach the defibrillator, let it assess his heart rhythm and shock if required. I understand you're a doctor.'

River considered the eyes on her, Mrs Herb's in particular, and knew that loudly declaring 'no, I'm not a doctor' would also not be helpful right now. But then neither would it be helpful if everyone, including the ambulance dispatch operator, assumed she knew how to work a machine that was going to deliver a huge electric shock. Jeeeeeeeeesuzzz.

'Yes... of literature,' she said in as low a voice as possible, hoping that the voice at the other end of the phone could hear. This wasn't true either, she was a BA, but it was the only way she could think of to debunk the doctor idea without causing mass panic.

'I see, madam. But you've had first aid training?'

'I have... the works.'

'Okay, don't stop the heart massage. Ask someone to bring the defib over and open it up for you. Then give the patient two rescue breaths, several compressions and attach the pads.'

'Okay, okay...' River realised she was at risk of being overwhelmed with instructions. 'I'm going to put the phone down now, but stay there, okay? Please stay there...'

The defib was summoned and the café owner brought it over and opened it up. Once the 'on' button was pressed, a loud, commanding robot-lady voice told her to attach the sticky pads to the side of the patient's chest.

River worried that Mrs Herb was going to go to pieces now that things were looking so serious, but actually Mrs Herb seemed to perk up at the sight of the defib.

'I'm River, what's your name?' River asked Mrs Herb.

'Evelyn.'

'Okay, Evelyn,' River said, 'I'm going to open Herb's mouth and give him two big breaths of air, then I'm going to pump those round and we're going to ask the machine if he needs a shock. Are you going to be okay with that?'

Evelyn nodded and wiped at her eyes, making the mascara smudge worse.

River tipped Herb's head back, pinched his nose closed and then took a deep breath and, her lips over Herb's, she blew hard into his mouth. It was a very strange experience, warm and not unlike a weird kiss. But she didn't have time to think about it because he needed a second breath into his lungs and then more compressions, compressions.

River undid the buttons on Herb's shirt, revealing a large pinkish chest, which, mercifully, only had an outcrop of sparse hair around his big pink nipples. She'd heard about people having to shave chests before putting on the defib pads. The machine actually came with a razor.

It was the work of a few fiddly moments to put the sticky pads in place as instructed by the calm robot-lady in the machine.

'Stand clear!' robot-lady commanded, loud and urgent, and much to River's surprise. She'd expected to be given a reading and to be told to press the shock button... but clearly this was an automatic model.

She did a backwards crawl away from Herb and urged Evelyn to do the same. Evelyn's hands were up over her face and she looked as terrified as River felt. What if she'd made a mistake... hadn't put the pads in the right place, hadn't done the compressions quickly enough? She could not bear for Herb to die on her.

The machine let out a truly terrifying, high-pitched zaaaaaaaaap, and Herb bounced up and down against the floor. No one moved, spoke, or even breathed in the moment that followed. All the air, all momentum left the room and everyone stared at the big American guy on the floor, willing him back to life.

'Stand clear!' robot-lady urged again and the machine whirred with the effort of charging up once more.

Evelyn began to cry once again and River was tempted to join her.

The enormous zaaaap sound zinged through the air for a second time and Herb arced up and down. Once again, total silence in the room. And then noisy, throaty, full of phlegm... Herb drew a breath.

'Continue compression!' the machine barked and as River leaned forward to begin the task again, the café door opened and paramedics in green overalls, bearing bags full of equipment, burst in.

'Over here! Over here!' River heard herself shout and at last she was able to step back and hand over to people who really knew what they were doing.

'How many shocks has he had?' one of the men in green turned to ask her.

'Two and we just heard him take a breath.'

'That's good, all good...'

An oxygen mask went over Herb's face. An IV drip went into his arm, and a stethoscope went over his heart.

'Yes, you've got it beating again, well done,' the paramedic declared and there was a cheering burst of applause. River could feel tears of relief forming in her eyes. *Go Herb*, she thought, *I hope you get a few more trips around the block. Jeeeeeeeeez.* She'd saved his life, for now anyway. She'd CPR-ed him back.

And then... oh God... tears spilling on to her cheeks, she immediately thought of the life she had not been able to save. If only it could be so obvious when people need CPR on their metaphorical hearts.

The paramedics were fast and slick. They had both Herb and Evelyn's names within moments, then they were bundling Herb onto a blanket and up onto a stretcher. Soon he was out of the café door and into the back of the ambulance with his wife by his side.

And everyone who was left in the café could breathe a huge, collective sigh of relief.

'You did real good, kid.'

River heard that familiar voice behind her shoulder. Had the ambulance guys even noticed that Franklyn Gregory was in the café? She didn't think they had. And she guessed they'd have been too busy and too professional to care.

'Yeah...' she said, quickly wiping her face and turning to look at him. 'I did!'

'Can I get you a drink? Or get you a ride? Or buy you a cream cake?' he asked.

'On the house, ma'am,' the owner added immediately.

'No, thanks,' River replied. She was feeling unusually calm again, but strangely hollowed out and now those tears were starting to fall again, even though she really didn't want them to.

'Sorry about your jacket,' she told Franklyn. 'And the 2.4 million views that's going to get.'

He shook his head. 'That doesn't seem like anything important now.'

He passed her some napkins and put an arm around her shoulders as she tried to dry her face again.

'No,' River agreed. 'I'm fine, I'm fine,' she insisted, 'just adrenaline, I guess. You need to learn how to do CPR. And after this, you're definitely coming to my party.'

Franklyn nodded: 'Okay, it's a deal.'

30

'Hello? Hi... you don't know me, I'm Tess Simpson, I'm a friend of River Romero who lives in number 44.'

The steel-haired gentleman who'd opened this door did not look very pleased to see her.

'I know there's been an on-going situation with the pool, so I promised River that I would talk to all the neighbours and work towards sorting it out. I work in finance, so I'm used to this kind of thing.' Tess was smiling hard and using her breezy I'm-so-on-your-side voice.

'I'd be happy to start paying the monthly maintenance again, but I'm not paying the fee to do the deep clean. That was all because of that situation with Mrs Papadoupolis...'

'Yes.' Tess was keen to cut that off, she'd heard this version of the story several times already. Mrs P had flirted with the pool boy, *allegedly*, Mr P had freaked out and ordered said pool boy off the premises and that's when the argument with the maintenance company had all begun.

'Okay.' Tess held up a small notebook and made a tick on her list. 'You might like to know that so far, everyone agrees with you.

They're happy to re-start monthly payments and have a pool again, but they don't think it's fair to foot the bill for the clean-up.'

'Yeah... but Mr P won't pay for the clean-up, so it is what it is,' he shrugged his shoulders. 'No pool.'

'Well, I'm going to try and make progress on the cleaning,' Tess told him. 'So hopefully we can get to a place where we can re-start monthly payments and all enjoy a pool again.'

'Good luck with that,' the man said and abruptly closed the door.

Undeterred, Tess moved on to the next address. She was glad she'd had the idea of doing this at 8 a.m.: almost everyone was in, but they didn't want to talk for long, as they had their full days ahead. What she'd told the previous guy was true; everyone felt the same. If Mr and Mrs P could just get over their differences and pay up for the deep clean, then the usual pool service could resume.

The problem was, Tess had broached the topic with Mr P yesterday evening and it hadn't gone well. Mrs P had now moved out (no word if the pool boy was still involved) and Mr P was clearly still very bitter. But Tess had decided, once she'd finished her questionnaire of the building's residents that she would go and take a much closer look at the pool.

* * *

When she went down and stood beside it, the apartment's pool was about eight metres long and five metres wide. There was no water in it and the bottom sloped from a depth of maybe a metre at the shallow end to two metres at the deep end. Not being much of a swimmer, Tess couldn't tell if that was deep enough to dive in or not. The bottom of the pool was full of debris: dried leaves, white plastic bags, takeaway cups, straws, scrunched-up packaging and paper. It was a mess, yes, but because of the dry LA climate, really not that much of a mess.

She couldn't help feeling that everyone was being a bit of a baby about it all. Rubber gloves, bin bags, a broom, some cleaning fluid and a hose were really all that were going to be needed here. And all of those things, bar the hose, were in River's apartment. Surely there must be some sort of hose somewhere around the pool, otherwise how would they fill the thing?

Why on earth would *she* don rubber gloves and clean out the apartment pool? Because she wanted to sit poolside, maybe more than anyone else in the whole building. She wanted to lie on a sun lounger, sipping at a cocktail and cooling herself in the water every so often. It was part of the LA dream she'd been sold. It was one of the things that had brought her over here. The reason there was a patterned, silky kimono in her luggage. And surely she was just a little concerted effort away from making it happen? So off she went for the gloves, broom, liquid soap and bin bags.

It was hot, of course, even by 10 a.m. But she had quickly started to make progress. The debris was almost entirely bagged up and now she just had to work out how to sluice the pool with water so she could scrub at the blue-painted concrete with soap and the broom.

'Tess, is that you down there?'

She looked up to see Larry leaning over his balcony and gave him a wave. 'Yes, hi!'

'What in the world...?'

'If I don't get in here and clean it, I'm never going to have a pool to sit beside for my holiday.'

Larry checked his watch and then told her he would be right down to help.

'You don't have to...'

'Yes, I think I do.'

And within five minutes, he was also in the pool with a broom and a bucket. He found the hose, connected it up, and wet the bottom and sides of the pool thoroughly so that their soapy brushes would glide along more easily. And as they scrubbed, they fell to talking about the things that Larry had so firmly insisted he didn't want to talk about.

'I'm sorry I flipped out on you the other day,' he said, 'and you were completely right, I reacted about the whole money thing in exactly the same way you reacted that first dance lesson.'

'Complete freak out because we were right out of our comfort zones?' she asked, scrubbing hard at a stubborn brown stain.

'I guess. And you have come back and made progress, which is really impressive. So I need to do the same... man up about my taxes.'

Tess looked up and gave him a smile then she turned her eyes back to brushing. She knew that for some people, it was easier to talk when they were doing something and not being eyeballed.

'I haven't properly filed taxes for about three years,' he admitted softly. 'I have a part-time job, three days a week, so I've just let my employer file for me and all the dance lessons I've done around that... well, it's been undeclared.'

'Okay,' Tess said.

'I would love to sort all this out, you know, but I'm terrified I'll land myself in a much bigger mess. I can't afford to pay back taxes.'

'Okay,' she said again, 'you need to believe me that I've heard much worse. It sometimes helps people to know that most tax offices are very busy chasing companies for millions of dollars in unpaid taxes and, as long as you are really straight with them, they are quite forgiving of people who owe a few thousand... or even a few hundred. You just have to explain it honestly, in the right way, and arrange a manageable payment plan.'

Larry nodded and even looked a little bit hopeful, which made

Tess want to hug him. Why did people get so stressed and upset about this stuff, when it was usually very straightforward to put it right? She put the blame on trauma at an early age from maths lessons.

'What about your pension plan... I think that's a 401(k) account in the States?'

He gave a dismissive wave and let out a sigh: 'No idea... I've had jobs in the past, money must have been paid in... but it won't be anything like enough...' he admitted. 'I don't know what I can do about that.'

'Let me do some research,' she offered, 'sometimes you can pay money into your pension and reduce your tax bill... or pay money to a charity and reduce your tax bill. Sometimes tax can be deferred and paid into your pension over a few years instead. All kinds of things can get sorted if you just bring in the right person – and that's me – to take a look.'

'I'm guessing you're expensive, though,' Larry said, 'a proper big company accountant an' all.'

'Larry!' she exclaimed. 'We're friends, and this will probably take me a solid afternoon to work out. You can treat me to a fish taco when it's done. How about that?'

'Tess, you can't sort out three years of unpaid taxes and a pension for a fish taco!'

'Oh, yes I can, especially for the person who is finally letting my dream of sipping cocktails beside my pool come true.'

When all the scrubbing and brushing was done, Larry turned on the hose and they blasted the inside of the pool with water. Some patches needed to be scrubbed again, so they got down to work until it was all looking properly, beautifully blue. The deck and courtyard all around the pool were scrubbed and hosed clean too and Tess decided, expense be damned, when this work was done, she would go online and order two sun loungers, two side tables for drinks and, heck, two fresh potted plants while she was at it.

'Shall I make you tea when we're done?' Larry asked. 'And start to give you the details you need?'

'Sounds like a plan.'

'Not that you need to do this today... or in fact anytime soon.'

'Today sounds like a good day to start.'

'But you might have plans,' he protested.

'Yup, I do have plans,' she said, 'but I can still fit you and your tea and your tax details in, so don't worry about it.'

'You really are a good person,' he said, leaning on his brush for a moment and meeting her eyes, 'look at everything you've done here. We're going to get our pool back and it wasn't even that hard. Just needed someone to talk to folks and then roll their sleeves up.'

'Ha...' the truth of this struck her, 'that's almost always the way, Larry,' she said.

'What are your plans after our tea?' he asked.

'Walk the dogs, and then I'm going to take the car to the Getty Center and see some big art in a properly swanky location.'

She didn't add what her other definite plan for the day was: talk to Alex. Actually, properly get him on the phone and talk. She was going to bug him with calls and messages until he finally picked up, she wasn't taking no for an answer. His breezy texts just didn't seem quite right to her. They were sent at odd times of day for someone with an office job. Yes, he kept telling her that everything was fine, but she had to find out how things really were.

31

River was getting much better at English country lane driving. She was heading to a little town called Kenilworth that Dave had recommended. He'd told her to sit in a beer garden, under a tree, drinking chilled, alcohol-free cider and write and write and write. When she got bored, she could walk around the village and through its big green park spaces and then she could settle down in another pub and write and write some more. Now she was bowling down the kind of English country roads she'd dreamed of... oak trees, beech trees, luscious hedge greenery flashing past her window. And she had two things playing. Her laptop was reading out an audio version of *The Merchant of Venice*, while her phone blasted her latest favourite playlist at her from the car speakers.

So her mind was hopping from Tupac and Dr Dre to Shylock and revenge. River knew it was always good to mix ideas, create mind cocktails because that was how new ideas formed. So the music blasted, the play's words rang out and the luscious English green went by as she moved the car from 45 mph to 56, baby, 56 mph. In California, she'd be breaking the law.

Who do we still want revenge on, she asked herself? Who will we feel it's okay to have levelled by the end of the play? Who is it okay to hate, today, right here, right now?

Tupac's next song was playing and out came his angry words about: 'this white man's world.'

The Shylock character can't be Jewish, or black or any other ethnic minority, Shylock has to be a rich, old, wasp *white guy*, it occurred to her. And he can try to explain himself to us, and we can feel nothing but sympathy for his lovely daughter, but when we take away his wealth at the end, it feels right. It's a satisfying ending. So that means everyone else in the film is not rich-white-old; they're young/poor/ black/ Latino/ disabled/ ethnic minority/ other... and that's how we make *The Merchant of Venice* work and be relevant and be something the kids can get right behind today.

Yes! Yes! Yeeeeees! River honked the horn several times with delight, startling a small group of cows. She couldn't wait to be in the pub with her chilled drink tackling this new angle on the rewrite. This would work. This was the key. This was finally how she would make this script sing!

And her first thought was not telling Philip and explaining how this was finally the breakthrough she'd been waiting for... her first thought was telling Dave, which she had to admit was a little weird. But she'd enjoyed every one of their coffees and dinners so far. It was so nice to have someone to talk all the creative dilemmas through with. He was a good listener and a good guy, and he seemed to understand. She would make him another dinner and they'd sit and talk rich-old-white-guy Shylock over with wine, coffee and cigarettes. And she'd ask him how his studio struggles were going. Was he winning? Was he finally tapping into his creativity? Maybe he would even let her see some of his work. To date, he'd been as secretive about what was going on in his studio as she had been about what she was tapping into her laptop.

'I'll show you mine when you're ready to read me yours,' he'd joked the last time they'd spoken about this.

And another thing... she was going to ask him to move back into his own house. It just seemed too ridiculous that a man with a broken ankle, on crutches, was living and working in a shed at the bottom of his garden when she had his entire, beautiful four-bedroomed house to herself. Plus it had rained heavily last night and she wondered if his garden room was totally watertight.

There was nothing, absolutely nothing ulterior about asking him to move back in. And she was sure he wouldn't read anything into it either. They were friends in art. Discussing art, creating art, talking late into the night about art, enjoying the thrill of being alive and creating work, that's what this was about. And it was work that required thought and effort, but that they could one day stand back and be proud of... well, that was the aim.

Yes, she was already planning what to make for dinner and what they would drink alongside it. She definitely wanted Dave to show her his art.

* * *

As Tess drove into the car park of the Getty Center, she remembered why she'd thought LA would be amazing to visit. These buildings were stunning; the setting was stunning and the blue sky and bright sun all around made her heart soar.

She parked up. This had been a drive along relatively quiet 'freeways' and not quite as much of a driving-a-new-car trauma as she'd expected. She checked herself in the car mirror. Hair, still blonde, still curled, still pink. She liked her breezy white blouse, tucked into a linen pencil skirt that she was wearing with wedgy espadrilles. She had earrings in and make-up on. She'd had time...

time to prep herself, time to fuss, time to accessorise with her sunglasses, her lipstick and her nice earrings.

And now she went into the modern building and was greeted like a friend (the Californian way). She bought the guidebook, but declined the headphones, and began to walk around the stunning rooms, slowly taking in every fabulous painting and sculpture... drinking it all in.

She looked at the views out of the huge glass windows almost as much as she looked at the art. She took her time. Sitting down on the benches, reading the guidebooks and really looking. And after an hour or so in the gallery, Tess found the Cézanne painting she'd been looking for and sat quietly in front of it.

When she'd first met Dave at a student friend's party, they'd drunk truly rank cider and talked about this very painting, Still Life with Apples. He was weirdly impressed that even though she was studying accountancy, she knew all about it.

And now, sitting here looking at it in the flesh, all these years later, she couldn't help thinking back to the lives she thought they might have when she married Dave. She thought they would stay in London and that they would work hard enough and have the kind of success that would bring them one of those houses... up a quiet street in Kensington: red brick, two storeys, just the right size for a small family. She'd thought he would be an artist... and a successful one. Someone who got her invited to glamorous gallery openings at the Serpentine... or to see Saatchi's latest exhibitions.

But it had got too hard, too hard for her to carve a career path in London with talented sharks at every turn, especially when she wanted to get off the career treadmill, at least for a little bit, to have children. So when a comfortable, but far less glamorous, opportunity had come up in the 'sticks' of Leamington, she'd not exactly jumped at it, but she'd persuaded herself it was the right thing to do. And Dave might like to say he gave up art when they moved up there and he took the school job to give them stability during her maternity years... but really, he'd given up on art some time before that. And moving to Leamington was about moving away from the crowd that he was ruthlessly comparing himself to, and considering himself as a failure.

Why had those guys had so much success when he'd fallen away? Out loud, she would say: 'Oh art, it's so subjective, his things weren't quite the right fit, the group he was with... they were moving in a different direction...' But really, in her heart, she believed it was because he just didn't want it as much as they did. He wasn't as obsessed with creating or as hungry for success as the others had been then and still were now. Occasionally, when she came across a Van Saint interview, she couldn't believe how he still managed to pull off such outward cool with the ruthless drive for money and success that she remembered even back when he was starting out. Dave had always been so much more relaxed, more fun, more easy-going and while that made him a lovely person to be around, it probably didn't make him a great artist.

Was he disappointed in himself? She wasn't sure. Maybe this desire to paint, mentioned every summer, meant that he was. She wondered how he was finding the painting... when she asked on their calls, he simply told her, 'Fine, fine, going well.' No further details.

Yes, Dave was easy-going, warm natured... the fun person in their relationship, while she picked up the organising, the running and the managing, not to mention earning the significantly bigger salary. His seven-week summer holidays... staring out of an art gallery window at an LA landscape shimmering in the late after-noon haze, she realised how jealous she was of his long and languid summers.

He was Mr Fun and she was Mrs Do Everything Else. That's how the chips had fallen in their marriage. And now that she didn't have him around, she realised that she was relaxing... easing out from under her burden of responsibilities and trying to work out what *she* liked doing and how to properly take care of all aspects of *her* life.

Are we going to get divorced? She asked herself the swift, sharp question, probing the tender spot she kept coming back to.

Probably.

When she came back from her trip that was probably the most likely answer. Dragging this weary, struggling marriage on through more years filled with nothing but effort... she didn't want to do that. The thought of packing up and leaving Ambleside, the thought of no more 'the four of us' – family holidays, family Christmases, family dinners even – that was all going to be unbearably hard. But surely better than carrying around resentment for her husband and for the marriage they should have had in her mind every single day for the rest of her life?

Somehow, she would find the courage and the strength to start afresh.

Long minutes passed as she stared at the Cézanne. She tried to just enjoy it, let it flood her mind, calm her feelings. But finally, she couldn't shake off all the thoughts in her head, so she went in search of the gallery's café.

* * *

Rice salad and green tea. This was the kind of thing you ate and drank when you were a gallery goer in LA. She scrolled through her phone as she ate. There was Natalie, taking unbelievably pretty pictures of herself and the new boyfriend against a background of dazzling blue sky. Dave had even posted a pic or two of the roses blooming in the garden, tagging her '@Tess will want to see these'. Was that River? Tess looked beyond the roses and saw an elegant woman with a mane of dark hair sitting at the table on Tess's deck-ing. There were two coffee cups on the table... she hadn't consid-ered that River and Dave might hang out together. She scrolled on... friends were posting summer holiday snaps, homemade birthday cakes, drinks in the garden, brand-new shoes. And there in her messages queue was all that Alex was going to give her right now:

All fine with me Mum, don't worry 😃

She still couldn't get him on the phone. It didn't matter when she phoned, he just didn't answer.

She happened to look up and, at a distance of several tables away, there was a tall, rangy man in horn-rimmed glasses, carrying a tray with a plate of food, who was looking at her. He smiled and approached. Then he seemed to stop and stare again. She smiled back, so again he came closer, still smiling and now nodding at her.

'Oh, my goodness,' he said, as he got to within a few feet of her table, 'you must think I'm a crazy guy. I'm not wearing the right glasses and I thought you were someone I knew. So I didn't want to be rude and not say hello, but now that I'm here, I realise I don't know you. Truly a senior moment, or at least a middle-aged one!'

This made Tess laugh.

'Oh, don't worry, we've all done it,' she said, 'walked straight past our closest friend and run across the street to accost total strangers.'

'Really? It's not just me then? And my goodness, you seem to be English. You're a long way from home.'

'Yes... I am.'

It wasn't something Tess would have done before... but maybe because she was in LA... maybe because her hair was now blonde and pink (even if she kept forgetting and would get a fresh shock every time she approached a mirror), maybe because she'd just looked through all those reminders of home and family and felt a pang of loneliness, she asked the friendly looking man with the horn-rimmed specs, bald head and almost quite tweedy jacket if he would like to sit down at her table.

And Nathan Ward, as it turned out he was called, was very happy to accept her offer. He pulled out the chair opposite hers and sat down, tucking his long legs under the table and arranging his long arms on either side of his tray. And Tess immediately had a sense that this lunch with a stranger was going to be delightful. She instantly liked Nathan and after they'd talked about the gallery and what they'd enjoyed looking at, the conversation got a little more personal. It turned out he was a professor of economics at UCLA, his two children were just a little older than Tess's, and unprompted, he added the detail that he and his wife had divorced two years ago.

'Oh… gosh,' Tess said and paused for a moment. 'I'm never quite sure what the right response to that is,' she admitted. 'Should it be, I'm sorry, because everyone hopes marriages will be happy ever after, or should it be well done for having the courage to move out and move on, because everyone I know who got divorced is glad they did it?'

'Ah well… and sorry to drop the divorce bomb,' he began, with an apologetic smile, then looked down at his tuna salad. 'I suppose it's a mix of the two. Sometimes, I'm truly sorry, and sometimes I'm truly glad…' he looked up at Tess again, 'and that is the truth of it. I have very mixed feelings. But my wife, ex-wife,' he corrected himself, 'she seems to be just fine. I suspect women, or some women, are better at adjusting and just coping with things. Whereas I am getting used to it… slowly. I suppose I may spend a little too much time by myself. And, apologies, I now seem to be at the 'pouring out my troubles to strangers' stage.'

Once again, Nathan was making her smile. 'It's fine, honestly,' she assured him. 'I've spent a lot of time on my own too, recently. And it's nice to talk.'

She couldn't resist asking him about online dating. 'Is that something you do? Does that make life any easier... or maybe it's worse?'

'Online dating?' he exclaimed, 'Well, my kids keep talking about this and I think they've even created a profile for me. But, that would quite frankly scare the beejeezus out of me. "I'm not ready," I keep telling them. I am definitely not ready. In truth, I am enjoying being by myself... it feels like a period of peace, a truce after a long and very draining war.'

'Fair enough,' Tess told him. *A long and draining war...* that's not what she and Dave were going through... in fact, it was more like a long and draining truce. And if her marriage ended, no, she wouldn't want to rush into another relationship, but she'd certainly want to see what online dating was all about. Surely that was one of the upsides of being divorced? Finally there was a hope of resuscitating your sex life.

Their conversation moved on to work, and she talked about her job a little. Maybe because she didn't know him at all... and he was such a careful listener, she confided about the promotion that didn't happen, and now this sabbatical when she was supposed to work out a new path for herself, not to mention the other 'mid-lifers' at the company.

'Do you enjoy teaching?' she asked him. 'I always imagine it must be rewarding to be involved with young people. I'd love to find a way to do something like that, at least some of the time.'

'Ah ha! Be careful what you wish for,' he replied, pushing his glasses up over the bridge of his nose. 'Young people are quite the challenge, as I'm sure you know. But yes, it is rewarding. And some of them even, very occasionally, say nice things about what I've taught them.'

They ordered coffees and talked on about all kinds of things including River's chaotic apartment, and the saga of the pool... until Tess felt it was probably appropriate to go. But there wasn't any doubt in her mind that she would like to meet Nathan again. And as she was wondering how to ask, without wanting it to be mistaken for anything it was not, he reached into a pocket and brought out a little card.

'This is old-fashioned, I know, giving you my card. But we can do the modern version and make contact on LinkedIn too... if you'd like, obviously.'

She thought he flushed up ever so slightly at those words.

'Oh, yes, I would like that,' she said, taking the card from him.

'We're always looking for guest lecturers,' he said, 'maybe there's an aspect of accounting, of personal finance, or company finance that you'd like to talk to my students about. Have a think about that and maybe we could meet up a little further into your LA adventure and talk it through? And I might have a colleague who could share some research with you for your work project... if that might be helpful.'

She liked the shy hesitancy with which he suggested this.

'Yeah... I'd really like all of that,' she assured him, 'it's been lovely to meet you and, yes, I'd really like to meet again and talk about that. Guest lecture?' She felt a little thrill; no one had ever suggested her for such a thing before. 'I'd be honoured.'

As Tess walked out of the café, she could almost feel the warmth of Nathan's look on her back as she held his card very carefully in her hand.

32

The Ambleside garden party was taking on a life of its own, as River began to realise she had created a monster. There was the stress of the A-list guests: Franklyn, of course, his wife and possibly his daughter too, then producer Phillip and the one or two friends he was bringing along. Then, foolishly, she'd messaged Franklyn and told him to invite some of his cast. And there were now 'a handful' of them coming too.

Dave had invited the entire circle of old art school friends, who'd been delighted to hear from him and had agreed to come – including Van Saint – plus their wives, girlfriends and plus ones. And then there were regular friends Dave thought he should invite, and the neighbours who lived in the even larger house on the other side of the road... because when you were having a garden party, it was only polite to invite the neighbours, apparently. So now, there were about forty-five people coming.

Forty-five people! River couldn't think when she had last entertained even two people in her own place. At first, foolishly, she had thought it would be easy enough: order booze, order some food. But it out to be unbelievably complex. You had to have glasses and plates and cutlery, because there was no way Dave was going to let her use Tess's prized items from the kitchen. You had to have somewhere to cook and heat this food and lay it out. You had to think about all these endless details: napkins and toilets, sauces and rubbish collection. Chairs? Where would she get enough chairs from so that forty-five people could park their butts? And what if it rained? The weather over the past few days had been freaking grey and cold and damp, more like fall in New York than any kind of summer she had experienced.

River found herself looking at the weather app on her phone literally every five minutes, but that was no help because for the evening of the party, it just displayed half a cloud and half a sun and a small outline of a raindrop... so really what did that mean? That all England's weather was going to happen all at once that night?

If she had hoped to get some help from Dave, she was sorely mistaken. Dave only did two things now: he stayed in his shed and painted, no doubt because he was feeling the intense pressure of his old art friends descending on him and wanting to see his new work, or he hobbled up and down the lawn, putting more weight on the ankle than he probably should, mowing the grass.

In fact, she had got so annoyed about this, that she had shot out of the kitchen and begun to shout at Dave in the middle of the lawn: 'It's not just about grass, you know!' she'd yelled.

Over the din of the lawnmower, he had no idea what she was saying. But he could see that she was upset, so he'd cut the engine in order to listen, though he may have regretted that when the full flow of her furious words hit him face on.

'What is all this with the freaking grass cutting?' she'd yelled. 'There are at least forty-five people, forty-five very important people who are going to be here in just eight days' time. There is a freak of a lot to do. Grass... grass is just something you stand on. No one cares. No one gives a shit if it's one inch long or three inches long. It literally makes no difference. But if there isn't enough booze, or enough food, or anywhere to sit or anywhere to pee then that makes a difference. This is Hollywood! These are Hollywood people. This is Franklyn freaking Gregory. You think he's going to come somewhere without any freaking chairs? Where am I going to get chairs, and napkins, and enough glasses? How big is the barbeque? Can you make fifteen burgers at a time? Where will I keep fifty bottles of wine and hundreds of bottles of beer cold? These are the important things.'

As Dave stood stock still and silent in the face of this onslaught, River wondered what he was thinking. Maybe he was considering that she had a point, maybe he was missing his wife. Perfect, freaking Tess and her multi-talented organisational skills that clearly kept this house and garden together.

'I suppose you're used to your wife just sorting everything out,' she had stormed, 'well, guess what, buddy? You don't get to invite twenty-five of *your* friends over and all you do is cut the grass. Maybe you got away with that crap with your wife – who, believe me, would not have been very impressed – but you do not get away with that crap with me. We are hosting this party, we have to get our shit together, *together!*'

Two togethers back to back, she couldn't help noticing, jeez, what terrible sentence structure. Then she tried to turn on her heel, but cork wedges and newly cut lawn do not make for a smooth heel turn. So she did a half-stumble instead and then stomped away.

She had to get back to her desk, back to her script. But now, sitting at her laptop again, her head was blazing. How to concentrate... how to get calm after all this upset?

* * *

Finally, in between bursts of scriptwriting, because Phillip was now demanding to see scenes and she had to get something to him – even though she was re-writing everything in line with her rich-old-white-guys idea – River wrote a list, to stop herself from going crazy.

Party priorities:
Booze – beer, wine, orange juice and oranges for sangria, vodka, tonic, limes, Coke
Food – hamburgers and vegan hamburgers for BBQ, burger buns, chopped lettuce, chopped tomatoes, pizzas to go in oven
Chairs – rent
Trestle table – rent
Glasses – rent
Paper plates, bamboo cutlery, paper napkins, bin bags, two big bins and ice to keep booze cool – buy

There. That wasn't so hard now, was it? She picked up her phone and searched for a place to order the rental items.

It was nearly four hours later when her phone beeped with a text:

I am mixing contrite cocktails in the kitchen. Would you like one?

Gimme five. And thank you.

Is that five minutes or five cocktails?

Maybe both.

When she'd put her last sentence in place for the day, she went down to the kitchen to see Dave. It sounded as if he may have forgiven her, but she was still prepared to make another one of her most humble apologies.

'I shouldn't have said those things,' she began, as soon as she walked into the room, 'I was stressing. I've never planned a party like this before... a grown-up party. I was rude and I'm sorry.'

Dave reached over and put something cloudy and lime-scented with sprigs of mint into her hand. At first, he'd insisted when he'd moved back into the house that he still cook in the summerhouse to be out of her way. But she'd told him she only spent half an hour in the kitchen anyway, so he'd given in and now he was in the kitchen for at least an hour every evening, making simple meals and, tonight, elaborate cocktails.

'No, River,' he began, 'I should be apologising.'

This took her by surprise.

'What you said was completely true. I always leave this kind of thing to Tess. In fact, I leave all kinds of things to Tess. Important stuff... boring stuff... admin stuff... she takes care of a lot for us.'

What he didn't say was that Tess loved being the organisational person. She was so into details and sorting things out when he was not. Like River, he wanted to go with the flow, be spontaneous, muddle through... let things 'sort themselves out'. But perhaps he'd underestimated the stress involved in being the details person. Perhaps Tess would have appreciated more support.

'But,' he said to River now, 'what do we need to do to get this party on the road?'

'I've ordered chairs and glasses,' she said, pulling up a seat at the kitchen counter and taking a big slug of the drink. 'I'm guessing we could drive to the supermarket and buy food and booze and paper plates there...'

'Absolutely,' Dave agreed. 'I'll clean up some of the big rubber tubs we have in the garage and we'll fill them with water and ice to keep the booze cold.'

'Good idea.'

'And what about loads of fairy lights?' Dave suggested. 'Why don't I buy lots of ropes of them to light the garden with? Logs for the chimenea, of course...'

'Are you starting to get excited?' River asked, making eye contact over the kitchen counter.

'Haven't been so excited for years,' he said with a smile and held her look. Yes... for all sorts of reasons, he hadn't felt so excited for years – and one of those reasons was this lovely and free-spirited woman who was once again hanging out with him and enjoying his company.

33

LA was opening out to Tess, now that she was less worried about driving away from her Studio City base. She'd taken the dogs out hiking into the hills several times. She'd visited two more major art galleries and she'd made a shopping trip to the famous Rodeo Drive, where she'd been in the mood to splurge on something memorable. She'd wanted to mark her trip, her freedom, her independence with a new watch, maybe, or a pair of posh earrings. But in fact, the delightfully knowledgeable sales assistants in Ralph Lauren and Banana Republic had persuaded her to part with significant amounts of cash on nine pieces of wardrobe hardware that she knew were going to completely change her style. She now owned two new work jackets that fitted like a dream, and were soft, comfortable and not too politician-y, three new cotton-silk mix blouses that she loved everything about, one foxy navy gabardine pencil skirt and the pair of black, slim-cut trousers that you search for your entire working life. And just to tip the shopping over into the extravagance she'd wanted, she'd also bought a pair of higher-than-usual camel-coloured heels and the kind of casual lightweight coat that keeps you warm, and keeps the rain off, but still proclaims: 'I understand fashion and have a finger on the pulse, but I don't take it too seriously.'

Back at the apartment, the pool had been filled and she'd already enjoyed her first swim and her first afternoon on the sun lounger she'd installed. But some of the best fun was still to be had in the twice-a-week sessions in Larry's apartment where he was stretching her, flexing her and making her think about her body and how she moved it in a way she had never done before.

As he'd said, the effect carried on long after class. When she walked down a staircase, when she sat in a chair, when she turned to speak to someone, she brought awareness to what she was doing physically as well as mentally.

He was helping her to relax and trust her body and it really did help her to relax and trust herself mentally too. She'd been so stiff and so closed off before.

'English weather, English repression, and office life at a desk,' Larry had suggested, showing her how to be at ease when she stood: shoulders dropped, arms by her sides not crossed or clasped defensively in front of her. Then got her to stand tall, to breathe, to hold her head lightly and enjoy all these different postures.

And now, after spending lessons on arm movements, lessons on leg stretches, lessons on torso and shoulder bends and turns, he was getting her to put them all together and in a work of clever dance-teacher alchemy, all the small practised moves were forming what he'd had in mind all along – the Argentinian tango.

'You're kidding me!' Tess had exclaimed. 'Me? Dance the tango? Ha ha ha.'

But Larry took hold of her waist and her right hand and began to swivel her around in some first, simple moves.

'Now, the important thing is,' he said, letting go of her and reaching for his phone, 'we are not going to have you dancing the tango like an English lady who goes to night classes. No... I've seen those videos. Horrible,' he told her. 'No. Instead, you're going to watch Lorena Tarantino and her dance partner, Gianpiero Galdi, dance tango and then you will begin to understand what it's all about. It's unstructured, with no set steps, so it's like life, it goes where you take it and where it takes you. This is the dance you did with your gorgeous beau when you were growing up in a strictly Catholic country and your mother and the priest were watching your every move on the dance floor. It's touch, but don't touch, move, but don't move... hold, but let me go. It's seduction, but also repression. Here, I'll show you.'

And he called up a video of a beautiful woman in a tight lace dress and impossibly high, strappy sandals facing a handsome man in a dark suit. The first thing Tess noticed was that their eyes were fixed on one another's faces. And then there was the breathing – the woman was breathing so deeply and so freely that you could see her stomach and chest rise and fall. Then she put her whole arm around the man's shoulder, so that her elbow was at his ear and their chests were touching, but their hips and legs were free. Then the music began and slowly, she danced around him; she leaned into and out from him. She flicked her leg up and wrapped it around his. Sometimes she would lead and he would follow, some-times she would go completely loose and he would carry her gently round in a circle, until she began to glide her feet back into the steps. It was totally mesmerising.

'I'm not going to be able to dance like that,' she told him imme-diately.

'You have too little faith.'

'But the dragging bit...'

'That's easy if you can trust your partner... okay, hold here and here,' he instructed, 'and then relax... no, really relax... even though I know that's hard for you,' he teased.

Tess tried to do as he instructed and after they'd made four attempts, she leaned into him, leaned against him, felt his hold round her waist and under her arm and after his encouraging: 'It's okay, I've got you,' finally felt able to put her whole weight into his arms and then for a few moments, she was that tango woman being gently carried in a circle around her partner.

Give and take... lean in and lean out... lead and be led. The dance was a metaphor, not just for seduction but also for a relationship. In her marriage and in her family, she had been the one who gave, who led, who let everyone lean on her and now she had become all rigid and tense and unable to enjoy being anything else.

'And flick the leg up, and round, as if you're coming back to life... waking from a daze, excellent!' Larry told her. But then it was time to do it again and make it better.

It was funny, Tess thought, as he clasped her to his chest and span her round fast enough to make her stomach flip, how he was so professional and so focused on the details that nothing about this hold or these moves was at all flirty or intimate. They were teacher and student, trying to get this difficult thing right by doing it over and over.

After more tricky tango practice, it was time for them to have their jasmine tea break. As she pulled up a chair at the kitchen counter, Tess saw an ominous white envelope with the words 'Important tax information' stamped across the front lying there. She had been working on Larry's tax situation for several afternoons and this was most likely the result of her efforts.

'I'm not opening that without you beside me,' he told her.

'Don't look so worried,' she assured him. 'I think this is going to be fine.'

'I'm not going to have to pay any extra bills?'

'Now it's you that has too little faith.'

She opened the envelope and unfolded the letter; she read what it said and then passed it over to Larry.

'Is it okay?' he asked, before looking at it.

'It's very okay,' she said.

As he took in the information that all of the money he thought he'd have to pay in tax was going to be waived because of the new pension payment plan Tess had set up for him, he looked as if he might cry with relief. 'You made my bill go away! This is incredible.'

'Well... kind of, the important thing is you have a new pension plan that you're going to get really focused on putting money into. I've tracked your other pensions down too and they're going to bring some money in when you're older, but this is the one you've got to get serious about now. And the more you put in there, the less tax you'll pay. But don't worry, you have me on your case now. I'll keep you right.'

And right in the middle of the appreciative high five Larry was giving her, Tess's phone beeped with a message. She expected something from home, but instead it appeared to be from the man who was the very latest addition to her contacts: Professor Nathan.

Would you like to meet me for a beach walk this weekend? Maybe bring those dogs you were talking about. I'd really enjoy talking to you again. Thanks, Nathan (the economics prof with the wrong eyeglasses).

'Oh, Tess, that surprise on your face. What is it?' Larry asked.

'Remember I told you about meeting a professor?'

'Ah huh...' Larry had something of a smirk across his face now.

'He's asked me to go on a beach walk with him.'

'Ah huh...' he said again, still smirking.

'So that's nice...'

'Nice? The handsome, divorced prof dish invites you for a beach date and you think it's *nice*?'

'It's not a date!' she protested.

'It is absolutely a date,' Larry countered, 'so how do you feel about that?'

'It's not a date!' Tess repeated. But then why did she feel so... so... flustered?

34

Alex had selected a really very picturesque bench for this phone call. There was grass all around – dotted with litter and the odd dog turd, to be fair – and a pretty tree in the background. He guessed it was a cherry tree but as this was high summer and the blossom had long gone, he wouldn't want to swear to it.

He was wearing a dark t-shirt, hoping that this would mean any dirt or stains wouldn't show up so much. But he would hold the phone close up anyway. He'd washed his face and tried to ruffle through his hair so it didn't look too untidy.

Right... time to stop stalling and just get on with call number one of three; he pressed the relevant button.

'Dad? Hello, hi, it's Alex...'

Alex looked at the image on the screen. There was the Amble-side garden, luscious with flowers and the shiny green grass of a summer's day.

'Hey Alex! Good grief! This is a surprise – do you need money? Are you on the run?' his dad joked, presumably in reference to how unusual it was for him to phone. 'How are you doing?'

'I'm good, enjoying the sun. Lovely, isn't it?' Alex said, clutching at the conversational touchstone that was the UK weather. 'Looks like you're out in the sun too.'

'Oh yes... yes, plans in action. I'm having a party along with the American woman who's over here. So trying to work out where to put the tables and chairs...' Dave swung his phone around the garden, so that Alex could take in two large tables out on the back lawn and a stack of chairs.

'Plus, we're going to light the chimenea.' Dave swooped the phone over the pot-bellied garden stove with a hearty pile of logs beside it. And now Alex remembered having friends over and sitting out beside the chimenea late, late into the night.

It all seemed so long ago, this lovely, English countryside life he'd once enjoyed, like something that had happened in another lifetime, or to someone else even... like the memory of a long-running mini-series that he'd watched several years ago, that was how detached he felt. From Ambleside, from his home, from his family and certainly from this jovial guy, only three inches tall, smiling and waving at him from his phone screen.

'How's work?' Alex's dad asked him next.

'It's good... I'm enjoying it,' Alex replied, feeling almost nostalgic for the office. That time too, seemed so far away. All that felt real to Alex was the horrible little room, the grinding sameness of every day, the pain of dragging himself from minute to minute and the decision, which had taken so long to make. But now that it was made, had let a vast and unbearable burden tumble from his shoulders.

'How's your leg?' Alex remembered to ask.

His dad held the phone over his leg. He was wearing a familiar old pair of navy sweatpant shorts and there on his foot, ankle and halfway up his calf was a grey plastic boot.

'The cast is off and the boot is on,' Dave said. 'Things are definitely improving. When are you coming to see us? Your mum will be back in another couple of weeks, are you going to come and see us then? Take a bit of time off? Loll around the garden in the sun. Drink a few beers with your old man?'

It sounded nice... but it also sounded like an invitation back to a place in the past, which couldn't possibly happen.

'Well... I'll take a look at my calendar and see what I can do,' Alex said, 'it would be great to catch up with everyone. When's Natalie home?'

'Not long after your mum, so we can have a big family get-together...'

Alex tried to imagine it: the garden, sunshine, beers, Dad cooking on the barbeque, Mum in the kitchen fussing over salads and sauces... Natalie on the phone, and then asking if Soph and Ellie could come over, and Mum doing that disappointed face, because this was supposed to be family time. Natalie suggesting she eat then go to Soph or Ellie's house... Mum looking practically tearful at the thought.

Maybe they should all have gone on Mum's big holiday, it occurred to Alex now. Then he could have said goodbye to them all properly.

God, it was all so complicated... look at that garden with its plants and chimenea, and now tables and chairs. All the choosing and shopping and buying and planting and deciding and cooking and all the *effort* required for everything. Alex had stood in front of the bathroom mirror before this call deciding what to put on his face so he could shave. Did he need the squirty stuff from the aerosol can his mother had given him? With its promises of being alcohol free, sensitive, creamy and protective? Or did he just need to froth up this bar of soap between his hands? Everything about modern life just seemed so needlessly complex and overwhelming. It was so depressing and he could not be bothered with any of it any more.

'Great to hear from you, Alex, but I think I may have to go now,' his dad said. 'River, the US lady, is approaching and she will be demanding my full attention. Why don't I phone you after the party and I'll tell you all about it?'

'Good idea,' Alex said brightly, 'I really hope you have a great time.'

'Thank you, I will give it my best shot. And what about you, Alex? Are you planning any good times?'

'Yes, definitely...'

'Good to hear.'

'Dad?' Alex could see that his father was about to hang up and he just wanted to hold his attention for a moment longer.

'Yes?'

'Just... have a good time. Be happy.'

'Yes! You too, buddy.'

'Goodbye.'

'Goodbye.'

35

The drive to the beach was not straightforward. Tess had missed not just one freeway exit, but two. So there had been painful detours and double-backs and one incident where she had found herself having to cross a six-laned highway with about 100 yards to spare before her turnoff. This had involved a substantial amount of swearing at the implacable lady from Google Maps and the two over-excited dogs in the hatchback of the car.

But now, according to her phone, 'her destination was on the right'. So, she drove into one of the huge, virtually empty car parks they seemed to have all over the place in this part of the world and tried to sit quietly for a moment or two to recover from the stress of the journey. But Burton and Wilder sensed immediately that the destination had been reached and they were far too pleased to let her sit for long. There was so much yipping, yapping and panting that she knew she would have to get out and put them onto their leashes.

Maybe it wasn't just the stress of driving that was making her nervous. She was wound up today because this was the day that Dave and River were having a party in her home. Dave had mentioned it a few days ago, almost in passing, and when she'd questioned him, he'd tried to play it completely down, until question by question she'd established that *about forty-five* people were coming! Forty-five people? They were setting up rented tables and chairs on the lawn, they were putting up a barbeque on the patio, using her beloved Smeg range as a pizza oven and... she couldn't help it, the whole thing was making her feel hugely annoyed and anxious. And what if something got damaged? Would it come out of River's deposit? Or Dave and Tess's home insurance? If it was a joint party, just what were the liabilities exactly? And even as she thought this, she had to tell herself: '*Aren't you the fun party girl!*'

And then there was the fact that she was meeting Nathan – that also felt stressful. She hadn't mentioned this to Dave. 'I'm going to the beach, walking the dogs,' she'd told her husband when he'd asked what she would be doing while he and River were ruining the garden.

She tried to put things into perspective: 'They're having some people round. You know what it's like, forty-five people say they'll come, twenty-five turn up; they'll have a few drinks and a burger and head off again. It will all be very sedate and boring. And as for me, I'm meeting a nice professor on a sunny afternoon for a dog walk. Again, it's all very sedate and boring. So shut up and calm down!'

She opened the car boot and clipped the dogs' leashes onto their harnesses. They each had a separate bungee cord lead that then clipped onto one leash for the walker to hold. This gave the dogs some space from one another, and prevented their leads from tangling, and it meant she couldn't be pulled in two different directions by the dogs. But generally, although the dogs liked walking separately, they also accepted walking together and didn't pull much. River must have done some careful training around that, because two chunky malamutes pulling against one walker would have been far too much struggle.

It was breezy, more so than Tess had expected. As she took the first paces from the car with the dogs, she reassessed her beach outfit choices. She'd gone with a knee-length wrap skirt, plus vest top, a floppy straw hat, sunglasses and she had changed her driving shoes for flipflops. Was she going to be too cold, she wondered? No, surely it would be fine. They could pick a more sheltered beach route and walk out of the wind. Also, the cloud was clearing, most likely it was about to get very warm.

She'd agreed to meet Nathan on the beachfront beside the ice cream shop, but she was a good fifteen minutes early. As she walked out of the car park, she saw there was a row of shops on the other side of the road, so she thought she would buy herself some juice. A nice chilly bottle of apple juice would boost the blood sugar and help with the nervy, almost fluttering feeling in her stomach.

One hand on her hat against the breeze, she crossed the road with the dogs and came to the front of the little food and drink store. For a moment, she considered bringing the dogs inside, but the shop looked small and cramped and, as Tom had told her, Burton and Wilder took up a lot of doggie real estate. She looked around for something obvious to tie them to and decided on a sturdy-looking ice cream advertising flag with a weighty base. Then she went into the store and spent several minutes trying to work out which of the Snapple flavours she wanted from the fridge. She was at the counter paying when the sudden movement of the flag caught her eye. The window behind the cashier didn't go all the way down, so she couldn't see what the dogs were doing, but she had the immediate suspicion that they were on the move.

'Oh! Oh no! Just a second!' she exclaimed, dropping her drink and rushing for the door.

No sooner had she stepped out than she could see the dogs

were off. They were running down the broad sidewalk with the flag still attached to the lead, still upright, racing behind them. It looked as if the flag was terrifying the living daylights out of them as the more it clattered and bounced behind them, the faster they ran.

Tess had already started running. Within several strides, she realised she had to lose the flipflops because otherwise, she was definitely going to lose the dogs and also, most likely several toes.

'Burton! Wilder!' she yelled. 'Here, here! Good dogs!'

She was clinging onto her hat and her sunglasses, while her skirt flapped like an open door in the wind. The dogs were going faster, so much faster than her. The gap between her and them was widening at every second.

'Burton! Wilder!'

The flag hit a kerbstone and fell over, which caused Burton to leap in panic into the road.

'Jezzzzus Chrissssssst!' Tess hissed.

She relinquished her hold on the hat, then the sunglasses, letting them both be snatched from her head as she ploughed on after the dogs.

A silver car made an abrupt tooting and screeching halt to avoid the dogs, then the flag, then Tess galloping in their wake, wrap skirt dangling.

Was that astonished face on the other side of the windscreen Nathan's? There was no time to check.

Tess's hips were burning in their sockets; the balls of her feet were stabbed by one hundred little stones and spikes as she ran and then the bloody skirt snagged on something poking from a railing and was yanked clean off. She didn't even look round, losing a skirt barely registered compared with the horror of what the dogs might do on the beach... mow down grannies, maim a toddler, break the leg of a random passerby. She had to catch them.

'Wiiiiilder! Here!' She hurled at the generally slightly more obedient one of the dogs, as they raced down a wooden staircase, flag rattling behind them, towards the beach. And there at the bottom of the stairs, they finally met their stop sign. An impossibly handsome guy in a short neoprene suit, a yellow-and-turquoise-clad Adonis with wet, curly blonde hair, caught hold of the flag base and finally yanked the dogs to a halt.

'Oh my God! Thank you! Thank you so much. Oh... God...' Tess could hardly get the words out, she was panting and sweating so much. She wasn't sure she'd run so far and so fast since her final appearance in the mothers' race at Natalie's primary school sports day.

Although she was now dressed only in a short vest top and some clean and white but fairly mumsy pants – pants UK not pants US – she was only registering the remains of her outfit in some small side-room of her brain, because mainly she was just completely traumatised... and completely relieved.

The dogs, now that they had come to a halt, were panting heavily too. Just like Tess, they were a bit chubby and unfit for this level of activity. Neoprene guy, maybe to stop having to look at her pants, was untangling the flag from the lead. When he'd managed this, he handed her the lead, told her he'd take the flag back to the store and then with her delayed thanks ringing in his ears, he headed up the wooden stairs.

Tess considered, for a moment, going back up onto the road to look for her skirt, glasses and hat – how she'd managed to keep the basket with her purse and car key tucked under her arm through the escapade, she had no idea. But she was too tired and suddenly it all felt incredibly humiliating. So instead, she sat down in the sand and as soon as she did that, the dogs also sat down beside her.

'Let's just take a moment,' she told them, patting the nearest one on the head, 'let's just sit here and gather our thoughts. Poor dogs,' she added, 'thank goodness Nathan didn't run his car into you. That would not have been a good start to this...' she realised she was about to say date.

But this really wasn't a date.

'Meeting,' she said instead.

She glanced down at the pants. Where they met the tops of her lily-white, English legs, several small curly hairs poked out from a deeply neglected bikini line.

'Tess! Tess! Is that you?'

She knew without turning round that Nathan was coming down the stairs. Putting her hands into her lap and wondering if it was too late to tuck any of those offending hairs away, she decided that it might be better to remain sitting in the sand. Within moments, Nathan, a picture of the preppie summer gent in a pale blue polo shirt, chino shorts and not the ubiquitous pair of trainers, but classy-looking leather sandals, was standing in front of her. She even liked the smart white cap he'd picked to protect his hairless head from the sun. He was doing what it was best to do in the absence of head hair: wear feature glasses, curate the stubble beard and maintain a fit physique. Stanley Tucci, she thought all of a sudden, the dapper American actor, that's who he reminded her of.

'Tess, hi, are you okay?' he asked. 'I had to slam on the brakes to avoid you and the dogs.'

'Oh! That was you! I'm so sorry...'

'Did they get away from you?' he asked.

'Well... yes!' Surely that much was obvious?

'Are you okay?' he asked again, then extending his hand added: 'Do you want me to help you get up?'

'Nathan... I've lost my skirt,' she cast her eyes down at her bare legs, paler than the sand, 'not to mention my hat, glasses and shoes.'

'Oh, my...' then from the crook of his arm, he took the creamy cotton cable cardigan she'd not even noticed until now. 'Could this help you?' he asked. 'Then we could go back out to the road and look for them.'

She opened up the cardigan's buttons, then stood up and wrapped it round her waist, tying it in place with the thick sleeves. It was a very nice cardigan. She wondered if his ex-wife had bought it for him, pre-divorce, or if he'd been talked into it by a helpful sales assistant.

He looked a little concerned for her, pushing up his horn-rimmed specs and running a hand over his chin.

'Let me take the dogs,' he offered, so she handed over the lead and they went up the wooden stairs and out onto the sidewalk there.

The skirt was lying in a heap just a short distance away, so Tess picked it up and shook it out. It had escaped lightly, with only a slight tear at the front where it had snagged. Further investigation uncovered the sunglasses at the side of the road, but they had been run over by a car and could only be put in the bin. The hat must have caught the wind and blown free, because a thorough search and even a request or two into the roadside shops didn't unearth it. And Tess did not like the smirk on the face of the girl in the chic little realtor office, who had clearly seen her running after the dogs and was still amused.

The flipflops were relocated, not far from the shop where all the trouble had begun, and it was a big relief for Tess to brush off her dirty feet and restore them to some kind of flipflop dignity.

'Can I buy you an ice cream? Or a coffee?' Nathan offered. 'Or maybe a brandy? And do you still want to walk along the beach, or have you had quite enough exercise for the day?'

There was just the tiniest little hint of mischief to this comment.

'Have I had enough exercise?' Tess repeated, with her own note of mischief. 'I'm guessing I looked pretty ridiculous sprinting across that road.'

Allowing himself just the smallest of laughs, Nathan said gallantly, 'I'm just glad you and the dogs are okay. It looked a little scary there for a few minutes.'

They did walk along the beach... for several hours in fact, head-long into the warm wind, with soft sand underfoot and the crash and toss of the sea beside them. It was beginning to feel like a real holiday at last, being somewhere so beautiful. She and Nathan walked and talked for mile after mile. They talked about their work and about their families. They covered the trivial stuff – shows they liked and favourite films – as well as more serious things too: worries about their children's career paths, their own career paths, politics, the future... It was a long walk, and a long, intense conversation, so when they were back at the wooden stairs, they were both tired and hungry.

'You know, about a mile from here, there's a nice beach restaurant, where we can get something to eat and drink, for ourselves and the dogs,' Nathan suggested. 'Would you like to do that?'

It turned out that Tess would, so she followed Nathan's car to the restaurant, where there was a table out on the terrace that allowed dogs.

'Seafood salad...' she told him, as she looked through the menu. 'I don't know if I have ever seen seafood salad on a menu in England, but over here it is the only thing I want.'

'Shall we ask them to give us each a small glass of wine?' Nathan wondered. 'I've discussed this in depth with my Biology colleagues and I'm assured that a healthy adult can process about one unit of alcohol per hour.'

So small glasses of fruity, icy-cold wine were supplied and the food, drink and conversation happened against a backdrop of the golden-pink sunset over the beach.

Marriages... the conversation took a turn for the extremely personal and Tess found herself wanting to know more about how Nathan and his wife, Lynda, divorced.

'Did you see it coming?' she wondered. 'Did things go wrong quite quickly... or did it take a long time to reach the conclusion... sorry,' she added, 'if you don't want to talk about this, I'll totally understand.'

'No... it's okay. I've thought about it so much, it's kind of a relief to talk through all the things I've considered,' Nathan told her, 'you know, we did couples' counselling for six months. We did all the things you're supposed to do. We raked up every single old grievance and explained it fully, without interruption, with "active listening" techniques, so we could fully understand each other's pain and apologise for it.

'We set a date and agreed that it would be a fresh start, a symbolic new beginning, and from there on, we wouldn't refer to the old arguments and old resentments, we would let them go. We tried to rekindle some of the physical side... err...'

Nathan made his slightly flushed embarrassed face and Tess quickly nodded and added: 'I've got you.'

'But really...' he clasped his hands together and tucked them under his chin, 'when I look back and think about all that now... it's like when you have a beloved, elderly family dog that you know is dying. But you do the expensive surgery that the vet says has only a slim chance of success because you'll do anything to keep that dog alive. But... the dog dies anyway. That's not to say it wasn't the right thing to try with all the therapy and everything, but our dog died.'

'Oh dear... I'm very sad and sorry for you and Lynda. It's not how anyone wants things to end.'

At this, Nathan gave a small smile and something of a shrug.

'I'm hoping it will turn out for the best. I have to hope it will turn out for the best. Otherwise, I become bitter and regretful and that is not where I want to be. It's important to enjoy living. And if it hadn't happened, I wouldn't be sitting here eating amazing seafood and looking out at this view with someone who is such interesting company. Come and sit over on this side of the table, Tess,' he suggested, 'you're missing the view.'

So Tess moved her chair round to his side and for some time, they sat side by side, enjoying the golden light over the waves dim down into dusky pink.

Then Nathan turned to her and said thoughtfully: 'I've been on my own for two years now and there hasn't been anyone that I've enjoyed talking to as much as you...'

Those words made Tess's stomach clench with a nervous excitement she hadn't felt for a very long time.

'I don't know where you are in your life and in your marriage,' Nathan went on. 'But I'm guessing you're not out here all by yourself because things are amazing...'

Tess shook her head at this and for several moments couldn't find her voice, but then she said: 'I suppose it's a bit complicated at the moment... sorry to use that old cliché.'

Nathan smiled: 'Well... things become a cliché because they sum up a common situation well.'

'I suppose so...'

She looked at him closely. He had very kind brown eyes behind those glasses and a closed-mouth smile that turned down a little at the corners. She liked the contrast of his clean-shaven head with the stubble beard over his face and chin. He had a healthy-looking tan, and with a rush of nervous energy, she realised she found him very attractive. Not just the way he looked but his whole self – he was so considered, so put together, so orderly. He was wearing casual summer clothes but they were immaculate and extremely well ironed. She liked the care that had gone in to so many things about him – the shiny leather cover on his phone matched his shiny leather wallet, she'd noticed earlier when he'd bought them a drink at the beach. And his car... it hadn't been anything flashy, but it had looked, not just spotless, but freshly polished.

Most important of all, Nathan wasn't Dave. Or anything like Dave. And after twenty-three years of Dave, that looked extremely attractive.

'I just want to ask, because it would be wrong not to ask...' he began, 'I very much hope we can become good friends... but could there be anything more than a friendship here?'

Nathan's shoulder was touching hers. He smelled like clean, lemony soap and laundry powder and Tess felt the kind of charged breathlessness she hadn't felt for years.

'I'm not... sure,' was her honest answer, given in a low voice.

Nathan's face was close, right up close, and she was going to have to decide right now whether or not she was going to kiss him.

36

The garden looked incredible. There was no other word for it. The tables were topped with snowy tablecloths, glasses, small vases filled with flowers and sparkling tea-light holders. The fairy lights had been painstakingly draped around every possible kind of support from cherry tree branches to the patio awning. Bottles were lying in tubs, ready to be doused in ice and cold water.

The grass was crisp and green. A stack of logs was piled at the ready beside the chimenea. The gas barbeque was all set and in the kitchen there was a fridge full of food, and as a backdrop to it all, an English country garden in the warm sunshine of a glowing August day. Lush, well-watered greenery, the perfume of roses and the liquid warble of birdsong.

It was beautiful. Dave walked round it all, making a tweak and adjustment here and there. Wanting everything to look and be perfect. He could not remember feeling so excited. His friends were coming, both neighbour friends and some teacher friends. River's producer was coming. Actors from Stratford were coming. And then... he had to pinch himself, Van Saint, Dean Vincent and some other long-lost friends from the art school days were coming... and icing on top of the cake... Franklyn Gregory and his wife had supposedly said yes.

'I know he's Hollywood A list, but Franklyn as a person was a man of his word,' River had told him, 'so... I think you should probably expect the man himself to be standing in your garden at some point this evening. So make sure your phone is charged and you can take some pictures.'

And at 8.35 p.m., the Franklyn Gregory show rolled into Ambleside. Just as the sky darkened properly, just when the fairy lights and tea lights moved to maximum twinkle, and the guests were two to three drinks in and sparkling with charm and enjoyment... just at the perfect entrance opportunity, when the backdrop was already set, Franklyn and Mena arrived. They were so extraordinary looking, Dave couldn't help noticing as he was introduced and found himself making small talk to this superstar and, quite frankly, supermodel. They were so trim, so dapper, so shiny. Their skin and teeth gleamed, their hair was like fake hair, it was so perfect. And they weren't overdressed, Franklyn was in a pair of pale jeans and a pale blue shirt, Mena in the sort of simple summer dress with floaty sleeves and a short skirt that Natalie would wear. But everything fitted beautifully and just looked so perfect.

'This is a gorgeous place you have here,' Franklyn *bloody* Gregory was telling him.

'Thank you so much... are you enjoying being in Stratford?' he managed, feeling totally star-struck and catching a glance at a work colleague over Franklyn's shoulder whose jaw was literally hanging open.

'Oh my gosh, we love it. It is so beautiful here. The countryside is just gorgeous. So green. Truly it's a privilege to be here. And doing Shakespeare. I mean, he's the boss,' Franklyn replied, 'he's the man.'

Dave was trying to picture River and Franklyn as a couple and he just couldn't see it. This man was so together... so focused, so professional. River... he looked for longer than he meant to in her direction. She looked amazing tonight... like some boho writer girl straight out of your dreams.

And while Franklyn and Mena were still in his garden... while he was still entertaining one of Hollywood's biggest current names, that's when Van Saint pulled up in his Ferrari, of course. For a glorious half-hour or so, Van Saint, Dean and Mitchell, who he'd once studied, painted and worked alongside, were in his garden, dazzled by this party. Dazzled by the celebrities, of course, but also by River, the actors, and the loveliness of the setting, the music and it all.

'This is incredible, Dave,' Van Saint told him, 'you've built a really interesting life out here in the sticks. It almost makes me think maybe I could leave the grimy, inner-city hell of east London for a lovely place like this.'

Dave snorted. He'd seen the glossy magazine articles. He knew that Van Saint (real name Jim Roberts btw) lived in a multi-million pound Georgian mansion, complete with glassed in rooftop pool and obligatory cinema basement in 'grimy, inner-city hell' east London.

Dave topped up their champagne glasses, let them play their own music on the speakers and listened to their talk of gallery events in Zurich, Basel, New York and Chicago.

'Come on, you must still wish you were part of the team?' Dean Vincent asked him, when several bottles of the good stuff had been drained.

'No... not really, I like teaching. It gives a lot back,' Dave said.

'Is it not boring as fuck?' Van Saint asked, leaning over Dave from his tall height, a sneer on his face. 'Don't you wake up some mornings and wonder why on earth you'd want to drive your fucking car to the same fucking school to look at the same fucking faces all over again?'

That was a surprisingly accurate portrayal of how Dave did, in fact, feel on some mornings of the week... but he wasn't going to give Van Saint the satisfaction of agreeing with him.

'You teach art,' Van Saint was saying now, 'but do you still make art? Hmmmm? Do you?' He jabbed at Dave's chest with his finger.

Dave remembered that Van Saint had always been confident, opinionated, and over-bearing but clearly his massive success had now turned him into a totally obnoxious prick.

'I do some painting... but it's a hobby. Just a hobby,' Dave muttered. But somehow, he must have glanced towards the summerhouse, because Van Saint was on it like a bloodhound.

He pointed and declared: 'To the summerhouse, to inspect the latest works by Dave Simpson, class of 1992.'

* * *

What time was it?

Dave had no idea: 4 a.m. – 5 a.m.? He was stumbling around, very much the worse for wear, in his own house. He'd put out the *fires* in the garden. God, that had been painfully hot and difficult work. There was definitely no fire anywhere any more. He'd seen everyone off the premises; well, he thought he had. A quick look round the living room had revealed either a pile of coats or someone asleep on the couch, but no matter, no matter. He would worry about that in the morning. Right now, he had to get to bed. Bed... bed... his lovely bed was calling. In the kitchen he held a glass under the tap, filled it with water and then took a sip or two. Then realised he'd had far too much booze for any mere glass of water to help. He was way, way beyond the water stage. This was going to call for truckloads of industrial-strength painkillers in the morning, but he didn't want to think about that right now.

Nevertheless, he kept hold of the glass and headed for the staircase, sloshing water in his wake. He had long ago forgotten about the ankle and went up stair by stair only dimly, right at the back of his mind, wondering why his leg was hurting so much.

Bed, bed... he needed his lovely big bed, up there at the top of the stairs. There was something, some other little mental tug, telling him there was a reason why he couldn't get to his bed. But never mind, never mind, he *needed* to get to that bed.

Dave pushed open the door of his bedroom, or at least, the bedroom he thought of as his, the one he'd shared with his wife for so many years and stumbled into the room. He threw off his jacket, his shirt, then undid his belt and buttons and let his jeans fall to the floor. Very fashionable and expensive jeans, by the way, that he had bought especially for this party, hoping to meet the approval of Dean Vincent and the legend that was Van Saint. Quite frankly – bollocks to the pair of them.

'Bollocks to the pair of you,' he said out loud. Water... water, where was his water? He felt around, located the glass on the floor and took another gulp.

Then, wearing only his boxers, and also his socks, because the thought of going all the way down there to take them off was quite frankly exhausting, he got into his delightful, oh-so-welcoming and comfortable bed. Oh! That was so good, so lovely. This bed felt more comfortable than it had done for weeks. Oh, why was this bed so delicious? Still, he was aware of just the vaguest feeling that he wasn't supposed to be here, which was ridiculous, because this was definitely his lovely, lovely bed.

He closed his eyes but then heard something... and thought he felt something move.

There was someone else here... or just right over there.

'Tess?' he asked out loud. 'Tess?'

He leaned up on one elbow and, eyes adjusting to the dimness, he looked at the other person in the bed. As it was now after 5 a.m., there was just enough daylight coming in from around the edges of the blinds for Dave to see who was lying beside him.

'River?' he said in surprise. For it was she. He saw the dark hair and the pale face still with the slash of red lipstick and the dark, smudgy eyes.

She was absolutely lovely, wasn't she? He had been thinking this for weeks, he realised with absolute drunken clarity. She. Was. Lovely. Gorgeous. So funny. Creative. Mercurial and delightful.

'River, I think you're absolutely lovely,' he said out loud.

* * *

Tess leaned in. Her lips brushed against Nathan's. She felt the roughness of his hair against her lip, then his much softer lip and the hesitant tip of his tongue. And she wanted more of this kiss, felt hungrier for kissing than she had for a very long time. It was sort of the same... it was still kissing... but it was also quite enticingly different too. She ran a hand over Nathan's very smooth, bald head. It felt satiny, sexy. So different from the hairy man she was used to.

She had no idea where this kiss was going to lead... but for now, it was a sensationally different kiss, happening right here on the terrace, under the sunset, on the California beachfront.

* * *

River opened her eyes and looked right at Dave.

She got up on her elbow too. And it didn't look as if she was wearing anything under that sheet. Not a stitch.

'Dave?' she asked, sounding blurry. 'You look weird and you're in my bed.'

'No,' he said, sure of himself, but sounding very blurry too, 'this is my bed. You're in my bed.'

'No, this is definitely my bed,' she said.

'You're definitely in my bed,' he repeated. 'And I think you're lovely.'

'Oh, you are sweet,' she said and she put her arms around his neck, which meant the sheet around her fell away and Dave saw exquisitely delicate boobs down there below the mouth that was moving in on his. Small, hard, white teeth bumped against his. He tasted warm wine mouth, wet and soft. Those delectable boobs were now pressed against his chest. Dave wrapped his arms around her and kissed back.

37

There was a phone ringing... ringing... ringing...

Tess opened her eyes. It was definitely her phone. She groped around the bedside table and her hand landed on the smooth glass of her screen.

'Hello? Hello, it's me,' she said, realising as she said the words that she'd not seen the number, and actually had no idea who was calling her.

'Mum? Hello, it's Alex!'

'Alex! Hello darling, how are you? Oh, it's so good to hear from you!'

She pulled herself upright in bed and all at once felt wide awake. 'How's it going? Oh, I can't believe it's you. It's been so long since I spoke to you.' She tried to rein herself in, she knew how he recoiled when she made too much of a fuss over him. But it was so lovely, so rare and so unexpected to hear from him.

'How are you doing?' she asked and bit her tongue, promised herself she would now be quiet, let Alex talk while she listened.

'I'm really good,' he said, and she heard the cheerfulness in his voice, 'work is going well and the weather in London – it's glorious.

It's so hot, it feels like a foreign city, you know, sun beating down on the concrete... drinks outside on the pavement tables.'

'Oh, I know... it's wonderful in the summer. Have you been to Hyde Park, or gone down to the river?'

'I've been walking and walking in Hyde Park, I love it. Been sitting in the deck chairs after work reading Russian novels.'

'Wow! That sounds pretty intense.'

'I've finished *War and Peace*... all 1,563 pages of it. Finished it! It was amazing. Totally blew my mind.'

'That's incredible. I've never even started it, I'm ashamed to admit...' Tess imagined her thoughtful son carrying the massive book around with him every day. In his bag on the tube, in the pocket of his raincoat... bringing it out as he sat on a deckchair in Hyde Park. She imagined her lovely boy, in the world of work, one face among millions in the sea that was London.

'I really miss you, Alex,' she told him. 'I feel so far away from you all... I would have loved to go on that family holiday, you know. Just to hang out with everyone again.' This was an acute feeling now that she could hear his voice. Sometimes she thought she was really fine, and pretty happy on her own, and at other times, like now, she missed everyone intensely.

'Is London okay? Are you making friends? Are you settling into work okay?'

Once again she was asking too many questions. Let him speak... let him speak!

'Yeah, I really like it,' he replied and Tess drank in his happy, upbeat tone. 'I'm learning a lot at work. It's interesting and there are people there that I really like. But you know me, Mum, I like to be on my own too. So it's a good mix. I'll have a busy, worky, sociable day, and then usually a quiet evening to just chill out, make my dinner and get my reading done.'

'Make your dinner! So how's your cooking coming on?'

'I can make burgers, I can make macaroni cheese, I can make chicken wraps... so I'm rotating these.'

'Chicken and veg tray bake, remember I showed you how to do that?' she suggested. 'But anyway, what are you going to read next?' she asked to keep him engaged, keep him on the line.

'Oh... I don't know... maybe continue in the Russian theme... more Tolstoy... or maybe Dostoyevsky. Something a little bit weighty... *Crime and Punishment* sounds like the kind of thing.'

Again, Tess pictured him, jostling for space on the tube with his eyes on the pages of his book, his face the picture of concentration. Maybe he should have done English Lit or foreign languages at university. Had Economics really been *his* choice? Or had she leaned him into it? Telling him what a good prospect it was for employers... always the sensible Mum. If she had been too strict or too bossy with him, it was only because she wanted so much for him... wanted the world... believed he had real talents and was someone who could do whatever he put his mind to.

But didn't every mother look at their children and think that? Because she felt the same about Natalie too, but there was a sensitivity, even a fragility to Alex that made him just a little bit more vulnerable than Natalie. Tess knew she had hovered over Alex and micromanaged... and she knew just how annoying Alex found this. There had been periods when he'd shut her out of his life and hadn't told her what was really going on – in that final year of school and final year of uni – until things had got to a crisis point and now she was always alert to the possibility that this could happen again.

'I miss you,' she said, putting all the love, warmth and feeling in her heart into those simple words.

'Muuuum! You're supposed to be having a great time, far too busy to miss us. What's it like in LA? What are you doing?' he asked.

'I've been visiting art galleries, I've been to the beach a few times, I've been hiking... and I started dancing lessons with this really cool ballet teacher who lives in the building...'

'You dancing? I'm trying to picture that.'

'Yes, I know... but I'm getting better, honestly! I've had an amazing haircut. I am now a blonde. Natalie is gradually coming round to the idea.'

'You are a blonde? Send a picture please, I can't imagine that.'

'I did,' she said. 'I sent it on "the fam" chat group. That's the one you never reply to, or acknowledge in any way, shape or form...'

'Sorry,' he said, sounding quite genuinely contrite. 'Sometimes those messages come at... well, the wrong times for me... and then I forget to look at them.'

'Well, take a scroll now, you'll see the new, improved, dancing, blonde mother.'

'Sounds like you're having a great time,' he said.

'Yes... I am. It's different, very different being away from you all... but I'm enjoying it.'

'I think you needed a change,' he said.

And it was funny to hear these caring and perceptive words from him.

'Yes... I did,' she agreed.

'You sound happy,' he said, 'and it suits you.'

'What about you, my darling? Are you happy?'

'I really am, Mum.'

Because they weren't video calling, she paid close, close attention to his voice, took in every syllable. And he did sound bright and genuine, relaxed and happy.

'Be happy, Mum, it's really good for you.'

'Yes, be happy, Alex. It's really good for you too.'

There was a pause; she imagined them both smiling at each other down the line.

'Well... I guess I better go,' he said finally. 'It's been really nice talking to you, Mum.'

'It's been lovely talking to you too, darling. I love you and we could do this more often.'

'Yeah... you take care.'

'Goodbye.'

'Goodbye, Mum.'

And he was gone.

Be happy... that was a nice thing for him to say. And an unusual one too. Tess lingered on the screen of her phone as the photo of Alex, taken a few years ago now, was still there.

And then a message flashed up:

What a lovely evening. I hope we can do that again sometime soon. Nathan. Meanwhile, I have an urgent question for you, please give me a call.

And all the memories from last night came tumbling back to mind. That kiss on the terrace... that other kiss in the car park...

And now what?

38

As soon as River woke, she could register only one thing: she was going to throw up. She pushed the covers off and ran to the bathroom. After ridding herself of some of the toxic remnants, the night before came vividly back to life. Wiping her mouth, then splashing her face with much needed cold water, she first of all tried to remember what had gone well, in those long hours the party had lasted, because she was pretty certain that quite a lot had not gone well.

Franklyn and Phillip... focus on these guys, she told herself. They were the important ones. From what she could remember, her time with them had gone well. And the important thing was, they hadn't stayed too long, which was good. Because now, she could smell smoke, a smell which seemed to be coming from her hair, her skin, every part of her, and it was making her retch into the toilet bowl once again, as she remembered a fire... jeeeezus, a big fire. And drama. And... Dave? She gave her face another sluicing over the sink. *Dave?* When she went back into the bedroom, she saw nothing unusual, nothing that didn't belong to her. But wait just one moment... the second pillow on the bed had a head-shaped dent. And now she remembered a kiss. A long and passionate kiss... but nothing else. Surely nothing else?

She had to get downstairs and find water and headache pills and maybe coffee or juice or whatever it was that you were supposed to take to make all this pain and nausea go away.

Too old for hangovers, she told herself, *far, far too old for hangovers*. Even the glimpse of sun that was appearing around the edges of the blinds looked too bright. River fumbled about the room, found her sunglasses and put them on. No matter that it was ridiculous to wear sunglasses indoors. These were exceptional circumstances.

She came down the stairs very slowly, worried about what she might find down there. She approached the kitchen gingerly, expecting to enter a room of utter chaos and disaster. The fire hadn't been in here, had it? Please, not in Tess's beautiful kitchen. She opened the door slowly... but in fact, on entering, she saw that most of the major clean-up had already taken place. Four large garbage sacks were filled and neatly tied in the middle of the room. The surfaces were all wiped down and the kitchen floor looked slightly damp. There was still a vast collection of glasses by the sink and a heaped box of empty bottles beside the sliding doors to the garden; she didn't really want to look into the garden because she was sure there would still be plenty of evidence of party damage.

The garden... that's where the fire happened.

Just as River was trying to remember the details and wondering where Dave was, he came bustling into the room wearing yellow rubber gloves and with two large pieces of metal in his hands.

'Oh hello! You're up...' he said brightly, but then he must have clocked her dark glasses, pale skin and ragged hair because he added quickly, 'Sit down, honestly, pull up a chair and I will bring you coffee, water, medicine, watermelon slices... whatever you need to get you back on your feet again. In fact, sit outside... I've cleared a soothing little corner away from the shards of broken, twisted metal,' he raised the pieces in his hands to demonstrate, 'and trust me, the fresh air will revive you a little.'

'Are you sure? It won't be too bright out there?' she whimpered.

'No... I promise, I've made a dappled corner.'

'Dappled... that does sound nice. Dave...' she was looking at him more closely now, 'you don't have any eyebrows.'

'No, I know, I think they got burned off. Now what would you like?'

'Burned off... jeeeezus. Well... water, medicine, coffee... maybe watermelon... that all sounds helpful.'

'Okay, go and sit, I will be right there.'

* * *

And he was.

River had been sitting in the promised dappled shade and within minutes, Dave appeared with a tray laden down with a cafetière of coffee, a little jug of milk, water, paracetamol and slices of watermelon.

Meanwhile, River lit a cigarette, inhaled and instantly regretted it.

'Oh my God, I feel dreadful,' she admitted, stubbing out the cigarette in the coffee saucer.

'Yeah... I've definitely had better mornings myself.'

'Thank you for doing all the tidying up.'

'Oh... there's still plenty to do in the garden. We're going to be picking up bottle tops and fag butts for the rest of your time here. But right now, you should concentrate on drinking some coffee and feeling better.'

River drank the water and then some coffee. She swallowed the headache pills and considered re-lighting her cigarette.

'Did you sleep in my bed last night?' she asked Dave, because she felt it was important to get this out into the open straightaway.

'Ermm... yes... not for long... I was confused.' Dave looked embarrassed. 'I went into the wrong room, out of habit. And...'

He paused.

'And?' she asked.

'I have to admit that I kissed you, River. You were quite keen at the time to be kissed, but considering how much you'd drunk, it wasn't very gentlemanly of me to take advantage.'

'We kissed?' River just wanted to clarify. 'That was all?'

'We had a very, very nice kiss... yes,' Dave said, searching her sunglassed face for a reaction to this.

River continued to sip at her coffee and stared off into the distance through her dark glasses.

'Well... these things can happen... and drunk kissing is... nothing.'

'No...' Dave said quietly. 'I suppose not...'

He picked up the drained cafetière and took it back to the kitchen with the words: 'We're going to need more of this, I think.'

To his surprise, when he came back out into the garden with the fresh coffee, River was still in the chair, but her head was in her hands and she was crying hard.

'What's the matter... what on earth is the matter?' he asked.

'Oh God...' the sound of his sympathetic voice, the fact he was crouching down to be beside her was making it all so much worse, 'everything is such a mess,' she blurted out, 'everything! The script's a mess, my money is in a mess, my apartment's a mess, everything is just one huge, fucking hot mess!'

She was crying without any dignity now, big racking sobs, snot coming from her nose.

Dave put a hand on her back and patted gently, which again was such a nice thing to do that she cried harder.

'It is...' she managed, 'it is all just such a freaking mess. Ever since Drew died. I just can't get myself together. Every time I think I'm getting it together... I just fall apart again.'

'I really, really hope I've not caused any of this...' Dave said. 'I'm so sorry if I did the wrong thing.'

'No... no... you're fine. You've been very kind to me...'

'You're really good fun, River,' Dave said gently. 'I really like hanging out with you. And if it's any consolation, your apartment will definitely not be a mess any more. That's one thing you don't need to worry about.'

River managed something of a small laugh in between bursts of tears.

'Oh God, the script...' she blurted. 'I just don't know... I don't know...'

'Isn't it always like this? You're working on something so hard, you just can't judge it any more...'

'Probably... probably... ohhhh...' a fresh round of tears.

'I don't know if it's any consolation,' Dave began, 'but the older you get, the more hangovers come with a side helping of huge existential dread.'

River turned to him and put her wet face against his shoulder, then she put her arms around his back and just bawled.

'You're okay...' he said, again patting her back and River considered what a kind man he was. He must be a lovely dad. This made her cry even more.

After several long, and for Dave's shirt, damp minutes had passed, there was something of a break in the tears. He thought maybe this would be a good moment to get her a fresh glass of water, some tissues and top up her coffee.

'Just stay right there,' he instructed, 'I'm going to be right back with supplies.'

'Do you have Xanax?' River asked.

'No... but I think I've got some full-fat Cokes and it looks like that's what you may need.'

River was left thinking: 'Full-fat? What the freak is that?'

When Dave came back, he had a cold glass full of ice and he poured half a can of Coke into it.

'Take a few sips of that,' he instructed.

River did and as the sugar and caffeine rushed into her bloodstream, she did start to feel slightly better. She took the tissues he was offering too and mopped up under her eyes and gave her nose several hearty blows.

'No matter how much you cry, the time to blow your nose always comes... you know, I think Simone de Beauvoir wrote that. It's one of her lesser-known quotes, obviously. But I used to tell it to Natalie a lot, when she was younger.'

And for a dodgy moment there, Dave thought he might cry too. How was Natalie? How was she getting on in Spain? He really needed to have a long chat with her and find out. God... he was honestly in danger of letting his whole family fall apart. And he had to do something about it. But first... River needed his immediate help.

'So... who is Drew?' he asked gently.

For several moments, River's lip trembled as if she was trying to decide whether she was going to talk or cry.

'More Coke,' Dave instructed and River took a long gulp.

'That is helping,' she said afterwards.

'Yeah... we used to call it the red ambulance at college.'

River even managed a slight laugh at this.

'Drew...' she began, a little unsteadily, 'he was the man I loved... so much...' tears slid down underneath her sunglasses, 'after Franklyn. And he got cancer... and he cheated on me... and he killed himself.'

'Dear God...' was all Dave could come up with, 'he really packed it in.'

And even though River was still crying, she was laughing too: 'Yes, he fucking did. What a fucker.'

'The fucker,' Dave repeated... not really sure what to say.

'Fucking fucker,' River said and took another long gulp of her icy cola. 'That was the exact sequence of events: he got cancer... testicular, you know, not pleasant, but not the end of the world. You lose a ball, you have to have chemo... and then he cheated on me with an actress, of course, because they're all such insecure bitches, who'll sleep with your boyfriend like it's having a cup of coffee with you... and then he kills himself. Saved up all his meds for weeks and took everything all at once having *emailed* the police station beforehand, and having left the apartment door unlocked so that someone with proper training would find him. Not me...'

'Dear God...' Dave repeated.

He was right beside River, his hand on her back, holding her tight, hoping he was helping in some way. Good grief, hangovers were vicious... barbaric at this age. He wasn't feeling too incredibly top-notch himself. Any minute now and no doubt his very own existential life crisis would arrive.

River added: 'And everyone thought... "Oh, what a relief, he had cancer, and he killed himself, so he was spared a horrible death"... but his cancer was not terminal. He could have done the chemo, and been cured. He could have had a full and normal life.

'He didn't kill himself because of the cancer...' she went on, holding a balled tissue to her face, 'he killed himself because no one was enough; nothing was enough. There weren't enough good reasons to live for him. And he just couldn't find mental peace. He was a writer like me and he was always churning, running and re-running over everything, fretting, overthinking and this was a way to finally get peace.'

River had wrapped her arms around herself and was rocking

gently: 'I never saw it coming, Dave, I never saw it coming...' she started to cry again. 'I've gone over and over and over the day before. We spent that day together; we were over the cheating, that was behind us. He was so happy that day, called every member of his family and all his favourite friends, he was so fucking happy... We were so happy. It was one of our best days. We got drunk on fizzy wine, we were dancing to Lou Reed... Transformer... remember? *Perfect Day*...' She gently sang the famous line.

'My favourite album,' Dave said. 'I like *Satellite of Love*...'

'Mine too... but I can never listen to it again because the next day... the day after our best day ever, he's fucking dead... fucking *dead*.'

River began to cry again, loud, keening, heart-rending cries.

'I'm so sorry...' Dave told her. 'I'm so sorry.'

He just stayed there, holding onto her, even though his knees were killing him and he could really quite do with a red ambulance himself, not to mention a pee... and jeeeezus, the state of the garden. He would have to get some professional help to put it right before Tess's return.

When the crying had abated, Dave found himself asking: 'Do you think Drew was the love of your life?' He didn't even know why, he hoped it would help her to talk about him more, but he had no idea... he was completely out of his depth here.

'Oh shit, I don't know...' River pulled tissues out of the box and blew her nose again, which Dave took as an encouraging sign.

'Sometimes I think you never love anyone as much as you love the very first person you love... that first love, it's so intense... so pure. But no one ever takes it seriously. Everyone thinks you're going to get over it. But sometimes, two young people just see straight inside each other's souls, don't they? And the whole world doesn't get it. The first time I fell in love – it was huge... took me years to get over it.'

'Sounds like something you should be writing about.'

River gave a weak smile at this.

'Yeah... maybe they'll ask me to do the *Romeo and Juliet* high school musical next. And then *Hamlet*, that's an obvious one... I'm seeing a whole series.' She managed another slight smile.

'Probably the script is going okay,' Dave said gently. 'And you have time, plus peace and quiet here to get it done.'

'Yeah...'

'Maybe you should go back to bed for a bit?' he suggested.

'Yeah... probably a good idea.'

* * *

Once River had downed the rest of her Coke and headed back into the house, Dave continued to deal with the garden carnage. He had bin bags and despite the oppressive heat and the thudding of his own head, he steadily worked over the lawns, flowerbeds and bushes picking up glass, pieces of metal, charred chunks of wood, paper plates, cigarette butts, and all the other pieces of debris from last night's extravaganza.

As he approached the summerhouse, he saw the pile of paintings and felt his stomach churn. He'd drunk a lot last night, but not enough to have blotted out that memory. He shook out the bin bag in his hands and knew exactly what he was going to do next.

As he crouched down over the pile of his work, the phone in his back pocket began to ring.

He was surprised to see it was Tess.

'Hello! What are you doing phoning me? Isn't it very early over there?'

'Hello Dave, how are you doing?'

They switched to video so they could see one another.

'It's not me you want to see though, is it?' Dave asked. 'You want to make sure the garden has survived.'

'Well... maybe,' she admitted.

'Don't worry, it's going to be fine. The lawn is going to need some TLC...' this was an understatement, Dave was planning to get the whole thing re-turfed before she arrived, 'but otherwise, we're in pretty good shape.' This was a downright lie... he angled the phone camera away from a flattened rose bush, but no need to get Tess all worked up. He could have a lot of the damage repaired before she got back.

'Did you have a good time?' she asked him.

'Oh... well... parts of it were fantastic... I mean, Tess, Franklyn Gregory was in our garden!' he said. 'But the pressures of being the host... they were pretty immense.'

His phone in his hand, he began to push the canvases into the bin bag.

'What are you doing?' she asked.

'I'm getting rid of the rubbish,' he said.

But she had spotted something.

'What are you throwing away there? That didn't look like rubbish.'

Dave suddenly felt very tired and very hungover. So much so that he sat down on the grass.

'No,' he said, 'these are my paintings... and I've decided to throw them away. Because they're absolutely crap. Boring, mundane, suburban, *hobbyist* crap.'

This wasn't just his opinion, some pretty important artists had told him exactly that last night. Yes, he'd been drunk, but he wasn't going to forget their laughter for a very long time... maybe never.

'Dave... can I see them?' Tess asked.

'Well... if you want to...'

Dave held the phone up and spread his blue canvases across the grass. They were different sizes, and all different shades of blue with abstract shapes painted across them... well, not entirely abstract shapes... those shapes meant something to him, but certainly hadn't meant anything to the 'experts' he'd shown them to last night.

Dave held his phone up over every one for a few moments in turn. He looked at them too as he did this. They had taken hours and hours of work and while he didn't for a moment consider them great art, he realised they meant a lot to him.

'They're lovely,' Tess said down the line, 'please don't think about throwing a single one away. If there are any in the bin bag, take them out now.'

'No, there aren't any in the bin bag, but quite a few went up in the chimenea last night.'

'What?'

'Long story,' he said, 'do you recognise them?'

'Yes... of course I do. There's that tiny little green shed perched on the path we had to walk down to get to the beach in Cornwall. And there are the flags, the rows of flags on the beach at Biarritz... that dazzling summer blue, you've got that just right. And I love the tiny figures... is that Alex, with a surfboard? And toddler Natalie with the spotty yellow-and-pink swimsuit?'

'Yeah...' he said, so pleased that she'd been able to read them all.

'They're lovely, Dave. I love every single one of them. You must have worked so hard.'

'You're too kind,' he said, and realised he had a lump in his throat.

'I want to hang them all up in the house... if that's okay with you?'

'Yes... that is okay with me...' he realised. 'As long as it's somewhere subtle... a little bit out of the way, you know... not hanging over the mantelpiece or anything like that.'

'I'll think of some good places. Are you enjoying the painting?' she asked.

'I found it really hard to start and I'm super critical of what I've done,' he admitted, 'but when I'm in the moment, painting, yes, I really enjoy it. But...' his voice went a little husky, 'as I suspected, I'm not an artist, Tess.'

Tess heard the deep note of sadness in his voice and felt a rush of love and sympathy for him: 'That's okay though, Dave... you don't need to be an artist. I think it's quite a tricky lifestyle.'

'Yeah,' he agreed, thinking of the weeks he'd spent watching River. She'd spent hours and hours locked up in her room and seemed to go through a whole range of artistic ups and downs every day. It looked totally intense and exhausting. 'But didn't you fall in love with an artist?' he asked his wife.

Tess, thousands of miles away, looked out through the big window over the balcony and into the bright blue sky of another LA day.

'No... I fell in love with you,' she told her husband. 'You're a very kind man. You're a good teacher...'

'I could be better.'

'You're a good dad,' she went on.

'I could be better... And I could be a much better husband too. I want to do much better at it all.'

'Yes,' she said, 'me too.'

And that was the truth of it. This conversation, this simple heart-to-heart was putting Nathan into perspective for her.

'Where do we start?' he asked her.

'I'm not exactly sure, but maybe with wanting it to be better... and more conversations like this.'

'Yeah...' he agreed.

And there was a long and thoughtful pause, before Tess said: 'Alex phoned me. It was very early in the morning for me, but it was lovely. He sounded really good. Better than I've heard him for ages. Really upbeat... really happy and settled. Sounds like he's enjoying work and London and making friends... all the things you'd want.'

'Yeah... he phoned me too, the day before the party. And agreed, he sounded great. It was really good to hear.'

'And how's River getting on?' was Tess's next question.

'Oh...' and suddenly the memory of kissing River came hurtling back to Dave and he felt nothing but a flood of guilt, 'she's pretty hungover today. I've given her coffee and Coke and sent her back to bed. She's in no state to help with the clear up.'

'Oh dear...'

'But I think her writing's going well, so that's good.'

'She must be getting to the end of her project...'

'I don't know... I suppose so...' Still Dave was thinking of that kiss and wondering how he would explain it to his wife... or if he should. 'And what about you? What are you doing today?'

'Oh... it's a pretty exciting day for me today... I've been asked to give a guest lecture on personal finance at the University of Los Angeles.'

'What?'

'Yeah... I met one of the economics professors there a week or so ago... and they've had this last-minute cancellation and were urgently looking for a replacement... so I've volunteered to help out. And after that... my dance teacher is taking me out for a fish taco... because I did his accounts for him and saved him about $7,000 and then he's taking me to LA's best tango dancing club. So it's a pretty big day.'

'Wow...' Dave looked around the slightly destroyed English suburban garden and told her, 'Well, that sounds completely epic...

I am totally jealous... your dance teacher?' he asked. 'Why have I not heard anything about you having a dance teacher...?'

Tess laughed. 'Wasn't the point of this holiday for me to go and do things on my own?'

'But... a tango club? That just doesn't sound very you.'

'That's what this holiday is all about.'

She sounded so well... so energetic and so happy, Dave couldn't help but notice.

'I hope your lecture goes really well,' he said. 'And that you have a great day... and I love you, Tess.'

'Thanks... you have a good day too. Love you too, Dave.'

Love you too... that wasn't quite the same, though, was it? He thought as he hung up. That was what you said to your children, your parents... even your friends. And she sounded so good. Tango dancing, guest lectures... the blonde hair.

Was she going to come back to him?

Going to come back to their marriage?

To the way things were?

Why would she?

39

The night before... the night before...

River was in bed trying to sleep off her hangover and tossing, turning, dozing, then tossing and turning again. She was searching her memory for what on earth had gone on at the party. She was thinking hard, trying to remember as much as she could, the good, the bad and there had definitely been ugly too.

It had begun beautifully; hazy, warm sunshine, a light breeze and the garden, oh-so beautiful, roses standing out in full bloom, tables with white table cloths, chairs, icy bottles of wine and beer cooling in tubs heaped with ice. Dave had rigged up speakers at the windows to play out over the garden and there was a cable so people could plug in their phones and play their own songs. And the most beautifully dressed guests had arrived. Dave's neighbours in linen suits and floral dresses, sipping champagne and making the kind of polite but delightful conversation that made you wish you'd been brought up in England.

Then the actors had arrived, all jeans or heels and minidresses, and the volume had cranked up a little. More laughter, more jokes, and cigarettes lit up in the garden. And then Phillip had showed up by swanky car from London with his girlfriend and a couple of friends in tow. River remembered what a good host Dave had been: circulating, introducing guests to one another, making sure everyone was talking and their glasses were full. He'd picked up on the importance of Phillip straightaway and had provided him with a welcoming glass of champagne and then a range of fancy soft drinks. Dave had run the barbeque and their old-fashioned hamburgers and elaborate kebabs had gone down a storm. And gradually, this sort of whispered anticipation had begun to build that Franklyn and the famous artists would arrive.

It had swelled and then ebbed a little as people got onto their third or fourth drinks and began to suspect that it wasn't going to happen. And then the party had got a little looser round the edges. River had put her favourite tracks on through the speaker... and Blondie, Beyonce and Tupac began to blast through the garden and a few of the actors began to dance on the lawn... especially to Blondie, everyone has to dance to Blondie's 'Heart of Glass': 'Oooooh ooooh woah oh!'

And then Franklyn had appeared. *The fucking fucker had fucking appeared.*

'You fucking made it!' River seemed to remember greeting him, wine bottle in one hand, cigarette in the other. Never mind, she also remembered that she looked absolutely gorgeous. She'd ordered some outrageously expensive, cutting-edge, summer dress on the internet – Essential Antwerp, well, when in Europe – along with high, clumpy heeled, pink ankle boots. She'd made her hair poker straight, done deepest smoky eye and slash of lipstick and looked totally boho summer hot.

'Hi River, what a fabulous house... what an awesome party,' he'd told her and she could tell he meant it. 'This is my wife, Mena.'

River remembered kissing this slinky blonde woman, who smelled ah-mazing and had skin like satin. She also remembered they all talked... and it was lovely and kind of totally cool. She had revelled in the feeling of enhanced reality that celebrities bring. People all around are noticing but pretending not to and meanwhile the celebrity is noticing being noticed and also pretending not to.

But she had to respect Franklyn, he totally owned it, bossed it even.

He and Mena talked to her, the hostess, for the longest. Then they began a gorgeously kind and thoughtful tour of the garden. Like visiting royalty, they went around, shaking hands and saying hello to every single person there. No one went without their moment in the Franklyn sunshine. Make that the Franklyn and Mena sunshine, because she was quite something. She was the wife for him and River could tell that he truly loved her. Phillip got senior Hollywood treatment, River remembered. And that was good... there was something else about Phillip too... but she couldn't remember it right now. No panic, it would come back, surely.

And while River was watching Phillip schmooze with Mena and Franklyn, there was this screech of tyre tracks and blaring music from the front of the house. When she'd gone round to look, she'd watched a ludicrous silver sports car pull up, then three guys and a woman in a satin slip of a dress piled out. The guy in the pink suit and flamboyant yellow shirt she knew straight away. That was Van Saint, one of Britain's most famous and most successful artists. She thought the guy in a more conservative blue suit was Dean Vincent... known for his work with Van Saint. The guy piling out of the back in a black shirt and jeans, she didn't know him. But she guessed these guys were all from Dave's art class. And the woman had to be someone's wife-slash-girlfriend, because she didn't look like the kind of person who'd hang around all day thinking artistic thoughts and being splattered in paint.

Dave's voice over her shoulder: 'Oh my God! You made it! You found us! Bloody hell!' Then a volley of laughter, followed by: 'It's so good see you again.'

Big manly hugs and back slapping all round.

And then there were some preciously glam moments of Hollywood clashing with the art world: Van Saint looking pretty surprised to be shaking hands with Franklyn Gregory.

'How do you know Dave?' he'd asked, sounding astonished.

'River,' Franklyn had pointed her out, 'she's a friend of both of ours.'

'Right...' This had cleared no confusion.

Having sprinkled the party with magical Hollywood sparkle, Franklyn and Mena had slipped off with kisses and more of those wonderfully scented hugs and: 'See you soon. Wow, great party, River.'

And then the neighbours with their delightful chat peeled off home too. So the actors, the artists, River and Dave were left and that's... that's when it all got wild.

Aware of the deep, pulsing pain in her head, River remembered The End of the Wine... and the ransacking of the entire drinks cabinet. And then Jimi Hendrix was blasting out of the speakers with that big heavy, throbbing bass and amp and electric guitar.

And it got sooo late and she got soooo drunk.

And the artists went into the summerhouse and hauled all of Dave's paintings out and they roared with laughter at his efforts. Dave was laughing too, but River... she could feel her stomach clench. It had clenched up then and it clenched hard now at the memory of this.

All those drink bottles scattered across the lawn, glittering in the firelight. And the artists opening the chimenea and first of all stacking in more and more logs and videoing the fire and laughing and drinking like crazy pirates.

Then they started to stuff Dave's canvases in through the door of the chimenea.

They were filming the whole thing and roaring with laughter and calling it 'the Suburban Death of the Artist'. (This, she had to admit, was freaking genius... but not at Dave's expense.)

And she was talking to Phillip and trying so hard to concentrate on what he was saying because it was... what was it? It had definitely been good.

But finally, she'd had to stand up, and put a stop to what those asshats were doing. She stumbled over to the chimenea in her clumpy pink boots, cigarette in one hand and scooped up all the canvases that were left with her other.

'Fuck off,' she told the artists, 'I'm keeping these ones.' And she stomped towards the summerhouse with the paintings in her arms. But something was missing.

She realised halfway to the summerhouse that her battered old Zippo lighter wasn't bumping against her hip. It must have fallen out of the handy pocket of her dress (those European designers, huh, a pocket in a party dress) when she bent down for the canvases.

She turned to see Van Saint, his face orange in the firelight, pull open the Zippo's brass case, pull out the fuel-soaked wadding and throw it into the already roaring fire.

'Stand back!' he shouted.

Then there was a thunderous bang and pieces of hot metal and fire exploded over the garden. Just like a mini, freaking *volcano*.

There were screams and shouts and that madman's maniacal laughter.

'Oh my God,' she groaned now, pulling the duvet over her head and wondering if she was going to throw up again. She didn't even want to remember the next bit. It was horrible. There were burning chunks of fire all over the garden. Chairs, napkins and tablecloths were on fire. The hem of someone's dress was on fire. And so much screaming! And then Dave had appeared, hobbling at speed from the kitchen with a large fire extinguisher in his hands. First the girl's dress was doused, then he darted from fire to fire covering everything in a muffler of foam. And soon the fires, the madness and the screaming began to damp down.

River had approached the three artists, who were still freaking filming.

'Which one of you is the sober one?' she asked first. The guy in the jeans, who wasn't the famous one, said he was.

'Okay, you guys need to go now,' she'd told them. And she remembered them making a fuss, just like the stupid boys at school parties... 'We were just having a laugh'... 'Don't be like that.' But, in fact, she really enjoyed being 'like that'... and told them to scram with no chummy goodbyes to Dave, who was still dousing sizzling metal with foam.

And... that was it! It was coming back to her. That was when she ran into Phillip. And he seemed so calm and sober and wise. He even helped with some fire extinguishing. Then, when things were finally calm again, he sat down with her and made her drink a glass of water.

And that's when he told her. 'Hey River, I hope you're not too drunk to remember this in the morning, but what we've seen of the script so far is great. It's really great. You are knocking it out of the park and everyone is genuinely excited. It's so good we've got extra funding, and we've got another big name on the project now. Oh, and park the Shakespeare-for-teens documentary idea for now, just focus on this script. Keep up the fantastic work and we'll speak tomorrow when your hangover has worn off. Okay... goodnight.' And he'd kissed the top of her head.

Yes... that was the good part. That was the best bit. It made all the other stuff... Van Saint, Dean Vincent and the chimenea, the ruined chairs, the ruined garden, the terrible, terrible head and godawful stomach almost worthwhile.

Oh, and kissing Dave... she could just about remember that. That had been a good part too. And Dave hobbling into the fray with the fire extinguisher – what a freaking, goddam hero.

40

It was about a week or so before the party that Dave had moved back into Ambleside. He'd chosen to sleep in the spare room because it was downstairs and had its own bathroom, so River still had as much privacy as possible. But he wasn't yet used to being in this room, so when he woke up at 6 a.m. the day after the-day-after-the-party and looked at the unfamiliar ceiling and then the pale green walls, it took him several moments to remember where he was. And what was that ringing sound?

Turning his eyes towards the floor, he saw his phone flashing and ringing at him. Natalie's was the name on the screen and 5.58 a.m. was the time. What on earth?

'Natalie?' he said, answering the call, 'Is everything okay?'

'Daaaaaaaaad!'

The heart-rending wail made Dave sit up bolt upright in bed.

'Natalie? Are you okay?'

'No, I need Mum! I can't get through to Mum.'

This was the life of dads, always the next-best parent in a crisis.

'What's happened, Natalie?'

And as the story unfolded, Dave appreciated, yes, this was, of course, a tragedy, but it was a teenage tragedy, not an actual real-life, panic-stations tragedy. But his lovely daughter was obviously in a total state and needed sympathy and very gentle handling.

'Natalie, honey, do you think there's any way you could get just an hour or two of sleep?' he asked. 'It would probably really help.'

His daughter seemed to be calming down a little now that she'd unburdened herself to her dad: 'Maybe,' she sobbed, 'I want to come home.'

'That's fine, you can come home,' Dave told her. 'I'll look up your flights and see what we can do. But why don't you just put your head down for a little bit? Get a little rest.'

And Dave, who was very keen to do exactly that himself, was on the point of winding up the call when his daughter added, 'And Dad, have you spoken to Alex?'

'Yes, he phoned just... just the other day. And he phoned your mum too. He sounds good. He sounds like he's finally settling in and starting to enjoy himself. I've not heard him sound so happy for ages.'

There was a pause from the other end of the line.

'I think it's weird,' Natalie said.

'What's weird?'

'He's phoning you, he's phoning Mum, he tried to phone me and Soph said he phoned her brother as well. He left me a voice-mail all about how he'd found true happiness and I needed to be happy and... what's going on with him? Do you think he's on drugs?'

Dave's heart was thumping a little too fast. He should not be smoking... that much he knew. He tried to slow up his train of thoughts – Natalie had been awake all night, she was barely making sense herself, and this was probably all an enormous teenage tantrum in a teacup... but... but... she had a point. It was a little weird. And what had River told him yesterday? *He was so happy that*

*day, called every member of his family and all his favourite friends, he
was so fucking happy... We were so happy. It was one of our best days.*

And then Drew had killed himself.

Jesus Christ.

Dave ended the call with Natalie as calmly as he could, telling
her to get some sleep and promising to be in touch very soon.

Then he threw back the covers and pulled on his jeans.

And with a terrible sense of fear, foreboding and guilt, all he
could think of was that maybe his beloved son, his darling Alex,
had not been doing so well in all those short and stilted phone
conversations. And maybe all those times he'd not answered, or not
called back were not because he was out having a great time in
London, but because he was having a terrible time and he didn't
know how to tell anyone. And maybe now, Alex was feeling better
because he'd decided to kill himself. Maybe even today.

It was very early, but Dave sincerely hoped River wouldn't mind
as he tapped on the door of the master bedroom door.

'River?' he said gently when there was no reply. 'River?'

'Go away!' she said finally. 'That would just be too complicated.'

'No, not that!' and if he hadn't been in such an agitated state, he
might have laughed. 'I need to talk to you about something and it's
really important.'

'Christ, Dave, it's so early. Can this not wait?'

'No!'

He came into the room as River pulled on a big sweatshirt and
pushed her eye mask to the top of her head. She didn't yet look
fully recovered from her hangover. Well, no wonder, it was six in
the morning.

'I need to ask you about my son,' Dave began, 'I don't know if
I'm being ridiculous, or if he's feeling suicidal.'

'Shit.'

He had River's full attention now. And for the next few minutes, he explained how hard it had been to contact Alex for weeks and how brief he'd been when they did get him and now he'd made these much happier calls to his family and to one of his friends.

'I remembered what you said about your last day with Drew,' Dave told her. 'And I'm really starting to worry.'

'Has Alex struggled before... you know, stress? Anxiety? Not handling things well?'

'Yeah...' Dave admitted. 'His last year at school and his last year at uni. They were both nearly a disaster and we had to help him a lot.'

'Is he sensitive?' River asked next. 'An overthinker?'

Dave had never thought of these words to describe his son before... but somehow, they clicked into place: 'Yes...' he said, 'he's very sensitive, bless him.'

'You need to get him on the phone,' River decided.

'No...' Dave knew that phoning would not do. It would not put his mind at rest. 'I need to get to London. I need to see him.'

If he ordered a cab, caught a train, he estimated he could be in London before 9 a.m. No, phoning would not do. Alex rarely answered his phone anyway. Dave had to see Alex in person. He had to make absolutely sure Alex was okay. Today.

'Is there anything I can do? River asked.

'No... no, you've helped so much,' Dave told her, as he turned to leave the room, but then he asked her: 'And what do I say to him when I find him? What's the right thing to say?'

River thought of all that frantic work she'd done to keep Herb's stubborn old Tennessean heart beating and then of Dave hopping with his plastic boot out of the kitchen with the fire extinguisher.

'You're the daddy, you'll know what to do,' she told him, 'Now go get your boy.'

* * *

Maybe because it was so long since Tess had been in a nightclub, she was in a state of hyper excitement. It was so dark and loud, so buzzing with energy and excitement. She was dancing with Larry, with Larry's rowdy friend, who sang and clapped while he danced, and with two women Larry knew – dancers, obviously, who span and twisted and made every movement look liquid and effortless, despite their high heels and tight, sparkly dresses.

It was too loud to say much. So she just smiled, drank chilly, lime-flavoured beers and *danced*, so proud of herself. Not just that she could partner Larry and understand which steps were needed, which move to make and how to make full use of the simple patterns she had learned, she was proud of herself for the lecture she'd given today.

The UCLA campus, the lecture hall and the 200-plus students... it had all been so much more of an event than she'd expected, but even though she'd been called in at short notice, she'd been really well prepared. Having children the age of these students meant she knew how not to bore them. She had great stories, good slides, interesting info and even a meme or two to keep them entertained as they were informed. She was rewarded with genuinely enthusiastic applause from the students and a trip to a nearby restaurant with Professor Nathan, who heaped her with praise and offered her a whole series of paid lectures next summer.

She had been very touched and a little overwhelmed. Her response had been to put her hands over his and tell him she would think about it.

'I have things to sort out at home,' she'd said, 'at work and with my husband. I'm honestly not sure where we are at the moment. And adding anything other than a lovely friendship with you into the mix is probably not going to help me... or you.'

Nathan's smile had turned up at the edges, crinkling the kind eyes behind the glasses. 'I'd be honoured to have a lovely friendship with you, Tess.'

'Just to be clear,' she'd smiled back, 'a lovely friendship does not involve kissing... I'm going to blame the sunset and the Chenin Blanc for that.'

This had made Nathan laugh. 'Well, it was good for me... you're the first *other* person I've kissed. Had to happen sometime. I felt like a college kid that night.'

'Yes! Me too,' she admitted, 'but let's not tell our college kids – they would be completely horrified.'

'It's a deal.'

So, it had been, and was still, a wonderful day. She was far too warmly dressed for a nightclub. She could feel sweat running down between her shoulder blades, and maybe a little bit of a fresh air break was called for.

Outside, in the breezy warmth of downtown LA, she pulled her phone out of her bag and wondered what her family was up to. Ah... messaging her by the looks of things: voicemail and texts...

'Muuuuum, muuuuum...' the tearful voicemail from Natalie began, 'we've broken up. I had to break up with him... he cheated on me...' loud sobs, 'he cheated... I need to speak to you... I need to come home. I just want to come home...'

And after a pause: 'Have you spoken to Alex, Mum? He left a message. It was so weird, I don't think he's okay... call me, Muuuuum.'

The texts were from Dave, and they had arrived very recently:

Have you heard from Alex today/tonight? I'm really worried about him. Can't get him on phone.

Going to London to see him.

Keep trying to get him.

And the absolutely useless:

Don't worry... I'm probably just fretting.

Tess scrolled through her contacts for the number of the airline she'd booked with. She'd paid for a flexible ticket, of course.

And it was time to come home.

41

Alex would be lying if he said he hadn't enjoyed planning his suicide. Finally, he felt motivated! He had a meaningful project. He was bringing certainty into his life, taking matters into his own hands and shaking off the terrible hopelessness he'd felt for weeks on end. He was no longer lying in his room, wasting his life, waiting for death to come to him. He finally had a goal and a purpose, something to work towards. In fact, he woke unusually early, got dressed and left his room in a hurry, knowing that today was the day.

Everything else was just a distraction now. Yes, flowers, trees and the summer were beautiful and full of life for now, but what did it matter? One day, the flowers would die, the trees would fall, and the whole city would collapse into the sea, forgotten by anyone that ever lived. It was all a lie and it meant nothing. Life was ridiculous, better to do away with it than suffer it for years on end.

No, there was nothing left to do. Nothing at all. Except die.

As Alex rounded the last corner of the street, the railway bridge sprang into view. It wasn't anything special: a grey, mass-produced construction for people and cars. The side of the bridge was punctuated with some boring graffiti, simple scrawls and patterns, in colours that had once been garish, but were now faded and almost gone. There was litter strewn across the pavement, old takeaway boxes and fag ends, all perfectly normal.

But as soon as Alex reached the bridge, he stopped dead and his hands began to shake. He put a hand onto the railing to balance himself and recognised the sick and panicky feeling of anxiety building up.

'Here we are...' he told himself.

Of course, he'd been to the bridge before. He knew the view over the side, of scrubby trees, gravel and train sleepers laid out before him, ready and waiting for him to just slip over the edge, and splatter to bits among the metal tracks.

But now that he was here, he quailed at the idea that *here*, in this grimy corner of the city, he would meet his *end*.

Had he really arrived at the end of his life? Would this be his final destination?

Why had he chosen here? Why had it not occurred to him to die somewhere real and natural, somewhere with hills and trees and grass and nature all around? Why did it have to be in this ugly place?

His heart was burning. He couldn't breathe. The fear in his chest was too much; he thought he might throw up.

As he stood there, slumped against the railing, he didn't know what to think. His mind wandered from counting the number of railings on the opposite side of the bridge to examining the pattern of discarded specks of gum covering the road.

This was not how he'd imagined it. In his mind, he'd pictured the moment as being somehow more profound. He'd thought that when the time finally came to throw himself off a bridge, he'd remember all the best things in his life, and count his blessings, and in that moment, he would somehow be peaceful and happy.

He tried to recall all the best moments of his life. His fondest memories of the people he loved. But he couldn't put his thoughts together into any kind of story. All that came back to him were recent memories, inconsequential conversations, like his dad talking about the chimenea. He hadn't even been able to get through to Natalie, had left her a garbled voicemail telling her to be happy and not worry about him, or something like that. Modern life had reduced the suicide letter to a shitty voicemail.

His head hurt from all this. Maybe dying was going to be just as confusing and pointless as being alive. But at least when he was dead, he wouldn't have to think about all these strange and endless thoughts any longer.

His breathing had returned to normal. His fingers trembled, but he felt strangely calm. He felt like he had thought everything, said everything, done everything, and felt every emotion he could. There was nothing left for him to feel, and now a strange numbness engulfed him, filling him with indifference. Nothing left to do. Nothing left to say.

He stared down at the cold metal rails below. There was a rumbling noise. A train was approaching the bridge at a rapid pace.

42

It was 8.45 a.m. and Dave was standing in the swanky foyer of the financial services company where Alex worked. This had made sense to Dave earlier this morning, as, tired and a little befuddled, he'd taken a taxi, then a train, then an underground train to get here.

Surely, if he wanted to see Alex, this is where he would be at 9 a.m. in the morning. Dave approached the bank of receptionists, who kept guard in front of the turnstiles where workers in smart suits were already swiping their passes and clicking in for the day.

'Hi there, I'm looking for my son... it's pretty urgent...' Dave hoped he wouldn't have to explain any further.

'Okay... what's your son's name and what department is he in?' one of the women asked.

Dave told them Alex's name and that he was a graduate trainee, but he couldn't give her any further information. He didn't know the department, of course. He realised with a pang that he should know, but that was the kind of detail he left to Tess.

'I'm not finding anyone by that name... why don't I put a quick call in to HR?'

Several minutes went past while Dave listened to the woman asking questions. He swung between desperate anxiety about Alex and wondering if he himself had completely lost his mind. Surely any moment now, they would summon Alex and he would appear in the hallway, cheery, and astonished, not to mention embarrassed, to see his dad here.

'I'm actually going to put the HR department on to you if that's okay,' the woman said, holding out her receiver.

And that was how Dave found out, even though the HR woman was bending company protocol, that Alex hadn't been to work for nearly four months. The company had no further information. The HR department had tried to contact him by phone, email and mail and not received any reply.

'Thanks very much, that's very helpful,' Dave said, sounding incredibly reasonable and calm, while inwardly feeling total panic.

Nine weeks. *Nine weeks?* That was all the time Alex had been with the company. And it had ended four months ago! What was Alex doing? Had he found another job? Was he working? Was he unemployed? Was he able to pay his rent? Had he moved? And above all... why hadn't he felt able to tell them? That was the biggest and most frightening question of all.

Dave did know Alex's address because he and Tess had dropped him off there two weeks before his job had been due to start... so he could settle into London, get his bearings, get to know his flatmates and prepare himself for the world of work.

But was Alex there? If Dave took the underground and bus out to that address would he find his son there? Not for the first time this week, he wished Tess was home. But also, he very much wished that he could sort this out. More than that, he wanted to sort this out. He needed to find Alex.

He looked at his phone... the battered old iPhone he'd had for four years now. Whereas Alex had a new one, bought for the new job... but he was still on the family plan.

Dave was already hitting the button, crossing every single finger and hoping that this very simple piece of parent surveillance would still work.

'Find my iPhone', he pressed, remembering the happy days of tracking Alex during his very first trips to the pubs of Leamington.

Please work, please work, please work, please work.

The signal was loading, four dots were coming into view... one was on the West Coast of America, one was in the south of Spain and the two he homed in on now were in London.

He identified his phone, then zoomed in on the other. The signal was live, Alex was there right now... it was in Croydon. Dave's heart began to hammer when he realised that his beloved boy appeared to be on a railway bridge.

As he rushed out of the building, he dialled his son's number.

43

'*Now!*' Alex said out loud, 'Just do it *now!*'

He pushed forward. He began to lift his right leg towards the edge of the bridge, when something crashed hard into the back of his left knee.

The force of the blow caused Alex to fall onto the pavement. He yelled, as the pain ricocheted through his exhausted body: 'Aaaah! Bastard, no!'

He heard the clang of metal on metal, and hurried footsteps. The knee was painful, yes, but something much worse had happened.

Someone had just saved his life.

He had finally built up the strength to finish himself off, and someone had *ruined* it.

He could hardly bear to look up; he didn't want anyone here, to try to talk him out of it. He felt unbelievably angry. What right did this random person have to interfere?

He felt a touch on his arm and forced himself to look up.

Bending down over him was a girl about his age, with long auburn hair and bright blue eyes. She was wearing a brown leather jacket, and had a large, vintage camera over one shoulder. She had perfectly smooth skin, and her face was flushed, vibrant and full of life and animation. Everything about her seemed young and healthy. And her smile was so wide that her entire face seemed to reach out to him. There was no cynicism in that smile.

'Are you all right?' she asked. 'I'm so sorry! I did ring the bell on my bike, but it never works, and then you moved really suddenly, and I couldn't cycle around you!'

She helped Alex up to his feet. 'What were you doing anyway, was that a calf exercise?'

'A... a what?' Alex stuttered.

'A calf exercise, was that why you thrust your leg out like you did? I do them a lot, whenever I've been cycling for more than a few hours, otherwise my legs seize up.' She laughed a clear, simple laugh and gave that radiant smile again. 'I'm yabbering on... are you okay?'

To Alex's astonishment, he realised that the girl had no idea what she had just done. She had no idea that she had saved his life. He was so completely confused by this bizarre turn of events that he had no idea what to say or think. He wobbled on his feet, then put out an arm to grab the railing. His head was spinning. The girl put her arm round him to help him stand.

'You lean against that railing, mister!' she said, propping him up against the barrier that only seconds before, Alex had tried to throw himself over. 'Have a good old lean right there! Gosh, that's such a lovely view over those train tracks isn't it? It's really got a cool, industrial, decaying sort of vibe, doesn't it? I'm going to take get a photo of it. This camera is brilliant, proper retro; you have to print the pics in a dark room and everything, and it's in black and white, for that sort of depressed vibe, you know?'

Alex had no idea how to keep up with this conversation. He noticed that one of the girl's lovely eyes had a slight squint. It gave her a unique look and brought a kind of energy and kookiness to her face. He found himself staring at her.

'I know!' she exclaimed, taking him by the arm. 'If you wouldn't mind standing just... there,' she said, moving him slightly to the left. 'Great! And then your arm leaning like that... and then just look nice and relaxed!'

And so Alex found himself posing for a photograph on the very bridge he had been planning to throw himself from. *This is ridiculous*, he thought. He felt overwhelmed by the utter weirdness of his situation and stood there awkwardly, not knowing what to say or do, against this onslaught of newness and surprise. As the camera clicked, he even caught himself posing.

* * *

Dave was on one of those cycles you can hire in London. He had already spent £60 on a taxi and now £15 for this bike. But nothing was too much, because he had to get there.

He'd sat in the taxi frantically consulting his phone about the fastest way to get to the spot and taxi had narrowly trumped train. But then, when the taxi had come to a halt at a road works snarl up, Dave had not been able to sit still. The phone dot was still on the bridge. Dave could hardly bear to look at it. Did it mean his son was still there... on the bridge deciding whether to do this or not? Did it mean just his son's phone was on the bridge? Or... did it mean that Dave was going to be too late...?

The agony of not knowing was unbearable. At least if he was running towards Alex that would be better than sitting here, so he'd paid the driver, jumped out of the car and realised immediately that with a great plastic boot on his leg running was out of the question. That's when he'd seen the rack of bikes.

Now he was rushing, faster than he could ever have imagined he could cycle, towards the scene, the phone instructing his turns. He was panting with effort and making every kind of bargain he could with the powers up there. He would be the best dad ever; he would be the best husband in the whole world too. Nothing, *nothing* would ever be too much trouble for him again. He would get fit; he would lose weight; he would attend every father and husband counselling session ever. Just please let him get to Alex. Please, please, please let Alex be okay.

'Just let me find him,' he begged, 'just let him be okay. I want to tell him that everything is going to be okay and we will look after him for as long as he needs us.'

Totally in the grip of adrenaline now, his legs pumped and he swooped down roads, round corners and through a wide park. Surely it couldn't be far now.

* * *

'There!' the girl said, letting out another peal of laughter. 'Thanks so much! Oh my God, what am I doing asking you to be in my photos?' She was suddenly embarrassed. 'I whack you in the knee with my bike, then I make you pose for my stupid art stuff! I have ADHD... I get distracted,' she confided. 'Are you okay?'

'I have no idea,' Alex admitted truthfully. He felt strange. The panic within him had subsided. The urgency, the bleakness, the misery of his situation was somehow less. Against all odds, he could feel the warm glow of a smile breaking across his face.

'I'm a huge, fucking disaster,' he said, his turn to confide now.

To his surprise, the girl burst out laughing at this. 'Aren't we all, though? You seem like a pretty okay disaster to me.'

Alex laughed too. He couldn't stop himself. It was a simple, short burst of laughter that bubbled up from him just for a moment. But even that tiny bit of lightness felt like it meant much more.

The girl laughed again too, for much longer than him. She didn't seem to know what she was laughing at, but seemed thrilled to be joining in. When the laughter stopped, he didn't know what to say. But she broke the silence.

'Well... it's good to laugh,' she said, 'really... if I could, I would laugh all the time.'

For a moment, they just stood on the bridge looking at one another, and then a car passed and that seemed to break the spell.

'Awesome to meet you, dude!' she said brightly, 'But I've got to be going! I'm moving to Edinburgh tomorrow, believe it or not, and I've still got a million things to pack...'

'Edinburgh?' said Alex, his brain was scrambling for information. 'My sister's at uni in Edinburgh,' he managed. Could this be enough of a connection? Could there be a chance this would somehow let him see this girl again?

'Oooh, let me give you my number then,' she added, quickly rummaging through her jacket, and pulling out a pen and a piece of card. 'My phone is broken, because I dropped it over a bridge, funnily enough. Ah, there must be something about me and bridges... so I'll have to write it down. If you have any problems, or if they have to cut your... they won't have to cut your leg off, duh, haha!' she gave another laugh. 'But seriously, if there's anything up, or you're in Edinburgh... give me a shout.'

She pushed the card into Alex's hand. On it, she'd written a number and below that, in neat, beautiful handwriting, she had written a name and her Instagram tag.

'Emilee,' he said, smiling, '@Emi-lee-wears-a-beret.'

'That's me!'

'Emilee,' he said again. Of course, she had a name like Emilee.

And, now that he looked properly, she was wearing a beret. It was the same shade of pink as her cheeks.

'Well... catch you later!' she said, giving him another wide and delightful smile. Then, in a single movement, she jumped onto her bike, swung her feet onto the pedals, and sped off into the distance. Alex was alone on the bridge once more.

He was still trembling, but he didn't think it was fear any more. In fact, it felt a lot like excitement. Nothing had changed. He was still a penniless, failed financial services intern, with insomnia, drinking issues, a disastrous room, depression, anxiety, suicidal tendencies and possibly no chance of employment ever. He still felt completely detached from his family and still had not even the slightest idea what to 'do' with his life, or where in the world to find truth, meaning and peace.

But he felt different. He felt a little bit interested in life. What happens next, he wondered?

A burst of sunshine broke through the trees and flashed against the train tracks down below, turning them bright gold. A girl with a camera, and a stream of wonderful nonsense had crashed into his world at exactly the right moment.

Calf exercises... depressed industrial vibes... Edinburgh...

He realised now that everything about the world wasn't hideous. It was possible for this world to contain bad and terrible things, yes, but also vintage cameras and bicycles and girls with berets and broad, bright smiles.

She saw things differently. She could take this miserable, broken world, and make it feel beautiful and cherished. Emilee had looked at the bridge and seen beauty in it. How did she do that? And how could he find out more about her?

'I'm alive!' he said out loud. 'I'm *alive, alive*. God, what a stupid bastard I've been! I'm so lucky to be alive.'

Someone was shouting his name... for a moment he thought he

was imagining it. But no, someone was definitely shouting his name.

'Alex! Alex! ALEX!!'

This wasn't Emilee's voice.

It sounded a lot like... how could that be? It honestly sounded like his dad.

He looked across the road and saw a bike hurtling at breakneck-speed down a hill towards the bridge. There at the handlebars, beetroot in the face, was his dad.

This day was already so full of astonishment that Alex didn't even question it; he just waved and smiled.

The bike slowed up a little as his dad crossed the final road, then pedalled right up to him. His dad didn't even get off the bike, just leaned over and wrapped Alex up in a huge and totally comforting hug.

'I've got you,' his dad said in a choked and muffled voice.

'Yeah,' Alex replied.

44

It was nearly 4 p.m. the next day when a taxi pulled up outside Ambleside. Inside, Tess was crumpled, exhausted, and wrung out in the way you can only be if you've had to sort out, pack up, organise, and leave in a hurry, then make a huge and exhausting transatlantic journey, while keeping up with intense emotional events involving both of your children. The plane had been delayed. And she wouldn't let Dave leave Alex to come and pick her up. So she'd done taxis, trains and another taxi to get here.

Now, she was completely jet-lagged, ragged at the edges, and also strangely surprised to be back, to be outside her home once again. It felt as if months had passed, not just four weeks, since she'd last been here.

There had been a lot of crying on the plane. She had cried over Alex... she had cried for Natalie and she had also cried because her adventure was now cut short and, all of sudden, over. From the plane window she'd seen some of the places that she might have visited in her final fortnight – the desert, Joshua Creek, maybe she would even have got to the Grand Canyon. *Never mind*, she'd told herself, *I can come back.*

'This doesn't have to be goodbye, in fact, I really hope it isn't goodbye,' she'd told first Nathan and then Larry. 'I hope this will be the start of a good friendship.'

'Yeah, you have to come back... every single year now,' Larry had insisted, 'when I will trade you tango lessons for tax returns.'

They had hugged outside Larry's apartment front door, when she'd come with the treats from her fridge and her fruit bowl, plus the news that for family reasons, she was all packed up and waiting for her cab.

'Thank you for everything,' Larry had told her, 'for sorting the taxes... for sorting the pool... and let's not forget River's balcony.'

They had laughed at that, remembering their first slightly crazy encounter.

'Yeah, she better keep that tidy, or else, you let me know.'

'Hang loose, Tess... and keep on dancing,' had been his parting words and they had made her cry.

Carefully, she had walked around River's apartment one last time, checking she hadn't left anything, cuddling the dogs, who would be off into Tom's full-time care in a few hours' time, and laying out her keys.

She imagined River walking into the now clean and peaceful apartment, enjoying the cleared desk and new bookcase, sitting out on the balcony with its new pots of plants, cooking in her pristine kitchen and taking a sparkling white shower... plus she now had a *basketful* of toilet rolls! She wasn't sure when River was returning; Dave had promised he would sort all that out and she just needed to get on the plane.

Yes, Dave had promised to sort that out. This was something different.

* * *

And now she was in the back of the taxi on the driveway in front of Ambleside. The roses growing up the front of the house were out in full bloom, the soft and blousy flowers lifting in the breeze. Everything looked so gentle compared to the vivid brights of LA. The house was pale limestone, the plants were gentle shades of pink and green and look at the door in that perfect, weathered shade of blue. She had picked that blue paint and Dave had applied it... five coats, she remembered. Four would have been fine, probably, but she'd thought why not do just one more to be sure?

They had done this.

Together, they had taken this old, tired and weary house and made a beautiful home for themselves and their children, built their family here.

Beneath the physical weariness, she realised how excited she was to see them all again.

She got out of the car, paid the driver and unloaded her luggage. The taxi was just pulling out of the driveway when the front door opened and there was Dave. Tess had wondered what it would be like to see him. Really *see* him.

And there he was, standing in the doorway of the family home they'd created.

Her husband looked both totally familiar and yet slightly different. His hair was newly cut, his face freshly shaved. He was in a pink shirt that she particularly liked and this was tucked into jeans with that fashionably stiff and unbroken look that she didn't recognise. Above the warm smile, she saw a hint of dark eye circles. No wonder, of course. Their son had *tried*... well... had certainly *thought* very seriously about killing himself.

And Dave had spotted it. Dave had found him. When Alex was on the very brink, Dave was the one who had been there and caught hold of him. Dave had told her that afterwards, he'd taken Alex straight out for a hearty breakfast, then he'd helped him to pack up and clean his dismal room. And together, with two small suitcases and a binbag of possessions, they'd made the taxi and train journeys home. Dave had been looking after Alex since then, day and night. Apparently, Alex had mainly been soundly asleep. And in the midst of all this, Natalie had also arrived home, bringing a drama all of her own.

Tess and Dave stepped towards one another now. He held out his arms and she did the same, hurrying towards him. Whatever she had thought she might feel about him after their time apart, in that moment it didn't seem to matter, as she moved into that warm, familiar and comfortable place.

'Hello, darling,' she said.

'Hello, Tess,' he replied, sounding relieved, 'it's so good to see you. I'm so glad you're back.'

'Hello,' she said again, hugging him hard and resting her face on his shoulder, 'it's good to see you too. But I am so tired.'

'Me too... unbelievably tired... I'm so glad you're back,' he repeated.

He put his face gently against hers and his cheek was softer than she remembered.

'Come in... come and see everyone... I'll get the luggage.'

When Tess stepped into the hallway, she registered the missing presence of Bella, who would always put a cold nose into her hand and thump her tail against the wall when Tess came home. Poor old girl.

Then she walked into the sitting room, expecting to see her children, but it was empty. Although it was clean and ordered, it had lost the pristine state that she had begun to keep it in. There were two sweatshirts on the back of a sofa, a pair of trainers had been abandoned on the floor, and a half-empty bowl of popcorn stood on the coffee table.

A thud on the ceiling suggested that someone, at least, was

upstairs, so she headed up the creaky staircase to investigate. There was a flurry of giggles from Natalie's room, so she went there.

'Hello!' she called from outside.

'Mum!'

Natalie bounded to the door and gave her a huge hug. Not the depressed and tear-stained Natalie she'd expected, but a bright, tanned, blonde girl, bursting with life and energy. Soph and Ellie were here, of course, what else could Tess have expected? They were sitting on Natalie's bed listening, no doubt, to every single tiny detail. Tess kissed them all hello and realised how lovely it was to see, not just Natalie, but the whole trio together.

'How are you doing?' she asked her daughter, full of sympathy.

'Oh, I'm not too bad... Soph and Ellie have cheered me up so much. And being here is so relaxing...' Natalie added. 'I've just been sleeping and Dad has been making us all our favourite things.'

'Has he, now? How nice of him!'

'Your hair looks really good, Mum,' Natalie added.

'Yeah,' Soph and Ellie chimed in.

'I was wrong about you going blonde,' Natalie admitted.

Tess smiled: 'Thank you... yes, I love it and I'm sure the boys in this family will notice eventually... and talking of boys, where's Alex?'

'I think he's in the garden, reading a book,' Natalie said, already turning back to her friends, who were giggling at her reply. Because when the three of them got together, they giggled at *everything*.

Tess went down to the kitchen and then out of the sliding door to look for her son. There he was in the lovely decked corner, laid out across a lounger in the shade, book in hand.

'Hello Alex, how are you doing?'

'Oh hi, Mum...' he sat up, put the book down and accepted the kiss and long hug she was desperate to give him. 'I'm doing well,' he told her.

She took in the smile and the pale face that had been out of the sun all summer. He was skinny too, with sharp cheekbones, thinner than he'd been when she'd seen him last, in London.

'And what about you?' he asked.

'Jet-lagged to hell,' was her honest answer. 'I don't know if I want booze, or breakfast, or to go and lie in a darkened room.'

'Maybe all three,' he suggested and she thought that maybe there was a hint of sparkiness in his voice that hadn't been there for some time.

'Yeah... so what are you reading?' she began, because she'd decided it was important not to ask any hard questions... maybe for weeks. Alex could just be here... enjoying some peace and quiet, taking good professional advice, and making sure he got well, really properly well before even thinking about anything else.

She only cared about him finding a way to be happy in himself. And the mummy comparisons be damned. Nothing was worth the kind of distress Alex had been in. Absolutely nothing was worth that.

* * *

Then there was someone else to go and say hello to.

As she approached the summerhouse, Tess could hear the tapping of a laptop keyboard. She knocked on the door and the tapping carried on for another moment, before there was a loud. 'Come in!'

'Hi River!' Tess began, opening the door to see the person she felt she already knew so much about.

'Hi! Tess! Oh my God, it's so good to finally meet you!'

River stood up and pulled Tess into a hug. Then they stood back and took each other in for a few moments.

Maybe because she was on a deadline, River was in saggy sweats and her hair looked a few days past a wash, but she was still so obviously, vibrantly good looking, Tess noted with something of a lurch. *This* was who had been hanging out with her husband.

'I feel like I know so much about you,' River began.

'Me too!' Tess agreed.

'Oh my freaking God... I bet there's a ton of stuff you wished you didn't know about me... like the state of my balcony and my bathroom,' she began in her husky, quick-fire way. 'Can I just apologise, seriously, from the bottom of my heart? I have no idea what frame of mind I was in when I left that place, but it wasn't a good one. I should never have let you deal with all that.'

'Don't worry, things are much better there now,' Tess said with a smile.

'I bet they are, you superwoman. And how are my doggies?'

'They're lovely! I really enjoyed hanging out with them. We went on some hikes and I took them to the beach...' she decided she'd leave out the flag and the near-death experience. 'I also met your neighbour, Larry, and did some dancing lessons with him.'

'Oh my God, Larry is so cool. He's like this legend who used to party at Studio 54, did he tell you all about that?'

'No! But he taught me how to tango and we cleaned out the pool together.'

'No way! You totally precious people... so we can go swimming again?'

'Yes... it's a lovely apartment.'

'So,' River wanted to know, 'did you have a great time away? Did you have a holiday and spend some proper time on yourself?'

'I did miss everyone... but yes,' Tess admitted with a smile, 'I spent a lot of time on myself. And it was a really good thing to do.'

'Seriously cute hair,' River noticed.

'Thanks.'

'You don't look like I was expecting,' River added, tilting her head to the side as if she was studying Tess. 'You look kind of cooler and more fun.'

Tess gave a little laugh. 'That's the LA effect,' she said.

'You look happy.'

'Yeah,' Tess agreed. 'I am happier than I was when I left, you know... despite everything that's happened.'

'Try not to worry about your boy too much,' River said, 'You guys have got him.'

Because she was in danger of crying if she thought about that too much, Tess asked River a question. 'So how about you? How's the work going?'

'It's going great,' River replied, 'it's been amazing to be here. It still is amazing and I don't know what it is about this summer-house. I love it. I've never worked anywhere so well as I work in this place. I may have to dismantle it and take it back to LA with me...'

But also, River knew, it was because she was loving what she was writing. Line by line it was at last working and coming out right. She didn't know how much longer she'd be at it... a week... ten days... but she did know that by the end, she and Phillip and hopefully the rest of the production team were all going to be very happy.

'Dave has really looked after me,' River added. 'That's a really good guy you've got there. He's super nice, but underneath that nice, there's this, you know, *mensch*, as we'd say in my part of New York. But you know that, right?'

Tess nodded.

'If you ever get fed up with him, you send him in my direction. Okay?' River gave her a wink and then added: 'we'll talk more tonight, but right now, there's this scene I'm in the middle of that I really need to get back to.'

* * *

When Tess went back into the kitchen, Dave was setting out treats onto two wooden boards and pouring three hefty glasses of white wine from what looked like a decent bottle.

'Will River join us?' Tess asked, but Dave shook his head. 'No, she's working... all the time. She says it's always like this when you get to the end. It takes over. She even has a special Mozart playlist for the final days on a script, to help soothe her brain and let her concentrate, apparently.

'When she starts a project, it's pop. Then the middle bit is rock-'n'roll and by the end it's Mozart and all his precisely placed notes are needed to make the final thing hang together, apparently.'

'That's very interesting,' Tess said, settling into one of the kitchen chairs. 'Have you been having some very nice chats with the crazily glamorous writer who's been staying in our house?'

Dave gave this comment a look that she couldn't quite fathom.

'Yes, I have... and she's certainly de-glamourised the artistic life for me. It's bloody hard work and she has suffered!' he added. 'So the deal is, she's moved to the summerhouse during the day, but she'll sleep in the spare room and she's got a rent reduction, obviously, and I've said I will bring her booze and meals on wheels until she is done.'

'That sounds like a pretty good deal...'

'Yes, I'm keeping her sweet... you never know. She's already told me her *mom* will get the invite to the Oscars, but maybe we can get to the after-party!'

This made Tess laugh. 'You'd like LA...' she told him, 'people drive everywhere.'

'How delightful.'

'And there is always somewhere to park.'

'Living the dream.'

'Now...' Tess's walk through the garden had raised quite a few questions: 'What's happened to the chimenea?' she began, 'and the rosebush that used to be at the corner is now a completely different one? And the grass...'

'Woah... not on day one... not on day one,' Dave insisted, 'it's all been taken care of, nothing to see. I will tell you all about that another time!'

So, once Dave had taken River her snack, he and Tess went to the sitting room together and, once the sweatshirt, trainers and popcorn had been removed, Tess lay flat out across the sofa, while Dave took up a seat at the end with Tess's feet in his lap. It was a pose they'd not sat in together for years.

'You look so well,' he told her, 'and I love your hair. I did say that when you first got it cut, but I love it even more in person.'

'Thanks...' she said. 'Looks like you got to the barber's too... and new jeans, was that party prep?'

He nodded and then told her: 'I've made some resolutions, serious ones, so you're not allowed to laugh...'

'I won't...'

'I've bought twenty lessons with a personal trainer...'

'No!' Tess had not expected this.

'I've signed up for an online course in healthy cooking and I've ordered an exercise bike... and a sauna bag – the bag is for stress relief, not weight loss. And,' he went on, before Tess could interrupt him, 'if you think we should do marriage counselling, or family therapy, then... let's do it.'

This was a lot to take on board all at once. A personal trainer, healthy eating, a bike and what the heck even was a sauna bag? A sauna, in a bag? Marriage counselling... family therapy... this was a lot to unpack.

'Wow...' she said simply. As she was the one who had learned how to tango and dyed her hair pink, she could hardly laugh. She had a suspicion that their friends might think they were both steering deep into midlife crisis territory... but no matter.

There was no need for her to ask what had brought all this on… it was obvious, and it looked like Dave was about to tell her anyway.

'That morning when I went to London,' he began, 'to find Alex… well, let's say it… to potentially stop Alex from killing himself… which, by the way, I did not do, the ungrateful little swine has informed me!' Dave could see that Tess was about to cry, so he put his hand over hers and began to tell her about the funny part too.

'Apparently at the crucial moment, this girl crashed her bike into him. Right there on that bridge, and they had a little chat… and she took his picture, gave him her number, and told him she was moving to Edinburgh.'

'Edinburgh?' Tess was trying to take all this craziness in.

'Yes… so he's planning to go and see her, sometime in the future, when he's feeling better… and Tess, he does need some help, of course he does. But he really does believe that the danger is over. We don't need to hover and hide the razor blades or anything…' Tess's eyes were spilling over now. 'Because he's promised, absolutely promised, to let us know if it ever gets even anywhere near as bad as that again. So we can trust him about this. It's in the open now. He's going forward and he really wants to be… alive.'

Dave gave her hands a reassuring squeeze.

'Life is so complicated…' she said, wiping at her eyes, 'they will both still need us for quite some time, won't they?'

'Oh, for goodness' sake,' Dave rolled his eyes. 'I would still love to have a heart-to-heart with my mum.'

'That's nice,' she said, feeling very comforted.

'So,' Dave went on, 'when I was rushing around London trying to find him…'

'It's amazing you found him,' Tess told him, 'no matter what he says about the girl with the bike…'

'I made a whole series of promises to the powers above…'

Tess smiled.

'That I would shape up in every direction of my life. I would get out of every single one of my ruts and bad habits and be grateful for everything I have, just as long as I could find him and he would be okay. So now... I've got to keep my side of the bargain.'

45

THREE MONTHS LATER

There was a time in her life when Tess might have felt nervous approaching the podium on a stage in front of the whole 6,000-strong UK and global workforce of her accountancy firm. But not today.

Today, she felt incredibly well prepared, ready for this, and really quite excited. It wasn't just that she'd rehearsed her talk until she knew it off by heart, checking each and every anecdote and joke with her harshest critics – Natalie and Alex – and it wasn't the Rodeo Drive outfit either, although as the lovely girl in the Ralph Lauren shop had told her: 'In that navy pencil skirt and silk blouse, you will slay, lady, wherever you go.' And it wasn't the blonde hair, with a now permanent pink dip at the bottom, expertly curled by her own fair hand. No, well, it was all of these, but it was also deeper. It was about the way she moved towards the podium; the way Larry had taught her, shoulders loose and down, head lightly balanced, relaxed, breathing well and taking up your space... taking your place in the world. And it was about the stable, new-found confidence inside.

At home, she saw that she was still central to her family, even if it was in a different way. At work, she had found that she could do things in a way that worked for her. She didn't have to fit in with anyone else's plan. And she wanted to inspire everyone here to feel the same way.

Plus, today was her fiftieth birthday... and there was a new necklace with three interlocking circles hanging at her neck, each one engraved on the back with a name: *Alexander, Natalie and David...* because on a day like this, everyone needed a lucky charm.

The CEO, John Lloyd, smiled generously at her and then began his introduction: 'I'd like to welcome our newest partner, Tess Simpson, to the stage. As well as the usual responsibilities of partnership, I'm delighted to say that Tess is bringing some new elements to the role. She's going to take on the additional title of Director of Midlife Wellbeing. If, like me, you're entering the second half of your life, then we want to look after, and in fact nurture, you here in a different way. I'll let Tess tell you all about it.'

So then she was on.

She smiled, took a breath and made eye contact with the crowd. 'Hello everyone... it's great to be here,' she began. 'I took a sabbatical over the summer and I did something I'd not planned to do... I didn't even want to do... and I'm still not very good at, but in all kinds of surprising ways, it has changed my life.' She paused, as she'd practised, for effect. 'I learned to dance the Argentinian tango. And it's okay to laugh,' she added, releasing a burst from the crowd, 'I know I would have. But that's why taking time out, shaking yourself up and letting completely new things happen is so important.

'It makes room for the unexpected,' she told them. 'It takes you out of your comfort zone, to uncomfortable places even, and it lets all kinds of interesting things happen here,' she pointed to her head.

'So our midlife wellbeing project is starting up with some really interesting ideas...' and she went on to outline the first offerings:

sabbaticals with purpose, tech classes – so everyone of any age could feel completely confident about using their work apps and software – new skills training, public speaking training, and the chance to give guest lectures and intern training both in the UK and in the US. Oh yes, Nathan had opened his contacts book and helped her to put some amazing opportunities together.

* * *

Much later that evening, the lights were dimmed, the music was turned up and the crowd of friends they'd invited to Ambleside for food, drinks and birthday cake sat down in a makeshift circle to see Tess and Dave, as promised, take to the kitchen dance floor.

Both were a little giggly with champagne, but they were confident enough about their moves not to need much Dutch courage.

Just before they began, Tess's eyes swept past the mantelpiece loaded with flowers and birthday cards. Right at the front was a special one with a photograph of a very familiar balcony, even more beautiful now because the plant pot collection had grown to include pink and purple bougainvillea and an enormous cactus. There was a more substantial cast iron table out there now and on top, a laptop, a white coffee cup, and the chunky glass ashtray from Ambleside they'd insisted she keep.

Inside, River had written:

Have a wonderful birthday, Tess. I will be raising a glass to you.
I know your family will spoil and cherish you.
Life is going so great over here. I've just inked the deal for my Hamlet/High School mash-up! A huuuuge cheque and another visit to Ambleside next summer! And I'm so excited that you guys are going to come and stay here. Dave can keep fit in the pool and Larry is so dying to meet him!

Thank you so much, guys. Last summer gave me everything I needed to get back on track... hey, I can even listen to 'Perfect Day' again and feel pretty okay about it. (Dave will know what that's about.)

Don't you dare get sad about turning fifty, Tess. It's the start of your third act. And the third act is always the best one.

Loads of love to you all,

River

A hush descended and Tess and Dave began the dance just like the couple on the video Larry had showed Tess all those months ago.

They stood opposite one another and they locked eyes.

Physically, Dave had changed in the past three months. He had kept his bargain with the powers above... he'd given up booze, changed his diet, and now took exercise every single day. He'd had to buy a new, slimmer suit for this party. He was off the high blood pressure pills and he'd even started *running*. And, of course, dancing... with his wife.

Helping his son, Alex, realising he loved painting and could turn to it at any time, remembering what a pair of monumental a-holes Van Saint and Vincent were, taking charge of his weight and de-stressing with exercise, not wine... these were all things that had served to give Dave a much greater sense of peace and of confidence in himself.

The unanswered questions had fallen away. The recriminations about what he could, or should, have done instead of the life he'd chosen were gone. Charging on a runaway bike down that hill towards Alex had put everything into crystal-clear perspective for him. He was going to keep Alex alive and help him to find his happiness; he was going to be a great dad to both his children, a brilliant husband and he was going to be able to cycle for fifteen minutes without dying. Everything else was nice, but not even remotely important.

Oh, apart from dancing with his wife... that seemed to help everything.

So now, Tess and Dave faced one another and breathed, waiting for the right beat in the bar to begin.

How had Larry described this dance? 'It's touch, but don't touch; move, but don't move... hold me, but also let me go.'

Tess approached and put her arm around Dave's shoulder. But the last three months had marked such a change between them that she now thought of him once again as David – just like when they'd met – not comfy old Dave.

Her elbow was on top of his shoulder, wrapping them close. Their chests were touching, but their hips and legs were free to tango.

Tess began with the steps around him, leaning into him and leaning out from him. Her leg flicked up and then twisted around his. To a growing chorus of claps and cheers from their friends, the dance went on, step after step, move after move. Sometimes she would lead, sometimes she would follow; there was now give and take... trust, support and understanding... in the dance, and in their lives.

As planned, the music changed from tango classic to 'La Vie en Rose' and they were going to make their 'wow' move, just as Larry had shown her and she had shown David. Chests together, she leaned in, felt his arm around her back and under her shoulder, then she relaxed, so easy when you trust your partner, and let him sweep her gently round in a half circle, before her feet picked up the steps again and they came to a standstill, wrapped tightly around one another.

Smiling, and suddenly a little embarrassed by the applause, Tess remembered Larry's words: 'Argentinian tango is unstructured, no steps... no rules... it's like life. It goes where you take it and where it takes you, and there is always something new to learn.'

For their third act, David and Tess were definitely going to be together.

And it was going to be good.

ACKNOWLEDGMENTS

It's been quite some time since I last had a book out and, although I was determined it was going to happen, I'm very lucky to have these people in my life, who encouraged me to keep going and Get It Done: the fam, Thomas, Sam and Claudie Quinn; my mum and dad; my awesome agent, Diana Beaumont at Marjacq; and my lovely author friends Shari Low and Maggie Ritchie.

Special thanks also to Sam Quinn, whose own writing inspired the chapters about Alex.

A huge thank you to Ross Hunter, Duncan Black, Niels Footman and all my Copylab colleagues for flexible working hours and for all the creative and grammatical inspiration! Massive thanks also to the members of the lockdown 'Virtual Pub Group' – without you there would have been no reading recommendations, no Zoom pub quizzes, no chilly garden wine drinking, no daft WhatsApp discussions and all the other nonsense that got us through those endless Glasgow lockdowns. Special mention to Jess Brodie, my new social media guru and co-conspirator at our life story service.

Hello Boldwood! It's wonderful to have a new author home. Thank you so much to my new editor, Emily Ruston, for great advice and for steering us through some very tight deadlines. I hope there are many happy publication days ahead.

And finally, if you were one of my readers before and you've come back to me after this long absence... thank you so much. This book truly is for you and I hope you love it.

MORE FROM CARMEN REID

We hope you enjoyed reading *Worn Out Wife Seeks New Life*. If you did, please leave a review.

If you'd like to gift a copy, this book is also available as an ebook, digital audio download and audiobook CD.

Sign up to Carmen Reid's mailing list for news, competitions and updates on future books.

https://bit.ly/CarmenReidNewsletter

ABOUT THE AUTHOR

Carmen Reid is the bestselling author of numerous woman's fiction titles including the Personal Shopper series starring Annie Valentine. After taking a break from writing she is back, introducing her hallmark feisty women characters to a new generation of readers. She lives in Glasgow with her husband and children

Follow Carmen on social media:

 instagram.com/carmenreidwrites
 facebook.com/carmenreidwrites

ABOUT BOLDWOOD BOOKS

Boldwood Books is a fiction publishing company seeking out the best stories from around the world.

Find out more at www.boldwoodbooks.com

Sign up to the Book and Tonic newsletter for news, offers and competitions from Boldwood Books!

http://www.bit.ly/bookandtonic

We'd love to hear from you, follow us on social media:

facebook.com/BookandTonic

twitter.com/BoldwoodBooks

instagram.com/BookandTonic

Lightning Source UK Ltd.
Milton Keynes UK
UKHW041032011021
391469UK00001B/219